MURDER AT SUGAR RUSH BEACH

A gripping crime mystery packed with twists

PAULA LENNON

Preddy and Harris Book 3

JOFFE
BOOKS

Joffe Books, London
www.joffebooks.com

First published by in Great Britain in 2022

This paperback edition was first published
in Great Britain in 2022

Cover art by Nick Castle

ISBN: 978-1-80405-215-0

CHAPTER 1

Tuesday, 1 January, 9.10 p.m.

The uncomfortable feeling in Detective Raythan Preddy's gut often crept up on him whenever one of his teenagers did not answer their phone. This queasiness was particularly acute tonight as he drove towards the flashing blue lights way ahead. The police radio had crackled a report of a possible stabbing at the giant marquee newly erected on Sugar Rush Beach in downtown Montego Bay. A young man was the victim, the voice said. No shots heard, but the victim was bleeding. The name Sugar Rush Beach meant nothing to Preddy at first as none of the locals ever used its official name. The area was more popularly known as Dowdy Beach, and Dowdy Beach had been the destination of his son Roman and a friend not an hour before.

The sun had retreated hours ago, and the car windows were down, yet Preddy's shirt clung to his skin as he tried to shake the feeling that the seventeen-year-old could be involved. The beachfront traffic was almost at a standstill, red brake lights indicating that there was nowhere to go. He drummed on the steering wheel with damp fingers, a deep frown etched on his face. Scores of people were leaving the venue on foot, dodging between nose-to-tail vehicles as they left the shadows of the white sandy beach and headed inland towards the relative safety of the brightly lit shopping district. The pointed canvas roof of the white marquee was visible in the distance, and Preddy wondered why no one had turned on the surrounding floodlights.

Sugar Rush Beach rarely saw any major action, except on special occasions like tonight, when it became a mass of badly parked cars and eager patrons. During the daytime it was just an extensive, neglected free beach, covering an estimated sixteen acres, used only by some carefree locals. With no changing rooms, restrooms or lifeguards, it was unattractive to others. Occasionally, an ice cream vendor or peanut man would ride across the sands hoping for a sale, but no higgler ever pitched a permanent stall there. The underused beach came alive a few times a year — when a stage show was held featuring raucous musical performers, or a week-long church convention took over with vociferous mic-toting pastors, or a jerk food festival was laid on, where the air turned smoky and delicious all day.

Preddy tried Roman's phone again. It rang unanswered. He activated the blue lights and siren on his otherwise unmarked police car, sending a piercing wail into the air. Some motorists tried to obey the plea by moving a few inches to one side, but there was little they could do to give Preddy enough room. In frustration he pulled onto the pavement, forcing some pedestrians to leap out of the way, and sped towards his destination, coming to a screeching halt in a cloud of dust.

He grabbed a torch from the glove compartment, and fumbling to get it on, set off running towards the huge tent. The sand pulled him backwards as it grabbed onto his sneakers. Overturned white plastic chairs were strewn around the beach, evidence that people had fled in a panic. A security guard tried to prevent him from approaching a large group of people standing around some bushes, but the detective brushed away his outstretched arm.

"Police, sir!" he shouted. "Move aside!"

As the torchlight fell on the victim, Preddy felt his breath escaping his body. Next to the Portaloos, beside the bushes, a young man lay on his back dressed in a white T-shirt and blue jeans. Not the outfit Roman or Ninja had been dressed in. The right side of the T-shirt was stained vivid red, above which was a company logo. Only the whites of the man's rolled-back eyes were showing. Another security guard appeared at the detective's shoulder. "Sir, you have to get back!"

"Detective Preddy, Pelican Walk Police," said Preddy without looking at the guard.

"Oh sorry, sir, didn't recognize you in de dark."

Preddy felt the victim's wrist for a non-existent pulse. "Get dem to turn on de floodlights, man," he demanded. "No film show not taking place tonight. All entertainment done."

The deceased appeared to be in his early twenties, youth forever frozen in his features. Preddy straightened up and glanced around. He was not on duty and hoped that the Summit police would turn up to take over so that he could leave the scene. This was not how he had intended to start the new year at all and he did not want the gift of a murder case. It crossed his mind that other officers who had heard the police radio would be thinking the same thing, but fear had lured him here first. Despite his reluctance to stay, twenty years of policing made him swing into action.

"Anybody see anything?" Preddy raised his voice. "Please talk to me if you saw what happened here."

Voices murmured all around him but no one piped up with information. Some tried to photograph the body, fussing with one another for space to get a better view, which Preddy tried to block. He looked at the security guards. "Get dese people back, please. As far back as possible."

The guards ushered the unruly spectators away from the crime scene. Preddy pulled out a pair of latex gloves from his pocket, put them on and stooped low. He lifted the edge of the T-shirt and glanced at the small round hole just under the rib cage. He checked through the victim's trouser pockets. A set of keys, no wallet, no cash. A smartphone lay vibrating in the undergrowth near the body, the caller unaware that they would never hear the owner's voice again.

Suddenly the floodlights went on and the beach lit up like daylight. A huge sign on a flagpole fluttered in the air. *Welcome to the Grand Marquee.* As Preddy got up and retrieved the shuddering phone, a man pushed through the crowd.

"Let me see him! Let me through!" The man looked down at the body and screamed. "My God! Jerome! Lord God!"

Preddy instantly noticed that the man was wearing clothes similar to those of the deceased — a logo T-shirt and blue jeans. His hair was cropped closely against his scalp and his thick eyebrows almost formed a unibrow on his caramel-coloured skin. He held a smartphone in one hand and a megaphone in the other.

"Come, sir." Preddy took hold of the speaker's arm and gently pulled him back. "Don't go any closer. Who is de person?"

"It's Jerome, my nephew." The voice was almost a whisper. "Jerome Baccus."

The detective searched his memory without satisfaction. "And you are?"

"Gavin Baccus. I'm running tonight's promotion and movie show. Lord God, look what they did to Jerome!"

"I'm afraid dere's nothing we can do for him, sir. I'm sorry." Preddy remembered the slogan now: *Baccus, We're Backing Montego Bay.* He had heard adverts on the radio, heard this man's cultured Jamaican-English voice, but had never paid attention to who the businessman was. Gavin Baccus was vying with one other businessman for the opportunity to develop this prime beach area and turn it into something outstanding, a gem of the Caribbean.

Gavin Baccus stared at Preddy's hand. "That's his phone, isn't it? I was ringing him."

Preddy stared at the screen, which was still vibrating in his hands showing the caller as *Uncle Gav.* "Yes, I'm sorry, sir." He pressed the image of the red telephone receiver and the phone fell silent.

The distraught man pushed his own phone into his pocket and massaged his temple. "Oh God," he breathed.

"When you last see him?"

"Just before the movie was about to start. He handles all my advertising, publicity and social media. He came up front to wish me good luck." His voice choked. "We had a quick chat, then the lights went out. The pre-movie promotion started running and he went off to reclaim his seat."

"You see where he was sitting?"

"No." The man shook his head. "Jerome came with his girlfriend, Eryka, but I didn't see where they were sitting. My sole focus was on making sure the projector was getting the adverts fully on the screen."

"Eryka who? Where's she?"

Baccus looked around as if noticing for the first time that the immediate area was almost devoid of people. "Eryka Malden. Don't know what happened to her." His tone was low, his face twisted in despair. "She must be here some-where, Detective."

"Let me have dis." Preddy gently removed the mega-phone from the man's grasp and put it to his lips. "Police here! If anybody saw anything, please make yourselves known to me." He watched the distant, thinned crowd, but no one broke through or attempted to reach him. "If dere is an Eryka Malden here, please come forward."

Preddy handed the megaphone back to Mr Baccus. "Please wait here, sir."

Preddy was relieved to see three constables from Summit Police Station arriving and he acknowledged the approaching men with a wave. One began unwinding caution tape around the scene. The other two pushed back the remaining rubber-neckers. Preddy's relief was short-lived. No other detectives had arrived on the scene, so there would be no opportu-nity to foist this murder onto anyone else. Superintendent

Brownlow, his superior, would not let this case go elsewhere once he heard about it. The Baccus name was familiar to many Jamaicans, particularly those with an interest in Montego Bay or greater St James, and Brownlow was an expert social climber.

Preddy glanced at his silent phone. No message from the still-missing Roman. At least his daughter, Annalee, could be accounted for. She was safely ensconced with her grandparents in Darliston, Westmoreland, and no doubt being spoiled and pampered.

The year could not have begun any worse. Last night had held so much promise too. He and his girlfriend, Valerie, had attended fireworks on Breathless Beach at the Freeport, celebrating the start of the new year. He had been feeling optimistic for his future and that of his beloved city. Now this. Same day, different year, more murder. The criminals were straight back to causing death and devastation without a pause for blessed contemplation. He stared up at twinkling stars that saw every speck of sand but could tell him nothing about the perpetrator. Night-time crime scenes in open areas were the worst. Here there were hundreds of potential murderers blending into the shadows and a good chance that the actual murderer was right there on the scene. It was time to bring in reinforcements from Pelican Walk — and quickly.

Preddy's first phone call was to Detective Sean Harris who promised to be on the scene in fifteen minutes. The Scotsman was in no hurry to leave Jamaica and seemed quite settled in Montego Bay. His original reason for being piloted into Pelican Walk as a secondee was to spy on Preddy for Superintendent Brownlow and Commissioner Davis. That investigation had come to an end, in Preddy's favour, yet the white man remained in the city. Much to Preddy's disquiet, Harris had finally admitted to secretly investigating another detective at Pelican Walk, although he refused to name the object of his attention. A foreigner on Preddy's patch knowing more than he did was unacceptable and distracting, but the Scotsman was a good detective. Preddy scowled and tried to put the matter out of his mind.

He placed a call to Detective Kathryn Rabino. She could always be counted on when he needed a calming presence around, particularly when dealing with fraught relatives and nervous witnesses, who loved her crystal-clear vocals. Even the craftiest of suspects had learned not to mistake the perfectly coiffed straight weave and extended eyelashes as signs of her being a pushover.

Preddy hesitated about phoning the fourth member of his team, Detective Javinia Spence. Visions of Spence sitting and reading bedtime stories to her young daughters flooded his mind. This was soon replaced with the thought of her angry face if she learned tomorrow that she had not been called on. The last time he had tried to be considerate of her family life, she had politely told him that she would take care of her own business. That her husband Mikey had a great relationship with his girls and, if she wasn't around, the youngsters would just treat him as a human trampoline and wear themselves out. Spence answered on the third ring and was through her front door before the conversation was over.

The purr of a large motorbike grew into a growl as it crept along the sand and was enough to inform Preddy which detective had arrived first.

"Happy New Year, Preddy," murmured Harris in a monotone.

Preddy winced at the noise. "Maybe next year."

The Scotsman shut off the engine, removed his helmet and shook his greying red hair free from his damp scalp. Even though he lived further away than the other detectives, his preferred mode of transport usually got him to scenes before the others, and with no need for sirens or lights. He dismounted and peered at the body. "Do we know who it is?"

"Victim's name is Jerome Baccus." Preddy jerked his head in the direction of Gavin Baccus, who had collapsed into a chair and was being hugged and fanned by a helpful bystander. "Dat's his uncle, Gavin Baccus."

7

"Gunshot?" asked Harris.

"De only wound I can see is a small hole dat went through his T-shirt. Puncture wound just below de rib cage." Preddy lifted the shirt slightly and shone his flashlight at the bloodied spot. "Stabbed wid something sharp wid a long point. Can't see another injury."

"One stab, straight tae the point," mused Harris. "Must have pierced the heart."

"Try move!" A familiar female voice echoed in the distance. "Move outta me blasted way. We have room for you at Pelican Walk, you know?"

Preddy smiled to himself. Detective Spence had arrived and clearly the new year had not tamed her, but sometimes being polite with the locals was completely ineffective. Spence was followed shortly by Rabino with her digital single-lens reflex camera hanging from a long strap around her neck.

"The pathologist is on her way, sir," said Rabino. "Might be a delay getting here though. She's coming from Sandy Bay."

"Tell me dat's Sandy Bay, Hanover, and not Sandy Bay, Clarendon?"

"Hanover, sir." Rabino smiled and began adjusting the settings on her camera for night photography.

"Okay," said Preddy with some relief. "I'm just thankful she's still on de island."

By now an area of twenty metres was completely cordoned off, yet a few people lingered to watch the aftermath. One disgruntled patron shouted, "So no show nah keep tonight?"

Spence rounded on him, eyes narrowed. She shone a torch in his face. "Dis is a murder scene, sir. If you have any information, let us know. If not, leave de area now!"

"Den you no can move de body and make we gwaan watch we show?" asked the man with some insistence while shielding his eyes from the glare.

"You no have TV ah you yard?" Spence set off towards him. "Come here, make me see if you have anything in you pocket you shouldn't have."

8

The man kissed his teeth, turned his back and quickly walked away. Spence returned to her teammates.

Rabino shook her head. "The nerve of some of them. Murder has become so routine to them that they just want the body out of the way so life can continue as normal."

"Just like Hollywood," said Harris.

Suddenly the area went dark again. The moonlight was almost non-existent, and the stars, although pretty, rendered little assistance with visibility. "A whe' de rass?" mumbled Preddy. "Lights!"

"De generator cut out, sir!" shouted a voice.

"Och, great," said Harris.

"We'll have to do what we can by flashlight," said Preddy irritably, wondering why the universe was conspiring against him on this of all days. "Okay, people, dis isn't good, but let's spread out and see if we can find de murder weapon or anything useful."

The detectives lifted the overturned plastic chairs. Newly purchased buckets of popcorn and bags of chips were scattered around, and the salty smell of hot fat lingered in the air. They searched the sand and the long grass beside the Portaloos. Preddy's phone rang, and, spotting the name, he quickly answered it. "Where are you, Roman? You trying to give me heart attack?"

"Just cool, Misser Officer. Me and Ninja inna Kentucky," said Roman in a chirpy tone. "De food sweet."

"Look how long I trying to get you," said Preddy, the accusation clear.

"Yeah, I kinda worked dat out, Dad. So many missed calls." There was no hint of apology in the youth's voice. "Had to turn it off just before de lights went out for de show. An announcement came over de tannoy . . . all phones off."

"Oh, of course," said Preddy. He could not begin to imagine a world where he would no longer hear his son's voice, even if it was cool and detached. "Didn't think of it, to be honest. Look, you guys should probably just get out of de area."

"De guy dead fi true?"

Preddy sighed heavily. "Yes, son. You see anything?"

"No, sir. People start scream and run so we start run too. Is only when we reach Kentucky car park, we hear dat is a guy get stab."

"Okay, well I'm on de case, so I have to get to work," said Preddy. "You and Ninja get your chicken and go."

"But is not even ten o'clock." The voice at the other end of the phone line was indignant. "Too early to leave downtown."

"I don't care what time—"

"Sorry, cyah hear you. Hello, hello?"

The phone went dead. Preddy was not fooled for one minute, but he knew that Roman would not answer if he tried to make contact again. Besides, the boy was never slow to point out that he would soon be an adult. Roman was keen on making his own decisions with as little consultation with either of his parents as possible. Preddy pocketed his phone and continued with his search, his eyes gradually becoming used to the partial darkness.

After about twenty minutes searching the sand and bushes, Spence said, "Over here!"

The other detectives made their way towards where Spence was directing a stream of yellow light. Rabino bent close and captured a photograph of the object of her colleague's attention. "Looks like an ice pick," she said.

Preddy lifted it to shoulder height. "Dat is definitely fresh blood."

Harris studied it closely and pointed. "There's a little etching on it . . . looks like a turtle. It doesnae look like an ice pick though, more like an awl."

"A wha'?" asked Preddy.

"An awl. Ye know, a tool used for punching holes in things like leather or wood," explained Harris. "Craftsmen use them a lot."

"Knowing our people, dey use it as an ice pick." Preddy carefully placed it into a transparent evidence bag. "What's de difference anyway?"

"This is much thicker, stronger," said Harris. "Ye can change the blades for different sizes and shapes depending on what ye're making."

"For murder, de blade size and shape don't matter," said Spence. "Whatever you use to pierce de skin, it going end badly for de victim."

"Aye, ye're naw wrong there," agreed Harris. "Any eye-witnesses?"

Preddy shook his head. "None dat have stepped up so far. Have to hope when de panic dies down somebody will come forward. Apparently Jerome's girlfriend Eryka is here somewhere. All I know from de uncle is dat Jerome worked closely wid him in his business, Baccus Design, doing mainly advertising and social media stuff."

"Oh, that Jerome," said Rabino. "Baccus Design is competing with the guy who runs All Angles. What's his name . . . Wesley Ashburn." She stood and placed her hands on her hips. "Jerome Baccus has written some pretty vicious things about Ashburn on social media. Those two parties seem more like enemies than business rivals."

"Wait," said Spence, her eyebrows lifting in realization. "Dis dead guy is de same one who wrote dat Mr Ashburn has no vision for Mo Bay and can't see further dan his pointed nose?"

"Same one," said Rabino.

"Och aye?" said Harris. "So this probably isnae some random stabbing then?"

"Maybe, maybe not," said Preddy. A swirl of thoughts skipped through his mind. "If he had a wallet, it's gone and he has no cash on him. I've got his phone, which he dropped in de bushes. Could be random, could be disguised to appear as random." He looked towards the few remaining people on the opposite side of the caution tape. "Now, where is Miss Eryka Malden?"

"Disappearing girlfriends." Harris scanned the surrounding beach. "Always a bad sign."

"Detectives!" Preddy spun around at the sound of Gavin Baccus's voice. "Found her. Or rather, she found me. This is Eryka."

"Hey presto," murmured Rabino.

"Make sure you don't shine any light on de body," said Preddy in a low voice.

Spence and Rabino moved to block the sight of the body, while Preddy and Harris took a few steps towards the approaching pair.

The girl was in her late teens, maybe early twenties, slim, dark-skinned, hair in thin braids down to her waist. She was dressed in white jeans and a yellow camisole. Her eyes were wide with shock. Mascara stained her cheeks.

"Eryka? I'm Detective Preddy, Pelican Walk."

"Hello, sir," she whispered.

"I'm sorry about your boyfriend," said Preddy.

She sniffed and nodded. "He was my very good friend, but not my boyfriend. I can't believe this." Her soft voice wobbled, her final words emerging as barely a whisper.

"Can ye tell us what happened?" asked Harris.

Eryka closed her eyes briefly then opened them again. "We arrived here around eight. I drove and parked down there." She pointed off into the distance. "We bought some popcorn from a stall and went to find seats. Then Jerome said he was going to say hello to his uncle and check that everything was okay for the nine o'clock start."

"Yes, he came and chatted to me for about ten minutes, as I said," added Baccus. "The operator shut off all the lights while we were speaking and started running the promotional reel. You know, showing visions of what the beach and entertainment facilities would look like if we won the development contract. Jerome said he was going back to sit with Eryka. That was the last I saw of him, disappearing into the darkness down the aisle on the far side."

"He never came back," murmured Eryka as her eyes brimmed with tears.

Baccus pointed. "He headed down there."

Preddy looked where Baccus indicated. Past the shadowy images of food and drink stalls were two lines of lime-white-washed stones, which formed a trail guiding patrons to the temporary bathroom facilities. "I guess he made a stop there . . . or planned to."

"Do ye know if he had a wallet or cash on him?" asked Harris.

"Yes, he definitely had a wallet on him, and a phone," said Eryka.

"Didn't find de wallet. We have de phone." Preddy tapped his trouser pocket. He wondered if he imagined rather than sensed Eryka flinch, or whether her movement was just the normal movement when tears were flowing. She leaned to one side as if trying to look past him for a glimpse of the body.

"You didn't go look for him when he didn't return?" asked Preddy.

"No. I just thought he'd be back when the adverts were over and the movie was about to start proper. I mean, he'd already seen the adverts and was involved in the production, so I didn't think he'd rush back to watch them with me." She sniffed into a handkerchief. "I'd never seen it before, so I was watching the screen. Didn't even notice how much time had passed. Next thing I heard screaming and somebody shouted that there was a man dead by the bushes. I went to look. It was dark so all I could see were the shoes, but I knew it was him."

"Ye didnae approach Jerome, tae check on him?" asked Harris.

"No!" She crossed her arms over her shoulders and rubbed them. "I just screamed and ran and kept running. Before I knew it, I was back at my car. I just leaned on it. Couldn't move. I didn't know what to do. I heard you on the loudspeaker, but I just couldn't move."

A private vehicle was let through the caution tapes and Preddy watched it crawl up the beach towards them. The pathologist, Doctor Sewell, tooted her horn as she neared the tent and Rabino held both arms aloft directing her to come forward. The lights of an ambulance went by shortly after the pathologist's car and the two came to a halt side by side.

"Let's walk to your car," said Preddy, eager to move them away from the distressing sight behind. They moved slowly, Baccus gripping Erica's arm as she wobbled along through the sand in inappropriate heels.

"We know this is very hard for both of ye, but do ye know who could've done this tae Jerome?" asked Harris.

"No," whispered Eryka. "He was a nice guy."

Baccus frowned. "If it wasn't just a thief, I'd put my money on Wesley Ashburn. That man had it in for us, from long time."

"You think he would go to dis length?" asked Preddy. "I thought dis was just a business rivalry? May de best man win and all dat?"

Baccus clenched his fists at his side. "He's been taunting us for weeks now. Trying to put us off as if he was sure that he would win the beach contract and we were wasting our time."

"If he was about tae commit murder, I doubt if he'd be hinting at it in advance," said Harris with barely hidden scepticism. "Murderers tend nawtae be keen on people knowing their intentions."

Baccus shrugged, his haggard face stricken with anger. "He was planning something, that's all I know."

"Do you have any ideas, Eryka?" asked Preddy.

"None at all." Her voice changed, hardening slightly. "You'll have to tell Jerome's so-called girlfriend about it. I don't speak to her."

Preddy and Harris exchanged glances. "Och, and who would that be?" asked Harris.

"Nicki Younis."

Baccus looked momentarily confused. "That girl Nicki is his girlfriend? Since when? Jerome said they were just friends. Actually, I thought you were his girlfriend as you're the one I always heard him talk about."

Preddy noticed a hint of pride cross Eryka's face at these words, but she said nothing.

"Where can we find Nicki?" asked Preddy.

"Good luck with that," said Eryka. "She lives in St Thomas, I think, but she comes to Mo Bay sometimes. They had a long-distance thing going on, although Jerome said it wasn't serious. She seemed to think so." Eryka reached into her jeans pocket and took out the remote key fob, activating the doors of a top-of-the-range blue Audi.

"We'll track her down through de phone," said Preddy with a glance at the luxury vehicle. "I imagine all de important contacts will be in here."

"Can I go now?" she asked. "I just want to leave this place."

"Yes, sure," said Preddy. "Let me take your number first."

Harris held the torch while Preddy wrote her phone number in his notebook, together with that of Gavin Baccus. The three men watched as she drove away.

"I need to get the guys to take down the marquee and pack up all the equipment," said Baccus, his voice rattling with emotion. "If we leave it till morning there won't be a thing left there, not even a chair. Even what they can't use or don't understand, they will take."

"Fine," said Preddy. "Jerome will be taken up to Cornwall Regional. We'll need to notify his parents."

"I'll phone my brother, Detective. Trust me, it will be better coming from me."

Preddy closed his notebook and tucked it into his shirt pocket. "If you think dat's best?"

Baccus massaged his temples. "It is, honestly."

"If ye think of anything else, naw matter how insignificant it seems, call us any time," said Harris.

Baccus nodded and headed off in the direction of the projector, which was being guarded by his assistants. All of them were smartly dressed in black trousers and long-sleeved white shirts.

"It's a shit start tae the new year for us, but can ye imagine what it'll be like for the Baccus family?" Harris said.

"A parent's worst nightmare." Preddy shuddered involuntarily. "We have to get dis killer."

CHAPTER 2

Detective Preddy turned his jeep into the driveway of Pelican Walk Police Station. The cream-and-blue building had received a lick of paint over the Christmas period and looked pristine on the outside — from a distance. Closer inspection revealed unfilled wall cracks, damaged windows and dangling roof slats.

A herd of six goats wandered aimlessly all over the long driveway. Some took up cool spots under the Julie mango tree, paying scant attention to the approaching vehicle. A nanny goat reclined under the richly coloured foliage of a croton bush. There she was shielded by deep green leaves spattered with red-and-yellow patterns, as if someone had flicked a paint brush at them from a distance. No one had any idea who the contented animals belonged to. Just before Christmas two constables had seized the herd from a flatbed truck as the driver could give no explanation for their presence. Despite appeals for farmers to come forward and claim the animals, no one had showed up yet, leading many to believe the theft came from outside St James. Preddy carefully avoided running over them as he parked. No doubt the

17

ruminants were destined for a pot of curry, but he did not want to be personally responsible for their demise.

Inside the lobby, Wilson was staffing the front desk, which served as first port of call for visitors. Preddy greeted him, then crunched the last bit of a mint sweet and exhaled into his palm. Satisfied that there was no trace of his potent ganja tea, he took the stairs in his usual style, two at a time, and headed straight for Superintendent Brownlow's office. The superintendent's door was open and he beckoned to Preddy before the detective could knock.

"So, we've started the new year pretty much like how we ended the old?" said Brownlow, his tone more despairing than angry. He leaned back in his chair and placed his hands on his plump stomach.

Preddy nodded as he took a seat opposite. "On a plus note, it wasn't a shooting. De state of emergency is still having a good effect. Way fewer shootings."

"Lord knows we're grateful for that," agreed Brownlow with a sigh. "Can't believe we're actually expressing gratitude for a stabbing. How the hell do we get the criminals to lay down all other weapons?"

"And dis is a new one," said Preddy. "An awl. Looks more like an ice pick, but it has a distinct look to it. Pathologist said de point went straight into de heart of Jerome Baccus. We're not releasing dat bit of information to de media by de way, just dat he was stabbed."

"What else do we know?" The superintendent picked up a pen and twirled it in front of his lips. "Please tell me we have a few good leads?"

"We have his phone so I can see all his frequent contacts and recent phone calls," said Preddy. "Hundreds of people were on de beach last night. Most scattered when de body was spotted, and so far no one has admitted to having seen or heard anything. Granted, it was dark because de floodlights had been turned off, and where he was found is partially hidden from de rows of seats."

"Is it likely to have been a random killing?"

"We spoke to de uncle, Gavin Baccus, briefly and he's basically pointing de finger at Wesley Ashburn. He's a rival businessman trying to win de beach-development contract."

"I've heard of him. He's the All Angles man." The superintendent pursed his lips. "Hmm, I can see why Baccus would think that. There's no love lost between them, although surely he would be more likely to murder the uncle than the nephew?"

"By all accounts de uncle was a pain in Ashburn's side, but Rabino sent me some links to social-media posts made by Jerome. All I can say is dey weren't nice," said Preddy. "He was at de marquee with a young lady named Eryka Malden, who says dey were just friends. Says Jerome was a nice guy. Maybe dat's her loyalty speaking, because from de little I've seen, he was rude and arrogant."

"Young people and social media, man." Brownlow looked disapproving as he tutted. He made a steeple of his fingers. "This Eryka Malden didn't see anything?"

Preddy shook his head. "She gave me de name of a girl who seems to be Jerome's real girlfriend, Nicki Younis. Detective Spence spoke to Nicki dis morning. She lives in Golden Grove, St Thomas, but says she'll come to Mo Bay dis evening."

Brownlow raised his eyebrows. "So she knows her boyfriend was murdered while on a night out with another girl? How did that go down?"

Preddy grimaced. "Not very well apparently, but she did know dat Jerome and Eryka were friends. I've asked Spence and Rabino to interview her, as she might open up to other women. It could be a pretty delicate conversation."

The superintendent gave a rueful smile. "Yes, I guess it will be."

"Detective Harris and I are going to see Wesley Ashburn. He agreed to talk to us, but he'd rather not come to Pelican Walk. Says we can meet him at his design studio on de Hip Strip dis afternoon."

"How did he sound? Nervous? Worried?"

Preddy thought about this for a few seconds. "Hard to tell. He'd already heard a newsflash when he woke up dis morning. Didn't sound surprised to hear from me. Didn't seem upset or sad, but den again, I've never spoken to him before so I don't know what he's like."

"I have." The superintendent leaned forward and spoke in a reverent tone, as if speaking of Norman Washington Manley, one of Jamaica's most cherished national heroes. "He's a very intelligent, sharp man, Preddy. As well as his design work, he's opened a nightclub and a restaurant down Dead End and has improved the city's offerings no end. He's a respected businessman. I would even go so far as to describe him as one of the stalwarts of Montego Bay."

"Yes, sir." *Here we go*, thought Preddy. *Trust Brownlow to see the bright side of his personality.* Social climbing was very much the super's thing, and he would not support any moves that might annoy the city's wealthy residents.

The superintendent stared at Preddy, warming to his task. "Gavin Baccus is not that well known to me, but if he gets the go-ahead to develop Sugar Rush Beach, he's going to be very influential in this city. Very influential."

"I understand, sir."

"I hope you do, Preddy. And please make sure the rest of your team does too."

Preddy fought to prevent a frown from creeping across his brow. "Yes, sir."

Superintendent Brownlow poured out two glasses of ice water and offered one to Preddy. "Anyway, it was probably an opportunistic murder," he said. "Some wasteman took advantage of the darkness, stabbed him and stole his money."

Preddy ran his fingers along the cold glass. "Dat's a possibility, sir," he said. "Doesn't explain why dey took money and left an expensive phone. I mean, I know it was dark, but whether de phone was in Jerome's hand or in his pocket, it would have taken two seconds to grab it. No way de murderer missed it."

"Probably feared it could be immediately traced and decided not to touch it."

Preddy took his time over downing his glass of water. It never ceased to annoy him that the brass could draw such quick conclusions and expect the detectives to do the same and deliver the murderer all within twenty-four hours. More recently, the Police High Command had begun attributing baffling murders to lottery scamming, before the specialist lottery detectives had even been assigned the cases. The pressure to wrap up murder cases was becoming all-consuming, not least because potential foreign investors did not find the crime statistics attractive and the government was running out of excuses and explanations. The tourists seemed to take it in their stride and continued to flock to the island, breaking records for arrivals each year.

"We'll look at all avenues, sir."

"All right, remember to keep me informed." The superintendent turned his gaze to his computer screen and Preddy took it as his cue to leave.

"I will, sir." He quietly shut the door behind him and headed to his office.

* * *

It was late that afternoon when Preddy and Harris drove along the low-lying coastal road. Once formally known as Gloucester Avenue, it was now named Jimmy Cliff Boulevard after one of Jamaica's favourite sons of reggae. The latter name had not yet caught on, and unbothered residents continued to refer to it informally as Bottom Road or, when talking to tourists, the Hip Strip. Both sides of the Hip Strip were taken up with businesses — cafes, restaurants, jewellers and craft shopping facilities — but the prime side held the all-inclusive hotels bordered by miles of white sandy beach.

Harris had his phone close to his nose reading something and ignoring the magnificent view. Many a time Preddy had thought about snatching it from him in an effort to find out what the Scotsman was up to, but he resisted the temptation. Commissioner Davis would pension him off with the slightest provocation, and any manhandling of Harris would be classed as assault and as such unforgiveable.

Instead Preddy peered out at the latest arrival in the metropolis — the Usain Bolt Tracks & Records restaurant, with its life-sized statue of the athlete doing his famous lightning-bolt pose. Then past the newly opened Spanish Court Hotel with its hundreds of extra new rooms, outside of which freshly washed taxis jostled for tourist dollars. Not being a coffee man, Preddy had never entered the new Starbucks that sat at the entrance to Doctor's Cave Beach, but it was clearly popular with better-paid locals and tourists alike. Jamaicans shamelessly loved all things foreign, particularly American, and would do anything to be seen with the familiar green cup.

Preddy smiled as he passed an attractive white building, which he was sure would test the creativeness of determined Jamaicans. The Island Strains Herb House catered to people with prescriptions for medical marijuana, and he expected it to encourage a healthy market in fake prescriptions. If the Herb House ever branched out into selling his favourite tea, it would be his new haunt.

He put the indicator on and Harris raised his head to see where they were. Preddy turned off beside the Canadian Consulate and headed up a short road to Miranda Hill, home to a small number of businesses and residential premises. Three other vehicles were sitting in the target car park.

"So, this is All Angles?" Harris stared at the impressive building. "It really stands out from all the other properties ye can see from the main road."

"Nice, man," said Preddy in admiration.

All Angles was two storeys of glass blending seamlessly into white walls. Not a large structure, but certainly a strikingly contemporary one. The building looked like something out of a design magazine: one of those glossy places that did not need to denigrate its outward appearance by putting up common signs or any bright colours. A large fountain sent sprays of fresh water into the air, and the calming sound deadened the noise of traffic from the heavily polluted main road. A batch of orange carp darted between the algae and lily pads in the surrounding waters. Coconut trees belonging to the neighbouring property sheltered the small car park. The elevated location presented a perfect view of the rippling blue water of the distant Caribbean Sea.

"I've driven past dis building so many times and just assumed it was an architect-designed house belonging to some foreigner," said Preddy. "Never knew dis was Wesley Ashburn's business place. He calls it a studio."

Harris smiled. "Och, naw the pretentious type, then?"

"No name signs anywhere. He's pretentious, all right. According to my kids, it's called humble-bragging." Preddy closed the car door. "Remember what Super said, now."

"Of course, I'll be at ma most polite." Harris pushed back his ginger fringe flecked with white strands and mockingly smoothed his hair down. "At least Super didnae suggest we wear ties."

Discreetly placed security cameras under the overhanging roof recorded the detectives' every move as they approached. As Preddy raised his finger to press a sunken black button, the mechanism came alive as if by magic and the glass doors slid open. A rush of air-conditioned draught pushed the temperature from high eighties to low sixties in a split second. A distinct click sounded as Preddy entered and a soft light flashed in his face, making him flinch. His fingers inched towards the weapon tucked in his waistband. He looked behind him. The same thing had happened to Harris — a click and a flash of light. Preddy frowned and wiped his hands on the sides of his trousers.

"Could've waited till I put ma best smile on before taking ma picture," muttered Harris. "Do ye think we should go out and try that again?"

"No," said Preddy. "You not going look good no matter what you do."

"Cheers," said Harris. "Thank God we wore jackets, it's bloody freezing in here."

"Good morning, detectives?" It was a question more than a greeting.

Wesley Ashburn walked across shiny white porcelain tiles towards them. A dark, middle-aged man, he was shorter than Preddy had expected, with a wisp of a moustache and black-and-white stubble. He wore a tan suit that swamped him, high-waisted trousers held up by a round stomach, and a bold red tie. He clutched a folder of papers with both hands.

"Good morning, Mr Ashburn. We spoke. I'm Detective Raythan Preddy. Dis is Detective Sean Harris."

Harris inclined his head slightly. "Mr Ashburn."

The man nodded his greeting at Harris. "I saw the jeep as soon as you turned off the main road." His voice was deep and he enunciated each word precisely.

"You still took our photos even though you guessed who we were?" Preddy was unable to hide his annoyance.

"Just security, that's all." Wesley Ashburn's left eye twitched as he spoke. "You can never be too careful in these times, can you, detectives? Need a record of all who enter in case of trouble."

Preddy stared down the host. "Not a bad idea," he said, "but people react differently to clicks and flashes of bright light, particularly people trained to listen out for certain sounds and react quickly."

"Oh." Wesley Ashburn's eyes moved to the right side of Preddy's waistband where his holster was partially visible beneath his jacket. "Yes, I get your point. We'll do something to make it less obvious."

"Nice place ye have here," said Harris.

"It's not bad." Ashburn spun on his heels. "Follow me, gentlemen."

The roof of the lobby contained a large skylight, which today looked onto the cloudless blue sky. There was no reception desk. The white walls were lined with the types of abstract paintings that designers seemed to adore. Preddy imagined that some of the paintings cost more than he earned in a year. Plants of all colours in expensive-looking terracotta pots lined the aisle, bringing the outdoors indoors in a calming manner. It was like walking through an elaborate greenhouse.

As they rounded a corner, they entered a vast open-plan area. A large glass-fronted minibar sat at the bottom of the white-tiled staircase. Miniature bottles of rums by Wray & Nephew, Appleton and Blackwells were in view.

"We'll go upstairs to the offices, if you like, but this area is where we exhibit our plans and designs." Ashburn waved a hand at the floor space.

There were at least a dozen tables spread out with building model designs in 3D. Two well-dressed men stood at the far end of the room studying the content on a table. They raised their heads only to briefly acknowledge the arrival of the new visitors.

"Couple of my colleagues," murmured Ashburn.

"This is some intricate stuff, right here." Harris pointed at a model. "That looks like a miniature of that twin towers hotel at the Freeport?"

Preddy looked at it. "You're right. Complete wid miniature swimming pool and deck chairs."

Ashburn smiled proudly as they studied his production. "We don't cut corners in our business. Only the best designers and architects work here. I don't work with people who just talk the talk."

"What tools do you use to build dese?" asked Preddy. He could see nothing that would require an awl to aid the design. These tiny structures looked like they were built using expensive technical equipment, not hand tools.

"Some are done with 3D machines which we have round the back there. We also have some other machines for cutting and chopping smooth lines. Modern technology works wonders in this industry if you have people who can operate them."

"How many of ye work here?" asked Harris.

"Five in total. The individual offices are upstairs. All guys I've known since I was young, kicking balls in the street and giving trouble." He smiled conspiratorially as he spoke. "Everybody trained right here in Jamaica and also did extensive training abroad. As the name suggests, we cover all angles . . . architect plans, design, fittings, landscaping. We even assess the potential of land for building purposes. We get plenty of tourists through the door. They see a bit of rock with a great view and think it's okay to buy it and stick a house on it. No thought to soil type, or erosion, or feasibility, or utilities."

Preddy walked around the tables. "Which one is Dowdy Beach?"

"Ah, we prefer its real name, Sugar Rush Beach, if you would, Detective." It came with a tone of admonishment. "To your left, just beside the Alvin Marriott."

Preddy would not have known that the wooden human head was an Alvin Marriott sculpture. More not-so-subtle bragging by Ashburn, but at least the man truly cherished the work of world-class Jamaicans. Preddy walked in the direction indicated, followed by Harris. Soon they were standing over the entertainment complex design, which took up a good ten metres of floor space — a sprawling model complete with a beach made of real sand embracing blue crystals representing the Caribbean Sea. This was a design to rival that of Emancipation Park in Kingston. There was a huge dome-shaped stage with thatched roof, cascading water features, royal palm trees, restroom facilities, raised gazebos and food huts, all set among perfectly landscaped surroundings. Preddy was pleased that the design was based around the giant trees that had thrived on Dowdy Beach for hundreds of years and provided natural shelter from the harsh sun.

Harris strolled along the table. "Looks good."

"To die for." Preddy stared at Ashburn, who avoided his gaze and dabbed at his flickering left eye with a handkerchief.

Harris pointed a finger at the model. "What's that track along the beach? For bicycles?"

"Oh no, Detective. That's a boardwalk. No bicycles allowed in that area. The only wheels that would go along there are baby buggies or mobility scooters." Ashburn pointed at another track before rubbing his hands together as if trying to dry them. "That purple line is the route bicycles would take. They have to go around the outskirts of the complex, not through it."

"Nice," said Preddy. The man was jovial, yet clearly unable to stop the involuntary tic that revealed his discomfort. He seemed to be trying to treat the detectives as if they were prospective clients or investors needing to be convinced, but his nerves were getting the better of him.

"So you and Gavin Baccus were going head-to-head in de final race to win de Dowdy . . . Sugar Rush Beach contract?"

Ashburn shook his head. "Gavin and I are rivals, I'll admit to that, Detective, but there's no way I would do anything to sabotage his plans. As for murder? That's not my style at all. I'll fight you on paper or on product design."

"Where were you last night?" asked Preddy.

"Am I really a suspect, Detective?" The eye jumped as he spoke.

"At this stage, we're just making enquiries tae try and solve a murder," said Harris. "There are lots of people we plan tae question. Please answer the question, sir."

Ashburn took a deep breath and failed to curb his spasm. "I was downtown. I'm not going to lie. Wouldn't be much point because I'm sure people saw me there. And yes, I did go over by the Grand Marquee to see what Gavin Baccus had laid on." Ashburn held up the palms of his hands as he watched Harris and Preddy exchange glances. "I did not go anywhere near Jerome Baccus, I swear! I saw him, but I stood way at the back behind the last row of chairs watching the promotion and eating my jerked chicken."

"Did you notice anyone approach Jerome or argue wid him?" asked Preddy.

"No. I only glimpsed him briefly. He was with a girl." Ashburn pointed at the 3D model. "Look, the marquee is about here. I stood right back there, and Jerome was about here. Gavin was up front. I could see him clearly and heard him with the megaphone. Half of Mo Bay did." Ashburn's eyes narrowed in recollection. "He gave a bumptious speech before the promotional film started running then sat down. The place went black-dark and I saw nothing after that. Next thing I was aware of was a disturbance by the Portaloos — people shouting, then screaming. I had no idea what was going on and hung around by the roadside watching as the area got cordoned off and constables told us to leave. It wasn't until hours later when I was going to bed I heard a newsflash that there'd been a stabbing. This morning they named the victim, and I was shocked."

Preddy watched him closely. "Jerome mocked you and your business on social media?"

"So he's a jumped-up, cocky millennial. Doesn't mean I'd kill him." Ashburn did little to conceal his bitterness. "If I was going to attack anybody, it would make more sense to go after Gavin. The boy was a nobody riding on his uncle's coattails. No manners, no class. Total nobody."

"His mam and dad didnae think so," said Harris. "In fact, they're quite distraught."

Ashburn bit his lip. "Sorry, that was a stupid thing to say. I didn't mean it like that at all, Detective. Look, I'm as sorry about this terrible killing as everybody else. Nobody deserves to die, but I don't know anything about it. I swear!"

"Can you think of anybody who might have been involved?" Preddy asked.

"You mean like my guys here?" Ashburn looked incredulous, but the eye began dancing again. "Of course we want to win the contract, Detective, but all of us earn very good money and have done for years now. If we don't get the Sugar Rush Beach contract, life will go on as usual. Other people interested in the beach development, particularly environmentalists, will still have issues. All Angles would just move on. You might want to speak to the beach vendors' association, as I know they've been complaining about getting airbrushed out of both prospective developments."

"Who would that be?" asked Harris.

Ashburn frowned. "Clean Living Association or something? Can't remember the proper name. It's a group of around ten people. They want us to find space on Sugar Rush Beach for every fisherman, fruit seller and peanut man in Mo Bay, and it's just not possible. They'll have to move on and find other places to hawk their wares."

Preddy made a notation and closed his notebook. He glanced at Harris, who nodded at him. "Thank you for speaking to us, Mr Ashburn. If anything else springs to mind, I want you to call us."

"I'll do that, Detective Preddy."

"We'll show ourselves out," said Harris. "Thank ye for yer time."

The detectives walked back to their vehicle.

"Glad ye didnae pull yer weapon on him when we arrived. Could've been a messy start tae the interview."

Preddy raised an eyebrow. "You noticed, eh?"

"How's the counselling going?"

Preddy did not respond.

"I told ye before, Preddy, talking about Norwood is the best way tae get the images tae fade. They'll never go if ye bottle it all up."

Preddy headed purposefully for the car door. "What do you make of Mr All Angles?"

Harris sighed. "There's definitely a mean streak lurking in the man, for all his earnestness. And that blinking eye isnae hay fever. Naw sure if I'm detecting 'murderer' though."

"Hmm." Preddy buckled up. "He put himself on de crime scene, smack in de middle of de sand, which saves us having to interview de owls and peeny-wallies. It also makes him a prime suspect."

"Super's going tae love that."

"Isn't he just?" Preddy turned and stared at him. "How's your private investigation going?"

"We're naw going tae start that again, are we?" said Harris, his exasperation clear. "Give up, Preddy."

"I hear you, Detective," he snapped back.

Preddy started the engine and turned on the music, though he was not listening to the reggae tunes. So far the Scotsman had only admitted to investigating one of the Pelican Walk detectives for corruption, but refused to say which one. Having excluded his own team, and a female detective on maternity leave, Preddy was left with seven detectives. Over the past four months, he had watched each detective closely, from their mannerisms to what they said, ate, wore, drove, and even where they lived. He had managed to narrow the list down to two: Iain Cotner and Des Willet. Neither man was a boastful sort. Both drove modest private vehicles, but seemed to dress in expensive clothes and shoes that would stretch any salary.

It annoyed Preddy that Superintendent Brownlow and Commissioner Davis had not seen fit to inform him that they were using his team member to investigate internal corruption. That was the remit of the Major Organized Crime and Anti-Corruption Agency, with its motto, *Taking the profit out of crime*. Instead, Harris was here playing undercover MOCA man with the full blessings of the brass.

He would not ask Harris any more questions. As his grandmother used to say, *Softly, softly, catchee monkey*.

CHAPTER 3

Thursday, 3 January, 8.30 a.m.

The detectives' workspace on the open-plan floor was almost empty. The area could accommodate a dozen people in pods, but it was rare that every officer was present at the same time. Most officers who had just arrived stopped briefly to put down their belongings and headed back downstairs. Harris locked his desk drawer and took a final gulp of hot coffee. Preddy was in the corridor watching him across the floor, and he acknowledged him with a slight nod. As the most senior detective at Pelican Walk, Preddy had his own office, which he had left to come and collect the team. Spence and Rabino chatted as they strolled towards the largest conference room in the building. Harris reluctantly followed, yawning in anticipation of the boredom ahead. It was too early for this. In fact, no time was good for this.

Prayer meetings. The police station's daily practice for the new year was being faithfully implemented. Allegedly, this bright idea had come from last year's anonymous survey of all officers for ideas that would make their working lives better. Harris had filled in the one-sided A4 page, whose tiny boxes strangely had not left much room for elaboration.

Somehow he found it hard to believe that anyone had voted to start the day with a prayer meeting, let alone that it was top of the list. Pelican Walk officers needed proper water facilities, better office furniture, modern crime-fighting technology and working motor vehicles with decent tyres, for starters. They also needed to acquire better weapons than the criminals. Harris had a feeling that top of the list had been pay rises, but the superintendent was unlikely to share such information. Harris was not minded to rock the boat, but he hoped that someone would put in an Access to Information request and dare the super to release the true survey results. He smiled wryly to himself. Commissioner Davis, the chief, would never allow it.

He caught up with his colleagues. "We really going tae do this?"

"Cho!" Spence kissed her teeth. "You too ungodly, man."

Preddy crunched on a mint and glanced back at him. "Boy, anybody would think we were leading you to de gas chamber."

"It's just half-hour, Detective Harris," said Rabino with a smile. "Not that painful."

"Speak for yerself."

"Not compulsory either," said Preddy pointedly. "If you fancy being de only person at your desk when de whole station is together, just remember: people will notice."

"Aye, I've already worked out how that would look," grumbled Harris.

"You no pray in Glasgow?" asked Spence.

"I guess people pray at home if they want tae. Ye wouldnae catch anyone praying in the office, unless they're about tae get roasted by the boss."

"Ah, blasphemous prayers," said Rabino. "If it's that bad you could always go on the front-desk rota. Someone has to be there, and Officer Wilson will want to participate some mornings. The only other people Super wouldn't expect to be present are those out on investigations."

Spence nudged Rabino in the ribs. "You shouldn't tell him dat. You not going see him in here before nine any morning again."

They lowered their voices as they passed the superintendent's closed door. The blinds were up, revealing that the room was empty, although his briefcase sat on his desk.

"If you buy that nice property you were eyeing up in Bogue Heights you'll be within a stone's throw from a church," said Rabino.

"I appreciate the warning."

"I'm sure Detective Harris will do his level best to attend as many prayer meetings with us as he can," said Preddy.

"I'm waiting for someone tae show me evidence that God exists."

Spence turned and gave him her best side-eye. "Eeh eeh? You still bawl out God name anytime something not going right though. I hear you plenty of time."

Harris shrugged. "That's just something ingrained and subconscious, not religious. I want evidence."

"Ah, evidence," said Preddy. "You should know better dan most dat sometimes dere is little evidence. You have to go on what your eyes and ears tell you and you own intuition."

Harris was not prepared to back down. "So far, ma eyes and ears tell me that there's way too many people being murdered on a daily basis for this God lark tae be real. Where was God when Jerome Baccus was being stabbed?"

"Busy stopping somebody else somewhere else in Jamaica being murdered?" suggested Rabino.

"That willnae cut it. There's more churches per square mile on this island than any other country in the world and people still think that praying is a good idea? What has it achieved?"

"God know what Him doing," said Spence. "It woulda much worse if we never pray."

"Hmm, that's a convenient way tae get around the issue. We can say it's working because there would've been more murders if it wasnae working? Not very scientific."

Rabino pursed her lips and let out a low whistle. "When you make that point to Super, I want to be present with my camera rolling."

"Me too," said Spence with a chuckle. "Me will bring snacks and drinks. Don't start de conversation widout me!"

The voices of already assembled staff echoed down the corridor as they approached the conference room. A mixture of officers was present, constables and detectives, male and female. The chairs had been piled up at the back of the room to make more standing space. Harris made eye contact with some of the officers and hid his feelings with a forced smile. At least there was an air-con unit in this room, and it was actually functioning.

The thick red curtains were drawn back from the windows, allowing light to stream through. It was a pity the windows weren't lower, as they were too high for anyone to get a glimpse of the courtyard. It would have been more interesting watching the birds playing freely in the trees and the goats chewing on leaves. The superintendent's original plan had been to hold the prayer meetings in the back courtyard. Harris was grateful this suggestion had not gained any traction. While the trees could have sheltered him from the powerful sunrays, they would have done little to quell the intense heat.

The superintendent was already in front of the podium, reading glasses perched on his nose, earnestly flicking through a Bible for a relevant passage. Harris sighed. A verse or two would be read, a couple of hymns sung, followed by eyes closed and heads bowed in prayer to a being that apparently lived in the clouds. It might be only half an hour, but it would try his patience, and he vowed that he would indeed try to avoid arriving at Pelican Walk prior to any future services or hide in an interview room.

Harris scanned the many sombre faces and noted the deceptively honest features of one particular detective. A detective who, according to the MOCA team, had strayed onto the wrong side of the law. A man who would pretty soon be under lock and key himself, if Jamaican justice worked. Yes, everybody needed pay rises, but there was no excuse for an officer of the law to take the criminal route. The investigation was proceeding apace and the takedown would happen soon. If prayer worked, that man was going to need a lot of it.

* * *

Preddy drove towards Sugar Rush Beach taking his favoured route along the high elevation of Queen's Drive, more popularly known as Top Road. While it was as equally busy a thoroughfare as Bottom Road, it contained only a fraction of the city's entertainment facilities — namely, a few small hotels that struggled to find occupants, being too far from the beach, and a couple of restaurants with panoramic views of the sea and planes approaching Sangster International Airport. It was for the glorious views that Preddy preferred this route, particularly the sight of the Freeport peninsula, where the yachts and cruise ships docked. He glanced at his colleague in the passenger seat. Having grown used to the scenery, Harris was preoccupied with his phone. Preddy tooted and waved at a parked traffic police car strategically positioned on a driveway partially hidden by an overgrown hedge, ready to catch speeding drivers using the smooth road as a racetrack. The police driver waved back.

Preddy turned right at the intersection of Top and Bottom roads, passing Fort Montego, one of the many forts built in the eighteenth century as part of the coastal defences. Two men with petrol-powered brush cutters were at work. Unwieldy tree branches had been chopped back, the wild grass cut into a decent lawn, the sea-facing cannons polished, and new benches installed. The fort had not seen much military action during its glory days, the cannons and guns being fired back then mainly to celebrate the British monarch's birthday. A newly erected sign told the historical tale using words Preddy would not have chosen had he been allowed to write the copy. The truth was, once upon a time, the fort was the lookout for British murderers, anticipating the return of Spanish murderers anxious to reclaim the land they originally stole, and which was subsequently stolen from them. That wording was probably less likely to appeal to tourists though, thought Preddy, although some would no doubt be amused by or sympathetic to the reality.

Preddy waited patiently as a coaster bus packed full of pink faces pulled out of the wide driveway of Walter Fletcher Beach and crossed in front of him to park at Fort Montego. Beside the fort was the Old Fort Craft Market, with colourful wooden huts where vendors sold the usual tourist souvenirs. Among the market's original features were an eighteenth-century wishing well where people could once throw coins, and the remains of an ancient artillery store.

Preddy turned into the driveway of Walter Fletcher Beach and pulled up under a tree, ensuring that his vehicle did not block the main entrance.

Harris looked up. "This us then?"

"Dis is us."

The gates were a few metres ahead and manned by a clerk who collected entrance fees. Preddy disapproved of local people having to pay to enter any beach. When he was a schoolboy, most beaches were free and easily accessible. In recent years the best beaches had been leased to all-inclusive hotel chains and were patrolled by security guards. Sugar Rush Beach, which adjoined Walter Fletcher Beach, was still free — for now. A six-foot-high chain-link fence topped with barbed wire separated the two venues, although visitors on either side could see one another clearly.

Preddy clapped his hands to attract the attention of the clerk and pointed at the vehicle. The man eyed him with a frown until recognition dawned on him, then he waved back. "You good, me boss!" he said. "Nobody nah trouble it."

Harris pocketed his phone and donned his sunglasses as he climbed out. "There's naw sign of tourists abandoning the Mo Bay beaches, naw matter what's going on."

"Good weather, great food, wonderful scenery and friendly people," said Preddy. "Dat's what tourists get. Dey're not under any threat. Of course, dey'll keep coming back." He removed his notepad from the dashboard and tucked a few pairs of latex gloves into his pocket.

"Thought the state of emergency would've been over by now. Didnae realize they could extend it. Did it without much fanfare too. Havenae heard any announcements for months from the politicians on either side of the pond warning visitors tae be careful."

"No one needed to warn dem to be careful anyway." Preddy pushed open a rusty side gate that separated the cared-for Walter Fletcher Beach from the neglected Sugar Rush Beach. "Is de foreign media take bad news and run wid it, trying to frighten people. Nobody in Mo Bay not murdering white people pon beach. Dat's never been de MO of our criminals and, luckily for de tourist industry, most foreigners know it."

"Aye." Harris followed him through the gate along a man-made track etched out of the long grass. "Well, they've put down many of the guns for now. If only we could get the chopping and stabbing tae go the same way."

"Indeed. And we've got our first awl killing — well, de first I've heard of anyway. Dat is one trend I don't want to see take off."

"An awl with naw fingerprints isnae a good start." Harris looked around him. "Amazing place. Two beaches side by side, one has lifeguards, changing facilities, go-carts, gazebos, a bar and bouncy castle. Cross the fence and ye've got the sea and sand, but nothing else. The potential is so obvious. It's hard tae believe the powers-that-be are only just getting around tae developing it."

Preddy gave a rueful smile as he traipsed through the sand, his eyes searching for anything unusual. "Oh dey've thought about it all right. Dey've been thinking about it for thirty years."

Harris grinned. "Och, the 'soon come' mentality?"

"Same way."

The Grand Marquee and food tents were all gone, but the row of Portaloos were still there. Not the sort of thing that opportunistic thieves around Montego Bay would ever consider stealing unless they were brand new. The area immediately around the murder scene was still cordoned off with yellow caution tape, which flickered in the gentle sea breeze. A sole constable remained on duty and looked relieved to see the approaching detectives. They greeted one another.

"All quiet?" asked Preddy.

"Yes, sir. Not even dog don't pass through here."

"Okay, you can go, Officer. We'll take it from here."

The detectives spent considerable time combing the immediate crime scene, looking for evidence that had been missed in the dark. Artificial light could not compare with daylight when it came to finding evidence. Discarded bloody clothing was foremost on Preddy's mind. They came up empty-handed and moved further along the extensive beach. Large black plastic bags of litter were grouped together with sheets of cardboard in a pile beside them. The rest of the beach was occupied by shirtless young men playing football, looking for all the world as if they did not care that a murder scene was mere metres away. For many, it would not be the first time they had been in close proximity to one. Other youngsters were swimming, doing somersaults in the warm salty water and screaming in delight. A tiny girl dashed into the sea with exultant cries, her braids bouncing in the air. None of the beachgoers seemed to care about the relentless sun that bore down on them.

"Is school naw back in?" asked Harris.

"No money, no school," said Preddy. "Or if dey're lucky, school two or three days a week."

A young boy was scrabbling around near the bags of rubbish.

"Hey!" Harris beckoned to him. "Ye dinnae want tae go playing in the rubbish. Ye'll get hurt."

The skinny boy looked up, the whites of his eyes clear as he studied the Scotsman. "Not playing in de garbage, sah," he said. "Me ah look glass bokkle fi carry go shop. Twenty dollar, dem pay fi a bokkle."

"Well, ye dinnae want tae be treading where there might be broken glass with bare feet. Where's ye shoes?"

"Me leave me slippers over deh so!"

"Put dem on and go over de other side go look bokkle," said Preddy sharply. "Police business over dis side."

The boy eyed Preddy warily as he moved aside, crablike. "Yes, sah."

Harris removed two hundred-dollar bills from his pocket. "Here, take this with ye."

The boy gave him a bright smile as he took the money. "Tank you, sah!" He paused and considered the white man for a moment, his shrewd eyes raking him from head to toe. "Dis can buy patty. Can get a hundred more fi buy box juice, please and tank you, sah!"

Harris handed the boy more money. "On yer way now, young man." He watched as the boy skipped away towards other boys. "'Please and thank ye,'" Harris repeated.

"He removed your option to say 'no.' Sorry for you today. When dere's more dan one of dem, don't give out any money." Preddy approached the pile of rubbish and pulled on his gloves. "Your new fan and him friends going overrun de car when we leave here, just watch. News spreads fast in dis place."

"Aye, well, they'll be lucky."

"Look at dis." Preddy lifted a bit of cardboard and pulled another piece from beneath it. "Placards. Check what's written on it." He threw a pair of latex gloves at Harris, who caught them deftly.

Harris squinted at the cardboard through his tinted shades. "Guess there was a demonstration down here sometime during the day yesterday? 'Naw beach, naw justice!'" He lifted another placard. "'Say naw tae apartheid beach!' Ouch, that one's a bit harsh. 'Naw development without local involvement!' Check this one . . . 'Black Lives Matter!' Didnae think anyone would need tae say that in Jamaica."

"You'd be surprised," murmured Preddy. He uncovered another message. "'Vendors are people too. We deserve a livelihood!' I guess dere's a hell of a lot more people dan we thought who are not happy about de plans for dis beachfront."

The warning alarm of a parish council rubbish truck sounded as it reversed towards the detectives at a crawl. Preddy flagged it down and ordered the driver to park a distance away. A worker riding on the back lowered his dust mask and shouted out, "Ah de garbage we come fah!"

Preddy waved his badge at him. "We're not finished here just yet, sir."

The driver leaned out of the window. "We can move a bit closer, Officer? Dem bag big and heavy to carry."

Preddy glanced at the bags then back at the men. "Give us half hour den you can move closer and take everything."

"Yes, bossie!"

Preddy turned back to Harris, who held up a placard. "'Livity Vendors Association says naw tae Baccus and All Angles.'"

"Ah, de beach sellers Wesley Ashburn mentioned," said Preddy. "He did say dey were unhappy about being displaced."

"Didnae see or hear of any demonstration yesterday?" said Harris. "It wasnae on the news."

"Me neither," said Preddy. "Guess it was quite peaceful. De national media would ignore it unless de participants set fire to something or blocked traffic. It would be in de local press though. De *Western Mirror* publishes Wednesday and Friday, so my guess is we'll see a report in tomorrow's paper."

Harris tossed the placard to the ground and reached for a black bag. He untied the neck and peered inside. "So the most we can say is that the Livity lot — whoever they were — arenae violent people?"

Preddy grabbed a different black bag and fumbled around inside. "Or dat dey weren't mad enough to act violently in broad daylight, where dey could easily be identified."

He could sympathize with their pain. Building a magnificent entertainment facility in front of unemployed people was like dangling a bone in front of a starving, chained dog. There would be deep bites to suture if and when the chain broke. Preddy had seen it happen before. "De parish council guys should have a good idea who makes up de Livity membership. We'll make a stop at de Union Street HQ and ask some questions."

When they had finished searching, they retied the necks and stacked the bags back closely together. Preddy looked towards the garbage truck and clapped his hands twice to get the driver's attention. With both arms outstretched, he beckoned the man to reverse. The driver gave a quick toot and started the engine.

"Let's get out of here." Preddy glanced at his jeep in the distance and smiled. "I'll let you lead de way. Your three new young friends are leaning on my door."

Harris grimaced. "Och, great."

"You'll have to learn to develop a harder heart. Dese kids work in teams and know how to charm people. Kindness will turn you into what we call a 'bruk pocket'."

"Ah well, as long as it doesnae get me killed."

"No comment," said Preddy.

CHAPTER 4

Detective Rabino stood at the entrance to the Pelican Walk canteen fanning her face with a notebook. She watched as Spence purchased bottled water and shared jokes with the cook's assistant. Every table was empty since it was still relatively early for lunch. The sizzle of frying chicken could be heard in the distance and the strong savoury aroma filled the air. Within an hour the indistinct voices of hungry officers would liven up the place. Their interviewee, Nicki Younis, had arrived, and Officer Wilson had placed her to wait in Interview Room Two.

"She got here earlier than I thought she would." Rabino took two of the ice-cold water bottles from Spence, leaving her with the third. "That's a good journey from Golden Grove. I'm guessing she got a bus to Kingston then picked up something to Mo Bay."

"Must have jumped outta her bed before cockcrow." Spence led the way up the stairs. "But den again, if it was my man somebody killed, I wouldn't have slept through de night anyway. Probably wouldn't even have gone to bed."

"Very true."

A couple of male constables greeted them in the corridor as they walked in the opposite direction. "Ladies, how's it going?"

"Everything cool, Officer Mitchell," said Rabino. "How are you, my good sir?"

"Not as good as you," said the always-jovial Mitchell with a smile. "Boy, it not getting easier."

"Hope you're not kicking off any more doors in Montpelier, Detective Spence?" said the other officer.

"You know me, Blagrove. If it need a good kicking, I going kick it! If it need a good shooting, I going shoot it!"

They all laughed as Blagrove pretended to shy away from her in mock horror.

"We have someone to interview right now, but don't worry, Spence won't be kicking or shooting. I'll watch her," said Rabino.

"All right. Later, ladies." The men chuckled and continued on their way.

"Any first impressions from speaking to Nicki yesterday?" asked Rabino as they continued down the corridor. "Or should I ask, any tarot readings tell you what to expect?"

"No first impressions, really. I could tell she was crying, as to be expected." Spence grinned at her colleague. "My tarot just said it will be a difficult week, but light is at de end of de tunnel."

"Oh, please." Rabino rolled her eyes. "Those things are so general. They could say that for every day of the week. I'd be more impressed if it said, 'A girl from the eastern part of the island will bring you some helpful information.' That's the only way you'd get me interested in those predictions."

"Heh! You not going satisfy unless dem predict de Super Lotto numbers too! Is 300 million dollar it reach now, you know? If I get dat, no more crime investigating."

"Yeah, right. You love it, girl. There's no way you'd give it up."

"Speak for yourself, missis. If my parents had money like yours, I'd run a bookshop or something calming."

"Bookshop?" Rabino smiled. "No, you wouldn't. Way too quiet for you. You thrive on excitement and the challenge of the unknown." She glanced at her as they reached Interview Room Two. "Here's to unravelling the unknown."

Nicki Younis got to her feet as soon as the door opened. She was a plump girl, medium height and brown-skinned, in a clinging bright yellow dress, which she pulled down from her hips. Her long, straight ponytail matched Rabino's, except that unlike the detective, Nicki's was not an expensive human import, hers being a mixed heritage. With her jet-black hair drawn back from her round face so severely, she looked very young for twenty-one, more like a schoolgirl. A gold stud was embedded in one nostril. She sank long, red-painted nails into her palms, which held a small face flannel.

"Hello, Nicki. Take a seat, man. Is all right." Spence removed a notebook and pen from her pocket and sat directly in front of her. "We spoke yesterday. I'm Detective Spence. Dis is Detective Rabino."

"Hello." Nicki nodded at them both.

"Thank you very much for coming in, Nicki," said Rabino. She sat at a slight angle, close enough to reach the girl if she needed to hold her. It wouldn't be the first time an interviewee passed out under questioning, however innocuous the questions.

Nicki gave a weak smile as she retook her seat. "I did plan to come up here today anyway . . . to see Jerome."

"Some journey though." Rabino pushed a bottle of water towards Nicki. "Here, drink this."

Nicki squeezed the bottle with both hands to cool her flannel. "Traffic wasn't too bad."

"We're very sorry for your loss," said Spence. "We going do everything in our power to catch de person who did dis."

"Thank you." Nicki spoke softly, her eyes fixed on her fingers, which she could not keep still, as if she was playing an invisible piano. "I know who did it. Tex Doran."

"Tex Doran?" Rabino leaned forwards slightly. "Tell us about him. Who's he?"

"Oh, so that faas girl forgot to mention him?" said Nicki. "Strange that."

"Which faas girl?" asked Spence.

"Eryka Malden." Nicki paused her distracting movements and her tone hardened. "She who has an old man supporting her but is always hanging around Jerome trying to buy him off! She don't even earn a cent of her own. Is married man she keeping. Big old tough grey-back married man she have buying her car and house and—"

"Okay, slow down a minute." Rabino hovered her pen over her notebook. "Take a deep breath and let's do this calmly."

"Drink some more water, man," Spence encouraged her.

Nicki obeyed. She took a long swig and wiped her lips with the back of her hand. "Sorry. It's just that I know that girl got Jerome killed. I knew it as soon as you said the two of them were together at the Grand Marquee. I did know Jerome was going last night, but he didn't mention taking company. We spoke earlier in the day and he said he missed me." Her voice cracked and she dabbed at her eyes, smudging her eyeliner.

"Did he say anything that indicated he expected trouble at the marquee?" asked Rabino.

Nicki shook her head. Her face became blotched and a frown disturbed her brow. "Didn't mention anything about that girl either. I just thought he'd be going with his uncle Gavin, since the two of them were working on the promotion material. Shows how stupid I was." She blinked and wiped her eyes again. "I should have known that girl would come flirting around him, even though she knew her married man would go crazy."

"You know anything more about Mr Doran, where he lives?" Spence asked while scribbling her notes. "Is a local man?"

"I'm not sure, but I think he's based somewhere in St James. His real name is Terrell, apparently, but people call him Tex."

"How did you come to hear of him, Nicki?" asked Rabino.

"Once, when I came to meet Jerome in Mo Bay — maybe a couple months ago — I saw Jerome with Eryka getting out of her car." She frowned deeply at the memory. "I asked him about her. He said to relax, she was just his friend, and she was dating an older man anyway. I wasn't convinced and went at him over it. He swore nothing was going on. Explained that the man, Tex Doran, bought her the Audi and he rented an apartment for her too." Her eyes narrowed. "Even gave her a credit card. But she wasn't satisfied. Kept hanging round my man! Trying to buy love from young man with old man's money. Damn skettel! Jerome just finished uni and started working, he didn't have half as much money to throw around as she did."

"So Jerome know a lot 'bout Tex." Spence drummed her pen on the table. "Did Tex know anything 'bout Jerome?"

"Guess he found out." Nicki spoke through gritted teeth. "Jerome's dead, isn't he?"

The oscillating fan whirred in the subsequent silence. Nicki shifted in her seat uncomfortably and reached for her water, holding it to her lips, the lack of movement in her throat indicating she was not drinking.

"Did Jerome ever say he was afraid of what would happen if Tex found out about him hanging out with Eryka?" Rabino asked.

"No. I doubt if the two men ever met. Jerome did say that nothing was going on with him and Eryka so there was no reason for either Tex or me to be jealous about any time they spent together." She sighed and studied a small stain on the table. "I was mad, but what could I do? I'm living way down in Golden Grove. I've been trying to find work in Mo Bay for months now so that I can move here, but nothing's come up. I was only seeing Jerome every other weekend and I knew that would be trouble if I couldn't move here. The long-distance thing, I mean."

Rabino nodded. "Well, you're right on one thing. Eryka didn't mention Tex Doran to us. I guess she didn't see him as a threat to Jerome either."

Nicki's hazel eyes flashed. "Trust me, Detective, that girl is the reason why Jerome is dead. She and she alone! That old man let jealousy get the better of him. I bet you any money he did it."

"We'll have a talk to Mr Doran, Nicki."

"You need to arrest him!" Her voice came in a shriek. "Lock him up!"

"Dat's not quite how we work." Spence got to her feet, her tone sharp. "We investigate and seek evidence before we arrest anybody, unless dey walk in and confess. Unlawful detention and false imprisonment not going get us anything except a lawsuit. Evidence we need, ma'am."

Rabino studied Nicki's dejected face and quickly added, "But thank you for the lead anyway, Nicki. We'll take it from here."

The two detectives accompanied Nicki to the lobby and waved farewell.

"Well, that was interesting." Rabino watched Nicki Younis disappear down the driveway, tugging the hem of her straining dress as she went.

"Preddy will like dis," said Spence. "We might get de case wound up before weekend start." She poked her colleague in her ribcage. "See, de tarot was on to something!"

"Still not buying it, lady."

"You know, talking to her on de phone, I wasn't looking for a coolie, but she look like coolie breed and Younis is foreign name," said Spence. "How she cyah find work in Mo Bay? Me wouldn't call her pretty, but she brown. Everybody look like she have work, whether dem have an ounce of sense upstairs or not."

"Don't say that too loud." Rabino winced in an exaggerated fashion. "Miss Younis is probably a family rebel. Trying to do things her own way without parental help or business connections."

"Hmm. Or maybe de type of work she want she cyah get? Dem sorta uptown people entitled, man. She will want to manage a bank, not start out as a cashier."

"You got all that from the interview?" Rabino looked at her sceptically. "Really, now?"

Spence's face crinkled into a mischievous grin. "Girl, you don't even begin to know de level of my intuition when I first meet people."

"Oh really? Do tell." Rabino folded her arms across her chest and leaned against the lobby wall, her eyes twinkling in expectation. "What did you make of me?"

"Dat was . . . five — no, six years ago, so let's think." Spence tilted her head to one side. "She speakey-spokey so she must stuck-up and lazy. She not going listen to anybody and going want to boss people around."

"Wow!"

"And dat was only after you stood up and said, 'Kathryn Rabino, pleased to meet you'," said Spence with a grin. "By de time you reel off your experience I was done wid you. Me say, me no want dat partner!"

The two detectives laughed, drawing the attention of the other officers in the lobby. Officer Wilson smiled at them, before burying his head back in his tabloid.

"And what did you make of me?" asked Spence. "Tell de truth, now."

"I thought, this woman will slap me down so hard if I don't agree with her and she'll cuss me out if I make a mistake. God help me if I step on her toe!"

"Damn, girl, me did come in so bad to you!"

"You still come in bad, so my opinion hasn't changed one bit."

They laughed again and turned towards the stairs. Rabino drank from her water bottle. "Glad to see you seem to have changed your opinion of our Scottish brother."

"Who? Change wha'?" Spence kissed her teeth, but there was no venom. "I still wouldn't trust dat white man. Him secretive like de first day him come here — more so, actually. I always get de feeling dat him hiding something . . . all when him ah laugh and joke wid we."

Rabino shook her head. "Suspicious mind you have there, lady."

"Well, as long as I don't have to take orders from him, I can work wid him." They approached the detectives' open floor. "Thought he'd have gone back to foreign long time. What him still doing here?"

"He loves the place?" suggested Rabino. "Wants to solve murders? Wants to do his bit for Jamaica?"

"Heh! You believe dat bull, yet you won't believe de tarot." Spence looked knowing as she lowered her voice to a whisper. "Detective Harris hanging around for a reason. Probably want Super job and him will get it too. De day him take over Pelican Walk is de day I put in for transfer."

CHAPTER 5

The St James Municipal Corporation, still known to everyone as the parish council, was situated at the five-storey Cecil Davidson Building at the corner of Union Street and Orange Street in the middle of the downtown business district. It was one of the few government buildings with a wide ramp and guard rails for easy access. The light-blue external walls had faded over the years, various sections spattered with dark water stains from the overhanging air-conditioner units. Inside, the female receptionist sat behind a desk facing the glass doors and, once the detectives had introduced themselves, she made a phone call. Minutes later, a young woman appeared clutching a large folder to her chest. She was small and dark with a bright, welcoming expression on her carefully made-up face.

"Detectives Preddy and Harris, is it? I'm Miss Brenner."

They greeted one another with handshakes. The woman turned on her kitten heels and indicated that they follow her. She led them to the end of a hallway and held a door open so they could precede her. "Come, let's go in this room — quieter over here."

"Thank you for agreeing to see us at such short notice, Miss Brenner." Preddy pulled out one of the heavy wooden chairs and settled around the long table. Harris sat down beside him.

She leaned forward and whispered, "You could have come a long time since, but they wouldn't get out of the only available meeting room. People say women like to talk, but these men . . ." She took a seat opposite Preddy. Her eyes twinkled as she smiled. "Anyway, Lord knows, I'm happy to escape my desk for a minute."

Preddy smiled back. "In dat case, I'm glad we were of service to you. Hope you can return de favour and help us wid dis murder case."

She gave a slight shudder. "It's terrible to hear that Jerome Baccus was murdered. Poor guy. I'll help in any way I can, sir."

"Will Jerome's death affect the decision-making process at all?" asked Harris.

"We don't envisage anything other than a short delay. Wesley Ashburn and his All Angles team will erect their own marquee on Sugar Rush Beach and do their presentation in two weeks' time as scheduled. We've rescheduled Gavin Baccus for the week after that, assuming he still intends to participate. We haven't heard anything to the contrary. A final decision on who gets the contract will be made within a month after that."

"You had a lot of protests about de development?" asked Preddy.

"Oh Lord, yes." Miss Brenner rolled her eyes and lowered her voice. "And we're not even responsible for the beach contract, we're just helping out. They should contact the Urban Development Corporation in the first instance, but everybody turns up here cussing. In the end, the councillors agreed to assist the UDC by taking on complaints and public comments. At least once a month they meet to discuss the matter."

"Good tae know councillors are listening tae the people's concerns."

Miss Brenner sized Harris up with a swift glance. "Between you and me, I wish they'd never offered a public consultation. It's a nightmare. We've been flooded with comments that we can't keep on top of — people worried about noise, beach access, cost of entertaining a family on a day out. Then you have groups like the fishermen, who say they should have a dedicated area to clean and cook fish. Those communities in close proximity to the beach have been most vocal, particularly the small-time vendors." She flicked through her thick folder, pausing to run a finger down a page of correspondence. "Believe it or not, both Baccus and Ashburn complained about aspects of the other's development too. I expected them to stay out of it, but both have been pointing fingers like bad-mind little boys. Ashburn says Baccus 'hasn't made adequate provision for solar energy as he obviously doesn't understand the sun'. Baccus says the All Angles sewage provision 'shows lack of basic thought and will be disastrous to the marine environment and beyond'."

"Charming gentlemen," said Harris with a glance at Preddy.

"We saw a whole heap of protest placards on Dowdy — sorry, Sugar Rush Beach," said Preddy. "Have a group called de Livity Vendors Association been in contact about de plans?"

"They certainly have, sir. Easier to deal with them though, despite the banner-waving. They're led by a calm Rasta man, goes by the name of Ras Bizzi. About a dozen of them were protesting right outside here yesterday morning in the hot-hot sun." She shook her head. "I felt sorry for them. They were here for about an hour, then Ras Bizzi led the procession down to the beach."

"So, no road-blocking, den?" said Preddy.

"No, you know." The woman smiled again, and her cheeks dimpled. "Some of the people were a bit boisterous, but Ras Bizzi calmed them down. The only reason the traffic snagged a bit was because drivers were slowing down to read the placards, then tooting their support. Our security man had an eye on the vendors, but we didn't even need to call the police. Every time any of them raised their voices or got aggressive, Raz Bizzi quietened them down. He said we don't need the fussing and fighting, we need to sit and reason."

"And did anybody invite dem inside to sit and reason?" Preddy was unable to keep the scepticism from his voice. Unlike Harris, he had a better idea of how public consultations worked in practice. "Or even promise dem a date for a sit-down meeting?"

"We're overrun, unfortunately, Detective, and so is the UDC." Miss Brenner had the grace to look sheepish. "We've got the Livity Association's list of complaints and suggestions to look into, and I'm sure the relevant stakeholders will try. Seriously though, can you imagine if we were to sit and meet with everybody who contacted us? It would be another two years before the project ever got off the ground. My understanding is that it's decades since the then-government threw out the idea of a major development for Sugar Rush, before I was born. This is the first time people seem genuinely sure something will be done. Even the mayor is excited."

Preddy nodded. It was true that he had been hearing about ambitious plans for Dowdy Beach from as far back as he could remember. Following each general election, the relevant government came in and extolled a fairy-tale vision for the beach. Plans were developed then changed when that administration moved on. The People's National Party and the Jamaica Labour Party had passed the baton back and forth over the decades and there had been no progress on any of the promises.

"You have a phone number for Ras Bizzi?" asked Preddy.

"Yes, sure." Her carefully manicured fingernail dug into a page and she reeled off the number. "He signed the letter on behalf of Livity, so I guess it's his number. I've never tried to call it. The correspondence is just on plain paper, not letterhead. I think it's an informal thing they have going on, so I wouldn't expect them to have an office number."

"Do ye know where in Mo Bay he usually hangs out?" asked Harris.

"He's an ital juice vendor who plies numerous beaches, apparently." She squinted in thought. "I've seen him down

One Man Beach before. Pushing a huge pink cooler on an old supermarket trolley. Long grey-and-brown dreads down to his waist. Not sure if he has a shop anywhere. Oh, and sometimes he's dressed in straw clothes, although he was dressed normally yesterday — cargo shorts and mesh vest."

"We'll try and contact him," said Preddy. "Other dan Livity, were any other people making a big noise around here? Like dey might take things into deir own hands?"

She smiled as she shook her head. "You know our people, particularly the men. They love rey rey and jump up, but if they see their mothers coming down the street, they shut up quick-quick."

Harris chuckled. "If it wasnae for that engagement ring, I'd swear ye didnae like men."

"My man, I love!" She spread the fingers of her left hand and admired the tiny rock. "And I've always been big on supporting police, men and women. Honest."

"I hear you." Preddy got to his feet with a quick nod at Harris.

Miss Brenner tidied her pages together as she rose. "I'm just glad that I won't have anything to do with the final decision. Plenty of people will be involved in that — PNP councillors, JLP councillors, UDC officers, even the mayor will get a say." She walked towards the door and paused with her hand on the handle. "From what I'm hearing, though, I think it's going to be a pretty close thing between Wesley Ashburn and Gavin Baccus."

As they walked to the car, Preddy's phone rang. "Okay, we're on de way," he said.

"Trouble at the ranch?" asked Harris.

"No. We're going to watch a film show."

* * *

As Preddy and Harris approached the Pelican Walk meeting room, the voice of Gavin Baccus could be heard inviting the audience to sit back and enjoy his vision of Montego Bay.

It was the only room with a forty-five-inch TV monitor, which was securely fixed to the wall to prevent theft and had a CCTV camera pointed straight at it.

Preddy pushed the door open. Rabino had rigged the TV to her laptop and she and Spence sat watching intently. Two standing fans had been commandeered from other rooms and whirred behind the seated detectives. The room was kept pristine and rarely used, except by Commissioner Davis when he came for a visit, and by Superintendent Brownlow when entertaining his superiors, including the mayor. At one point, Preddy had expected it to be assigned to Detective Harris, but the Scotsman had surprised him by insisting that he preferred sharing space with the other detectives and did not want an office. It took some time before Preddy worked out that this was a strategic decision on Harris's part, rather than one based on a need for camaraderie. The open plan allowed Harris to watch and hear the target of his private investigation.

The meeting room could comfortably seat at least six officers around a large table and had scuffed leatherette seats to cushion their behinds. An unused glass jug and matching glasses stood on a locked wooden side cabinet. Preddy believed it held alcohol — he could not imagine the brass holed up in the room sipping just iced water.

Rabino looked up as the door closed behind the men. "I'll restart it, sir, though you haven't missed anything."

"No popcorn?" asked Preddy.

"No popcorn," repeated Spence. "Carrot cake is here though." She slid the plastic container along the table towards him. Harris intercepted it and took a slice before pushing it towards Preddy.

"Och, this is nice," muttered Harris with his mouth full. "Mmm."

"All you shouldn't eat dem things," said Spence in a disapproving tone.

"Ye saying I need tae watch ma figure?" Harris patted his flat stomach and stared at her.

"Not saying dat at all. Your face already red and your hair match it. Carrot not going help your complexion at all."

Harris smiled and pulled out a chair beside her. "It's great having colleagues who really care, Detective Spence."

Preddy took a slice of cake and looked at the screen. Rabino restarted the video. The brief introduction by Gavin Baccus was followed by a professional voice actor, who lauded the greatness of St James parish and anointed Montego Bay as the jewel in its crown. The voice explained the plan for the tourist city to be the most coveted entertainment spot on the whole island, rivalling those of the wider Caribbean.

"How on earth did a beautiful piece of beach like that get the nickname 'Dowdy'?" asked Harris.

"No idea," said Rabino. "And the worst thing is if a tourist asks for Sugar Rush Beach many of the locals don't know where it is. The name Dowdy has stuck. People use it on posters and flyers."

"Guess all dat will change when de mega-development takes place." Preddy pointed at the screen. "See, Baccus has neon signs saying Sugar Rush Beach. Wesley Ashburn has too. You should see his model development — some pretty nice features, no expense spared on de miniature design."

"Although both Baccus and Ashburn say each other's plans have got problems," added Harris. "Trying tae undermine each other."

"Dis vision look good, man," murmured Spence.

The camera panned in and out to the more spectacular entertainment features. The uniform bamboo huts were made to look thrown together, Robinson Crusoe style, but were clearly an earthy feature of the design. What looked like fishing boats run aground were actually dining facilities with benches and tables running the length of the vessels. Even the beach bar was built to resemble Noah's Ark and stood out against the magnificent backdrop of crystal-blue sea. There was a huge stage with an oval-shaped covering, which could be retracted or inflated depending on the weather. An unusual-looking waterfall formed the frontage to the stage, the water cascading gracefully down stone-grey tiles etched with images of Jamaican fruits.

"I could sit dere all day and stare at dat waterfall." Spence sighed.

"They'll never let that run all day," said Rabino. "You can bet it will only be turned on during performances. Not that they'll mention that aspect, obviously. This promo is designed to focus on the features they know people will like, without highlighting any of the downsides."

Preddy frowned. "Baccus has less trees in his vision dan Ashburn. Ashburn kept lots of de old trees in his design."

"Baccus has less trees, but he also has less stalls and shops as well," added Harris.

Preddy nodded. "Yes, less stalls and shops equals less chance for Livity Vendors to get one."

"Looks like Baccus is quite interested in having plenty of green space though. The lawns are quite extensive. Nice tae relax on after a swim."

Spence shook her head. "No way will dey let visitors walk on any lawn. De place will be full of 'Keep off de grass' signs."

"True," said Rabino. "Just like Emancipation Park in Kingston, and Turtle River Park in Ochi. Grass to look at, not to walk on, lay on or sit on."

"Ah, I get it," said Harris. "Shame though, but at least there'll be gazebos tae rest under, and both men have factored them in."

Rabino glanced at him. "Well, I haven't seen Wesley Ashburn's design yet, but which one would you prefer, as a tourist?"

"Och, I'm naw a tourist." Harris squirmed slightly in his seat.

Rabino smiled. "Come on, you know what I mean."

Spence looked at Harris. "No offence, but trust me, whoever wins dis development opportunity is thinking mainly of tourists. Whether Baccus gets it or Ashburn, de ultimate goal is de almighty tourist dollar. Nobody really gives a rat's 'bout what Jamaican people like or want."

"Ooh!" Harris grimaced. "That sounds a bit harsh."

Preddy glanced at him. "Not harsh at all. We know how tourism works on dis island, and it has never worked wid de feelings or needs or wants of de average Jamaican in mind. Most kids can tell you dat Dunn's River Falls is in St Ann, but de majority have never been there."

"And never will," concluded Spence. "Way too expensive."

Harris nodded slowly. "I see. At least both design companies are highlighting free entry though, so that's something."

"Yes," said Rabino. "There's been such an outcry over fees to attend what used to be free beaches all over the island, that I guess the government decided to keep entry free. Look at Baccus's fancy bar though. I can just imagine the price of drinks and they'll be priced in US dollars."

"De Jamaican dollar dead and buried long time," said Spence in resignation.

Rabino continued, "They'll make the money from the small shops — the cook shops, especially as you can't bring your own food or drink. Then there'll be money earned from the candy-sellers, clothing stalls, craftsmen—"

Harris indicated with his chin as a flood of colour and attractive craft items held by toothy smiling Jamaicans dominated the screen. "Look, he calls that area an 'artisan village'."

"Hah! See it deh!" said Spence triumphantly. "Fancy name to attract tourists. 'Artisan village', my backside. Give it a year after whoever wins it den you hear say it cyah run widout a fee and *bam*! Fee charge."

"Not a bad prediction," said Preddy with a smile.

"Which is why the Livity Vendors Association are none too happy," said Harris. "They were protesting at the parish council offices yesterday — and at the beach — about being left out."

Rabino tore her gaze away from the screen and looked at him. "Yesterday?"

"Aye, yesterday in broad daylight. Protested on Union Street then at Sugar Rush Beach. Makes ye wonder if they did more than just protest, maybe got violent. They're against choosing either businessman as they're going tae be left out either way."

Preddy looked at Spence. "I have a feeling you would like Ashburn's vision. No pretentious name for de shopping area either."

"I going look online later and see if I can find it," said Spence. "I well want to see what Ashburn has in mind to beat dis."

"De question is whether Ashburn had murder in mind," mused Preddy. "Would he go to such an extent to derail Baccus and win de contract? He's a nervous man, but I don't know whether dat is guilt or just him being anxious at being questioned by police."

"Wait till you hear what we got from Jerome's girl, Nicki Younis," said Rabino when the half-hour promotion came to an end.

"Eeh hee," Spence interjected quickly. "She done decide whodunit long time. Quicker dan any TV detective!"

Preddy stood, stretched and walked around the long table. He pulled out a chair and sat facing the team with his back almost touching the TV. "Tell me more."

"Love triangle," announced Rabino.

"Might even be love hexagon," Spence corrected her.

"Nicki says Eryka Malden has a boyfriend, married older man named Terrell 'Tex' Doran and that he's our murderer."

Preddy massaged his palms as he leaned across the table. "I knew dere was something about dat girl Eryka. Her face changed when I asked if she had any ideas who could have killed Jerome, but she failed to mention him."

"And I guess Mr Doran's motive is the one as old as the hills?" said Harris. "It's always all about love or money, or love of money."

"Quite," said Rabino. "We don't know how long the two of them have been an item, but apparently Tex bought Eryka a new car and pays rent on her apartment."

"Jealous boyfriend . . . works for me." Preddy flicked through his notebook as he spoke. "I wondered how she could afford a criss new Audi at her age, so dat explains it." He found Eryka's phone number. "Let's bring her in for a chat, stick her in an interview room and see if we can get her to talk. In de meantime, do we know where to find dis Tex Doran?"

"No, sir," said Spence. "Nicki thinks he's local, but she don't know where him live and him name not coming up on any records."

"De name is not familiar," said Preddy. "But if he can run his household and find money for girls, cars and apartments he must be quite well off. Wonder what his wife thinks about it, assuming she knows?"

"If they have a joint bank account she'll likely know," said Harris.

Spence kissed her teeth. "Any woman dat knows her husband is spending millions on young girl and puts up wid it is a damn idiot!"

"Or addicted to the cash, so she just stays put and bears the humiliation," said Rabino.

"Still a damn idiot though," insisted Spence. "Not me, never!"

"Right, first things first," said Preddy, "I have de Audi's plate and dere's only one dealership in St James. Should be able to get Tex Doran's contact details widout consulting de reluctant Eryka. We need to question her again though."

"We'll find her, sir," said Rabino.

Spence finished her last piece of cake and used a napkin to scrape everybody's crumbs into her plastic dish. "I can't wait to hear her story."

Preddy eyed her as he walked towards the door. "I'm sure you'll be at your most gentle and understanding wid her?"

"Absolutely, sir."

Harris grinned as he stood. "Make sure the CCTV is working in whichever interview room ye use for Eryka. I want tae see actual proof of Detective Spence being gentle and understanding."

Spence gave him the side-eye, but her tone was friendly. "You can gwaan talk!"

Preddy was relieved that the relationship between the two had improved considerably over the last five months, although they still butted heads from time to time. He attributed the thaw in relations to Harris standing up for Spence against a murder suspect's claim of police brutality, which Harris insisted had been self-defence on Spence's part. Superintendent Brownlow laid the matter to rest, and the so-called victim was now a convicted murderer languishing at Tower Hill Correctional Facility in Kingston.

"Okay, people, it's been a long day." Preddy held the door open. "We'll pick dis up again tomorrow."

Harris squeezed past him. "I think I'll go and make some further checks about that awl. It's an unusual-looking thing. Might come up in an online search."

Preddy watched the Glaswegian head down the corridor towards the detectives' open-plan floor and wondered if he was really going online to do any investigating about the murder weapon, or just going on the computer to further his own personal investigation. A feeling of intense irritation ran through the Jamaican detective. He forced himself to dismiss it and concentrate on the more important matter at hand.

CHAPTER 6

Detective Preddy glanced at his watch. Valerie was late for dinner and he felt some relief that, for once, he was not the one delayed or rescheduling. He could only pray that he would not be forced to abandon his girlfriend mid-meal. He had travelled straight from Pelican Walk without going home to change, and Valerie had planned to travel directly from her Grove Street lab to meet him. The venue was the open-air restaurant on the front terrace of the Wexford Hotel, a mid-market boutique hotel on the Hip Strip, which during daylight provided a captivating view of the turquoise sea and the luscious greenery of Old Hospital Park. The terrace restaurant, Rosella's, had always been a tranquil place to dine, and now its recent refurbishment made the site that much more attractive with its plush banquet chairs and low lighting adding to the intimate ambiance. It was still early evening, and two couples, the only other diners on the terrace, were seated at a good distance from his table.

He turned his attention to the brightly lit park. Now that the sun had gone down the park visitors had increased in number, encouraged by the presence of security personnel, to sit under the gazebos and on wooden benches. Soon the unlicensed food vendors would be out selling jerked pork and chicken, with fried festivals and hard dough bread. A peanut man would appear, pushing a cart up and down the road, balancing a portable furnace of hot roasted peanuts and ignoring toots from annoyed motorists. All sellers were banned from inside the park grounds, which were gated at either end and protected by a low orange wall topped with wrought-iron railings. Instead, the mobile chefs pitched their carts on the pavement close to the railings, visible under the streetlights, knowing that the tantalizing meat odours would soon lure customers in their direction.

The haphazard activities of the informal trade made the streets look unkempt and lawless, but nobody had died from food poisoning so far. Either the cooks were extremely diligent in their handling of the raw meats or the patrons had strong constitutions. Preddy had developed a degree of apathy towards these unruly entrepreneurs, who found a way to earn a living under cover of darkness without robbing people or breaking into homes. With no social security or other government benefits to claim, this was as good as it got for thousands of breadwinners. As long as the stagnant economic situation persisted, the city — the island even — would be managing a delicate balancing act. The rage of dejected young men was like a dam ready to burst, with only a wall of entrepreneurship, lottery scamming and foreign remittances saving the city from a flood of social unrest.

Preddy glanced towards the sea and could make out the shadows of slow-moving catamarans carrying pleasure-seekers back to their villas and hotels via the spectacular coastline. For most carefree foreigners, Jamaica was a place of bliss and relaxation where their only concern was which sunscreen to use and whether to indulge in ice-cold Red Stripe beer or opt for potent Wray & Nephew rum. Crime would rarely encroach on any aspect of their sun-fuelled vacations.

The waitress approached and he ordered a glass of coconut water. He leaned back and turned to study the sea again and was lost in his thoughts when he felt a warm pair of lips on his cheek.

"Hello, baby." Valerie circled his shoulders and hugged his chest. "Sorry, just some last-minute stuff to finish at de lab, but here I am."

Preddy reached behind and pulled her around in front of him. She stooped and kissed his lips, then gracefully tucked her floral dress beneath her as she took a seat opposite him.

"You look beautiful, as usual." He smiled warmly at the woman he loved. "Light of my life."

Valerie ran her own private forensic laboratory in Montego Bay and one in Kingston. Having once worked alongside Preddy in a government laboratory many years ago, she understood more than most about the long, uncertain hours in the force, why dates had to be broken and rear-ranged, why patience was an absolute virtue. She hung her handbag by its straps on the back of her seat and tucked her bobbed hair behind her ears. Even after a hard day's work her eyes were bright and attentive.

"I look a mess and I feel tired, but de thought of seeing you did dis to me." She waved her hands at her face and gave him a beaming smile.

"Dat's what I like to hear." Preddy used a menu to fan her face and she closed her eyes, savouring the coolness. "Somebody who really want to see me. Nowadays is only Spartan get crazy when him see me, and I know him doing it just for food."

"You and dat damn bird!" Valerie laughed. She reached across the table and squeezed his hand. "Poor love, I can assure you I'm not here just for de food, although I can't wait to get some escoveitch fish. Anyway, stop feeling sorry for yourself. Most people are happy to see a handsome, strapping detective."

Preddy grinned. "Not if dey have something to hide. Usually, I turn up and introduce myself, and everybody goes quiet. De ones who recognize me start moving away before I even get near dem."

The waitress returned with the coconut water, which Preddy pushed towards Valerie and ordered another one for himself. Valerie grasped the glass and swallowed gratefully without pausing for breath. "Oh, you don't know how much I needed dat."

The waitress glanced from one to the other. "You ready to order your meal now?"

"More dan ready." Valerie pushed away the menu. "I'll have escoveitch fish, rice and peas, and coleslaw."

"I'll have de same," said Preddy. "And bring a bottle of house white too, please."

"And some still water," added Valerie. As the waitress left, she stared at Preddy. "Feeling fed up and unloved, eh?"

"You read me too well, madam. I'm okay though — honestly. You know what it's like. Superintendent Brownlow wanting answers yesterday. Commissioner Davis publicly sticking up for us, privately sticking de knife in."

"Dey should count demselves lucky to have you," she said. "You going see de psychologist tomorrow?"

Preddy's eyes flicked towards the dark sea then back to her. "Yes, man. Ten a.m. sharp. Wrote it down like you said and put an alert in my phone." He hated lying to Valerie, but felt it was the only way to keep the peace. As far as she was aware, he went to counselling sessions once every fortnight. To date he had attended only one session and had not lasted the full hour at that. Talking with other humans about the bloody Norwood incident was not his thing.

"You sleeping better now though, so it must be working? You slept all through de night wid barely a murmur last weekend."

"Dat's because you were beside me." He watched her closely. As much as he cherished his own space, there were times when he remembered what it was like to have the noise of a wife and kids at home to keep him grounded and maintain a sense of normality. "You should move in, you know. I've told you. Get rid of your apartment and move into mine."

"Timing's still not right." She shook her head. "I really do want to though, you know dat?"

"I know."

She played with her fork, dragging it along her napkin. "Have to make sure David is on board. You know how teenagers stay. He's only just given up on de idea dat me and Norman will ever get back together."

Preddy nodded with understanding. "Don't want to be kids, not ready to be adults. Teenagers are hard work."

It had taken Annalee and Roman a good two years to accept that Valerie was a permanent fixture on the landscape. They had long given up trying to change the subject whenever he talked about her. His daughter had surprised him recently by asking if she could visit Valerie's lab one day. The four of them had dined together in the city a few times during the summer holidays, while Valerie's son, David, remained with his father in the family home in Kingston and steadfastly refused to visit his mother's apartment in Montego Bay. Preddy was aware that this hurt her, although she played it down. The boy would eventually have to accept the inevitable, and Preddy was ready and willing to make friends with him as soon as he did.

The steaming plates of food arrived and they tucked into the delicious fish. "So, how's de Baccus investigation going?"

Preddy waved his fork at her. "We're not going to talk murder, remember?"

"Hah! So you say, Mr Detective. I usually give you ten minutes before your mind goes dere. It always does. I just pre-empted you."

"My mind is staying on dis festival. It's de best thing ever. When I try to make it, it never tastes quite like dis." He savoured the sweet fried roll, chewing appreciatively. "I hope we'll have places selling food like dis when Dowdy Beach is developed."

"See!" She stuck out a sandaled foot and tapped his leg.

Preddy smiled and sighed deeply. He would always spare her the gory details of any investigation, but she was right, his mind rarely left his latest case. "So far, so messy. We've got plenty of upset people all over de city, vendors and residents who either don't want de development or want a different development. We've got Jerome frequently taunting his uncle's business rival on social media. And now into de mix goes a wealthy sugar-daddy — it would appear our victim was spending a lot of time wid de man's girlfriend."

"So, Jerome was not a popular young man, den?"

Preddy poured white wine into their glasses. "Not at all, but what can we do? Popular or not, we have to put his murderer behind bars."

"I'll drink to dat." They clinked glasses. "How's Annalee doing? I know you've been missing her."

"Back to school today, for both of dem." Preddy paused to sip the cold wine, revelling in the crisp flavour. "She was keen to see my parents, and dey were overjoyed to see her, so I let her stay in Westmoreland. Can't lie, it was strange. First Christmas holiday where she hasn't spent at least half her time wid me."

"Hmm, get ready for de time when she wants to spend de entire holiday wid friends and not see any family."

Preddy winced. "I don't even want to think about it."

"Still, Roman came."

"And went every day. I swear he only came because he made a couple of new friends down here over de summer and it was convenient to stay in Ironshore. Easy ride back and forth to downtown." His sipped his wine again. "Him getting a bit mouthy, but I don't say too much. I remember being much worse at his age."

Valerie smiled warmly. "I can't imagine you back-chatting your dad."

"Oh, I would. I'd do it from a distance though and stay hiding in de bushes after. Tried to gauge when he'd calm down to know when to return." A faraway look crept into his eyes. "If he wanted me to sweep de yard, I'd complain dat it would soon be covered in leaves again, so why bother. Dat used to get him mad."

Valerie chuckled and her eyes twinkled. "Ah so you did lazy?"

"Very. Compared to my friends in our village I was spoiled. Dey had to carry water from a standpipe early every morning before school. We had piped water in our home, and I could get up late. Rarely would I ever wash a single plate. Mum never complained. When I look back on it sometimes . . . My parents were angels. Still are."

"You changed somewhere along de line though."

Preddy looked thoughtful. "Mum took sick, just after I finished my A-levels. For about three months she had cramped hands and found it hard to grasp anything, even a spoon. I realized just how much she did for us kids and started doing my part." He smiled. "Dad was shocked at de new me. We grew much closer after dat."

"You grew into a man dat he could be proud of. Don't worry about Roman, it will all soon start to become clear to him too. I know it's de same wid my David. Boys need deir dad's influence though, so I'd never try to interfere. He seems happy at uni and I'm confident things will work themselves out."

They ate and talked for almost two hours and waved away the enticing dessert menu presented by the eager waitress. Another waitress wheeled a trolley past containing a sumptuous-looking chocolate cake and glass bowls of ice-cream sundaes.

Valerie gave a low moan as her eyes followed the trolley right to the customers' table, but she waved away Preddy's silent question. She sat back and patted her stomach. "Dat was good."

"You coming back wid me?"

"Have to be up early tomorrow, remember," she said. "I should go home."

"I'll get de bill." Preddy stood up, took her hand and pulled her to her feet. "It's not even ten yet. De night is young. I'll have you home by midnight — promise."

They shared a long, lingering kiss. "You've convinced me, Detective."

CHAPTER 7

The usually vivid-blue skies carried more than a hint of rain, and some streetlights were still on as the sun was yet to make an appearance. The temperature was soothingly cool and the air smelled free of all pollution. Preddy jogged through his Ironshore neighbourhood, his long legs making easy work of the route. He pounded the pavements, ever alert, glancing at the neighbouring properties. This was a middle-class residential area with other apartment complexes as well as some large villas with well-tended gardens and one or two nice cars in each driveway. An aggressive dog barked behind a hedge and ran the length of its enclosure, growling while it kept pace with Preddy. The detective never carried weapons when he ran as he expected trouble from neither man nor beast and never got any. He crossed the road to give the neighbours a chance to sleep peacefully rather than to appease the agitated animal. He quite liked dogs, but if one ever escaped and bit him it would be the last thing it ever did.

After a full hour he returned home feeling energized, his soaking vest clinging to his torso. As he put the key in the lock, he felt a light tap on his bare shoulder. He spun around and bent low, arm raised to fend off attack, only to see a bunch of green feathers above his head. Spartan cheeped, flew up into the air and hovered at a distance.

"You must crazy," Preddy admonished him, his heart pounding. He stared at the bird in annoyance then instantly demurred. "Sorry, I'm just jumpy. Come, come back."

Preddy could have sworn the parakeet looked disgruntled before it flew away. He entered the apartment and opened the side window, which was the bird's usual entry spot. It visited him regularly, three or four mornings every week, but had never tried to enter by the front door before. He smiled to himself. At least the bird was feeling at home. Soon it would want its own key. *Well, I've upset two animals already and de day has barely begun*, he thought. *Not a good sign.*

Preddy showered and stared into the mirror as he shaved. Not a wrinkle in sight, but the salt-and-pepper colours were evident, the creep of the salt growing more pervasive. He did not resent the signs of having survived nearly fifty years on the planet. He pulled on his chinos and a long-sleeved shirt. In the kitchen he threw a handful of green ganja leaves into a large cup. The boiling water hit the leaves and he inhaled the comforting odour. People could say whatever dismissive nonsense they liked about the herb, but as far as he was concerned ganja tea was the best tonic to start the day. Most of his colleagues loved coffee, and the island produced the world's finest, but to him there was no comparison.

He finished off the beverage and licked his lips. The idea of breakfast did not appeal and he could go entire mornings without food without feeling queasy. Besides, today was Friday and he liked to try and arrange for the team to have a hefty lunch together on Fridays, although it rarely panned out. More often than not some unforeseen emergency would demand their attention.

He checked his phone and was relieved to see that no calls had come in. If it was not a lead to help him solve the Baccus murder case, he did not want to hear it. He listened to the headlines on the radio and was pleased that the announcer led with happy news for once — the saving of Cockpit Country, one of Jamaica's best-loved ecological sites. A rugged rainforest spanning the parishes of Trelawny and St Elizabeth, rich in plants and animals, it was previously being eyed up by foreign mining conglomerates for bauxite exploration. Nothing had changed over the centuries — there was always some opportunist coming from thousands of miles away looking to exploit the island's natural resources. At least for now the government had rejected the idea and promised to set boundaries covering an estimated 219 kilometres around the region.

Preddy secured his windows, pocketed his phone and picked up his briefcase and keys. He thought about leaving corn on the window ledge for Spartan but decided against it. The property manager inspected the grounds at least once a day and Preddy did not want to fall foul of the regulations. People expected him to set a good example, and even though he was not perfect, he would do his best.

His phone beeped and he frowned at it. A notification for the 10 a.m. appointment with the psychologist, an appointment he was not going to keep.

Another message popped up, this one from Valerie reminding him about the same meeting. He sighed. The Norwood images were becoming less vivid, yet refused to go away completely. Bullets flying, blood flowing and young men screaming, the result of his ill-conceived raid on a den of hoodlums with a team of overwrought cops seeking revenge on their fallen colleague. Talking to Spartan about Norwood was helping soothe his nerves, but no one was likely to accept or believe that. Even Valerie thought it was a joke. The idea certainly would not be supported by the psychologist, who had to justify his pay. After all, if patients took to healing themselves by talking to pets and stray animals, that element of therapeutic practice would quickly become obsolete.

* * *

Preddy entered Pelican Walk Police Station through a side entrance and avoided Superintendent Brownlow's office as he made his way to his own. He was not sure whether the super knew about his broken appointment schedule and the detective did not feel like subjecting himself to an interrogation if he did.

He closed his door quietly behind him and pulled down the blinds. He turned the radio's volume knob anticlockwise before turning the power on. The cool sound of rustling leaves took over the airwaves and he reclined in his chair, staring at some notes he had made the previous evening. He had proof from the Audi dealership that Terrell Doran was the registered owner of the car driven by Eryka Malden and now he had the man's address. The salesman had promised to send a copy of Tex's photo ID to the detective immediately and Preddy was eager to see it, yet the WhatsApp icon on his phone stubbornly refused to show notification of a message.

He glanced back at his notes. The luxury car had been purchased a year earlier, which was a good indication of how long the affair with Eryka had been going on. The salesman had given Preddy a phone number and explained that it seemed to be out of order — he had been trying to contact the owner to bring in the vehicle for its complimentary one-year service.

Preddy tried the number and listened to it ring before cutting out. Maybe it was not a bad thing that his prime suspect did not pick up. If Tex Doran was the murderer, it might be better to tackle him long before he even guessed that they were on his tail — ambush him at home or work.

A few minutes later Preddy's phone beeped and he grabbed it eagerly. Not the message he was hoping for. The psychologist's office number was saved in his phone as *Not Today Doc*. He messaged back that unfortunately an emergency situation had arisen and he regretted not being able to make this appointment.

He trawled the internet for information on Terrell Doran, to no avail. The phone beeped again. He opened the message and stared at the passport of Terrell Andre Doran. The image lost its sharpness as he enlarged it.

Tex was a plain-looking, ebony-skinned man, with afro hair about an inch high. He was born in Montego Bay and aged sixty-two now. Preddy shook his head. Just another middle-aged man growing older, struggling to keep the attention of a twenty-something girl, throwing as much money at her as possible and ending up transformed by jealousy. Being extravagant rarely worked for long, leaving the men bitter and resentful at the loss of women they considered "property". Preddy had seen it happen year after year, a story as old as the hills with the same ending — violence.

Tex Doran resided in Westgate Hill, a moderately wealthy enclave overlooking the city. Preddy wondered what Tex did for a living and why the searching online drew a blank. A few stories of charitable functions he had attended with a Suzanne Doran were all that popped up, and most of the content focused on the kindness and good works of Suzanne. He guessed Tex was one of those secretive rich people who did their best to stay under the radar and avoid enquiries from the tax man.

Preddy pushed the notepad to one side, opened a locked drawer and pulled out another used notepad. These notes were not for sharing or discussing with anyone. Many of the jottings made little sense to him, even though he had written them. Some were mere snippets of conversations, overheard words that could be clues to piecing together a jigsaw puzzle, information gleaned over months by watching and listening to even the most innocuous of comments made by Harris and the superintendent.

Superintendent Brownlow had slipped up recently and asked Preddy how Detective Cotner was doing. Iain Cotner had never been a member of Preddy's team, so the question had hung in the seconds of uncomfortable silence that followed. Preddy could still remember the superintendent's slight look of horror and his failure to immediately compose himself upon realizing his mistake, how he had stammered and enquired instead after Detective Harris's welfare. One was a dark-skinned Jamaican, the other a pale Scotsman, and their identities could not be confused. The superintendent had never been a good actor, and Preddy had taken great pleasure watching him bluster and change the subject.

He smiled wryly. The super never asked him how Spence or Rabino were getting on. Maybe not so strange, as the Jamaican detectives were expected to just get on with it, while the Scotsman's every suggestion and request was given careful consideration by the High Command.

Preddy's phone rang. Detective Rabino was calling. They had a visitor in reception.

CHAPTER 8

Detectives Preddy and Rabino watched Eryka Malden through the one-way mirror of the interview room. Eryka wore a sleeveless red dress and her braids were twisted into a messy bun at the nape of her neck. She reminded Preddy of a customer-service representative at a popular phone store, except for the many gold bangles on each wrist. She rested the sides of her hands on the table and rubbed her palms together. Her mascaraed eyes flitted around the bleak room. Nothing to view but grey walls, a white plastic table, matching scratched chairs and one mirrored wall in which she could see her own reflection but not the detectives behind it.

"Well, she looks like she doesn't want to be here, so dat's a good thing," said Preddy.

"Such an innocent face. Wouldn't figure her for getting herself into a mess like dating a married man," replied Rabino.

"Let's see if she'll continue de cover-up. Ready to do your thing?"

Rabino smiled. "Always, sir."

Preddy pushed open the door and Rabino entered in front of him. "Hello, Eryka, I'm Detective Rabino. My

75

colleague, Detective Preddy, you already know. How are you?"

Eryka gave a weak smile of acknowledgment at Preddy and shook Rabino's hand. "Hi, Detective."

"Hello again, Eryka," said Preddy.

The interviewee's eyes went from one detective to the other while they took seats facing her, and those eyes anxiously followed the notebooks placed on the table. She licked her lips as Rabino uncovered her pen.

"Thanks for coming to see us at such short notice." Rabino offered her a broad smile. "Sorry it's a bit warm in here, but we don't have any fans available at the moment. You okay?"

"Yeah, I'm good."

"Right, great. I know you already spoke to Detective Preddy about the night Jerome was killed. We were hoping that now you'd had a chance to think about it, you might be more clear about any possible enemies Jerome had?"

"No . . . not really."

"Nobody at all?" asked Preddy.

Eryka stared at the table. "I only know he was fussing with Wesley Ashburn on social media from time to time. The two of them taunting each other, but other than that . . ." She waved the back of her hand in the air to end her statement as if swatting at an invisible insect.

Rabino leaned forward and stared at her earnestly. "Think carefully, Eryka. We're trying to gather the names of all possible suspects. I know you must be desperate to see Jerome's killer jailed and we need some idea of who to talk to. We don't want days to turn into weeks then into months, because if this case goes cold we may never catch the murderer. Speed is everything in a murder investigation."

"There will always be people who didn't like him that I don't know of." Eryka rubbed her hands together again and her bracelets jingled. "I've known him since high school, had a crush on him back then. We used to hang out with others anywhere free — the shopping mall, the beaches, the park.

We were quite good friends, but I wouldn't expect him to tell me everything. The murderer was probably just somebody who asked Jerome for money, and when he refused, they stabbed him."

Preddy fixed her with an icy glare. "Stabbed him through his ribs and pierced his heart. Dead within seconds."

Eryka's throat constricted visibly and her eyes grew moist. "I don't know how they could do it."

"You wouldn't be covering for anybody now, would you?" asked Rabino.

The question was met with silence. Eryka mopped her eyes delicately with the knuckle of one finger, careful not to smudge her make-up.

Preddy tapped his notebook firmly with his pen, a monotonous beat, the sound exacerbated in the silence. The noise dragged Eryka's nervous eyes to his and he held her gaze. "Does de name Tex Doran ring any bells?" he asked.

Eryka dry-retched and pushed her chair back, bringing her head close to her knees. Preddy reached for the waste bin and used his foot to shove it towards her. "Use dat if you must."

Eryka pulled the bin closer. Nothing emerged from her painted lips except the sound of heavy breathing.

"Look at me, Eryka," demanded Rabino. "Look at me."

The girl raised her head and stared at a mark on the table as if her lids were too heavy to raise any further.

"We gave you every chance and you said nothing," said Rabino. "Do you know what that means? It means now we're thinking you knew that Tex Doran might have something to do with Jerome's murder."

"I'm even thinking dat maybe de both of you planned it," Preddy added. "You set up Jerome, led him to his death, knowing Tex Doran would be waiting for him. You're an accessory to murder."

"No! No way!" Eryka shook her head violently. "I was not involved at all. I loved Jerome, not Tex! Tex is just . . . somebody who helps me."

"Somebody who helps you? Dat is what you call him?" Preddy pulled his notebook closer and turned back a few pages. He held it at an angle to prevent Eryka from reading it. "Tell me if I've got dis right. He bought you a brand-new Audi Q7, he pays rent on your apartment, gave you a credit card and pays all de bills?"

Eryka covered her eyes with both hands and made a groaning sound.

"Talk, Eryka," said Rabino gently. "Let's hear all about it. We have no time for games and if you obstruct this investigation, it will be very bad for you. But if he did it and you knew nothing about it, that's a different thing. Either way, your cooperation will go a long way to what happens to you."

Eryka reached into her bag, fished out a white flannel and wiped her face, staining the cloth brown and red. She sniffed a few times before she spoke. "I haven't spoken to Tex since the murder. He kept ringing my phone, but I didn't pick up. I mean, he's always ringing me, so it's not unusual. Sometimes I pick up, sometimes I ignore it. Gets on my nerves, to tell the truth."

The more the woman spoke, the colder Preddy felt towards her. "It must get on his nerves even more dat he can't even get hold of a woman he is spending millions of dollars on. Why take his money if you won't even take his calls? I'm guessing he bought de phone too?"

Eryka tried to deflect Preddy's hostility by keeping her eyes on Rabino. She softened her tone. "Tex is nice, just a bit overbearing. Always keen to know where I am and what I'm doing, you know?"

Rabino nodded. "He's an older guy, so I guess he believes he has to work hard to prove himself and keep you. How long have you known him?"

"Nearly two years now. We met when I was doing night shifts at the university bar, down Dead End. He used to come down there to drink and chat. Seemed lonely to me. Before long he was inviting me out, taking me for meals." She paused and gave Preddy a defensive look. "You don't know how it is when you have nothing and somebody with money starts to show an interest in you. I did think he was too old for me — he's sixty-two, I'm not even twenty-one. It was nice to have the attention. The relationship was quite platonic for months. Yes, I knew he was married, but when he offered to find somewhere for me to live . . ." She shrugged her shoulders.

"Did he know you spent quite a lot of time wid Jerome?" asked Preddy.

"Yes," she whispered. "I told him it was purely a friendship. Sometimes he got mad and we argued about it, but he usually backed down. I told him he couldn't expect me to give up my friends — male or female."

"You said you loved Jerome," said Rabino. "That doesn't sound like purely a friendship to me?"

Eryka closed her eyes briefly and winced. "Yes, I loved him. I wished he was my boyfriend and hinted at it all the time. He wasn't interested in a serious relationship with anybody. I mean, he has that girl Nicki Younis, but he's said many a time that she's more into him than he's into her. He hardly ever went to that bush in St Thomas to see her. She was the one running after him, coming to visit him in Mo Bay all the while. I was biding my time, hoping he'd get tired of her, hoping our relationship would develop."

"And taking him out and buying him things to show your love," added Rabino.

"Yes. I got the — Tex bought me the Audi about a year ago and Jerome absolutely loved it. Wasn't hard to get him to go anywhere with me after that. Sometimes I'd let him drive it with me in the passenger seat, but not often, in case Tex ever spotted us. He would have killed us." She seemed startled at her own words. "Oh, I didn't mean that!"

"Go on," said Rabino. "Tell us about you and Jerome."

"I bought him presents. I gave him a leather wallet and belt for his birthday a few months ago. Took him out to dinner too and paid for everything. We joked because he was putting on weight with all the fine dining." She looked sheepish and studied her nails. "He was a great guy and I couldn't help myself. I guess love turned my head."

"You think hate turned Tex Doran's head?" asked Preddy. "Had he ever met Jerome, threatened him?"

Eryka shook her head. "As far as I know, the two never met. Jerome would have told me if Tex ever came near him, I'm sure of it. They both knew what each other looked like from photos on my phone."

"Do you have a recent photo of Tex?" asked Rabino.

Eryka scrolled the gallery on her phone and held it up towards the detectives. Rabino glanced at it before handing it to Preddy.

"Send dis photo to my phone," said Preddy. Tex was smiling happily when the picture was taken, enjoying the company of the younger woman. Much more relaxed than in his sombre passport photo. "You still have my number?"

"Yes, sir." She took the phone and began clicking.

"You ever been to his home?" asked Preddy.

"He has a house in Westgate Hills, but I've never been there." She looked embarrassed. "His wife lives there with him. He also has property in Miami, so he spends a lot of time off the island. He comes and goes all the time."

"We haven't been able to reach him on de phone number we have," said Preddy.

"That might be the old one. Wait, I'll find it. It's the local number he's been calling me from since last week, so he's here on the island somewhere." She read his number from her bright pink phone and repeated it slowly as Preddy scribbled it down.

"Ah, de last digit doesn't match what I have. Next time he calls you I want you to answer de phone," said Preddy.

"I don't want to talk to him!" Eryka's eyes grew wide and pained. "I'm staying at my sister's place so he can't find me. Suppose he's gone mad? He has a key to my place and I haven't been back there since the murder, because I don't know what he might do."

"He might have something to confess to you." Preddy spoke abruptly. "Just say hello and let him do all de talking."

"I'm afraid he'll know something is wrong, that I've been talking to you!" wailed Eryka.

"If he has any sense, he'll know we're looking for him," said Preddy. "He must know we'd hear about him at some point."

"It's in his interest to come forward and clear his name if he's innocent, Eryka," said Rabino." You might want to tell him that."

Eryka dabbed her eyes and nodded.

Preddy looked at Rabino and gestured to the door. Rabino reached across the table and patted Eryka's hand gently. "You did the right thing in the end, Eryka. Thanks for helping us."

"If Tex did it, I hope he gets life." Eryka fixed her bag over her shoulder. "He didn't have to do it."

"You won't let him get away with it, will you?" said Rabino. "You'll tell us if he lets anything slip?"

"Absolutely." Eryka nodded forcefully. "We need to bring back the death penalty for murderers."

* * *

Preddy and Rabino escorted Eryka out of the police station and stood in the lobby watching her walk down the long driveway. The double doors to the canteen were propped open and Detective Spence was visible at a four-seater table facing the detectives.

"Might as well get lunch," suggested Preddy as the odour of oxtail drifted through the air, awakening his tastebuds.

Spence looked up from her pineapple juice.

"You couldn't wait, madam?" Rabino asked.

"Look here, woman, me thirsty." Spence crunched a piece of ice. "Wasn't sure how long you were going to be and I was dying. Look like somebody set off a false rumour dat a reward is on offer for information on de Baccus murder, because plenty idlers been ringing and me tired fi talk."

"Hold dat thought till I get some drinks," said Preddy.

"Another pineapple please, sir," said Spence.

"You see Harris anywhere?" asked Preddy.

"Not looking for him," mumbled Spence into her glass.

Preddy decided to let it go and looked at Rabino. "What you drinking?"

"Soursop will do for me, or if they're out I'll have guava, lots of ice." She squinted at the counter, behind which the cooks were busy. "So we're not ordering food?"

"It not quite ready yet." Spence glanced at her watch. "She say to give it half-hour."

Preddy strolled towards the counter and spotted Harris through the side window talking on his phone in the court-yard. His first thought was to step outside and beckon him to join them for lunch, until he noticed the small bronze laptop that Harris held so dear tucked under his armpit. Preddy paused and watched him, wishing he could lip-read.

A beige SUV drove slowly past Harris, who pocketed his phone as he walked behind the vehicle and was soon out of view. Preddy left the canteen, ignoring the quizzical looks of his colleagues, and strode out through the front lobby. He slinked along the outer wall of the building, peering around the corner as stealthily as a mongoose watching a mouse. The unfamiliar vehicle came to a stop right beside Harris's motor-bike. Preddy whipped out his notebook and wrote down the licence plate number.

Harris walked up to his motorbike and stood with his back to the SUV driver's door, but his mouth was moving and Preddy knew he must be speaking to the occupant. Much to Preddy's annoyance, the driver did not exit the SUV. Instead, they wound the window down slightly and the Scotsman turned his back to Preddy, who tried unsuccessfully to read Harris's mannerisms.

"Hello, Detective."

Preddy nearly jumped out of his skin. He spun around and nodded at the officer just leaving the station. "Oh, Officer Timmins, hello."

Timmins viewed him with suspicion. "You all right, sir?"

"Just getting a bit of air, you know?"

"Strange place to stand for air, sir, in de flower bed."

Preddy collected himself and glared at Timmins, saying nothing.

The young officer seemed to remember his position. He smiled genially. "Your shoes going get dirty over dere, sir. Better you go under de mango tree, go cool down."

"Yes, dat's an idea." Preddy glanced back at the SUV, where the conversation was ongoing. He wanted Timmins to leave. "You off out, den?"

"Have to go collar a pickpocket dat some people hold down Creek Street. Apparently dey're literally sitting on him."

"Best thing for him," said Preddy. "At least dey not beating him."

"Yet." Timmins grinned. "He's cursing whole heap of claat and if he dares to mention anyone's mother, dey are sure to finish him off."

"Hmm, yes. Can't let dat happen." Preddy peeped around his shoulder and the window of the SUV closed. The car crept forward towards the rear wall to do a U-turn. Harris backed up as it manoeuvred around him and walked towards the back door of the station.

"Rass," muttered Preddy.

Preddy looked at the contented goats chewing earnestly at a row of pink hibiscus. He picked up a small stone and aimed it at the flank of the largest goat, then hid under the lobby archway. The animal gave a startled grunt and ran across the driveway followed by two others.

The SUV screeched to a halt and the driver wound down his tinted window to see whether the animals were in front of the bumper. Eventually, he climbed out. He was a short, dark man with a bald head, dressed in a T-shirt and jeans. He checked the bumper and cursed at the unharmed goats, who had already settled under an almond tree. The man climbed back into his vehicle and drove away.

Preddy scribbled in his notebook. When he looked up, Timmins was scowling at him.

"What was dat about, sir?"

"Er . . . nothing, Officer. You go get de pickpocket before dem kill him."

Preddy tucked his notebook into his shirt pocket and re-entered the building. It was unfortunate that Timmins, Pelican Walk's resident animal lover, had witnessed the scene, but as far as Preddy was concerned the goats were living on borrowed time anyway. He headed back to the canteen and took a seat beside Rabino.

"Wow!" Rabino raised a bottle of juice towards him. "We thought you'd run out to pick guavas and make the juice yourself, sir."

"Sorry, ladies, just had to make a phone call. Took a bit longer dan expected."

"Didn't know if you were coming back, sir, so I got my own," said Rabino. "Didn't get a drink for you."

"Dat's okay, we'll soon have company in de form of Harris, so I may as well order something for him." Preddy turned slightly so that he could see the open doorway. "I think he'll come down when he can't find any of us upstairs."

Spence pointed at the menu. "Food ready. It looking and smelling good. I don't know what to order, but I going clean me plate."

They discussed the merits of three main courses — oxtail with butter beans, curried chicken or mackerel rundown — and whether any was a better choice than the soup of the day, red peas soup with yam and dumplings. The food was subsidized and the cooks were good, so any meal served up was not only tasty but also a hefty portion. Preddy preferred to do Friday lunch off the premises, preferably at one of the beachside restaurants where they could sit within touching distance of the sea, but this was going to be a long and busy day, so it was better to do a short lunch and get back to work.

"Ah, here's Detective Harris," said Preddy. As Harris's hands were free, Preddy guessed that the treasured bronze laptop was under lock and key somewhere safe from prying eyes.

Harris pushed aside two empty bottles from his side of the table as he took a seat next to Spence. "Hello, team. Thirsty work, eh?"

"What you drinking?" asked Preddy.

"Soursop juice will be fine, thanks."

"Either of you ladies need another one?" asked Preddy.

Spence quickly raised her empty bottle. "I wouldn't say no. Me throat still dry."

"Okay, I've got all de food orders." Preddy looked at Harris. "What you eating?"

"I'll have the curried chicken, I think, with callaloo rice. That should go down nicely."

Within a few minutes Preddy returned balancing a tray of drinks. Behind him was a cook carrying two trays of food, one at shoulder height and one at waist level.

The cook beamed at the detectives. "Okay, people, grab you food. I have oxtail for Detective Preddy wid plenty pepper. Chicken for Detective Harris with plenty gravy. Mackerel for Detective Rabino with green bananas and yam." She smiled at Spence. "And I know my lady would want red peas soup!"

Spence grinned. "You know me well. I hope you put plenty dumpling in it?"

"Yes, man! Nothing less."

Spence moved back as the large bowl sent hot steam towards her face.

"Jesus." Harris mopped his brow. "It's ninety degrees in the shade and ye're drinking hot soup?"

"You can feel de heat from over dere so?" asked Spence curtly.

"I can imagine de heat from over here so," Harris replied, adopting his best Patois. He fanned himself with a napkin in an exaggerated fashion.

Spence kissed her teeth. "Eat you chicken and leff me alone. Me ah enjoy me food." She dipped her spoon into her bowl and took up a heap of soup. "Bwoy, it nice!"

"I'll take yer word for it."

Preddy handed out the drinks and gave the tray to the cook, who headed back to the kitchen.

Spence rested her spoon for a breather. "I had an interesting phone call with Gavin Baccus," she said. "Nearly hung up on him because I didn't realize who he was when he started talking. Looks like Wesley Ashburn and his company are not as wealthy as dey seem. According to Gavin, dat property where All Angles is located doesn't belong to Wesley Ashburn — it's leased at a peppercorn rent from a rich client. All dose 3D models and diagrams you see he have dere? Nothing more dan show, apparently. None of dose deals have gone through. He's living on air."

Harris raised an eyebrow as he scooped up his rice. "And how does Mr Baccus know this?"

Spence shrugged. "Dey are arch-rivals, I guess Baccus did some deep digging. Probably spent a lot of money himself to get dat information."

"Or he made it up," said Harris. "Wesley Ashburn seemed a bit nervous, but if he was hiding poverty, he made a pretty good job of it."

"True. De property is convincing." Preddy took a long sip of mango juice. "Money goes to money though. I've been hearing dat since I was in high school. Rich people like to do business with other seemingly rich people. Anyone walking into All Angles will feel dat dose guys know what dey're doing."

"Aye, well, Mr Ashburn did say he'd be happy tae help further, so we'll get a chance tae question him further. Money is always a great motive for murder. I'll see if I can corroborate anything Baccus said."

"I texted a photo of de awl to Gavin Baccus, but he said he'd never seen it before," said Spence. "Didn't recognize de carving on it either."

"Had a look through multiple websites maself and couldnae find anything remotely like the turtle design," said Harris.

Preddy sighed deeply. "We've not shown it to anyone else, but we'll have to turn it over to de media soon. Put it on TV and in de newspapers, see if anyone recognizes it. No reward will be on offer. I'll run it past Super first, because if de calls start coming in, I might need to ask him for a few extra pairs of hands." Preddy took a large forkful of oxtail and savoured the spicy flavour. He noticed the cook watching him and gave her an appreciative thumbs up.

"Eryka Malden was an interesting one," said Rabino. "Took her a while to get talking, but she finally admitted that Tex Doran knew of Jerome and was jealous. It sounds as if Tex spent a small fortune on her, and she spent a good deal of his money wining and dining Jerome, trying to win him away from Nicki Younis."

Spence shook her head. "Young girl always ah give old man bun. Old man should know dat too."

Harris looked confused. "Bun?"

Rabino smiled. "Bun is . . . well, burn. Basically, it means to two-time someone. So if you hear that someone's giving their partner bun it means they're cheating on them, not feeding them pastries."

Harris grinned and spiked his chicken. "Something tae remember for future reference."

"You bringing him in, sir?" asked Spence. "Tex Doran?"

Preddy stared into the air. "I've been thinking about it, but he may spill all to Eryka in a heart-to-heart, so I'm going to wait him out a bit. See if anything happens by tomorrow."

"Tomorrow is Saturday, sir," said Rabino. "I'm not down to work tomorrow, but I can come in if needed?"

Spence swallowed a mouthful of soup. "Me neither. I'll be available any time if you call me though."

"I'll be in," said Harris. "Got a couple of things I need tae do."

Preddy narrowed his eyes as Harris took a drink of juice, all the time keeping his gaze on the Scotsman. He had no doubt that Harris had things to do that no one should know about. Harris seemed to grow embarrassed under Preddy's scrutiny and turned back to his meal.

"Dat's fine." Preddy put down his glass. "In de morning you and I are going to do some beachcombing, Detective

Harris. See if we can find out more about Livity Vendors Association."

"Och, and there was I hoping ye were going tae suggest going for a swim."

"De only thing I have to suggest is dat you don't give any more kids any money."

CHAPTER 9

Detective Preddy glanced at the clock on his living-room wall and returned to the gas stove. He had more than enough time to make it to the homeless charity kitchen and down to the beach to meet Harris. Preddy stood only in his boxer shorts as he stirred the huge pot of soup with a long-handled ladle. The savoury aroma was heavy with a mixture of chicken back, hard yellow yam and starchy coco, plus plenty of soft white yam. The latter was a new addition. He smiled to himself as he checked the texture of the food. The men who patronized the kitchen could be quite picky, and his only thought when one boldly told him that he had never been a fan of hard yam since his youth was, "Really?" Another man had more subtly declined the tuber, and on questioning him Preddy discovered it was not choosiness but problems with untreated teeth. At the time Preddy had chided himself for never having given any thought to the dental situation of the hungry men, but he took some comfort from the fact that every customer, without exception, made short work of the tender meaty bones.

Preddy reduced the heat to the lowest flame and headed for the shower. For a long while he stood perfectly still as

89

the cold water cascaded down his skin from head to toe. He wished it was half as easy to wash away the violent images that invaded his mind at night, preventing peaceful sleep, and were in no hurry to retreat. Most mornings Spartan would listen to him recount the gory details of the failed Norwood incursion and how it made him feel, but the parakeet was MIA, and Preddy feared the bird was still offended from yesterday.

He soothed his nerves with a large mug of ganja tea. Once refreshed he pulled on blue jeans and a burgundy West Indies cricket shirt and reached for his sneakers. He retrieved a large cardboard box and cushioned it with old newspapers before heaving the soup pot into it. Carefully, he carried his hot burden down to the jeep and made sure it was secured.

Back indoors he collected Styrofoam cups and bowls. The government's ban on single-use plastics and similar materials was soon to come into effect to protect the environment from the heaps of garbage that washed up daily on the beaches. Every few months there were beach-cleaning activities, yet the plastic bottles, scandal bags and food containers returned, usually after a heavy shower of rain, washed down from the hills and gullies where residents suffering poor refuse collection services had disposed of them. Some disgruntled residents, tired of waiting for the refuse trucks and reluctant to contaminate the gullies, set fire to the unwanted rubbish, thus creating another public health nuisance.

Preddy was enthusiastic at the idea of the plastics ban, yet he wondered if the supermarkets would continue being generous in their donation of cups and bowls when the more expensive biodegradable replacements came on the market. The cost of the ingredients came out of his own pocket and he never begrudged that expense. Without the donations of free containers, his trips would cease to be weekly. He carefully closed the rear door of the jeep and set out slowly on the drive downtown.

As usual, carefree tourists were up early and headed for the beach in coaster buses and on foot. The charity kitchen was out of sight for most tourists. The intrepid few who walked off the beaten path and found themselves on that side road would see a large group of men either standing near the door of the kitchen, or if it was not open, sitting across the road on the pavement. Some even lay down and slept on cardboard overnight to be front of the queue. They were usually half-dressed and always unkempt, but Preddy had discovered that beneath the exterior they were men who could hold their own in conversation, who could have been any middle-class man — and some indeed had once been considered well-off by Jamaican standards.

He had heard their stories. One was a deportee from Georgia in the United States who had overstayed his visa and been unable to find employment since returning to the island. Another was a divorcee who had fallen out with his entire family because of the way he had treated his wife and children. *"She naggy-naggy inna me ears too much, dat's why me and she couldn't 'gree."* Another had been injured in an on-the-job accident for which he had never received compensation and had been ripped off by unscrupulous lawyers. Only one man accepted full responsibility for his plight, admitting that he had lost numerous jobs due to poor timekeeping and boisterous backchatting to his bosses. *"If me coulda kibber me mouth, me woulda still have money and somewhe' to live."*

The men waved at him and flocked to the kitchen door as soon as his vehicle pulled up. Preddy smiled and waved back. They knew the drill now. There was no point rushing his vehicle, because no food would be handed out there. A male cook came out and helped Preddy bring the pot inside then collected the bags of sturdy cups. The detective greeted a female volunteer who was finishing mopping the floor. She was young and plump with a ready smile. He was always glad to see young people doing their bit for the elders who had lost their way.

"You no get no spoon dis time, Misser Preddy?" asked the girl as she watched her colleague place the bags on the countertop beside the sink. She fended off the hungry men

91

who had pushed their heads through the open door and closed it behind the detective.

"Rass," mumbled Preddy. "Forgot dem, sorry."

One of the men pressed his nose through the iron grill that separated him from his first and probably only meal for the day. "We no need no spoon, boss. A food we want."

"From me mouth can open me good to go, sah."

"Put de food inna de bowl, gi' we. Watch how quick we done it."

"All right, all right, people," said the cook cheerfully. He opened the hatch and wiped down the countertop. "Food coming up in five minutes. Who say chicken back soup?"

"Yes, sah!" The men murmured their appreciation as they gathered round. No one could get them to form an orderly line and the charity workers had long stopped trying to force them.

"You staying, Misser Preddy?" asked the female worker as she pulled on a white apron.

"Not today." Preddy shook his head. "Have a business appointment I have to keep — you know what dis city is like."

She nodded. "Me understand. Ah gwine scrub out de pot for you and you can pick it up later, you hear?"

"Will do. Thank you." He popped a mint into his mouth and drove away.

* * *

Preddy spotted the red hair of Detective Harris before he saw the motorbike. Harris was parked at the planned meeting spot on the private drive of a courier delivery company just off the Hip Strip. Preddy knew both the owner and the security guard, so getting a parking spot for Harris was easy. The Scotsman was casually dressed in long, white tailored shorts, a white T-shirt and brown sandals, and looked like any tourist. He was engaged in conversation with the guard and did not see the jeep. Preddy tooted and Harris turned to wave at him before quickly ending his conversation.

"He likes ma bike." Harris removed his sunglasses as he climbed into the passenger seat. "Hope it'll be safe."

"It's safe," Preddy assured him. "As much as he might like it, taking a police officer's bike for a joyride is not something dat de average person would do."

"Didnae think there was such thing as an average Jamaican?"

"De ones dat know not to fuck around wid police property are average enough. De others are crazies dat we need to put away."

"Aye, I hear ye."

They cruised along the Hip Strip, stopping at various beaches to search the white sands for signs of the Rastafarian salesman. No need to stop at the world-famous Doctor's Cave Beach or the prestigious Cornwall Beach, as the security teams would never allow vendors to wander all over their exclusive, picturesque properties. Finally, at Blossom Beach, Preddy narrowed his eyes and slowed the vehicle to a crawl, having focused on a distant figure. Preddy pointed at the slim man with flowing grey dreadlocks, the tips of which brushed against his waist. Beside him stood a bright pink igloo cooler balanced on a rusty supermarket trolley.

"Dere's our man."

"That's him, all right. Let's go meet Ras Bizzi."

Preddy pulled up under an almond tree, sheltering the vehicle from the penetrating sun. The heat of the day was barely lowered by the sea breeze, and the only people feeling any coolness were those fully immersed in the crystal waters. The detectives alighted and trudged through the sand towards their target.

"This is good," said Harris, polishing his sunglasses. "Och, I love the feel of sand between ma toes."

"Stay focused, Detective."

There were few tourists on Blossom Beach, which, because of its small size, had never caught the attention of the hotels and remained in government hands. The tourists that came were mainly people actively seeking to meet and talk to the locals, explorers unconvinced by the offerings of the all-inclusives and happier to see the real Jamaica. Some were there hoping to buy cheap weed having been directed to the spot by helpful locals. Most beachgoers were absorbed with the sun and sea and paid no attention to the detectives. A few people studied the odd couple closely.

"See de Norwood Babylon ah come!" shouted a youth, and all heads immediately turned in Preddy's direction. "Preddy bad as yaws!"

"Yer reputation precedes ye," mumbled Harris.

"Misser Harris, ah true she Scotlan' Babylon bad too?" said another youth.

Preddy glanced at his colleague's pink face. "Pot meet kettle."

A man rode past, skidding along the sand on a moped with a cooler strapped onto the back seat. "Creamy! Creamy! Ice cream me have yasso!"

Children screamed their appreciation as they chased down the mobile dessert man, their bare feet making better progress than his tyres.

Ras Bizzi was oblivious to the attention of the two men advancing on him. He opened his cooler and removed four ice-cold bottles, holding them deftly by the neck between his slender fingers. He waved the bottles at a group of people, one of whom reached out, took a bottle and seemed to be studying the crude label. Ras Bizzi was quite tall up close, with a narrow face and a jutting, bearded chin. He wore a waistcoat made from some form of dried grass and a matching skirt, with flip-flops on his feet, yet his look was not feminine and he could have been more properly compared to a gladiator. A beaded chain hung round his neck to his chest, the end of which held a large African map carved out of coconut shell.

"Guess you like his skirt, eh?" said Preddy. "You and he should get along just fine."

"Definitely suits this weather. Trust me, if they added kilts tae the police uniform, ye'd quickly learn tae appreciate it."

"No. Wouldn't happen. No man would wear dem . . . except you."

"Might test the theory yet, Preddy."

Harris peered into the open cooler. It was full of transparent plastic bottles balanced on broken chunks of ice. The contents were various coloured juices, labelled carrot, mango, pineapple, aloe vera, lemongrass and ginger. One greenish bottle, which seemed to be a blend of many natural plants, was labelled "purity".

"Ras Bizzi?" said Preddy.

"Yes, who need I and I!" The Rasta spun around and glanced at Preddy before turning his full attention to Harris. Ever the salesman, he quickly moved closer to his cooler and spoke slowly and politely. "Yes, sir? What would you like?"

A wooden handcart laden with large green coconuts was parked nearby. The seller was a shirtless man in coloured shorts that stopped mid-calf. He had a shiny bald head speckled grey and a tufted grey chest. "Cool jelly coconuts right here, sir?" the man said quickly, hoping to draw Harris's attention.

"Go weh, Moses." Ras Bizzi waved a backhand at him. "Is ital juice dem want."

Harris shot an apologetic look at the second man. "Naw coconuts for me."

"What can I and I get for you, sir?" The Rasta man's newly acquired accent seemed to belong to some unknown part of America. "Would you like the fruit juice or a nice plant juice? All fresh and natural with no preservatives, ready-made this morning, sir."

Harris drew his gaze away from the cooler and smiled at him. "We can stick with Patois. I like it much better than whatever that was. I'm Detective Harris, Pelican Walk."

Ras Bizzi grinned, displaying sparkling teeth. "Oh, I did hear seh one white Babylon inna Mo Bay, ah you?"

"Ah me." Harris inclined his head slightly. "One white Babylon. This is Detective Preddy."

The dreadlocked man remained jovial as he glanced from one man to the other. "I and I never know seh Babylon start walk beach ah look juice?"

"Not looking any juice dis time." Preddy waved his badge at him. "We're looking for de head of de Livity Vendors Association. I'm told dat's you?"

"Yes, you find I. Ras Bizzi at your service, Misser Preddy. What I can do fi you?" He glanced at the coconut man hovering at his side. "Dis is Moses, he's a Livity member just like I and I."

Moses expertly chopped open a green coconut with a machete, sending the displaced husk skidding across the sand. "I hope is something good you come to tell we, Detective?" he said.

"We're investigating a murder," said Preddy. "De murder of—"

"Wow!" said Moses.

"Murder?" The Rasta man took a step backwards and pulled on the tiny grey locks that formed his beard. "I and I don't know 'bout dem ting deh!"

"Naw need tae panic, gents, we just want tae ask a few questions," said Harris.

"Who get murder?" asked Moses.

"De victim's name is Jerome Baccus," said Preddy. "He was murdered right next to de Grand Marquee on January first. You must have heard about it?"

Moses handed the coconut to his customer and pocketed the money. He stood akimbo with his machete pointed at the sand. "Me did hear 'bout it, say somebody stab him up kill him."

Ras Bizzi tossed his flowing locks from side to side. "Ah pure wickedness a gwaan inna dis world and Jah-Jah nah sleep!" His attention was suddenly taken by foreign accents carrying in the distance. "Me ah listen to you, Officer, talk." He gripped his trolley and began pulling it. "Moses, I and I ah go down so, where some white man a swim."

"All right, Ras. Me right behind you."

"Officer, we can walk and talk still." The Rasta man struggled to turn the stubborn trolley, whose wheels were not built for sand. "I jus' ah go look two sale."

"Fine, go ahead." Preddy whipped out his notebook as he walked alongside them. "What is your real name, sir?"

The Rasta man's eyes flickered and he looked concerned. "I and I no have no business wid police, you know? I is a quiet, clean-living man wha' no do no wrong to nobody and no break no law. Never."

"Really?" Harris glanced at the cooler and removed a bottle, which he held out towards Preddy. "A handwritten label with naw company name or address? Naw even a phone number." He replaced the bottle in its original position, tucking it firmly under the melting ice.

"Indeed," said Preddy. "You have a food handlers' permit? Food Safety visit your premises and give you de go ahead to sell homemade drinks?"

Moses scowled as he pushed his cart. "Bwoy, you too rough pon we!"

Preddy shot him a cursory glance. He assumed the two vendors were of a similar age, probably just over sixty. They were a curious pair, Moses with his shiny grey-black pate and Ras Bizzi with his waist-length greying locks.

Ras Bizzi frowned, but his tone remained polite. "I not gwine lie, Officer. I no have no permit, no license, no nutten. Govament people tell I say I need dis and dat, before I can sell. But nobody helping wid money to feed I kids. Nobody nah offer I no suitable premises to make nutten. I haffi do I ting to survive. Just dis selling I do, boss. Dis is not no big crime. I nah rob, nah fight, nah kill."

"Real name?" Preddy tapped his pen on his notebook. "I'm guessing Ras Bizzi is not what your mother gave you."

"Bennett Shaw write pon I birth paper." His voice was calm. "A slave-master name. I no want it. Ras mean Duke. I and I prefer to claim my crown pon my island. Slave-master can take white man name and gwaan back a dem country."

Preddy wrote as the man spoke. "We won't argue about it." He gazed down at the chunks of ice in the igloo. "Where's your ice pick?"

"Ice pick?" Ras Bizzi looked confused. "I and I no sell ice, boss, so I no need ice pick. Dat ice is just to cool de juice."

"You need ice pick, sir?" said Moses. "Me no have no ice pick, but de machete can bruk ice good-good?"

"No." Preddy looked at him impatiently. "I don't need no damn ice pick."

"What we want is information on who might want tae hurt the Baccus family," said Harris. "We understand that the Livity members are really upset with the men who run Baccus Designs and All Angles."

"Not vex to kill, sir." Ras Bizzi closed his cooler and stared at Harris. "People well vex though. Is 'bout twenty member gwine ban from walk Dowdy Beach when dis project start and everybody have fambily to feed. Nobody nah listen to de likkle man. Ah me haffi speak up and try help dem."

"And ye speak for everybody, do ye?" asked Harris.

"Well, not everybody, because I nah defend people who wah sell dead animal. Dem come pon beach a skin pig and cow and a pluck chicken. Rasta scorn dem ting deh! I and I no touch dead animal, neither meat nor skin nor bone."

"I see," Harris nodded.

The Rasta turned his attention to Preddy. "White man not gwine notice, Officer, but you must notice wha' gwaan a Mo Bay. You no see de rich people dem just a get richer and de poor man a get poorer? Jamaica dollar nah buy nutten again."

"Ah true," said Moses. He took out his exasperation by bringing the machete down with full force against a coconut, slicing off the top. "It hard, man."

Harris looked at him. "What's yer full name, sir?"

"Moses Fearon. Not guilty of a ting, Misser Officer."

"Politician wicked," continued Ras Bizzi. "PNP wicked and JLP wickeder. Look all Cornwall Beach we used to can go pon? Now dem sell it off to rich foreigner. If you no have money you cyah go pon good beach. Marcus Garvey ah turn inna him grave. Haile Selassie I, too."

Preddy studied his face, noting that, unlike Moses Fearon, Ras Bizzi never changed his soft tone. "Where were you on de night of January first, Mr Shaw?"

"I and I don't love dat name."

"Answer de question, sir."

"All ah we were down dere, at de marquee." He scowled. "Nobody wasn't stabbing nobody. We was seated watching de promotion like everybody else. I did well want to see what Baccus have to show, cause I know him not including any ah we. When people start run, we run too. I is a man what don't like hang round any kind a violence. A peace and love I and I deal wid, even when people ah try bring we down."

"So ye didnae notice anybody missing from yer group at any time?" asked Harris.

"No, sah. After de lights go out, I never notice anyting except what a show pon de movie screen in front ah me eye. If a man or woman get up, me no know 'bout it."

"Me run when everybody run too," said Moses. "Never see a ting. Couldn't believe me go beach to go watch likkle free movie and someting like dat happen."

A customer approached and the Rasta man reopened his container. "Look fi wah you want drink, my girl," he encouraged her. The girl shuffled her fingers through the melting ice. "A two hundred fi de carrot, sista, it have in ginger. Nice, you see!" She paid him and skipped away, turning the bottle to her lips.

Harris mopped his brow as he watched the girl. The drinks looked tempting and were much needed, but it would not do for policemen to be seen buying anything from an illegal vendor. Everybody had a smartphone these days to capture wrongdoing and were quick to put it on social media for comments and likes.

"Where did you go after de murder?" asked Preddy.

"I catch bus and go home, sah, go meditate." Ras Bizzi stared earnestly at Preddy. "Rasta man no deal inna murder. When you ever hear 'bout Rasta a kill nobody?"

"In recent years?" Preddy closed his notebook and used it to pat his chest. "Let me see now, Safari Farr put a few bullets in Jody-Ann Gray at close range for just 250,000 dollars. Is sheer luck she didn't die."

"Dat man is not true Rastafari, boss! Me no know what religion him a follow. Jah gwine sen fire fi bun some people!" The Rastaman did a little jig of frustration, his locks bouncing on his shoulders while his arms flailed. "Real Rasta man innocent."

"De Coral Gardens Rastas weren't all innocent, if memory serves me right, regardless of what dey now say."

Ras Bizzi looked at Preddy, who sensed that the Rastafarian was waiting for further information. "Everybody out fi Rasta man. White man come do wha' dem want do in dis country. Chiney man come too. Coolie man come too, same ting. But if I light up likkle herb, dem fling I inna jail. Any business I try start, dem close I down. If you no white or brown you cyah do business a Mo Bay. But I hear tourism minister ah come talk 'bout prosperity inna Mo Bay. Prosperity fi who? A dat me wah know."

A local crowd had gathered behind him, listening to his soliloquy. They cheered and clapped loudly when he finished. "Talk de tings, Ras! Tell dem!"

"Same way it go!"

"Ah you know de ting, Ras!"

Preddy and Harris exchanged looks, acknowledging the end of the questions. "Thank you for your help, Mr Shaw," said Preddy. "I know you don't deal wid police, but we're at Pelican Walk and we're trying to find a murderer. If you hear anything you can contact us dere."

"I hear you, boss." Ras Bizzi nodded.

"You too, Mr Fearon," said Preddy.

"Yes, sir," said Moses.

Ras Bizzi gave Harris a look of apology. "I and I nah try cause you no offence, Misser Harris, cause I know not all white man is de same."

"Naw offence taken," said Harris with a short bow of his head.

They trudged towards their vehicle.

"That 'I and I' business was giving me a right headache," said Harris.

"Hmm, he's a bit of a character. Colourful in looks and speech."

"Ras Bizzi suits him way more than bland old Bennett Shaw. Cannae blame him for naw using it."

Preddy turned and glanced back at the Rastafarian. "He's a real cool cucumber. I expected him to get all hyped up when I mentioned Coral Gardens, but he let it go."

"What's Coral Gardens about?" Harris climbed into the jeep. "That's the area next door tae Ironshore, is it naw?"

"Same place." Preddy buckled up and started the engine. "From I was born, I've been hearing about it. April 1963, so we're going back a long way, but Rastas — particularly St James Rastas — all remember it. Prime Minister Bustamante sent police into de Coral Gardens community to round up Rastas after dey killed a man. Seven Rastas were killed. Some were arrested and beaten and had deir locks forcibly trimmed. It's a painful story. Dere's a whole exhibition dedicated to Rasta at de Cultural Centre, if you want to learn all about it."

"Have tae check that one out. It was over half a century ago though, and he seems a peaceful soul. Maybe he just wants tae let bygones be bygones?"

"Maybe," said Preddy. He pulled away from the beach. "If so, he's de first Rasta I've come across who does."

CHAPTER 10

Saturday, 5 January, 6.53 p.m.

Detective Preddy had long left Pelican walk and was now heading home from the supermarket, chatting with Valerie on the phone. She was in Kingston and due to return to Montego Bay tomorrow night. Tomorrow he would drive to Discovery Bay in St Ann for a hopefully stress-free day with Roman and Annalee and get back in time to pick Valerie up from the Knutsford Express coach depot at Harbour Circle downtown.

He parked at his apartment complex and unloaded bags of groceries. He usually preferred to make his own health drinks, but after seeing the Rasta man's concoctions earlier he had picked up some ready-made lemongrass and peanut punch. He nudged the car door shut and nodded hello to his neighbour as he hobbled to his front door.

He kicked off his shoes, dumped the bags on the counter-top and headed straight for the remote control. He estimated a good volume level to stop at before the sound penetrated the walls and annoyed his neighbours. While unpacking his purchases in the kitchen, he listened to the seven o'clock prime-time news. The first few minutes had gone, which was no loss. The national news was blatantly Kingston-centric, so there was no chance that the appeal he was hoping to hear had already been aired. The appeal was for people to come forward and identify the pointed weapon used in the murder of Jerome Baccus.

He switched on the air-con unit, enjoying its familiar comforting purr as he sorted out a tiny portion of rice to refrigerate for Spartan, in case the bird had forgiven him and returned for breakfast in the morning. He gave his meal thirty seconds on high in the microwave. The newsreader started talking politics, highlighting the bad behaviour of both political parties in parliament that day. Preddy strained his neck to catch a glimpse of the TV screen where the male parliamentarians were waving their file pages at one another and shouting aggressively, while the females joined in slapping the tables and jeering their opponents. Preddy shook his head. This was the example being set for Jamaica's youth. *Monkey see, monkey do*, he thought, and turned back to his food, dousing it in hot pepper sauce.

Preddy took a seat on the couch and stared at the TV as he ate. After fifteen minutes the newsreader finally shone the spotlight on the parish of St James. It began with footage of the Grand Marquee being erected early in the evening on first of January, when the sun was still up. The video camera panned around the food and drinks stalls, where people were stocking their wares. Gavin Baccus was directing a group of young men on the layout of the plastic seating. Next came a shot of the Portaloos, beside which the body was found. The newsreader made the point that within three hours of the footage being taken, Jerome Baccus was stabbed through the heart.

Preddy scanned the area, taking in as many of the faces as possible. A photograph of a smiling Jerome appeared on-screen, followed by a still of the murder weapon. The camera zoomed in on the distinctive design of the awl's handle — a good clear shot of the turtle motif, to Preddy's relief. Two special hotline numbers were emblazoned below while the voice appealed for viewers to contact the police if they had any specific information on either the murder or the murder weapon.

Preddy wondered — not for the first time — whether there was a possibility that the murder had been random after all. Many volatile people inhabited the island and the vast majority of them were not St James residents. In fact, since the state of emergency had taken hold, St James had given up its unwanted crown as the most murderous parish on the island. The title had been seized with some zeal by the criminals of St Catherine, with Clarendon a close runner-up and Kingston not far behind. The Grand Marquee could well have been infiltrated by criminal visitors from other parishes who had come to Montego Bay for nefarious reasons. Any one of them could have had a chance encounter with Jerome that resulted in a sudden act of violence.

Preddy placed his plate on the arm of the couch and sat forward as his eyes caught the familiar face of one of the ushers placing the chairs. The bald man was undoubtedly the same member of the Livity Vendors Association who had been with Ras Bizzi on the beach earlier. Moses Fearon, the sinewy coconut man. Preddy reached across a side table for his copy of Friday's *Western Mirror*. He stared at the front page, which carried the story of the vendors' protest, complete with pictures of their militant placards. Members of Livity were listed by name from left to right beside the by-line. It was the same man, all right.

Preddy sat back, a deep frown etched in his brow. Moses had been present at a morning demonstration waving a placard with the other Livity vendors, yet by evening he had been back as part of the Baccus marquee crew. Somehow he had neglected to mention this secondary job to the detectives. Moses's attire had been different too — the newsreel had shown him wearing the usher's uniform of a crisp white shirt and black trousers, while in the newspaper photo he had on long shorts and a vest and looked quite downtrodden. Why would Moses Fearon have been helping Gavin Baccus if he was dead set against any model proposed for Dowdy Beach by either Baccus or Ashburn? First thing on Monday morning, Preddy would try to find Moses Fearon.

He finished his meal while watching the rest of the news. The newsreader had moved on to the case of a missing person last seen at a party in Claremont two weeks prior. This was followed by a report of a fire destroying a six-room uninsured board property in Santa Cruz. Every week there was at least one of these fire stories, accompanied by interviews with the distressed occupants standing among smoking wood and zinc. The reporter signalled an advert break, and Preddy took the opportunity to try and find something less stress-inducing to watch.

He flicked through the channels until he found an adventure movie that had already started. It would be good to watch mindless adventure for two hours and not have to think of anything serious. He stretched his long frame across the sofa and tucked two cushions under his head. He had watched *Indiana Jones* many times already, but he still found himself chuckling at the best parts and urging Indie to escape. The irony of having become his father did not escape him. Maybe it was a rite of passage and all adults did this running commentary on films while their adolescents rolled their eyes and vowed never to be so annoying when they grew up.

As the movie came to an end, his phone rang and his first thought was to ignore it. What he wanted to do was grab a nightcap and get to bed. He reached across the coffee table and glanced at it, then quickly answered. "Hello, Eryka."

"Detective Preddy, good night. Sorry to bother you, sir."

"No bother at all." There was hope in Preddy's voice as he spoke. "Tex call you?"

Silence filled the air for a beat before Eryka said, "No."

The hesitation left Preddy wondering if she was hiding something. "You sure? Talk to me." Silence followed. Frustration filled the detective as he waited. "Eryka, you still dere?"

"Yes, sir. I wanted to talk in person. I can come see you tomorrow?"

Preddy frowned. He worked many hours overtime without claiming a dollar or complaining. As dedicated as he was to the Jamaica Constabulary Force, he was entitled to time off. His family was also entitled to his time, and one of his New Year's resolutions was to ensure they got it. Besides, he had not warmed to the girl, who he saw as an unrepentant user of men, and he was not inclined to change his plans to accommodate her even for an hour. "Actually, I'm not around tomorrow. Monday morning okay wid you? Say, nine?"

Eryka seemed to think about this for a while. Preddy waited, wondering if she expected him to change his mind. He thought about doing so, but resisted the idea. The meeting was not to relay a confession from Tex Doran, so it could wait until Monday.

"Can we make it nine thirty, instead?" she asked.

"Yes, dat's good. You sure you all right?" He thought about what could be bothering her. "I have a grief counsellor I can put you in touch wid . . . should have provided it before but it slipped my mind."

"No, I'm fine, sir," she assured him. "Just need to talk about something that just came to mind. It will keep though."

"All right, see you at nine thirty on Monday at Pelican Walk."

CHAPTER 11

Sunday, 6 January, 6.25 a.m.

Sunlight crept up on the window giving the bedroom's white walls a yellowish tint. Preddy lay still for a few minutes revelling in the complete silence of an exhausted city that had expended all its energy on a marathon weekend party. The serenity was soon broken in the gentlest of ways, the relentless tapping of sharp beak on glass forcing the detective out of bed. He stretched and padded his way barefoot towards the kitchen, relieved that his feathered companion had not deserted him for good. Time and speaking to Spartan were good healers. He removed the small dish of rice and stared into the fridge, contemplating whether to take something for himself, and decided on a bottle of coconut water.

Spartan began cheeping incessantly and spread his green wings as Preddy approached the window.

"I know you not really glad to see me. Just glad for de food, eeh?"

When the window went up, Spartan flew straight onto Preddy's shoulder, fastening his tiny feet on bare skin. The parakeet pecked the detective's chin twice before fluttering down to his wrist.

"Good morning to you too. Maybe I was wrong. Maybe you have some feelings after all." He tickled the tiny crest that crowned the bird's head and had led to Roman christening him Spartan. He placed the dish on a table. The bird's yellow beak made short work of the rice. Preddy stared at the innocent being. It was strangely comforting that a creature so tiny and defenceless was trusting of someone who could end its life between two fingers.

"Today is family day, Spartan. What you think about dat?"

The bird turned its head slightly, as if acknowledging the question, yet refusing to be distracted from the goal of filling its craw.

"Dat's right. Make haste eat." Preddy took a long gulp of coconut water. "I have an hour's drive ahead to St Ann. First stop, Seville Great House. Dose kids need to get some culture. Everything can't be electronics and technology. History lesson first, den Puerto Seco Beach to swim . . . which reminds me to find my trunks."

Preddy filled the kettle then headed toward his bedroom. He smiled as he uncovered a pair of floral swimming trunks tucked away at the back of a drawer. Heavily creased from lack of usage, they needed the attention of an iron, which he had no intention of using. He flapped the material in the air a few times then spread it on the bed before returning to the drawer and pulling out a large beach towel.

The phone rang. No doubt the early-morning caller was one of his offspring checking that he was awake.

On seeing the caller ID, his stomach rose and sank in a discomforting manner. Detective Javinia Spence. In all the time he had known her she had never contacted him at the crack of dawn to pass on any good news, and certainly never on a Sunday. Somehow he knew that he would not be driving to St Ann that morning, would not even be leaving St James.

He winced as he pressed the green image. "Please tell me something good, Spence? You won de Super Lotto and have my share ready?"

"Wish I could, sir." Her voice was sombre. "Dey just found a female body in de gully at Cherry Walk."

Preddy's stomach did another robust somersault and he rubbed it with his left hand, a movement meant to calm, yet it had no effect. His temples began to thud, forcing his eyes to narrow. There was only one female he knew of who lived at Cherry Walk, but he mouthed the question anyway. "Who?"

* * *

Preddy pulled up at the crime scene. Cherry Walk was a high-elevation, prosperous district where residents had a perfect view of the bustling city, with the sea and mountainous region beyond. The area had become well populated over the last twenty years and was dominated by private housing schemes comprising modern town houses and four-storey condominiums. The wide roads and well-kept pavements saved the area from the feeling of congestion that affected so many modern developments. This zone of urban tranquillity was home to Eryka Malden, her unit rented for her by her besotted older lover Tex Doran.

A police officer stood beside a gully speaking into his phone. A crowd of half-dressed residents gathered close to the low-rise wall were peering down and commentating on the scene below. Lack of rainfall had left the gully mainly empty of water, and it was thankfully clear of any litter. Preddy leaned over the wall and saw the object of their attention about six feet below. A female in a blue dress lay on her back, eyes closed, legs bent at an unnatural angle, arms at her sides. Long braids partially hid her face. A pool of reddish brown coagulated around one of her ears.

Rabino was already in the gully taking photographs of the body. A constable stood with his back to her, looking out for any rubberneckers who might have been contemplating breaching the gully wall. Most of the wall towered over a sheer six-foot drop, except for where a narrow set of concrete steps ran to facilitate access for clearing and cleaning of the area. As Preddy headed towards the steps Spence broke away from speaking to a male resident and walked up to her boss.

"What do we know?" asked Preddy. A sense of weariness mixed with self-loathing was threatening to overcome him, and he fought to appear upbeat and focused.

"It's definitely Eryka, sir." Spence pointed at a large grey stone covered in red stains. "Dat must be de murder weapon."

"Let's go get a closer look."

A car came to a screeching halt beside them and a woman jumped out, startling the detectives. Preddy barely managed to grab at her arm to stop her getting past him.

"Lord God! Not me sister, not me sister!"

Despite her face being contorted in anguish, Preddy could see the resemblance. "No, ma'am. I'm sorry. You cannot go near her. I'm sorry, you hear?"

"Is me sister. Let me go!" she wailed and struggled to pull away, but Preddy held firm, fearing she would miss the steps and fall head-first down onto the concrete.

An elderly female onlooker grabbed the woman's shoulders and pulled her into her ample bosom. "All right, baby," she said in a soothing tone, "You cyah go down dere. Never mind, me love. She gaan to Jesus. Only Him can help har now." The distraught woman collapsed into the good Samaritan's arms and sobbed loudly into her chest.

Spence rubbed the crying woman's back. "I'm so sorry, ma'am. You stay right here wid de lady. Don't go down dere."

Preddy walked down the steps, followed by Spence. His stomach had not stopped doing painful things since he received the news, gnawing on itself, refusing to settle. He barely knew Eryka and could not imagine the pain her sister must be feeling. The idea that she might be murdered had not crossed his mind for a second. She had remained on his radar as a means of getting to Tex Doran, not as a potential victim. He should have spoken to her, pressed her on what was bothering her. Now here she lay, her youth stalled forever. He groaned involuntarily.

"You all right, sir?" asked Spence.

"Yes, man. Didn't get any tea, dat's all."

Preddy's ears were alert to the distinct sound of a large-engine motorbike. Harris attracted the attention of a group of young men, who tore their eyes from the crime scene to admire his wheels.

"Ye can look, but dinnae touch," Harris warned.

"No, sir! Not troubling it."

Harris attached his helmet to the motorbike and ran down the gully steps to join the others. "Poor girl," breathed Harris as he stared at the body. "Do we know how she got down here?"

"No." Spence shook her head. "All we know is some child passing saw de body and showed it to his father, who called de Area One emergency number. He knew it was Eryka as he'd seen her driving her Audi around."

"Is de car here?" asked Preddy.

"Yes, sir. It's in what dey say is her regular spot." Spence pointed to a bunch of keys near the dead girl's hand. "Guess dose belong to her."

Preddy murmured a greeting to Rabino as he crouched beside the body. Eryka's once-neat black braids were frazzled and matted in blood. "Looks like she took a blow to de head."

"More than one." Rabino took a few steps back and photographed the wider area then allowed the camera to dangle freely at waist level. "Someone was determined to finish her off."

"She called me last night." Preddy got to his feet and closed his eyes briefly, remembering. He wished his gut would quit its nauseating behaviour. "I don't know why, but she wanted to talk to me face to face. I agreed to meet her at Pelican Walk tomorrow."

"Ye think somebody made sure get tae her before she could get tae you?"

111

"Dat's exactly what I think." Preddy stifled a groan. "Damn, I should have pressed her on what was bothering her. She didn't sound upset though. Didn't sound as if it was a life-or-death matter."

"What time was that, sir?" asked Rabino.

"Around ten, maybe closer to half past."

Rabino nodded. "At least we have an idea of the time-line. She looks like she's been laying here for several hours. We'll see if Doctor Sewell can narrow it down."

"Her sister is up top." Spence glanced up at the crowd, from which a high-pitched wailing could be heard, although the wailer was not in view. "We might need a medic to calm her down."

"Did Eryka not say she was staying with her sister?" Rabino looked at Preddy.

"Dat's right," Preddy recalled. "Said she wanted to stay away from Tex."

Rabino looked concerned. "The sister sounds like she's in a bad way, so I don't know what we'll get out of her."

Preddy frowned. "Wonder who called de sister?"

"Let's go ask her," said Harris.

"De ambulance soon come," said Spence. She looked at Rabino. "I'll cover up de body if you done take photograph?"

"Yes, go ahead, girl. I have enough shots."

Preddy took a deep breath. "Get a wrecker to come and take de Audi. We'll get de lab guys to see if dere's any evidence in it tomorrow. You hold onto de keys."

Preddy followed Harris back up the steps and over the gully wall. Eryka's sister sat on an upturned crate with head in hands, shoulders shaking as she sobbed. The elderly woman stood beside her rubbing her back. The sister looked up as Preddy gently touched her shoulder. "I'm Detective Preddy from Pelican Walk. Dis is Detective Harris."

The woman shook her head and groaned from her soul. No words came from her lips.

Preddy's stomach clenched as he gazed at the anguished woman. The feeling that this was a preventable tragedy would not leave him. "What's your name, ma'am?"

The woman beside her answered. "She say she name Alina Malden. Poor chile."

"Alina?" Preddy crouched down in front of her. "We're very sorry for de loss of your sister, ma'am."

"Dem kill me one sister. Me cyah believe." The words came in a soft croak and a sob trapped in her throat.

"Who told you she was here, Alina?" asked Preddy.

"Nobody. She was staying wid me last night and now she here dead!"

"I know this is very hard for ye, Alina," said Harris softly. "Can ye tell us what happened last night?"

Alina inhaled and wiped her face with bare palms. "She leave out of my place after ten, say she going home to pick up her clothes. Dat's all I know."

"Where do ye live?" asked Harris.

"Up Brandon Hill. She come stay wid me after dem kill Jerome, and look, see dem come do her same way!" She mopped her brimming eyes. "She shouldn't leave out last night. I tell her say she can wear my clothes anytime, but she say she need to get dem."

Preddy scribbled in his notebook. "You know what particular clothes she was referring to?"

"No, sir." Alina held her head as if it was too heavy to manage the strain of its weight without reinforcement. "I don't know why she leave me house. My clothes can fit her although dem no nice like hers. She have plenty nice clothes from dat man give her money."

Preddy looked at her. She had almost spat the words "dat man" and he knew it could only be Tex Doran.

"She called me," said Preddy. "Probably just after she left your home. You know why she would have called me? What she wanted to talk about?"

"No, she never say a thing to me about calling police. I had been trying to do things wid her to take her mind off

Jerome, but it was impossible. We watched de prime-time news at seven, because she wouldn't let me change channel." She sniffed and exhaled loudly. "Dere was a big piece on Jerome and Dowdy Beach. She never take her eyes off de screen. After dat I put on *Finding Nemo*, and dat is what we were watching before she get up suddenly, say she going out to get clothes."

"You never worry when she didn't come back last night?" asked Preddy.

"Not really. She was down, you know? I just thought maybe she want to be by herself without me fussing round her." She dabbed her reddened eyes. "I tried to call her around midnight to wish her good night but she never pick up. I sent her a text den went to bed. She's a girl who always reply to text. I wake at five o'clock and no see no reply. Is like me heart stop! Me know something wrong. Me fly come up here cause me know!" She began sobbing again.

"We should check if she made it into her apartment." Preddy glanced at Harris, who nodded in agreement. "Alina, you have a key to her apartment?"

"Yes, me have it in me pocket."

"We need to go inside and take a look around," said Preddy.

Alina's hand moved towards her jeans pocket. She hesitated and glanced at Harris. "Dat old man she keeping tell her not to give anybody key to de place. Tex Doran him name."

"Let us worry about Tex Doran, Alina," said Harris. "We're here tae help Eryka. We need tae go inside."

"All right." Alina stood up and Harris grasped her elbow and steadied her. "If is dat man do dis to her . . ."

"You think he would?" asked Preddy.

"Him is not a good man! Him have good wife and him want my sister. Big man like dat should know better. Me tell her not to deal wid him, but she no listen. Now look!"

Preddy and Harris followed Alina up two flights of stairs. She stopped at an olive-green door with two leafy plants in terracotta pots on either side of a coir welcome mat. The detectives waited while Alina fumbled, trying unsuccessfully to get the key into the lock. She cried out loud in frustration.

"Here, let me do it." Preddy carefully removed the key from her shaking fingers and opened the door. The decor was not what he had expected of a vibrant young woman. The interior was spacious, with pale orange walls, but seemed overwhelmed by dark matching furniture, chunky chairs and old-fashioned floral vases he had not seen since the eighties. A beige-and-black-speckled granite countertop was all that separated the functional kitchen from the blended living and dining area. He guessed that Tex Doran had presented it to Eryka ready-furnished to suit his own tastes. The place was neat, all cushions and throws in place, books lined up perfectly on shelves. There was no sign of any disturbance.

"Eryka lived alone?" asked Harris.

"Yes, I've only slept here once since she got de place. I never like dat man and I never wanted to be here if him just decide to stop in." Alina led the way to the rear of the property. "Dis is de bedroom."

A wardrobe, chest of drawers with a stool tucked under it, a nightstand on either side of the bed, a few clothes on the bed — otherwise nothing was out of place. Preddy opened the wardrobe and rifled through the wide array of dresses and jackets. He felt around in the pockets, coming up empty each time. Harris opened the chest of drawers and lifted out some of the T-shirts and vests before replacing them. Alina watched them, dabbing her eyes tearfully as they searched.

Eventually Preddy turned to some clothes on the bed, a pair of floral shorts, a plain white sleeveless vest and a red sweater. "Looks like she took dese out to wear but changed her mind." He held each item in the air, examining each briefly before pushing them into an evidence bag. "Maybe dere's a good reason she wanted dem."

"I have nuff shorts she could wear, but none nice like dat," said Alina. "Me never see dem before."

A pair of distressed pale blue jeans hung over the back of a chair with a red T-shirt. Preddy held the jeans aloft and the attached belt fell to the floor. "Look too long for Eryka. You recognize dese?" He retrieved the belt and threaded it back through the loops.

Alina peered at the clothing. "She don't have no jeans like dat."

"Man jeans." Preddy felt around in the front pocket, pulled out a piece of crumpled paper and smoothed out the creases. "Receipt from Devon House I-Scream for two eight-ounce cups at one o'clock on de first of January."

"Must be Jerome's gear," suggested Harris. "Nobody over thirty would wear those cut-out knees."

Preddy felt around in the other pockets and found nothing. "Guess he changed his clothes here before going down to de Grand Marquee." He rolled the outfit into a ball and slid it into a large evidence bag. "Wonder if Tex turned up and saw dem together?"

"Possibly," said Harris. "And I imagine he'd have been pretty angry."

Preddy moved towards the nearest nightstand watched closely by Alina, who rubbed her upper arms as if cold. He lifted an elaborate frilly doily, revealing a downturned multi-picture photo frame. The stills all contained images of Jerome and Eryka. A single upstanding photo frame contained an image of Eryka posing with a stiff smile and Tex beside her beaming broadly. On the opposite nightstand was a photo of just Tex standing outside the Bob Marley Museum in Kingston with the musician's image above his head.

"Tex is on display," Preddy said. "Jerome is covered up."

Harris turned and glanced at it. "Must be tiring, trying tae remember which man is likely tae turn up and when."

"She was a good girl, Detective Harris," said Alina.

"Sorry, Alina, I honestly didnae mean any offence."

"Well, she was good . . . until dat man came into her life. If it wasn't for him, my sister would be alive right now."

116

They returned to the open living area. "Can't tell when last I saw a whatnot." Preddy ran his eyes over the paintings on the walls — market scenes, seascapes, fruit bowls.

Harris scanned the room. "A whatnot?"

"Old-time furniture. My parents have one from de seventies."

Alina walked towards a piece of chunky upright dark furniture. "Dis him talking, sir."

The wooden structure was six feet tall with a flat-screen TV in the middle, surrounded by drawers and shelves containing china ornaments, Christmas cards and seashells.

"Hmm, a whatnot," said Harris. "More tae Tex's taste than Eryka's, I guess."

Preddy waved the evidence bags in Alina's direction. "We going hold on to dese things for a while."

"Yes, dat's fine." Alina rubbed her eyes, which seemed to have run dry. Exhaustion was evident in her voice. "Take anything you want, Detective."

"I want you to contact me if you think of anything, day or night," said Preddy.

She raised her eyes to his. "Eryka called you," whispered Alina. "It didn't help her."

Preddy took the kick to his gut with no obvious outward sign of pain, while his intestines twisted like someone was wringing out a wet cloth. "Trust me, Alina," he said.

Alina sniffed and nodded. She picked up a picture of her sister and ran a finger along her face. "Young-young girl. She shouldn't lose her life like dis."

"We'll do everything tae find the person who did it," promised Harris.

"We won't stop until we get him." Preddy locked the door behind them and handed her the key, giving her hand a comforting squeeze. "We will get him, I swear."

"Thank you," Alina murmured.

"I want you to go home or go to relatives," said Preddy. "Don't stay around here, it will only upset you more."

She nodded. "I'll go home. Daddy died years now. Mummy live in Boscobel, St Mary, but she not so alert nowadays. Doctor say she have early Alzheimer's."

"I'm sorry to hear dat," said Preddy. He leaned over the balcony and pointed out Detective Rabino, who was talking to a constable. "Go to dat lady wid de long ponytail. She'll get somebody to go home wid you."

Alina slowly walked away.

"Ye shouldnae told her that, Preddy."

"Told her what?"

"That we'll catch the murderer. We might naw. What will we say tae her if we cannae catch him or her?"

The Scotsman's tone of admonishment together with Preddy's own inner torment was enough to send a red mist over the Jamaican detective. He rounded on the foreigner, eyes blazing. "Detective Harris, we're going to catch de murderer."

Harris's face grew red and his temples throbbed. "Suppose we dinnae get him? Suppose we cannae prove who did it?"

"We'll get him."

"Ye keep saying that, but it doesnae make it true." Harris raised his voice in exasperation. "We cannae go around making promises we cannae keep."

"Listen to me, and listen good." Preddy took two steps towards him so that their bodies were only a foot apart. Perspiration crept down his brow as his chest heaved and fell. A look of disgust was imprinted on Preddy's face. "I going catch de murderer. You can continue doing whatever bloodclaat work you doing for Brownlow and Davis. Good luck to you. De rest of us will give dis murder one hundred per cent."

Harris bit his trembling lip and stared back at Preddy through blazing green eyes.

"You have something more to say? Say it." Preddy flexed his fists at his sides. "No? Well, get on your damn bike and ride on. Enjoy de rest of your Sunday, Detective." His parting glance was radioactive with malignant intent.

CHAPTER 12

Monday, 7 January, 8.20 a.m.

Harris was glad for a legitimate excuse to dodge the prayer meeting. After yesterday's revelation of a dead woman dumped in a gully, he did not know how anyone could continue to pray. Sunday was the most hallowed day in the Christian week, yet people were still being murdered and their God did nothing.

He exited the lobby of Pelican Walk behind Preddy, who had worn a permanent scowl into work that morning and snapped at whoever spoke to him. The Scotsman, having concluded it was not in his best interests to resurrect the spat of yesterday, said little. One or more murderers were at large. Bringing them to justice was what really mattered, and unity was the only way it could be done.

He caught the jeep keys that Preddy threw at him. "So ye trust me tae drive today?"

"Easy route to Westgate Hills, not many potholes. You should make it widout pain to my tyres or my backside." Preddy pushed a newspaper onto the floor as he climbed into the passenger seat. "All I know is I don't want dat motorbike of yours alerting de whole neighbourhood to our arrival."

Harris raised his nose and twitched it. "Do ye smell something?"

"What?"

"Dunno. I'm getting a whiff of something . . . herbal?"

"Like cough sweets?"

"Och, stronger than that."

"Peppermint tea." Preddy avoided his colleague's gaze. The flask of ganja tea beneath his seat was now tightly corked, but some had spilled in the footwell during the drive to Pelican Walk.

"Must be it." Harris started the engine and began to inch backwards.

"Hey," said Preddy. "Watch de goat, man."

Harris manoeuvred around the animal, which seemed not to appreciate either the weight or speed of the vehicle, and lumbered off at a leisurely pace. "I'm actually thinking about turning the bike in. Giving it tae Super tae reassign."

Preddy looked at the Scotsman. "You serious?"

"Aye, I'm serious." Harris swung onto the main road and set off towards the highway. "I want ma jeep back. The jeep's much better when ye have tae carry things around. And like ye say, there are times when ye need tae be inconspicuous."

"You might want to be careful about how you run dat conversation and who hears it. Lots of officers never had de choice of bike, car or jeep because of funding problems," said Preddy. "Took dem only two days to find you a bike — and it's a brand-new one."

"Someone will be glad tae get it, I'm sure."

"Someone. Someone not at Pelican Walk. Our guys will be left to continue to share transport or use deir own. And I wonder where your jeep went to? Whichever station has it will be forced to hand it back. Not a good look for you. People know favouritism when dey see it." Preddy reached for the radio control and turned the channel to instrumental reggae as if trying to drown out his colleague. "Turn right at de next stoplight."

Harris did as ordered. He was yet to master the ins and outs of the Police High Command's methods of getting or distributing vehicles, although he had long been aware that there was an issue. "Tell ye what, I'll make a special request that the bike stays at Pelican Walk. Maybe Super'll go for that?"

"Knowing Brownlow, he'll let you keep both. Dat will go down really well . . . you being able to pick and choose which mode of transport suits you."

Harris decided to drop the touchy subject. There would be no getting on the good side of Raythan Preddy today, which Harris attributed mainly to the demise of Eryka Malden. He tried to catch Preddy's eye. "Let it go, Preddy. It's not yer fault she's dead."

Preddy kept his head rigidly straight and stared ahead. They remained silent for two miles, until Harris came to an unfamiliar crossroads.

"Which way here?"

"Take de next left and it's a straight road to Westgate." Preddy looked at the map on his phone. "Crown Drive is de second road on de left."

Harris risked a glance at Preddy. "Pity we dinnae have time tae get a warrant for this."

"You know how long dat would take?"

"Unfortunately, aye, I do."

Harris turned onto Crown Drive and slowed to a crawl. The windows retracted and the detectives studied the frontage of the properties, none of which had numbers that could be easily seen, an all-too-familiar situation in the city and indeed throughout the island. Harris pulled beside a young man leaning against a wooden gate. "Hello, do ye know which one is Tex Doran's house?"

"Jus' up de road, on dis side. You soon reach. Is a yellow house wid one big-big mango tree in front ah it."

"Great, thanks."

The vehicle continued its crawl.

"Wonder if dis is it?" said Preddy.

"Hmm, well that's a yellow house and that's a massive mango tree."

Preddy squinted past Harris's shoulder. "Actually, dat's not mango. De leaves are too feathery, like a fern. Looks like a tamarind tree, but no fruits so I'm not sure. Continue up a bit."

Harris hesitated and continued to stare at the house. "He did say just up the road."

"You have to remember dat for many Jamaicans, 'just up de road' can be ten metres or it can be two miles. Distance is all relative."

"Don't I know it."

"Move on."

Harris increased his speed and continued driving until Preddy pointed out the target property. "Over dere. One yellow house, one huge mango tree."

The iron-grill gates to the sprawling single-storey house were closed and the long driveway and double garage empty of vehicles. A tall, thick hedge prevented passers-by from getting a good view of the garden.

The Scotsman checked the stone pillars on each side of the gates. "Cannae see a buzzer anywhere."

Preddy shielded his eyes and stared at the property. "De verandah grill have on padlock. All de window close front and side."

"Doesnae look like anybody's in."

"I'm in. Well, I'm out, actually."

A slim, fair-skinned Black woman rose from behind the hedge. Abroad-brimmed straw hat held her thick greying brown hair in place.

"Mrs Suzanne Doran?" said Preddy.

"According to the worthless piece of paper I got from the registrar, yes, sir, that's me."

Preddy and Harris looked at each other.

Suzanne walked around the hedge and stood behind her gate. A full-length apron protected her pink blouse and black jeans from the dirt. Her rubber gloves were heavily covered in soil and in one hand was a muddy trowel. "How can I help you?"

"I'm Detective Preddy, dis is—"

"That is Detective Sean Harris, yes I know. I've seen you both on TV." She wiped her perspiring brow with her bare arm and stared at Preddy. "You were the one who led the death charge on Norwood, weren't you? Or are you still not admitting to it?"

Harris took one look at Preddy's narrowing eyes and tightening jaw and stepped closer to the gate. "Nice tae meet ye, Mrs Doran." He took off his sunglasses and smiled at her. "We were actually hoping tae speak tae yer husband, Terrell. Is he available?"

She switched her hazel eyes to Harris and an arrogant expression crossed her face. "You're a day too late, Detective Harris. Tex flew out of Sangster Airport yesterday, courtesy of Caribbean Airlines."

"Och, where's he off tae?"

"Fort Lauderdale."

"Do ye know how long he'll be gone for?"

"He's just gone shopping. He'll be back Tuesday morning." She studied the detectives with intense eyes. "Why, what's happened?"

Harris gave her an apologetic look. "Can we go inside and talk, Mrs Doran? It's really important."

She pointedly stared around at her gardening and then at the sky. "I want to finish out here in case the rain comes down. Should've done this a long time ago."

Preddy took a deep breath and his eyes scorched hers. "Mrs Doran, we're dealing wid a murder. Two murders. Your weeds can wait — our investigation cannot."

Her eyes flickered. It was the expression of someone not used to taking orders or being challenged. She tossed the trowel into the flower bed and slowly removed her gloves. "Guess we better go inside, then."

She removed an electronic fob from her apron pocket and within seconds the gate purred its way open. She led the men up the verandah steps, unlocked the grill and directed them into the sitting room. The decor was noticeably similar to that in Eryka's apartment: large, dark, chunky furniture and flower arrangements in old-fashioned vases that could not claim to be cute. Patterned carpet covered most of the tiled floor with a few rugs scattered throughout. The air carried the delightful smell of cornmeal porridge and nutmeg. Suzanne removed her hat and tossed it onto a chair. Her grey-brown natural hair sprang free and she shook it away from her neck. She spun around to face them, arms folded across her chest.

"I guess this is about Jerome Baccus?" she said.

"We'll get to dat," said Preddy. "Where was your husband on Saturday night?"

Suzanne frowned. "Here, as far as I know. Why?"

Preddy's eyes were on hers and his voice unfriendly. "As far as you know? So, if he had left, you wouldn't know?"

"This is a very big house, as you can see, Detective. We're not dating and curling up in front of the box on Saturday nights anymore. We're not newlyweds, we've been married for decades."

"But ye would know if he was in or out, surely?" Harris maintained a polite tone.

"He keeps his own space, I keep mine — which is mainly in the library. I went to bed before him Saturday night and when I woke up Sunday morning, he was right beside me." She raised her shoulders and glared at Harris. "What is this about, Detective?"

"Did Tex seem upset at all?" asked the Scotsman.

"No, he was fine. Are you going to tell me what you want with my husband?"

Harris glanced around the room, taking in photos of the couple. Most were at formal occasions with both in smart dress. Tex was standing side-facing in some of the photographs. In others his head was bowed or looking away from the photographer. A few photographs of Suzanne alone, expensively dressed and coiffed, were dotted around the room. There were no photos of any children or external family.

"Was yer husband's trip tae Fort Lauderdale booked a while ago?" asked Harris. "Or did he just take off unexpectedly yesterday?"

"I'm not going to answer a single question until you tell me what you want with him. Jerome Baccus was killed last week, not Saturday night. What does my husband's whereabouts on Saturday have to do with anything?"

"Eryka Malden was murdered on Saturday night," stated Preddy.

Suzanne Doran's hand went to her throat and her eyes widened. "That girl."

"Ye know her?" asked Harris.

Suzanne pushed her hat off her chair and slumped into it. "Well, no, I don't know her, Detective Harris." Her voice was irritated. "But as you're here, I guess you know that my husband does." She knitted her brow and rubbed her temples. "I know of her. What . . . what happened to her?"

"We found her body yesterday morning," said Harris.

"And you think Tex has something to do with it?" Her voice was incredulous as she looked from one detective to the other.

Harris studied the long fingernails that massaged her brow. "Do ye naw think so?"

"No, I do not, Detective!" she shouted. "My husband is not a murderer. The girl was his plaything. I've known about what he's been up to for months now. He's just a stupid old fool, but he's not a murderer."

"You knew about dem?" asked Preddy. "Did you challenge him over de relationship?"

"There was no *relationship*. Tex said she was dating Jerome Baccus, which made sense to me as they are of a similar age." She gave a sour smile and waved a hand dismissively. "I considered it a midlife crisis. It wouldn't last too long."

"We know de affair has been going on for around a year, not months," said Preddy.

She shrugged yet failed to appear nonchalant, despite her best efforts. "A few months, a year . . . what is that compared to three decades?"

"Were ye aware that he spent a lot of money on Eryka Malden?"

"Yes, Detective Harris. I guess you're talking about the apartment and the car? I found out about those a few weeks ago. He also gave her a credit card, can you believe it? Idiot." Her eyes narrowed and she stared at the chandelier. "I saw a credit card statement in the glove compartment of his car addressed to an apartment in Cherry Walk. That girl had been buying herself clothes and jewellery and dining at all the best places in town. I guess it was Jerome she was buying for, as on most of those dates I can account for my husband's whereabouts. Paid for by him though, the old fool. Urgh! The stupidity of men who think with their cocks and not their brains . . ."

"Where were you Saturday night, Mrs Doran?" asked Preddy.

She stared at him defiantly. "Right here. On my computer, writing a short story. I like to dabble in literature. Can't say I'm good at it, but if you don't practise, you can't improve."

"Do you mind if we take a look around?" Preddy glanced into the utility room, where a wicker laundry basket stood next to a stainless-steel washing machine.

Suzanne Doran was on her feet in seconds and blocked Preddy's access. She closed the door firmly. "Actually, I do mind."

Preddy gave a slight bow, stepped away and glanced through the back window. Outside was a small pool with a few multicoloured sun loungers stacked beside it and an immaculate lawn surrounded by citrus trees.

Harris crouched down beside a wooden sideboard and came up with a piece of broken purple glass. "Had a wee accident?"

Suzanne stared at him. "Yes."

Harris used his chin to indicate the area on a shelf near Suzanne's shoulder. "This broken glass matches those two vases behind ye."

"It came in a set of three. I dropped it."

"Ye dropped it?" Harris ran his finger down a crack in the wall immediately above where he retrieved the glass. He smiled at her. "Gravity's a strange thing. Ye dropped it and it went across the room and landed on the wall. How'd that happen?"

"You sure Tex didn't throw it at you?" asked Preddy.

"My husband is not a violent man! Unlike certain people with a badge and a gun," she added with more than a hint of venom aimed in Preddy's direction.

"We just have a few more questions, Mrs Doran." Harris hoped that Preddy would not do something that even he would not be able to support him on.

"I'd like you both to leave, right now, Detective Harris."

"Can ye . . . ?"

"No, no and no." Suzanne strode towards the front door and yanked it open. "I'm going to get back to my gardening. You're looking for answers in the wrong place." She stood back and allowed the detectives to exit, followed them out and closed the door firmly behind her.

"We'd really like tae get in touch with Mr Doran." Harris tried to hand her a business card, but she pushed her hands firmly into her pockets and glared at him.

"I'm sure you would, Detective. He knows where Pelican Walk station is. He'll find you. I'll warn him to wear a bullet-proof vest." She stormed away to retrieve her gloves and turned her back on the detectives.

As soon as they had passed through the gates, the electronic locking mechanism was activated. From behind the hedge came the sounds of weeding again, and Harris mentally pictured her stabbing the weeds with the trowel.

"That went well," he whispered. "Cannae take ye anywhere."

Preddy gave him the deepest side-eye. "Don't you start. I'm not in de mood."

"I hear ye." They climbed into the jeep and Harris started the engine.

"She knew where Eryka lived," mused Preddy. "I wasn't betting on dat at all. She's a strange character, pretty and ill-tempered wid it. Full of chat. I bet she attacks Tex non-stop behind closed doors."

"The lady's definitely got an attitude problem." Harris completed a U-turn and set off back down the road. "Ye think she could've done them both, Jerome and Eryka? I mean, I could see her going after Eryka, but naw Jerome. If anything, she would've been glad that Eryka had a young boyfriend. She wouldnae have known it was platonic."

"Not sure she has murderer written on her. Still, even if she's not involved, she's got to be thinking dat her husband may have killed dem both."

Harris slowed down as they passed the young man who had given them directions. "Found it!" he shouted, giving him the thumbs up.

"All right, cool, bossie!" The youth grinned and waved back.

Harris turned back to Preddy. "Convenient that Tex has suddenly left the country. Do ye think he'll be back tomor-row as she said?"

"He damn well better be. Tex Doran has a lot of ques-tions to answer."

CHAPTER 13

All four detectives were in the evidence room with the door closed and blinds down. A faint smell of mosquito repellent lingered, although the room had been sprayed half an hour before for Harris's benefit and aired out. Preddy had hung a "Do Not Disturb" sign on the door knowing that other officers, except Superintendent Brownlow and Commissioner Davis, would respect it. The commissioner had not yet returned from his Christmas break, so that was one less intrusion to worry about.

The large room was filled with filing cabinets and cupboards containing evidence of various murder investigations. Every one of the storage facilities was labelled and secured by lock and key. Cardboard boxes of solved cases were piled up in a corner, taking up space and gathering dust. A wooden table in the middle of the floor could seat six comfortably. Harris, Rabino and Spence were seated with glasses of ice-cold water before them. Oscillating fans whirred overhead, yet the detectives still used papers and notepads to help cool the warm air.

Preddy stood beside a whiteboard at the front, next to a low podium, on which sat a basket of coloured marker pens.

The whiteboard was covered with a list of names written in black ink. Preddy tried to maintain a calm demeanour, although what he really wanted to do was kick the boxes all over the room. The murder count was going in the wrong direction for his superiors, the general public and, more importantly, himself.

"Okay, people, speak to me," he said.

"Two victims known to each other, close friends. Got to be the same murderer?" offered Rabino.

Preddy nodded. "I think we can agree dese two murders are connected, not random," he said. "Dere's a strong possibility it's de same perpetrator. I'm thinking Eryka saw something on de news, something dat triggered off a memory, and she wanted to talk to me about it."

Eryka's name was already on the board under the heading of potential witnesses, together with that of Gavin Baccus. Now Preddy turned and wrote her name in large letters at the top next to Jerome's. She had moved from possible witness to victim.

"Oh, we found a pink phone smashed to pieces on the banking just above the gully, sir," reported Rabino. "I'm pretty sure it's the same one Eryka had in the interview room. The murderer probably used a stone to batter it. No sign of the SIM card."

"Ye could be the last person she spoke tae, Preddy, we'll never know."

Preddy felt the bile creeping up to his throat and tried to focus. "She watched de seven o'clock news wid her sister. Afterwards dey watched a film and Eryka headed out midway through it. She called me and set off for Cherry Walk in her blue Audi, a distinctive-looking vehicle."

"Most people at de apartment complex knew it was her car although few seem really to know her," said Spence.

"So, the killer could have followed her or already been on the complex looking out for the car," said Rabino.

Preddy frowned. "Pathologist said de blow dat killed her came from behind. She was already dead when de other blows came." He slapped the palm of his hand against the board, almost knocking it off the stand. "Damn, I should have pressed her to find out what was bothering her."

"I bet Tex Doran was bothering her," said Spence.

Preddy tapped the name "Terrell Doran" with his pen. "We need firm evidence, but he's got to be de main suspect."

Harris pushed back his ginger fringe and dabbed at his brow. "Aye, Eryka's dead and he leaves the island hours later. Wife Suzanne's got tae be suspicious of her husband, although she's covering for him. Either that or she's involved herself. She knew exactly where Eryka lived."

Preddy put an arrow beside the name of his chief suspect Terrell Doran and wrote the name "Suzanne Doran" followed by a question mark.

Rabino tapped at her lips with the top of her pen. "Husband and wife could be working together, I guess. Maybe she's one of these 'stand by your man' types who won't give up on her husband no matter what."

"But all dat money him spending on young girl." Spence shook her head. "I would expect her to kill her husband first, before she bother go kill girl."

"We know what ye'd do." Harris grinned. "Suzanne was hostile and defensive. Sounded quite fed up with Tex. Naw sure if she loves him, but she's sticking with him despite the infidelity. And there were signs he's prone tae violence. She said she dropped a vase, yet there's a dent in the wall."

"She stopped me dead from going into de utility room," said Preddy. "No chance to check for any evidence. Whoever did it was bound to have blood all over deir clothes."

Rabino looked thoughtful. "We still don't have enough for a warrant to search the house. Super will go mad if we find a judge to sign one off based on circumstantial evidence and then find nothing."

Preddy smiled ruefully. "Dat thought did cross my mind." It had more than crossed his mind, it had stopped en route, zigzagged and implanted itself at the forefront of his brain. Interfering with Big Men could sound the death knell on the career of any police officer, whether celebrated or infamous.

"Tex could've taken the clothes with him," said Harris. "Disposed of them in America if he had any sense. He has plenty of money tae buy new clothes. He's naw going tae wash them abroad and bring them back."

"True." Preddy tapped Eryka's name again. "Talking of clothes . . . she told her sister, Alina, she was going home for clothes. Alina has clothes dat can fit Eryka, so I can't think why she would have gone home for dat reason."

Rabino shrugged. "It does seem strange, in the middle of the night too, but some people don't like wearing other people clothes, even their sister's."

"A serious ting." Spence nodded. "Me and my sister used to come to blows over it as teenagers and we wouldn't be any different now."

"Jerome left a shirt and jeans," said Preddy, "so it could be Jerome's stuff she wanted to get and hide from Tex, not her own."

"That would make sense," said Rabino.

"But we still have naw idea why she called Preddy," said Harris.

"No, we don't." Preddy studied the whiteboard. He scanned it then swung back around to face them. "Ah, nearly forgot. What I did see on de news was a guy from de Livity Vendors Association. Moses Fearon."

"Och, the coconut guy? The Rasta man's sidekick?"

Preddy nodded. "Him same one."

"Don't know him," said Spence. "We've had a look at de footage from de seven o'clock news, sir. It's same as de ten o'clock news."

"Didn't spot anything out of the ordinary," said Rabino.

Preddy opened his briefcase and took out the *Western Mirror*. He handed it to Rabino and pointed. "Dis guy."

Spence leaned over her colleague's shoulder and looked at him. "I don't remember seeing no protestors on de news."

"Me neither," said Rabino.

"He wasn't a protester, not at de time de TV footage of de Grand Marquee was taken," explained Preddy. "He was smartly dressed in a long-sleeve white shirt and black pants for de film show."

Harris took the paper from Rabino and studied the man, then looked at Preddy quizzically. "I dinnae get it."

"Moses Fearon is two-faced." Preddy wrote Moses's name below that of Terrell Doran and added "Livity Vendors Association" in brackets. "All of de vendors are up in arms about de proposed development. Mr Fearon had been on Dowdy Beach dat morning wid other association members, waving placards and complaining about being side-lined. By evening, he was back and helping wid de organization of chairs for Baccus. De TV footage is much clearer dan his newspaper photo, but I'm certain it's him."

"A man operating on both sides of the fence," said Harris. "That'll take some explaining."

Rabino frowned. "And what would be the connection between Moses Fearon and Tex Doran?"

"We need to find out if dere is one," said Preddy.

"Pass me the newspaper again." Rabino reached out for it. "Need to take a few copies."

Spence looked at her. "De photocopier not working, but it wouldn't show him face so good anyway."

"De copier break down again?" asked Preddy.

"It no have no ink." Spence kissed her teeth. "Odette say she can't get money to buy cartridge till end a month. Damn foolishness."

No money for ink. Preddy closed his eyes briefly, gritted his teeth and silently counted. "Okay, get another newspaper on de road. Vendors always have back copies. I want to hang on to dis one."

"Does dis mean you not looking so closely at Wesley Ashburn again?" asked Spence.

"Not ruling anybody out yet." Preddy shook his head as he scoped the whiteboard. "For all we know, it could be dat Wesley Ashburn is connected to Moses Fearon. Maybe he sent him to go look a job wid Baccus?"

"Keep your friends close and your enemies closer," murmured Rabino. "Do you want us to go trawl the beaches and see if we can find Mr Fearon, sir?"

Preddy thought about it for a moment. "Not yet. Being two-faced is not a crime. We need something more on him before we question him."

"A real tangled web," said Harris.

"We going untangle it," said Preddy with determination. "One way or de other."

* * *

As Preddy headed towards his office he could see Superintendent Brownlow in the distance chatting to Odette, the administrator. Preddy sidled into the men's restroom and held the door slightly ajar, watching until the superintendent had lumbered past. Preddy exited the room and, glancing over his shoulder, saw his superior beckon to Harris and the two men walk off in the opposite direction. Preddy frowned and continued to his office. Inside his temporary sanctuary he closed the door and leaned against it. Through the windows above his desk he could see the Caribbean Sea in the distance, meeting the sky in a perfect blend of blues. Everything appeared deceptively beautiful and serene.

The state of public emergency had so far quelled much of the rampant killings. Flooding St James with police and soldiers, imposing curfews and random searches, had made considerable impact on the runaway murder rate. Undoubtedly, many of the parish's most wanted men had fled with their high-powered weapons when the lawmen arrived en masse. Rumour had it that many had crossed the borders in market trucks, blending in with the sellers of fruits and ground produce, while other more innovative hoodlums had sought transport in caskets hauled by hearses. Some of the bad guys inevitably remained, biding their time, their AK-47s well hidden from law-enforcement teams.

Jerome and Eryka had been murdered despite the silencing of the guns. Every living person was made up of a thin layer of skin, covering a delicate heart and a fragile brain. A sharp-pointed object and a thick stone were all that had been needed to blot out human lives. The most determined of murderers would always find a way.

Preddy peeled himself off the door, walked toward his desk and threw down his briefcase. He stood on tiptoe and peered through the window, trying to see if the Scotsman and the superintendent had gone outdoors for their little confab. Neither man was in view.

He sighed. Criminally inclined detectives were a rarity in his experience. He had seen young constables get involved in crimes and then been allowed to resign from the JCF. Few were ever incarcerated for their lapses in morality. Two years ago, Officer Lindon Nembhard was jailed for aiding and abetting a murder, and Preddy was instrumental in nailing the young cop. Officer Franklin, another misguided soul, had been transferred to another station for lying and insubordination. He was now the problem of the underworked police in Portland, the calmest parish on the island.

Preddy unlocked a drawer, pulled out a notepad and stared at his hastily written notes. He was convinced that Detective Iain Cotner was the man on the High Command's radar. Preddy had traced the details of the bald man with the beige SUV who had nearly hit the goats when visiting Harris. The man was a real estate agent and part of one of the largest, most profitable franchises on the island. Preddy's first thought on discovering this was that the matter could have been innocent. After all, Harris had mentioned many times that he was searching for a suitable property to buy. However, this would not explain the Glaswegian's surreptitious behaviour in the rear courtyard. No one conducting an innocent conversation would stand with his back to the participant for so long.

Preddy concluded that Harris must be watching one or more properties that the real estate man either had on his list

135

or had recently sold. That would give Harris a good excuse if he was ever spotted lurking in a part of Montego Bay where he was not expected to be found. The thought cemented in Preddy's head when he recalled Rabino's comment to Harris about his house-hunting in the Bogue Heights area. From the start of his property search, Harris had said he was not keen on Bogue — despite the lovely houses — because of the nearby sewage treatment system. Whatever reason had brought Harris out to sneak around that up-and-coming district had nothing to do with buying property.

CHAPTER 14

Monday, 7 January, 2.35 p.m.

Detective Preddy locked his office door and headed to the rear of the station where the forensic examiners were busy with Eryka's ride. The blue Audi sat on the concourse under a canopy roof with all four doors open, rims sparkling, looking to all the world like a show vehicle. Another car was parked alongside it, an old Hyundai abandoned at the scene of a bungled robbery attempt on a gas station. The Hyundai remained dusty and unloved while two officers were giving the crossover SUV their full attention. Both officers were dressed from head to toe in white and wearing latex gloves. One was examining the boot while the other poked around under the driver's seat.

Preddy approached the driver's door. "Any prints?"

The officer stood up and stretched his back. He pointed at a trolley table, on which lay a box of forensic equipment. "Two clear sets of prints on tape. Both match de victims Eryka and Jerome. Took dose from de door, rear-view mirror and steering wheel, as you would expect. Other prints are on de window, but too smudged to get a clear pattern."

Preddy glanced at the driver's window. The stunning model would attract attention wherever it went, particularly from young men. "Like maybe somebody pressed deir palms against it, looking in?"

"Very likely." The man nodded. "My windows must have prints from newspaper man, candy seller, juice seller . . ."

"Quite. Mine too." Preddy gave him a wry smile. "What else we got?"

"Not much. It's a clean car. De only hairs picked up are synthetic, which I guess came from her braids. No blood, dried or otherwise. Umbrella and belt on de passenger seat. Glove compartment has tissues, a mirror, shades. No signs of a struggle in here. Nothing out of place."

"Not a scratch?" said Preddy.

"Not a scratch." The specialist folded his arms and stared at the vehicle. "Nice set of wheels, zero to sixty in five point seven seconds. Not many people in Jamaica wid one of dese. Must be fifty. . . sixty thousand US? Probably de first and last time I'll get to touch one."

"You and me both," said Preddy. "Maybe we'll get to ride in one as passengers someday. One not attached to a murder victim."

"We can dream."

Preddy put his head through the door, careful not to touch anything. "Nice interior, clean."

"Nothing untoward at all, sir."

Preddy nodded as he backed away. "Okay, if anything changes let me know."

"Will do, sir."

Preddy wandered around to the officer examining the trunk. "How's it going round here?"

"Oh, hello, sir." The tall officer almost bumped his head as he rose from the boot. He turned off his miniature flashlight. "Everything in here is as I'd expect it to be. Spare tyre, oil can, jack. Otherwise it looking clean."

"Ah, Detective Preddy, found you."

Preddy winced at the sound of the familiar deep voice, a voice he had hoped to avoid for the rest of the day. The forensic officer grinned at Preddy, who winked at him before spinning around. He walked towards Superintendent Brownlow, keeping a pleasant expression, which was not reflected in his superior's face.

"Walk with me, Detective."

The two men slowly walked the grounds of the police station, through the courtyard, under the now-fruitless mango tree, past the seized unlicensed or uninsured vehicles and around the front of the building.

"I hear that a tap in the second-floor restroom got smashed this morning?" said Brownlow.

Preddy stared straight ahead, avoiding eye contact with the superintendent. "An accident, sir."

"Oh? My understanding is that officers heard a distinct bashing sound and thought a plumber was working, but only you were in there?"

Preddy was not even aware that anyone had opened the door at the time. "De person misunderstood, sir. I turned on de tap, no water came out. I turned it again, it broke."

"And you thought you would beat the water out of it?"

It had not been Preddy's intention to abuse the pipework, but taps were meant to dispense water, not air, and its stubborn refusal to do so had led to his momentary lapse in behaviour. "Not at all, sir. Didn't realize I was applying too much pressure."

The superintendent drew to a halt under an almond tree. "Let me explain something to you, Detective. I know you haven't been near the psychologist, despite your promises." He held up a hand to stop Preddy speaking. "Decided to solve your problems yourself. Just know that I'd be shirking my responsibilities to the other officers if I didn't make a note on your record. We've discussed it before. You are a danger to them, to the public and to yourself if you're on edge."

"Sir, if I'm a bit shaken it's nothing to do wid Norwood, I just—"

"I'm not finished." The superintendent glared at him. "You're a grown man and I can't drag you to the doctor.

That's way beyond my remit. It will be noted on your file as failure to follow direct instructions."

Preddy felt like a teenage boy again, caught out by a teacher for failing to attend the after-school club to learn speech and drama, instead enjoying playing with the informal cricket team. He remembered the threat of being reported to his parents if he failed to comply with school rules. He decided that, like then, the only way to appease the regulators was to be contrite.

"Sir, I've been so much better lately . . . sleeping like a log. Can't remember de last time I had an adverse reaction to a gunshot. I can assure you I am no danger to anyone. I would take myself off de job if dat was ever de case, sir."

The superintendent gave a short mirthless laugh. "You had me until that last sentence. You would never take yourself off the job." He continued his walk, passing beside a purple hibiscus bush that had lost most of its colourful leaves to ruminants. "Talking to a professional about what happened in Norwood is a good thing, not a punishment. You need to tell someone what is on your mind."

Preddy took a deep breath. "Believe it or not, I have been talking to somebody. Well, not somebody really . . . something."

"Something?" The superintendent rubbed his heavy jaw as he turned to check the detective's expression. "I know you're not going to tell me you've started practising obeah?"

"No, sir. Experiments show dat talking to pets can have as good an effect on de mind as talking to a person. Better even, because you get to speak without fear of being criticized or judged. Animals are de best listeners."

Superintendent Brownlow narrowed his eyes. "Is this your attempt at humour, Detective?"

Preddy sighed and wished he had not been tempted to explain his position. His spiel did not sound half as sensible out loud as it had in his head. "No, sir."

"Damn it, Raythan, man! You can't say you haven't been warned. Commissioner Davis is always watching your records and asking about you and Harris."

I'll bet he is, thought Preddy. *Watching and waiting for an opportunity to crown the Scotsman King of Pelican Walk.* "I understand, sir."

A pair of overconfident goats wandered near to the men. "These damn goats still here?" asked the superintendent in annoyance. "I thought Wilson was going to deal with it."

"Timmins is on it, sir. He says dey'll be taken to a farm in Trelawny by Wednesday."

"Good. This place turning into farmyard, and we're not farmers."

Preddy did not respond and the two men walked in silence for a minute.

"So, first Jerome Baccus and now Eryka Malden," the superintendent finally said. "These waters are getting muddier. What are you doing to clear them?"

Preddy frowned. The man did not see the irony of demanding results while knowing the investigation was likely to become hamstrung by a lack of Harris's full concentration. "We're on it, sir. Every member of de team was on de scene at Cherry Walk." He paused before forcefully stating, "Sunday morning, when sun barely rise."

"I know, I know. "The superintendent waved a conciliatory hand in the air. "Still, I want a report by close of business tomorrow. People want to walk the streets of Mo Bay feeling unthreatened and go to bed feeling safe. They're depending on us. Nobody cares whether we get any sleep or even whether we go to bed."

Preddy had long accepted that the public probably did not care about the officers' working lives either — that they rarely had running water and were forced to keep the bathrooms stocked with kegs and buckets, that soap ran out early in the week and hand towels were scarce. "Yes, sir."

"The press will be crawling all over us for updates, and I want to be able to assure the public that we have concrete plans for solving the murders." Brownlow turned and headed to the station entrance, leaving Preddy behind. "Tomorrow evening, Detective."

"Tomorrow evening, sir."

Preddy watched his superior's lumbering form disappearing into the lobby. Brownlow would not last a day in a detective's shoes. The man had never been face-to-face with an M16 nor been shot at, nor had to shoot at anyone. Still, Preddy did not want the superintendent's job. He did not want to sit in a cosy office and issue instructions to detectives to go solve murders, while offering them little basic help to do so. It was not entirely Brownlow's fault, as the career officer was a cog in a grinding wheel within the hierarchy. The respective governments were an issue: politicians making promises to officers that they had no intention of keeping, while assuring the public that robust crime strategies were in place. Then there were the helpful foreigners, whose contributions in cash and kind could never be accounted for or fully utilized. Last year a batch of body cameras had been kindly donated by Japan, yet to date none had been distributed, because they did not fit the police uniforms.

Preddy sighed and stared at the well-fed, contented goats. Maybe he should seriously consider taking up farming in Trelawny. He looked at his watch. Nearly four o'clock. Tomorrow could not come quickly enough. If the aviation industry and the gods did not conspire against him, tomorrow he would get to question Terrell Doran.

CHAPTER 15

Tuesday, 8 January, 9.43 a.m.

Detective Preddy stood in his office at Pelican Walk filing paperwork in a cabinet, his back to the door. The soothing sound of rustling leaves played on his radio in the background, helping to steady his nerves. He had woken up with the same headache that had accompanied him to bed, and not even a mug full of ganja tea had forced it to leave. Eryka's unnecessary death was on his conscience and refused to be shaken off.

A knock at the door made him wince, but he did not pause his work. There were not enough hours in the day already, and too many sheets of paper littered his desk. "Come in," he called over his shoulder.

"Sorry to disturb you, sir." The administrator, Odette, stood in the doorway. "A Mr Terrell Doran wants to speak to you."

"Oh good." Preddy closed his cabinet and sank into his desk chair. "Put him through on line two for me."

"Not on de phone, sir. He's in de lobby." She looked at him warily as if expecting to be told off. "I told him it would be better to make an appointment, but he said you'd want to see him."

"He's quite right." Preddy was back on his feet in a second. This morning might turn out better than expected after all. The plan had been to go looking for Mr Doran at midday, not for him to waltz into Pelican Walk without ceremony. "Put him in Interview Room Two . . . no, actually, put him in Room Four. Give him some ice water. I'll be five minutes. Thanks."

"Yes, sir." She closed the door and disappeared.

Preddy grabbed his notebook. He picked up an empty manila folder, slid some blank sheets of paper into it and headed to the open-plan area. There was no sign of Harris but for his custom-made Ray-Bans. The Glaswegian never went outside without them.

Spence was on the phone speaking earnestly to someone. She rolled her eyes and pointed at the handset in exasperation as Preddy approached. His eyes went to Rabino, who had just hung up her phone and was reaching for a pen.

"We've got Tex Doran downstairs in Four. You got time to do dis wid me?"

Rabino scribbled something on her notepad. "Yes, sir." She quickly wound her long ponytail into a bun and fastened it before joining Preddy in the corridor.

"Whose idea was it to put him in Room Four? It's so dingy in there. No natural light and no fans."

Preddy grinned. "Ideal place for him, I thought."

Rabino smiled. "Oh, I see."

"We will of course treat Mr Doran with de courtesy dat we give all suspects."

"Absolutely, sir." She glanced at Preddy as they walked along side by side. "This is a little unexpected, isn't it?"

"Must be fresh off de plane from Florida. Can't believe it myself, but glad I don't have to chase him down."

"He didn't bring a lawyer with him?"

"No, he's on his own. Confident or plain brazen, not sure which."

"Could be his strategy," said Rabino. "Makes him look cooperative, as if he doesn't have a thing to hide."

Preddy nodded. "We'll see if Mr Doran is cunning or believable."

They descended the stairs, Preddy still looking out for any sign of Harris. He could not be with the superintendent as Brownlow had gone to a meeting in Kingston and his door was locked. Preddy imagined that Harris was holed up in one of the conference rooms far from prying eyes.

As he passed a casement window, he heard what sounded like the Scotsman's guttural laugh coming from outside. He pushed the window and put his head out, looking towards the rear of the building. Harris and a uniformed Guardsman Alarms engineer were standing next to a small concrete hut, inside of which was the panel box that held the circuit breakers and main controls for the police station's electronic security system. It facilitated internal and external surveillance as well as alarms. The men seemed to be deep in conversation, and although Preddy strained his ears, they were too far away for the voices to carry.

Rabino paused near the foot of stairs. "You coming, sir?"

Preddy frowned and drew his head in. "Yes, coming." He had toyed with the idea of calling out to Harris, before dismissing it. Harris would no doubt be annoyed at having missed Tex Doran, but Preddy was more than ready for any criticism the Scotsman might dare to level.

"Wouldn't it be something if Doran just confessed?" mused Rabino. "Put his arms out in front of him and said, 'I did it because I was mad.'"

"Dat would make me de happiest person in Jamaica," said Preddy with a smile. "Somehow I don't think it will happen though. We going have to do some work."

Preddy knocked on the door of Interview Room Four and pushed it open. Tex Doran was standing with his back pressed against the grey wall. He was casually dressed in black jeans and a skin-tight white muscle shirt. He unfolded beefy arms and pulled out his seat.

"Mr Doran, good morning. Dis is Detective Rabino. I'm Detective Preddy."

The man stretched his hand out to shake both of theirs. "I hear I'm a wanted man, so here I am." His deep voice was strained and he seemed to be making an effort to keep it level.

Preddy studied his features. Tex Doran was clearly determined to stay young. Doran's efforts in respect of his inch-high hair were misguided, Preddy thought. He doubted whether it had ever been jet black in the man's life, but now it was as black as coal. Doran's upper body showed evidence that he regularly worked out with weights, although his stomach showed a slight bulge. His shaven chin showed multiple specks of grey amid the black. He seemed to struggle to sit, settling uncomfortably on one cheek with his legs stretched to the side of the table.

"Problem wid your knees?" asked Preddy.

Tex rubbed his right knee. "Stumbled and fell when I was going up the plane steps at Sangster. Wasn't watching where I was going. Two days now it hurting, so it made shopping a bit of a pain."

"You'll have to get on to your insurance company," said Rabino, smiling at him. "Get some physio and let them pay for it."

Tex tried to smile back. His eyes were flat and expressionless. "It's not bad. And you know paperwork takes forever in this country. They behave as if computers were never invented. Making a claim would be more stress than it's worth. I'll live."

"Just want to confirm dat you're here voluntarily and happy to help us wid our enquiries?" said Preddy.

"Of course." Tex glanced around the tiny room. "Bit stuffy in here though, not much air."

"Sorry about dat." Preddy sounded as sympathetic as he could. "No other rooms available at de moment, so we just have to make do." He leaned over his notepad. "Thank you for coming to see us. I guess your wife has spoken to you?"

He winced as if in pain. "I was in Fort Lauderdale and got an urgent message to call her. Couldn't imagine what it could be. When she said that Eryka was dead—" He choked up and coughed to clear his throat. "I just couldn't believe it. Not my Eryka."

"So how did dat go?" asked Preddy.

"How did what go?"

"De conversation. I mean, your wife called you to tell you dat your mistress was dead."

Tex narrowed his eyes. "As you know, Suzanne is well aware of Eryka. There was no awkwardness to the conversation, Detective. And no, I didn't confess to my wife that I killed her, because I didn't. I was in shock . . . still am." He searched Rabino's face as if looking for understanding. "Haven't slept a wink for the last two nights and took an earlier return flight this morning."

"We're investigating two murders, as I guess you know," said Rabino. "Eryka Malden and Jerome Baccus."

"I heard about Jerome Baccus's murder, long time. I only just heard about Eryka's." He spread his thick fingers, which were ashy from lack of moisturizing lotion. "Look at me, I'm still shaking."

Preddy glanced at the large hands, which were indeed shaking, then back at the suspect's eyes. "Do you know of a man by de name of Moses Fearon . . . coconut man?"

"Never heard of him. The only Moses I know is in the Bible."

"He's part of an organization known as de Livity Vendors Association."

Tex shook his head. "Don't know of them, either. What is this?"

Preddy leaned forward and held his gaze. "Mr Doran, do you have any information about de murders of either victim?"

"No, I do not, Detective." His tone was adamant. "I can't tell you how hard it hit me, because you wouldn't believe it. Eryka was a lovely girl, beautiful and sweet."

"And in love with Jerome Baccus," added Rabino.

Tex scowled and his voice hardened. "That was just a dalliance. She hung around with him, but he had nothing to offer

147

her. Pain in my backside, that boy." His eyes flashed nervously. "Not that I hated him . . . well, not enough to kill him."

"You know who did?" asked Preddy.

"No!"

"On de night Jerome Baccus was killed, where were you?"

"At the Grand Marquee, like everybody else." His eyes flicked between the faces of the detectives. "Like half of Mo Bay, I wanted to see what the plans were for Dowdy Beach. I went to Baccus's presentation and planned to go to Wesley Ashburn's. Still do."

"So you saw Jerome and Eryka together?" asked Rabino.

"No, I did not. The place was heaving with people and I had no idea they were there. I mean, I would expect Jerome to be there because I know he was working on the publicity and marketing issues, but I didn't know Eryka was going. I'd called her earlier in the day and invited her to dinner, but she said she wasn't feeling so great and fancied an early night." He clutched his hands together and stared at them. "Guess her health improved."

Preddy leaned back and stared at him. "You were at de marquee. Your girlfriend, who you've been spending a lot of money on, was at de marquee, and so was de man who she threw you aside for? Do you know how dat looks?"

"Of course! Look, I know nothing about his murder, Detective. I came to see you because I have nothing to hide. I didn't even call my lawyer, because I know that he'll tell me not to talk, but I want to talk. I want to clear my name right now!" His speech was impassioned. "I did not kill the Baccus boy and I certainly did not kill Eryka. I hear that she was found in a gully at Cherry Walk. I'm pretty sure you know I got her that place at Cherry Walk. I would never throw that beautiful girl into no dirty gully!"

"Where were you on Saturday night, the night Eryka was killed?" asked Rabino.

"At home, I swear. I got in around six, six thirty and never left. Took a dip in the pool, had dinner with Suzanne. She went to her library on one side of the house, I went to my mancave on the other. Well, it's a little room at the back. I was in there listening to music, playing solitaire. Went to bed around eleven. Suzanne was already asleep. Didn't leave my bed till 4 a.m. Got to Sangster airport just after 5 a.m."

"What happened to de clothes you had on dat night?" asked Preddy.

"My clothes? They went in the laundry. Kicked them off by the pool." Tex Doran's dark eyes fluttered. He gave a nervous laugh and looked off to one side as if thinking deeply about something upsetting. "Actually, I remember them getting wet, and you know that chlorine is not good for clothes. I threw them in the washing machine to get the bleach off."

"You washed your own clothes?" Preddy did not bother to disguise his scepticism. "Single men tend to wash clothes. Not many married men do. Is dat something you usually do?"

He shrugged. "Not really, but I didn't want them stained. No point leaving them to dry and get spoiled. The helper doesn't come in until Wednesdays. She does the washing and cleaning."

Tex Doran closed his eyes, and Preddy wondered what was going on behind the lids. "What happened wid Jerome and Eryka, Mr Doran?"

"If something happened and you snapped, you need to tell us, Tex." Rabino encouraged him. "Maybe Jerome did or said something that made you mad? You reacted badly on the spur of the moment."

The detectives waited, but the suspect kept his eyes closed. He placed his elbows on the table and raised his fingers to knead his temples.

"Eryka cursed you for killing Jerome," continued Rabino. "You realized she never really loved you and you killed her. Even good people do bad things. We can put in a word for you with the prosecutor, about how you were provoked, if you tell us all about it."

Preddy nodded. "It's better if you come clean now. We can say you cooperated and were truly remorseful. We—"

"No!" Tex slammed his palms on the table and made to get up. He winced and grabbed at his injured knee, falling heavily back into his seat. He groaned as he spoke. "I did not kill Jerome or Eryka. Look, Eryka already asked me if it was me who stabbed Jerome. I told her no. It wasn't a lie. I have no idea who his enemies are. The only thing I know is that according to Eryka, he was seeing a girl named Nicki Younis. I know nothing about this Nicki, but maybe she was mad with them? Maybe she killed Jerome for cheating, and then was so angry at his loss that she decided to kill Eryka?"

"We did speak to Miss Younis, last week," said Rabino.

"Well maybe you need to get hold of her again. Eryka said Nicki hated her. Women can be real evil bitches, way worse than men." He blinked twice and his eyes widened. "Sorry, no offence, Detective Rabino."

Rabino inclined her head. "None taken."

"You're looking at me, you're looking at the wrong person. I won't pretend that I've shed any tears over the Baccus boy. That would be a lie and I'm not a great actor. Eryka meant the world to me. Killing her is not something I would contemplate for a nanosecond. I really want you to catch the person who did it."

"Do you think your wife hated Eryka?" asked Rabino.

"Hmm, what?" Tex knitted his perspiring brow.

Rabino stared at him. "You did say, women can be real evil bitches."

"Suzanne? What are you saying?" Doran looked incredulous. He rubbed his hands together as if trying to dry them. "Suzanne has her ways, but she would only get her hands dirty in the garden. She has too much pride to go confront another woman. No way would she commit murder. Hell, if she was that way inclined, I'd be dead by now!"

Preddy studied him. His hands had begun to shake again. "We know you spent millions on an Audi, an apartment, clothes, entertainment, plus gave her a credit card. Suzanne obviously knows all dis too. Are you saying she just calmly let you spend all dat money and never once said an angry word?"

"Whoa! I didn't say that, Detective." Tex waved an open palm in Preddy's direction. "She said a whole lot of angry words. Cursed and quarrelled and banned me from the bedroom for a week. We're still a couple and sleep in the same bed, but it's rare we spend much time together when awake. I have my quarters and she has hers. She focuses more on her own interests — her friends, gardening, charities. Had to give her a separate bank account." He smiled wryly. "She said I could throw away my own money if I wanted to, but I wasn't going to use hers. There is no way Suzanne would murder anyone for my tired old backside."

"And you're sure you can't tell us anything more?" asked Rabino.

Tex shook his head. "I cannot, Detective. I'm a businessman, not a murderer."

* * *

As they watched Tex Doran leave, Preddy stared at his limping gait. "He says he loved Eryka, and he's all cut up about her death, but strange he didn't ask how she died, isn't it? Didn't ask if she was shot, stabbed, chopped, strangled, beaten — nothing."

"That's true," agreed Rabino. "You think it would be top of his list of questions. The only information the public has is that her body was found in the gully covered in blood. We're the only people who know exactly how she died."

"Ah." Preddy snapped his fingers. "I'm going to get hold of Damian Slone, remember him?"

"Of course, nice guy . . . always cracking jokes. Sorry he left the JCF."

"He's in airport security now and seems happy. I want you and Spence to do a run to de airport. See if Damian can give you access to CCTV footage of when Tex Doran boarded Caribbean Airlines. See if you can find Tex stumbling or struggling to walk anywhere."

"Yes, sir. So, not convinced by his performance then?"

"He's still our prime suspect. It's always about love, hate or money, one or all of de above. If he's lying about his knee, dere's a good chance he's lying about Eryka's murder."

CHAPTER 16

Tuesday, 8 January, 11.50 a.m.

Detective Harris was holed up in a meeting room, the furthest one from the hive of activity on the open-plan floor. He sat facing the closed door with his personal laptop open in front of him, reviewing split screens. While it was true that the Jamaica Constabulary Force was not awash with cash, it was disheartening to know that at least one detective at Pelican Walk was not prepared to live within his means. Everything was in short supply at police stations throughout the island: office furniture, working vehicles, high-grade weapons, surveillance cameras and motivated staff. Pounding the streets in the hot sun to little acclaim could not be easy either when rogue officers were sullying the good name of their honourable colleagues. The men and women determined to give their all to crime-solving in Jamaica really must have law enforcement in their blood.

Harris would miss Jamaica when he left. Despite its many troubles he was in love with the island, its breath-taking scenery, lively people, delicious food and sometimes less-than-tasteful music that usually carried a strong message. His plan was to return to Glasgow in early summer. He could not bear the thought of returning any earlier, picturing the cold and darkness that would greet him. It would be an unbearable change. He missed his three children. Although they Skyped almost every other day, it was no real substitute for being able to hug them or play-fight or argue over the TV. He had promised them they could visit Jamaica at Easter and was looking forward to introducing them to a unique way of life.

He looked up as he detected a shadow behind the blinds on the windows separating the room from the hallway. Although the lurker could only see the back of his non-police-issue laptop, Harris was on alert.

The room was completely silent. Not even the old aircon unit was on, as the noise would attract attention and Harris preferred to bear the heat rather than be disturbed by someone popping in to check why it was rattling away. The shadow moved on and he turned his attention back to his split-screen reading with absolute concentration. A few minutes later came a sharp knock on the door simultaneous with it being pushed open.

Harris was caught off-guard as Preddy marched towards him, walked straight around the table and sank into a chair next to him. Harris fumbled, trying to close down the screens that had held his attention. He clicked a few buttons and pulled up a set of financials.

"How's it going?" asked Preddy.

"Er . . . I think Baccus could be right about Wesley Ashburn's company, All Angles." Harris tried to appear calm. A flush of blood turned his face crimson, an involuntary act that had followed him since boyhood and one he had never been able to conquer. "They're functioning with a heavy overdraft according tae this report."

Preddy leaned closer to Harris's shoulder and stared at the screen. "So, getting de contract for Dowdy Beach would really help pull Ashburn back from de brink?"

"Aye, it's a lifeline that he would've grasped with both hands."

Preddy frowned. "Or maybe he grasped an awl instead."

Harris began to lose his redness and his tone became more even. "Why stab Jerome though? Why naw get the man whose death would probably end the challenge for the project — Gavin Baccus?"

"I've been thinking about dat." Preddy's eyes flicked on every inch of Harris's screen as he spoke. "Wesley Ashburn knew de committee couldn't just award him de contract if Gavin died. Sure, de other candidates have been whittled out, but dis is a public procurement matter, which has to be clean and seen to be clean. De candidates who didn't get through to de final round would have wanted a second chance. If Gavin died, de committee would have had no choice but to run de whole competition again."

"I see." Harris nodded slowly. "Makes sense when ye put it that way. Disrupt Gavin's life by murdering his nephew and he becomes less enthusiastic about securing the project. The committee notice his lack of enthusiasm and lean towards Ashburn. Clever of Ashburn, if it was him."

"We've just seen Tex Doran, by de way."

"Seen him? He was here?"

"Gone now. Rabino and I interviewed him."

"Ye didnae call me?" Harris stared at Preddy and frowned. His temples throbbed as an overwhelming sense of frustration took over.

"Didn't know where you were, Detective." Preddy gave him a slow smile. "Knew where everybody else was except you. Fancy dat?"

Harris clamped his lips together and turned back to the screen. Raythan Preddy would forever remain resentful at being left out of the loop, but that had been the call of Commissioner Davis and the Major Organised Crime and Anti-Corruption Agency. If neither the commissioner nor MOCA had seen fit to apprise the other detectives of the undercover operation, it was not Harris's place to do so. He was here to do a specific job and he was going to do it no matter whose backs went up and how many death-glares he faced. Further angering Preddy would not be a good move though, and Harris silently counted to ten before speaking.

"How's Tex Doran looking as a suspect?"

"Looking very good actually," said Preddy. "Was at de Grand Marquee de night Jerome died. Doesn't have a solid alibi for de night Eryka was killed. Says he was at home, like his wife said. Spence and Rabino doing some research on him at Sangster airport."

"We know he really went tae Fort Lauderdale though?"

Preddy nodded as he stood. "Not something he could lie about. Claims he injured his leg boarding the outgoing plane. I think he could have injured it dragging Eryka out of her car or over de gully wall."

"So our suspect list isnae going down?"

"Could be going up. Tex Doran is pointing de finger squarely at Nicki Younis."

"I've read the notes Rabino and Spence took from their chat with Nicki. Didnae see anything suspicious in relation tae Jerome." Harris was glad to see Preddy on his feet and moving away. "Nicki obviously had naw love whatsoever for Eryka. Definitely worth a follow-up."

"Hmm, wouldn't mind meeting dis lady in de flesh." Preddy paused at the door. "Apparently she's staying wid her grandma just four miles from here. Ready to go?"

"Naw quite yet. I just need tae finish something off." Harris hesitated before adding in Patois, "Me soon come."

Preddy opened the door. "No problem. Shout me when you ready. I'll meet you in de front car park."

As the door closed, Harris breathed a sigh of relief. Remembering which matters he should discuss with Preddy and which were solely between himself and Superintendent Brownlow could be a strain at times. He wondered if Preddy had glimpsed anything on the screens when he'd entered. The investigation was coming to a close soon anyway. Before long, the criminal detective, the target of a whole year's surveillance, would be taken down. The MOCA team leader had said that the final act had begun and they would be ready to make the arrest within a week or so. Soon this would all be over and he could get back to routine policing and stop hiding from his suspicious colleagues. How he longed to get back to regular detective work.

* * *

Traffic was thick on the highway, making the journey from Pelican Walk to Sangster International Airport slower than usual. Spence drove her jeep along the well-maintained thoroughfare referred to by the Jamaica Tourist Board — but no one else — as the Elegant Corridor. A truck overladen with concrete blocks for the burgeoning construction sector crawled ahead, followed by an equally burdened cement mixer spitting dark-grey, noxious fumes. Annoyed motorists drove behind the vehicles with arms hanging out the windows and encouraged the truck men to speed up with rude hand gestures. The gridlock would ease off once they came to the roundabout, when those heading for the airport would be the first to escape, leaving the others to veer onto either Top or Bottom Road and continue towards the city centre.

"Damn traffic," grumbled Spence. "I can't wait till dem build de bypass and send dem big truck 'bout dem business. All dem vehicle shouldn't be pon main road wid bus and car."

"Agreed." Rabino wrinkled her nose and fanned her face as the smelly fumes filtered through the air-con unit. "It'll be a few years yet. We have to wait on the Chinese government to sign the cheques every time we need a new highway."

Spence kissed her teeth. "And dem not signing a damn thing unless dem can bring Chiney man over to work. No Jamaican company can get government work once Chiney show an interest."

"On the plus side, they're much better than we at meeting deadlines."

"Ah no lie." Spence gave a grudging smile. "If dey say one year it take one year. If we say one year it take four.

"And we'll want more money for cost overruns."

"And drinks breaks," said Spence. "'We cyah work wid-out two beer, boss man!'"

Both detectives laughed.

Spence shook her head as her vehicle made small progress. "I going put de siren on and blast dem out of de way!"

"Er, can you not do that, madam?" Rabino glanced at her in mock disapproval. "Remember what Super said about scaring the tourists?"

Spence chuckled. "Dat blasted man no have no sense. Couldn't believe de foolishness de man talking 'bout we must be mindful dat people from other countries get nervous when dem hear siren and we don't want dem to think of Mo Bay as being overrun wid police."

"Well, he says that's because the international media are always looking to write something bad about the state of emergency, and so far there's been nothing bad to report. He's not wrong there."

"Dat part is true, girl. If you leave it to de foreign press, dem will scare away visitors. No matter dat no gunman not pointing gun at tourists." Spence pulled up at a traffic light, another hindrance to progress they could have done without. "Just hearing police sirens shouldn't frighten a soul though. For all dey know we rushing to pick up pickney from school!"

"You ever do that?"

"Of course! One day me drop dem girls off at school and never realize dat lunch bag leave pon back seat. Me put on de siren and make such a noise you woulda think is wanted man me ah run down."

They both laughed again.

"Remind me when we leave airport to take Bottom Road," said Spence. "Need to see if we can find dat coconut man, Moses Fearon."

"Strange man," said Rabino. "Working for Baccus and complaining against Baccus at the same time. Shady as hell."

A male BMW driver tooted behind as the lights changed colour. Spence glared at him through the windscreen mirror for longer than was healthy.

Rabino poked her gently in the side. "Hey, don't give him the time of day, girl. Let's go. We've got CCTV to watch."

Spence peeled away. "My tarot said I going get into an argument and must avoid it at all costs," she said. "You're good at dis prediction business. Maybe you should take it up as a side-line?"

"No chance. Anyway, I'm pretty sure it would be frowned on by the JCF. I'll stick with photography. Much more calming, and I meet some nice sensible people at class."

Spence scowled and pretended to be offended. "I just know you wouldn't be suggesting me not sensible though?"

"Wouldn't dream of it, sis . . . I want to live."

Spence gave a sigh of relief as she spotted the sign ahead for the airport road. "Speaking of meeting nice people though, you still seeing dat guy?"

"Marvin? Yes, he's really something. We'll be going on our third date on the weekend."

"Heh! Great news. By dis time next year I want to buy new hat and heels!"

Rabino laughed out loud. "Idiot."

"I don't care what you want to seh." Spence stole a glance at her colleague. "At one point I was convinced you and dat white man was going to become an item."

"Really?" Rabino half-turned in her seat and looked surprised. "Never entered my mind. We get on just as well as any other detectives, I think."

"I'm pretty sure is not just me was getting suspicious. Preddy too."

"Never. How'd you know that?"

Spence shrugged. "I watched him watching you both having a conversation. He looked from one to de other like him eye wah pop out! Me did want to laugh, but me decide to mind me own business and just enjoy de joke. Poor Preddy look like him did a suffer, him so vex!"

"You never said." Rabino gave her a look of reproach. "Boss man has nothing to worry about. Marvin is much more my type — tall, dark and handsome, plus modest and thoughtful."

"Yes," said Spence triumphantly. "Marvin is de one. I can feel it."

"I wouldn't start saving for a new outfit if I was you, but if you're hunting down a new suit you can go check out Jacqui Morgan's posh boutique. Yes?"

"You must mad. Haven't set eyes on dat lady since she dash way Judge Guthrie. I would never set foot back in dat expensive place, not even for your wedding of de century."

Spence turned onto the airport road, which was congested with tour buses, taxis and private cars. Some vehicles headed for the departure area, stopping at inconvenient spots, including the no-stopping zones, to quickly unload baggage before ticket fines were dispensed. Others continued to the arrivals section, the distracted drivers trying to spot newly arrived passengers while avoiding ticket clerks. A white woman driving a car with rental plates came to an abrupt halt in front of Spence and opened the driver door. Spence gritted her teeth as she manoeuvred around it. The foreigner smiled and mouthed a silent apology as she climbed out and quickly shut her door.

Spence did not return the smile. "Shoulda run her rass over," she mumbled.

"There's a space, pull over." Rabino pointed to a space separated by a pair of yellow lines. "Let me ask this guy if we can park here." She leaned out of the window and spoke to an attendant, who directed them to an appropriate spot.

Spence shut off the engine. "Right. Time to see if Tex Doran is a liar, or whether de only tag we can pin on him is 'Stupid Old Fool'."

CHAPTER 17

Tuesday, 8 January, 1.20 p.m.

Detective Preddy allowed Harris to drive his jeep while he sat in the passenger side reading through notes, raising his head only to point out the memorized potholes along the way. Harris was well used to the overcautious advice and accepted it with good grace. They drove through the winding hills under lush overhanging trees and into the small upscale Portobello district on the outskirts of Montego Bay, a hillside area offering good views of the sea.

"So . . ." Preddy turned slightly in his seat so he could see the Scotsman's reaction. "What's wid de Guardsman Alarms guy earlier?"

A muscle in Harris's cheek twitched and his fingers clenched the steering wheel. "Och, just had an issue with the circuit breaker, I think. Something was causing the CCTV tae malfunction. Cannae be too careful when it comes tae security."

"And since when were you assigned to deal wid Pelican Walk security?"

Harris regained his composure and replied slowly, "What with an expensive piece of machinery like the Audi, and all the longing glances it was getting, I just thought we should make sure all alarms and cameras are working properly."

"Hmm," said an unconvinced Preddy, "I see."

Soon they located a property known as Blue Coat Inn, where an elderly lady ran an Airbnb operation. It seemed to be the in thing now — people using private houses to earn much-needed US dollars, and the government threatening them with all sorts of penalties if they did not register the properties and declare their earnings. This was the address Nicki Younis had given Spence and Rabino as her place of accommodation. There were no signs indicating that the property was anything other than a large private house. It was the only one with bright blue walls, so could not be missed. The house cast a sizeable shadow over a lawn of weed-filled grass. There was no gate or fencing around the property, so Harris drove in and parked on the driveway.

The sound of laughter hit them as soon as the engine went off. On the front-facing verandah were tables occupied by a Black family — three men and two women, all dressed in long shorts and vests with knapsacks beside them, ready for a day of exploring the city. They spoke with acute American accents. Empty plates lay before them with traces of hard-dough breadcrumbs, while the distinct smell of salt-fish and callaloo lingered in the air.

The front door was wide open with a huge coir welcome mat on the threshold. Preddy smiled at the group as he walked up the verandah steps. "Good day. How is everybody?"

The heartfelt responses ranged from "Fine" to "Good" and even a "Great."

"Looks like we came too late, missed a great meal," said Harris with a warm smile.

"Oh my Gaahd," said one of the men with considerable enthusiasm. "The saltfish and callaloo is awesome, and the fried dumplings are like nothing you've ever tasted in your life."

Harris tucked his sunglasses into his pocket then pointed at Preddy. "His fault we missed breakfast. Made me drive much too slowly."

"You coming to stay here?" asked another man. "It's really quiet and friendly, and Miss Bea is a lovely lady."

"Not at dis time." Preddy scanned the verandah. "We just came for a look around."

A lady who seemed to be the youngest of the group stared at them knowingly. Her face broke into a warm smile. "You guys a couple, huh? Good for you."

Preddy lost his own smile and frowned deeply. Two men in plain clothes coming to look around an Airbnb, neither wearing wedding rings. He should have known better.

Harris moved closer to Preddy's side and fluttered his eyes, giving his colleague a look of adoration. "It's complicated."

Preddy shot him a withering look while trying to maintain a pleasant face. The contortion gave him the appearance of someone suffering a considerable amount of pain. "Isn't it just?" he muttered.

"Ah!" The young American woman nodded with understanding. "Don't go letting nobody tell y'all how to live your lives. Y'all only got the one."

Preddy shifted uncomfortably. "Er, is Miss Bea around?"

"Yeah, she's round the back, I think." She pointed. "If y'all go down that way, there's like a standpipe. I'm pretty sure she's down there."

"Thanks," said Preddy. "See you later."

He quickly headed off in the direction she had pointed, with Harris on his heels.

"Don't do dat again, Detective Harris. Ever."

"Jeez, Preddy, ye have tae learn tae calm down." Harris chuckled. "We didnae want them tae know we're police. Let them think whatever makes them happy."

"Don't do it again. You can't say you never hear." Preddy continued walking around the side of the house. Ahead a lady stood with a bucket wedged under a pipe attached to a giant black water tank.

"Miss Bea?"

She turned and waved. "Yes. Hello there." She was a strongly built woman in a pink day dress resembling a nightgown. Her grey hair was parted down the middle and plaited in two bunches, each tucked behind an ear. Ankle socks and sandals finished off her attire. She turned off the pipe, wiped her hands on her dress and hurried towards them. "Is who dis now? I wasn't expecting anybody else today."

"Hello, Miss Bea. I'm Detective Preddy from Pelican Walk. Dis is Detective Harris."

"All right, Misser Detective." She looked at Harris. "Hello to you too, sir."

"Hello, Miss Bea. Pleased tae meet ye."

She tilted her head to one side and studied the Scotsman with sympathy. "Poor thing, you look like sun ah burn you. Come stand under de tree, man." She walked backwards, beckoning them to follow.

"Okay, thank ye."

Preddy smiled and glanced at Harris, whose flushed face seemed no redder than usual, but people meeting him for the first time usually assumed he was suffering. "He's used to it, Miss Bea. Don't feel sorry for him."

They stood under the broad green leaves of an almond tree, which was decidedly cooler than the open ground. "Is what happen why you reach up here?" Miss Bea looked nervously from one detective to the other. "Me tell dem de likkle money me making from Airbnb can only pay light bill and water bill. You know how much my property tax raise? Eighty per cent! Ah no joke business."

"I know exactly what you mean," Preddy nodded in agreement. "I'm on an apartment complex and our last property tax bill jumped from 40,000 to 92,000. Way more dan 100 per cent."

"Ah so government wicked and tief!" She shook her head in resignation. "What we can do?

"Never mind, ma'am. Is not taxes we come 'bout and you not in any trouble wid police," Preddy assured her. "We looking for one of your guests, Nicki Younis?"

"Oh, Nicki. She just gone down de road to pick up melon and pawpaw from one of me neighbour. I going make

smoothie for de foreign visitor dem. Dem love it, you see."
She beamed, and her eyes crinkled at the corners, the only
wrinkles on an otherwise unlined face. "Nicki soon come
back."

"Do yer guests usually run errands for ye?" asked Harris.

She shook her head. "Not really, but Nicki is not an
ordinary guest. She stay up here a few days every month.
I don't charge her much because I know her family. Her
granny and me used to go school back in de day. Sometimes
Nicki will do any likkle thing about de place without me even
need ask her. She's looking for a job in Mo Bay, so I don't
want to pressure her too much for money."

"I assumed she came from a family of money," said
Preddy.

"Dat is true. She and her family don't get along though."
Miss Bea lowered her voice. "You know young people . . .
parents want dem to do one thing, dey want to do another.
She say she going down de Freeport tomorrow to interview
for a . . . what she say, BPO job?"

"Aye," Harris nodded. "Business process outsourcing."

"Oh, me don't even know what it mean. Me just say me
hope she get it. Time hard inna Jamaica, sir." She glanced
at Harris. "You not gwine feel it though, Detective Harris.
People wid foreign money no feel it like we."

"I'm naw rich by any means, Miss Bea," said Harris.
"I listen tae the talk shows a lot and I know many people
are struggling." He turned and indicated the leafy surroundings. "Good thing ye've got all this beautiful land and great
weather tae help ease the pain."

She smiled. "Guess it's better dan working and living
in snow."

Preddy decided to steer Miss Bea away from their dis-
cussion on the cost of living, despite her obvious need to
unburden herself. "When Nicki came to stay in de past, did
she ever bring a boyfriend wid her?"

"Oh, de boy who dead de other night? Jerome? Him
come here maybe two time. De way how she talk about him,

you'd think he'd be here every night every time she come."
She looked at Preddy. "To be honest, I don't think he could
have been dat into her. Sometimes as she reach here she
phoning him to come over and him don't come."

"Guess she's been quite distraught since his death?" said
Preddy.

"She's been much quieter, but she still wants to get away
from country life in St Thomas, so she's still determined to
come live in St James." Miss Bea rubbed her throat, the bones
of which stood prominent under her skin. "When she got
back dat night, she didn't even come and say goodnight as
she usually would do. She just go straight to her bed. Is next
morning before I hear dat Jerome dead. Is a terrible thing!"

Preddy and Harris exchanged glances.

"Miss Bea, January the first was the night of the murder." Harris watched her closely. "The night Jerome died,
Nicki was in Mo Bay?"

"Yes, she came up same day. Dis is actually de longest
she has ever stayed wid me."

"What time did she get up here on de first?" asked Preddy.

"Let me see . . ." Miss Bea stared into the sky. "Got here
maybe around four in de afternoon. Said she was going to
give him a New Year's surprise as he didn't know she was
coming up."

"Phew! It hot, man," said Preddy. He stared at Harris
and wiped his forehead with the back of his hand. "Miss Bea,
you think we could go inside and maybe get some ice water?"

Harris locked eyes with Preddy and a silent message
passed between them. "Aye, I'd kill for some water." Harris
fanned his face with an open palm. "Ma throat's parched."

"Yes, of course, detectives. Come." Like a mother hen,
she hurried in front of them, glancing over each shoulder to
make sure her chicks were close to her wings. "I should have
thought of dat myself instead of having you out here burning
up. Back door open. Come."

Inside they walked through a utility room to the large
kitchen. Below the louvre windows was a six-hob gas stove.

Two giant white fridges stood side by side, a bread bin on top of one, while the other was stacked with dome-shaped food covers. "Most people surprised to see two fridge," she said, as though it was something she was used to repeating. "One is mine and de other is for guests. I want everybody who stays here to feel at home so dey all have free use of de kitchen. Dey can cook or use de microwave."

"Good idea," said Preddy. Miss Bea reached into her cupboard for drinking glasses. "We'll just go through," he continued. "Is de sitting room dis way?"

"Yes, go through, sir. You'll see a dining table down de hallway." She reached for paper handtowels and began to polish the glasses. "Me coming."

Preddy and Harris walked slowly through the long hallway. On either side were closed doors, six in total. "We'll never work out which one's Nicki's," said Harris.

"You're right," said Preddy. "Damn."

They continued through to the dining room where the lighting was dim, yet the wear of the furniture showed plainly. A large wooden table with eight chairs arranged around it took up a good portion of the floor. A wicker basket of oranges, grapefruits and ripe bananas was in the middle. Christmas decorations were still up. Little white plastic angels with immovable blonde locks jostled for position with shiny-coloured baubles on a small Christmas tree standing in one corner. The sideboard was empty except for a bulging cardboard box so full the flaps could not be closed. Preddy peeped inside and saw a variety of Jamaican trinkets — wooden coasters, straw fans, fridge magnets, headscarves decorated in black, green and gold. A blank receipt pad was next to the box. Each sheet had a carbon page behind it. Preddy turned over a leaf and smiled to himself. The lovely Miss Bea was clearly doing a side-line selling cheaply made souvenirs to foreigners at high prices. He pointed his discovery out to Harris.

"Twenty-five US dollars for a set of four coasters," exclaimed Harris. "Probably cost a dollar tae make."

"Shush, she coming."

The woman appeared with a tray and planted the ice water in front of them in long glasses. "You want anything to eat or you all right?"

"This is just fine, thank ye." Harris drained his water appreciatively.

"Dis is a much bigger house dan it looks from outside." Preddy gestured at his surroundings. "Looks like a good place to relax."

"Lots of space," agreed Harris, smiling warmly at their host. "Short journey from the city, yet far enough tae feel like ye're in the countryside."

"It's a good size, man." Miss Bea beamed. "My late husband build it. He knew what he was doing, because he always said when we too old de likkle pension not gwine do much, we need to rent out rooms. De place big and de rooms spacious and have en suite."

"Is dere any chance we can see inside de rooms?" Preddy took a long drink from his glass.

"That would be really great," said Harris.

Miss Bea lowered the tray to her side, her expression hesitant. "Well, dere are six guest rooms and all of dem are occupied. De Americans have two rooms, Nicki has one, a Canadian man has one, and some people from Kingston have de other two."

"Miss Bea, could we see Nicki's room?" asked Preddy. "She's probably de least likely to mind, since she not paying much for it."

The landlady was momentarily flustered. "Well, she soon come, so maybe you should wait for her?"

"Just a quick glance," said Preddy. "It's really just to check de size and space."

Harris gave her a wink. "Just a few minutes."

She smiled at him. "All right, I don't think she'll mind too much." Miss Bea rustled in her dress pocket for a key. "Come make me show you which one."

Preddy turned his head to one side, his attention drawn to the sound of a motor vehicle tooting as it came to a stop outside. He could not see through the window from his vantage point, but he guessed that either Nicki had returned or transport had arrived for the Americans.

Miss Bea opened the bedroom door and the detectives stepped in. The room was indeed light and spacious with a king-size bed taking up a great portion of it. A small suitcase sat on a chair, its dirty wheels dangling over the edge. Miss Bea tutted as she removed the suitcase and placed it on the ground. Various clothes were sprinkled on the bed. Harris wandered over to the dressing table, which contained cosmetics and jewellery.

"Bathroom dis way?" Preddy pointed at a closed door.

"Yes, I don't think—" started Miss Bea.

A car door slammed, and the vehicle took off again. They all heard a loud American voice from the front verandah. "Wow! That's a huge melon, Nicki."

Another American voice said, "Here, lemme help you."

A pleasant-sounding Jamaican woman replied, "Thank you."

"Nicki come." Miss Bea sounded relieved. "Make me go and get her."

As Miss Bea left the room, Preddy quickly pushed open the bathroom door. He did a swift assessment. Not much to be seen, a long bath towel on a shower rail and another folded on a vanity unit. Shower gels, soaps and a face flannel. He closed the door.

Harris shuffled the things on the dressing table. "Got anything?"

"Nothing." Preddy moved to the open wardrobe. He stood on tiptoe and peered over one of the shelves.

Voices were approaching, the lady of the house in urgent conversation with her guest, who sounded annoyed.

"Can I help you?" Nicki stood in the doorway, hands on hips and an anything-but-hospitable look on her face.

She was wearing flared red culottes and a sleeveless orange blouse. Her long hair hung loosely from her shoulders down to her wide waist.

"Dem just dis minute come in." Miss Bea hovered anxiously at the young woman's shoulder, looking as if she would rather be elsewhere.

"Yes, you can, Miss Younis," said Preddy. His voice hardened as he glared at her. "You lied to my detectives about your whereabouts de night Jerome Baccus died. You were right here in Mo Bay. You can start by telling us all about dat."

Nicki's shoulders slumped. There was petulance about her mouth. Her hands slid from her hips to her sides. She glanced at Harris, who leaned against the wall and folded his arms across his chest as he stared back at her.

An American voice called out, "Miss Bea, honey?"

"Oh, excuse me. Must go see what dem want." The woman disappeared and Preddy beckoned to Nicki. "Come inside and close de door."

Nicki obeyed and sank onto the bed.

"Talk," ordered Preddy.

Nicki sat with her hands at either side of her body, palms down on the bed. She kneaded the cotton bedspread with her fingers as a cat would do, except it did not appear to be making her feel comfortable. She bowed her head and stared at her sandals. The gold stud in her nose was distracting, and Preddy stared at it while waiting for her to speak.

"Jerome Baccus is dead," said Harris. "Eryka Malden is dead. Ye can talk tae us here or in a cell at Pelican Walk. Take yer pick."

"As soon as I heard that girl was dead, I knew you'd come blaming me." Her voice was soft, having lost all of its aggression. "I didn't do it. Neither of them. As there is a God, it wasn't me!"

"You were questioned about Jerome's death." Preddy flicked over the pages in his notebook. "If you had nothing to do with it, why did you neglect to mention dat you were in Mo Bay?"

"I don't know. Because I didn't want her — Eryka — to know, I guess. Didn't want her to be able to crow over me." Nicki's hazel eyes crept up to meet his as she shrugged. "I know it sounds stupid, but the plan was to surprise Jerome by popping up at the Grand Marquee. When I saw him with her, I knew there was no point. They were talking and laughing. I realized I was wasting my time."

"So ye were there at the marquee on the night he died," said Harris. "Ye want us tae believe that ye just walked away and left them?"

"But it's true! That's exactly what happened." Nicki pulled at strands of her black hair, dragging them in front of her eyes as if to hide her shame. "I was heartbroken. It was clear to me that she was going to win Jerome. I stayed at the back of the tent and started watching the presentation. I saw Jerome talking to his uncle Gavin, then he walked off into the darkness. My eyes went back to the screen, trying to keep my mind off him. It must have been about fifteen or so minutes later that people started running and screaming. They'd found the body. I went and glanced at it." She winced and rubbed her stomach as if waiting for a bout of nausea to pass. "I got away as fast as I could. I just didn't want to be there, didn't want to believe he was gone."

"De man you say you loved is dead and now de woman you thought took him from you is also dead." Preddy fixed her with an unblinking glare. "I don't believe in coincidences. You either did it or set it up."

"You've got it so wrong, Detective Preddy. I knew I was beaten. Eryka had the Audi and the money to go with it. I had . . . no chance with Jerome. I would never kill a man I loved." Her eyes became steely. "While I wouldn't shake hands with the bitch who took him from me, I wouldn't kill her either. I didn't leave here Saturday night. Ask Miss Bea, ask the Americans. We played cards all night, didn't go to bed till around three. Got up Sunday morning around nine and helped Miss Bea make breakfast. It wasn't till late that evening I heard the news report about Eryka Malden's death."

171

Preddy wrote as she spoke. "We'll verify your whereabouts."

Nicki noticed Harris scouring the room with his eyes. "You can search anywhere you want, detectives. I don't know what you expect to find, but feel free to look." She got up, unzipped her suitcase and strewed the contents on the bed. "Here, look."

Preddy glanced at the contents — a few sleeveless tops, shorts, underwear, body spray. "Where are de clothes you wore on Saturday?"

Nicki walked towards a laundry basket and held up a pair of jeans and a white linen blouse. "Right here." She threw them back in the basket and flung open the wardrobe. "Here's the rest of my stuff. Two trouser suits and a skirt suit."

A knock on the door and Miss Bea's voice came tentatively from behind the wood. "Everything all right in dere? Me can come back in?"

Preddy opened the door. "Yes, ma'am, come. We were just finishing off our chat, but we have a few questions you might be able to help wid." He stood aside and let her enter.

"Tell him where I was on Saturday night, Miss Bea!"

"Right here playing cards and winning every game, by de sound of things!" said Miss Bea. She gave a small smile. "De Americans won't be so quick to want to play Nicki again."

"What time was dat?" asked Preddy.

"Me would say from around nine o'clock, because I asked Nicki to bring hot chocolate to me bedroom and she bring it and ask me for card pack and dominoes." Miss Bea spoke with conviction. "I asked her if de visitors weren't going out, but she said dey were tired after being out all day and just wanted to play games. I could hear dem all night, but it didn't bother me. If my guests are happy, I'm happy."

"We'll talk to dem on de way out." Preddy looked at Harris, who nodded his satisfaction. Preddy turned his attention back to Nicki. "Miss Younis, when you planning on leaving Mo Bay?"

"I'll be going home on the weekend unless I get offered work tomorrow." Nicki brought her arms up and rubbed her plump shoulders. "I brought enough clothes to be ready for an immediate start because they said they want workers ready to work."

"If you do leave Mo Bay, make sure you leave a contact address in Golden Grove." Preddy stared at her, taking in the earnest features. She was a woman wronged, an unhappy creature, but his gut was not sensing a murderer. "Good luck, Miss Younis. And whatever you do tomorrow, do not start off your interview wid lies. People who lie and hide things usually get caught out in de worst possible way."

CHAPTER 18

Tuesday, 8 January, 4.08 p.m.

The sound of female voices emitted from behind the door of the Pelican Walk evidence room. Rabino and Spence brought their conversation to an abrupt end and greeted their colleagues as they entered. Harris pulled out a seat beside Spence, turned it around backwards and sank into it, resting his chin on the back. Preddy headed straight to the whiteboard and drew a black mark through Nicki Younis's name.

"Oh, it's like that is it?" Rabino spun from side to side in her rotating chair as she watched him. "After all the lies she told us?"

"It is," said Preddy. "She has an alibi for Eryka's murder. She was at de Blue Coat Inn in Portobello wid a lot of witnesses."

"Doesnae have one for Jerome's," said Harris. "She admitted tae being at the Grand Marquee that night. Says she fled when everybody else did. We believe her."

Rabino raised a well-delineated eyebrow. "So we're definitively treating this as a same murderer case?"

Preddy nodded. "No doubt about it in my mind. Whoever killed Jerome killed Eryka and did her because she knew something."

"Well, don't cross out Tex Doran," said Spence. "Underline him, circle him, blow him up!"

Preddy perched on the edge of a desk and folded his arms across his chest. "Tell me more."

"We've seen him on video, limping, before he even got near the airplane steps," said Rabino. "He climbed out of a taxi in the departures area. Grabbed his suitcase and tried to walk steadily towards the automatic doors, but you could see it even then . . . he was struggling with his right knee."

Spence got up and moved to the side of the table. She shook straight her trouser legs. "See him here." She demonstrated the suspect's movements, taking small steps and slowly dragging her right leg.

Harris smiled. "Always helps tae have a visual."

"And get this," Rabino continued. "When he got to the plane steps . . . it's like he pretended to stumble. He was up and rubbing his knee. One of the flight attendants ran over to check on him, then he hobbled up the stairs in front of her."

"Such a bad actor." Spence retook her seat. "I coulda do so much better dan dat."

"As I thought," said Preddy. "So wherever he picked up dat knee injury, it was not at Sangster airport."

"Tex Doran isnae going tae admit tae anything, and Suzanne Doran isnae going tae give him up," said Harris in frustration.

"Yes, she's de one who would have to deliver. She's not much of an alibi for him, but she's sticking to it." Preddy underlined Tex's name. "We'll have to work to break his alibi ourselves."

"Maybe pick up both of dem at de same time," suggested Spence. "Put wifey in one room and husband in another. Make sure dey see each other, but don't let dem talk. Dat might cause one of dem to break."

"Naw a bad idea," said Harris. "But I have a feeling we wouldnae get Suzanne down here without a warrant, even if we asked nicely. Something tells me she dislikes police way more than she dislikes her husband's shenanigans."

"Agreed," said Preddy. "Anyway, Tex is back on de island after two days away and doesn't look like he plans to run again. Maybe he used his time off to come up wid a plan and thinks he's smarter dan us."

"If him plan bad like him acting, we must get him," said Spence.

Preddy turned back to the whiteboard. "I want to see how de rest of our suspects are stacking up. If we can eliminate dem and focus on Tex, dat would be de best thing." Preddy reached down in front of Rabino and picked up the evidence bag containing the awl. "We don't get any decent leads on dis yet?"

Spence shook her head. "Not from my calls and I've been through a whole heap."

Rabino flicked through her notepad. "The best I've got is a gentleman, Mr Hibbert, who called earlier. He says the wood is lignum vitae, as old as he is, and no one uses that to make tools anymore. Apparently, cedar is cheaper and more plentiful."

"How old is he?" asked Harris.

"Eighty-two." She smiled. "At first he said eighty-one, then he remembered he had a birthday last month. Sounds like such a nice old thing. Kept calling me 'me lub' after every sentence."

"Did he know where dey were sold?" Preddy stared at the antiquated wooden handle.

"No. Says he hasn't seen those sorts of tools since 'me was a dandy young bwoy in de fifties'. His long-deceased father used to have tools made with lignum vitae handles, but not an awl."

"Hmm," muttered Preddy. "De handle barely shows any sign of wear and tear."

"Aye, wood shrinks and splits when it dries, so the person who treated it must've known exactly what they were doing," said Harris with a degree of admiration. "A professional craftsman."

"Made back in de days when things were made to last," said Preddy.

"So we could have an octogenarian murderer, or someone who borrowed or stole it from the elderly owner?" said Harris. "Great."

Spence groaned. "Don't say dat. We no have no old-old people as suspects. It better be someone younger who inherited it."

"It's definitely someone younger." Rabino drummed her fingernails on the table as she spoke. "Stabbing doesn't take much effort with a blade as sharp as that, but few eighty-somethings could haul a body — dead or alive — over a gully wall. I'd say the killer is strong and physically fit."

Harris nodded his agreement. "We need tae get in touch with Wesley Ashburn again. Hopefully, he willnae lawyer up. See what he has tae say about his messy financial situation."

"Yes, we'll do dat." Preddy stared at Wesley's name. "Mr Ashburn has no alibi for Jerome's murder, he was right dere at de Grand Marquee. It's not beyond imagination dat he could have killed Eryka just to throw us off track, get us to focus elsewhere, but is he dat cunning . . .? I wonder."

"By the way, we didn't spot Moses Fearon on any of the beaches," said Rabino. "Not a jelly coconut in sight. Didn't see Ras Bizzi either."

"Dem probably sell off all de water and juice and gone home early," said Spence. "Just as well as we wouldn't able to resist buy de water. Sun hot out ah road, man."

"Tell me about it," muttered Harris.

"We don't seem to have addresses for either of dem." Preddy searched through the pages of his notebook. "If you don't find Moses tomorrow, I'll get some constables to go flush him out. Maybe Timmins can help."

"Timmins? Eeh hee? Maybe not." Spence chuckled to herself and Preddy frowned.

"Looks like you upset him, sir," Rabino explained with a smile. "Says he has to get the goats moved quicker than planned to protect them from you. Didn't elaborate though."

"Oh, dat was just a misunderstanding between us. He'll get over it."

Preddy glanced at his watch. It was rapidly approaching 5 p.m. Their working hours were so uncertain that it was rare for any of them to work less than fifty hours a week. He picked up the awl and locked it away in a drawer. "Right, feel free to call it a day if you like. If anybody needs me I'll be in my office for another hour or so."

* * *

Preddy did not quite make it to his own office. Odette intercepted him midway to inform him that Superintendent Brownlow wanted to see him. Preddy could see his superior through the open blinds. Brownlow was reclining in his plush seat and seemed to be speaking, although he was not on the phone. The detective placed an ear against the door and listened, but the thick wood held whatever the man was saying, trapped within its pores. Preddy straightened up in frustration and knocked loudly on the door.

The superintendent reached forward across his desk and clicked the depressed button on his dictating machine. "So, what happened to that report I've been waiting on, Detective?"

Although the man's demeanour was calm, Preddy knew him well enough to figure that he was unhappy. The promised report was not close to being prepared, and Preddy could not believe Brownlow was really expecting him to give chapter and verse on the two murders already. "Didn't think it was worth giving you a half-finished document before I had anything concrete to report, sir."

"So, where are we at, Detective?" Brownlow sipped cool water from a glass while his eyes remained fixed on Preddy.

Preddy gave him a *Reader's Digest* version of where the cases were at, Brownlow interrupting him to bark questions that Preddy could not answer. On days like this it was clear that the brass had no idea of the complexity of murder investigations. It seemed that the superintendent and the commissioner thought the detectives were supermen with answers to everything, and particularly so since Saviour Sean Harris had come on board. Gathering suspects was an intricate skill that required ears to the ground followed by careful questioning, listening out for what information was volunteered and what was concealed. Elimination of said suspects took time and patience, which could run into many days, weeks even. The brass should have had a level of understanding above that of the average person, who assumed every murder could be solved within forty-eight hours.

"So you and Harris are going to have another conversation with Wesley Ashburn later?"

"We're aiming for sometime tomorrow, sir." The superintendent's brow puckered in disagreement and Preddy could not resist adding, "It's been a long few days, and like you said, sir, I don't want to stress or endanger my team. I'm looking after everybody's welfare to de best of my ability."

"Hmm." Brownlow pursed his lips and studied him. "Gavin Baccus has been calling me . . . and calling other people. You need to go see him first."

"Well, I did intend to speak to Gavin Baccus again, sir, but he wasn't top of my list."

Superintendent Brownlow narrowed his eyes. "Move him up your list, Detective."

Preddy clenched his fists in his lap. Intuition told him what was coming, but he wanted to hear it from Brownlow's lips and decided to face down the super's wrath. "Why, sir?"

"I told you, because he's been calling." The superintendent had the grace to look uncomfortable and shuffled his ample behind on his chair. He refilled his glass and took another gulp of water. "You are leading the investigation and he'll take comfort from what you say, rather than from anything I say. I want you to reassure him that we are doing everything in our power to solve his nephew's murder."

Preddy knew he should hold his thoughts, but he could not help himself. "Jerome's parents have been calling too, and dey want reassurance too. Eryka's sister is going out of her mind. Now what? Gavin has been calling de commissioner, de mayor? Gavin is more important because he's a wealthy businessman eager for his grand project to be given de go-ahead?"

"Remember who you're talking to, Detective Preddy." Brownlow raised his voice and leaned across his desk, straining the tight khaki collar around his thick neck. "Nobody's stopping you from running your own show. It's your case for now, unless you want to let someone else take over while you go spend time with the psychologist?"

"Someone else?" sneered Preddy. "I wonder who?"

Brownlow stared at Preddy without blinking. "You go give Mr Baccus the reassurance he needs and then you can go talk to Wesley Ashburn."

"Yes, sir." Preddy placed his hands on the chair arms and squeezed the fabric as if trying to free the foam underneath. "Is dat all, sir?"

"This is not personal, Raythan. I am not in a great position either." The superintendent sighed and leaned back. His look changed to one of concern as he studied his lead detective. "How are you doing anyway, man?"

Preddy's eyes remained steely. "Not good enough for some, apparently."

"You can go, Detective."

Preddy kicked back his chair, which scraped noisily on the wooden floor. He banged the door shut behind him. Down the corridor he stormed and almost smacked into Rabino as she came around the corner.

"Oops! That was close. You all right, sir?"

"Yes. No. Actually, come wid me a minute."

Rabino followed him into his office. He closed the door after her and leaned on it.

Her expression was anxious. "Do I need to sit down, sir?"

Silence followed, except for the gentle whirring of the fan and the distant sound of traffic on the highway.

"You're scaring me, sir. What happened?"

Preddy shook his head. "Just Super being annoying, nothing new." He went around his desk and sat heavily. "Take a seat. I promise dis won't take long."

Rabino waited on the edge of her seat.

"You trust me one hundred per cent, yes?" asked Preddy.

"Of course, sir."

"Dis is something I want kept strictly between de two of us. I want you to do something for me, but right now I can't tell you why. All I can tell you is dat it is important."

She shifted in her seat, crossing one trousered leg over the other. "Go ahead. If it can be done, I'll do it."

"Must be about a year now, maybe more, since Detective Harris said he's been looking to buy property." Preddy tried to think of the least offensive way to address the situation. "I know you gave him some real estate brochures and you always refer him to places up for sale."

"That's right, sir."

"You ever hear him mention somewhere named J Lane?"

"No, I don't think so." Rabino scowled as she stared at him. "Never heard of it. Why?"

Preddy took a deep breath. "I need a list of dose properties or copies of any real estate brochures you gave him. If he mentioned visiting areas dat you didn't refer him to, I want to kn—"

She held up a palm to stop him speaking. "What is this about, sir?" Her tone had deteriorated to one of deep annoyance. "I know you said you can't tell me why, but I want to know. Why do you care where he wants to live? I mean, he probably won't buy anything except a holiday home if he's going back to Glasgow. As long as he's not moving to Ironshore, what's it to you?"

Preddy stared at her indignant face. She was one of the smartest yet most easy-going detectives he knew and as a team member she never challenged him in the way Spence did if she disagreed. Rabino had a much more diplomatic way of dealing with issues, but he could not blame her for confronting him now.

"It's not what you think, Kathryn. Dis is not about where he lives or whether he stays in Jamaica."

"You're not going to tell me, are you?" She stood up scowling and headed for the door. "I'll get you the information before I leave, sir."

"Thanks." Preddy hated asking her to do this and knew that his request was out of order. "Remember dis is between de two of us. No way should he ever hear about it."

"Agreed." With her fingers on the door handle she turned and looked at him with something resembling sympathy in her eyes. "I think Harris is a good guy, despite the fact that you two don't always see eye to eye and he can be too outspoken for his own good. Whatever this is about, I hope you know what you're doing, because if anything gets to the ears of Commissioner Davis and he has to choose between you and Harris . . . you know which way he'll go."

As the door closed behind her, Preddy let that awful thought sink in.

CHAPTER 19

Wednesday, 9 January, 8.16 a.m.

Detective Preddy swigged hot ganja tea from a flask and listened to the calming melodies of Dennis Brown while driving to the downtown office of Gavin Baccus. The gentle crooning of the Crown Prince of Reggae did little to reduce Preddy's annoyance. Even Spartan had seemed to sense that all was not well in his human's world. The parakeet had taken one look at Preddy's morning face, spread his bright green wings and flown away from the windowsill, leaving the detective feeling guilty.

Preddy inhaled deeply. Here he was, heading to personally reassure Gavin Baccus of their determination to solve his nephew's murder. Meanwhile back at Pelican Walk, there were cold cases that the Police High Command were not worried about clearing up. Some were unidentified people, others were poor people whose relatives had no political or social power to attract publicity or achieve justice. Little resources were put into pursuing the murderers, and many cases never got even a fifteen-second mention on the TV news or a paragraph in the local newspaper. The victims placed top of the leader board of investigations were those who ticked all the relevant boxes — money, complexion, social standing. Being a foreigner, or even having dual nationality, went a long way towards the pursuit of justice for those unfortunate enough to have met a violent end on the island.

The detective tooted at a male driver who had the nerve to turn off and drive the wrong way onto a one-way road. The man made a rude hand gesture. Preddy gripped the steering wheel and concentrated on the road ahead rather than chasing the offender down. There was work to do: two recent murders to solve, and the day that lay ahead would not benefit from unnecessary distractions.

On the passenger seat sat a pile of real estate leaflets and pamphlets Rabino had given him. Harris had said he would try to get hold of Wesley Ashburn this morning. The Scotsman was determined to avoid morning prayers so he would be sure to avoid Pelican Walk, but Preddy wondered whether Harris would even try to find Ashburn at all and how much time he would spend questioning the man if he did. Harris was preoccupied with other things, even though he showed enthusiasm for the murder investigations. At this moment, the foreigner was probably with someone or in a place named J Lane.

The words "J Lane" had disappeared into a minimized tab on Harris's computer when Preddy burst into the conference room the day before. So far Preddy had failed to find any person, road or area by that name, despite intense internet searches. Last night he had spent a good few hours going through the real estate brochures searching for clues, to no avail. He had tried to remember which communities Harris had casually mentioned where he had planned to scope for houses. As much as Preddy disliked that Harris was running his own private investigation, he had no wish to jeopardize it by asking too many questions in public, and already rued asking the loyal Rabino for help. He winced as he remembered how, yesterday evening, she had knocked on his office door, handed him the papers with a sharp, "For you, sir," and quickly walked out.

Preddy's thoughts moved to the possible target of Harris's attention, Detective Iain Cotner, a veteran detective of ten years who had come from St Catherine via a stint in Kingston and had been at Pelican Walk for about five years. Cotner was a hard-nosed man who rarely joked and always vociferously defended the notion of law and order. To Preddy he seemed an unlikely candidate for corruption, but the MOCA investigators were highly trained professionals who only hunted down serious offenders. Although Cotner was not quick-tempered or prone to snap, Preddy did wonder whether even the calmest of men might not react violently if cornered and threatened with losing their freedom. He hoped for Harris's sake that he was not involved in something that could turn out too hot to handle.

Preddy grabbed two mints from the glove box and crunched on them as he turned off the main road. An illegal taxi stopped abruptly in front to let out passengers on the corner, blocking the smooth flow of traffic. Motorists behind Preddy instantly complained with their horns, an unholy tune of frustrated noise, which interrupted Dennis Brown's melody. Preddy squeezed the jeep past the taxi, cursing under his breath, and made a mental note of a prominent sticker in the back window. He would set Highway Patrol on the unruly motorist another day.

Preddy turned onto the huge car park of Overton Plaza, which was usually chock-full of vehicles but at this early hour was sparsely occupied. The three-storey plaza contained a mixture of hairdressers, restaurants, medical facilities and clothing boutiques, as well as a few offices. He cruised along, trying to recognize which unit was that of Baccus Designs.

Eventually he rolled down his window and asked a parking attendant. The man pointed, indicating a second-floor unit. From the outside it looked like an ordinary office unit, nothing like the ostentatious property that housed Wesley Ashburn's All Angles. He parked, climbed the steps two at a time and rang the buzzer on the white wooden door.

While he waited, he rested his briefcase on the balcony's iron railing and looked down onto the car park below, watching people arrive. Ordinary, hard-working people, minding their own business, making a living and just trying to enjoy their lives. Preddy was well aware that among the good people of Montego Bay, any one of them could be a pickpocket, thief or even murderer.

The door clicked and he turned around.

"Come in, Detective Preddy. Wasn't expecting you to reach so early, but I'm hoping you have something for me?"

Preddy shook Gavin's hand. His eyes were sunken, the skin around them noticeably darker than his brown complexion. "I hope you'll be encouraged to know dat we have a team of four working on Jerome's case, and Eryka's. We're doing everything we can, sir."

"I'm still in shock." Gavin turned and walked down a corridor lined with drawings of property developments. He motioned Preddy to follow him. "You know it's got to be the same person who killed them both, right?"

Preddy's voice was grave. "We are looking at de possibility of a connection between the two, but stranger things have happened."

"Who do you have in mind?"

"We'll talk about dat, sir."

Gavin Baccus entered his office and pointed at a leather chair facing his desk. Behind his desk on the wall was a full-scale map of Montego Bay which for once made the city look as if it held 110,000 people. Most maps made the city appear tiny and insignificant. The magnolia walls on either side were covered with enlarged images of the old city. Preddy walked past the seat he had been offered and paused in front of the map. It highlighted every major street and included every side street, half of which had not seen a name plaque in years, having been broken, stolen or vandalized.

"I want one like dis." Preddy leaned in closer. "We have good paper maps at Pelican Walk, but none of dis size. Google Maps doesn't pick up half of dese side streets."

"Yes, I find online maps a waste of time and you know what they say, 'If the map can't locate it, the map is wrong.' The road is always there." Gavin paused beside his desk. "Oh, can I get you some tea, coffee, water, Detective?"

"I wouldn't mind some water, thanks."

Preddy continued to study the map in Gavin's absence, then turned his attention to the photographs, which offered a glimpse of the city from long before he was born, when glamorous shops owned mainly by people of English and Jewish ancestry lined the high street. A time when shopkeepers took great pride in their frontage and added carefully constructed signage instead of painting uneven letters. A time when there were few motor vehicles and no potholes to avoid, when pavements were even and used by pedestrians rather than by unlicensed vendors. The wall on the opposite side displayed photographs of Sugar Rush Beach in its current unloved condition, surrounded by larger coloured drawings, artist impressions of the proposed new development.

Gavin handed Preddy a glass of cold water.

"Thanks. Where did dese old photos of downtown come from?"

Gavin stared past the detective's broad shoulders. "Oh, most came from the archives at the National Library in Kingston. I bought them as small images and got one of my guys to blow them up, with the library's blessing, of course. Some came out clearer than others."

"I wouldn't mind buying a few, but I have no time to go to Kingston for now."

"Well, the good thing is, Detective, if you want them, you don't need to traipse to Kingston anymore. You can access the digital archives online. Not sure what they've uploaded for St James, but you can have a look."

"I'll do dat." Preddy took a seat. "I like how you've surrounded yourself wid de city."

"I love this place. Despite the violence, overcrowded streets, undisciplined motorists . . ." He waved his hands as if these were beyond his influence. "We've got the weather, beaches, food and friendly people. What can you do if the city's in your blood? I want to make this place better. We cannot let murderers take over and ruin it."

"I agree." Preddy brought his briefcase to his lap and removed a newspaper, which he pushed towards Gavin. "You recognize de man in de photo?"

Gavin gazed at the photo. "Which one?"

Preddy leaned over and pointed. "Dat one. Moses Fearon?"

"No, I don't think so." Gavin held up the paper and squinted at it. His tone became dismissive. "Oh, Livity people. They were always around making noise, writing letters, demonstrating . . . misguided people led by that preachy Rasta Man. Some people won't accept that progress requires sacrifice. Seem to think they can stay put in their rickety shacks in prime locations while the twenty-first century continues around them."

Preddy raised an eyebrow. "So, you don't remember seeing Mr Fearon before?"

"No, should I?"

"I won't ask you to view de footage from immediately prior to Jerome's murder, because I don't want to cause you any further distress. I can tell you dat Moses Fearon is in de frame, dressed in usher uniform — black trousers, long-sleeved white shirt — setting out chairs under de marquee on your behalf. His daytime hustle is selling jelly coconuts on beaches and roadsides."

"I didn't do the hiring." Gavin reached for a pair of rimless glasses and polished them with a napkin. He placed them on his nose, magnifying his light brown eyes, and studied the photo again. "I asked an employment agency to send me ten people to work from 6 p.m. till midnight. Those were the planned hours anyway. Actually I wanted until 2 a.m., but what with the state of emergency, the council said we had to be done and off the beach by midnight." Gavin fumbled around in a drawer and handed Preddy a business card. "That's the agency. Jerome did the final liaison with the lady there — you know, getting the names and printing name badges with our logo on it."

"Did Jerome do background checks?"

"No, man. The agency did that. At least, that's what they said." Gavin removed his glasses and stared at Preddy. "You think this guy, Moses Fearon, tricked his way onto the site and killed Jerome? That I could have been paying the man who murdered my nephew?" His voice cracked.

"I haven't come to a firm conclusion yet, sir." Preddy glanced at the card and pocketed it before scribbling something in his notebook. "His presence could be totally innocent. As you know, dere were a lot of people at de marquee. Most took off before any police officers arrived. We still have a lot of enquiries to make and leads to follow."

"Bet you Wesley Ashburn sent him. I wouldn't put it past him to come up with something like that. He wants Sugar Rush Beach, bad."

Preddy maintained a straight face. "Our enquiries are continuing, please be assured of dat, Mr Baccus. Everybody at Pelican Walk is committed to catching de person who did dis and we won't rest until we do."

"You know he has no money, right? Ashburn, I mean?"

"My detectives are following up de information you provided. Thanks for dat." Preddy's eyes went back to the photos on the wall. As far as he was concerned he had done all the reassuring Superintendent Brownlow could expect him to do. Now he wanted to leave and get back to work. "You have any questions for me? I'll answer what I can, but at dis point dere's not much else I can tell you."

"Did you get any information on the awl? I saw it on the TV news. That was good coverage."

"We've had a few calls, but dey haven't led to anything meaningful yet." Preddy stared at him. "You recognize it?"

"No. Wish I hadn't seen it to be honest." Gavin closed his eyes. "Now I'll never get away from the vision of that tool being plunged into Jerome's heart."

"I'm very sorry, sir." Preddy got to his feet.

"They should bring back hanging," muttered Gavin. He rose and walked around his desk.

Preddy walked out ahead of him but did not respond. Sometimes he thought hanging would be a good idea too, but there were many heart-wrenching stories of innocent people on death row in the USA. Sometimes the justice system got it wrong, and it took the dedicated people of the Innocence Project to prove the injustice and set them free. Maybe hanging should be reserved only for killers caught in the act who could not deny their guilt.

Preddy paused at the door. "You wouldn't happen to know of a person or place named J Lane, would you?"

Gavin Baccus thought for a moment then shook his head. "Never heard of it. Is it important?"

"Could be." This was not a lie, Preddy told himself, and there was no reason to admit that the question had nothing to do with the murder investigations.

"If it's a person, it could be in the phone book. I know the names of most roads in the city, but that could be a new one. J Lane, hmm? Then again could be a jogging lane, could even be a shipping lane or something similar."

For a moment Preddy went still. He had not considered this angle.

"Was that helpful?"

"Very." Preddy shook hands with the man. "Thanks for your time, sir. Again, sorry for your loss."

"Thank you, Detective. Please stay in touch."

* * *

Back in his vehicle, Preddy stared at the cover of the real estate brochures. The Overton Plaza car park was beginning to fill up and the parking attendant would soon start identifying loitering drivers to send on their way, yet the detective knew he could not concentrate on driving without another look inside the brochures. Preddy made himself comfortable. He had no intention of moving anytime soon.

After a few moments looking over the brochures, the attendant tapped on his window. Preddy whipped out his badge and pressed it against the glass. "Police business," he mouthed.

"Okay, sir!" The man quickly moved away.

The back of one glossy pamphlet contained the names of local estate agents, one of which was the man who had driven the beige SUV to meet Harris at Pelican Walk. Preddy had skimmed it last night and not drawn any link to anything suspicious, but he studied it now with clearer eyes. His heartbeat increased as he stared at the relatively new Unity Hall luxury complex, Unity Court.

He distinctly remembered Harris commenting that Unity Hall was a beautiful, leafy district with wide roads and great sea views. The complex itself was nearly five years old, consisting of twenty two-storey houses and eighteen two-bed apartments in a single tower block with a roof garden. What was interesting to the detective was the unique feature that other upscale residential developments could not boast — a tenpin bowling alley with automatic LCD scoring. He stared at the tiny picture depicting residents, white and Black, posing with bowling balls. Behind them were ten neon-lit bowling lanes labelled A to J.

This was it. A different lane. J Lane.

"Well, well, sneaky Mr Harris," murmured Preddy.

Preddy knew of only one public bowling alley in the whole of Montego Bay — Jamzone, a state-of-the-art facility boasting twelve lanes at Whitter Village near his home in Ironshore. The Unity Court set-up was a private residents' bowling facility, not one that anyone could stroll into off the street. A deep frown spread across Preddy's brow. No Jamaican detective could afford a property in Unity Hall, not with legitimately earned money. Rabino was the daughter of a now-retired attaché and the only detective he knew of whose parents had real money, yet he was sure Unity Court would be a stretch even for them. Harris had sworn to him that the undercover investigation had nothing to do with either Spence or Rabino, and Preddy believed him.

He read the fine print in the exclusive property's description. If Detective Iain Cotner had recently taken up residence in this swanky place, he was definitely earning his bread elsewhere.

CHAPTER 20

Wednesday, 9 January, 10.38 a.m.

Detective Preddy drove away from Overton Plaza, forcing himself to put Harris out of his mind and concentrate on the immediate job at hand: nailing a murderer. A killer who had entered a packed beach under cover of darkness and slid a six-inch steel point into a man's heart. A killer whose encore had been bashing in the skull of a young woman and tossing her away like trash. Preddy's stomach churned when he thought of Eryka and how he had allowed his prejudices to surface above good policing and intuition. He might have considered her behaviour immoral, but it had not been illegal, and no woman deserved to be murdered or beaten for living her life the way she chose.

So far the parish of St James had recorded four murders for the new year. Way below the figures for the start of the previous year. Of the other two killings, one was a knife stabbing and the other a machete chopping. The once-barking guns were temporarily silenced by the swell of law enforcement, but determined lawbreakers would always find another, quieter way. Like most right-thinking people, Preddy desperately wanted a return to the old Montego Bay where residents left doors and windows open overnight and the only bangs were fireworks and backfiring cars.

The awl was the only piece of real evidence held on either murder and, so far, no one could place it. If the awl was a locally made tool, and if Rabino's octogenarian tipster was correct in his belief that it was extremely old, then perhaps it could be traced to a high-street store long since disappeared. Photographic records of old Montego Bay should be in the National Library's online database, and Preddy thought about heading straight back to Pelican Walk to look at them, but distractions awaited him in the office and he needed peace and quiet for this research. The St James Parish Library had free accessible computers and was as quiet as one could get, plus there were always helpful staff to answer any questions.

On Meagre Bay Road, Preddy turned into the library's attractively landscaped grounds, continuing down the long drive past a bust of national hero, Marcus Mosiah Garvey, and parked. The library was a sprawling single-storey orange building set on a generously sized estate that took over most of the short road. The unoccupied stone benches on the lush lawns would be overrun with students from the surrounding high schools by lunchtime, drawn by not only the books, but also by free internet access. Uniquely for a building in the downtown centre, it was laden with leafy food-producing trees — breadfruit, banana and coconut — which also served a secondary role of providing much-needed shelter for patrons who preferred to sit reading outside. Preddy locked the vehicle and headed indoors.

"Hello, Detective Preddy. Long time, no see." The librarian acting as receptionist wore a floral dress, short blue jacket and a bright smile.

Her face was unfamiliar to Preddy and he stared at her quizzically. "Oh, remind me?"

"I'm Ellen. You were here summer before last with your kids, girl and boy."

"You must have a good memory to remember dat, Ellen."

"Not really." She delivered another beaming smile. "Most people see you as a hard man, but when I first met you in person, you were just like any other dad. I heard you tell them to read more books and put down the tablets. Always a good sign!"

Preddy's lips curled. "I try my best, but de older dey get, de more dey rebel."

"Way of the world." She laughed. "How can I help you, Detective?"

"I want to get online access to your archived photographs of de city, de high street and main shopping areas."

"Sure, follow me." They walked along the polished wooden floor and she showed him into an open-plan zone containing a row of computers, two of which were occupied.

"Come, I'll put you on the one in the far corner so you get total privacy. It's cooler in that area too."

"Thanks."

She turned on the computer and brought up the National Library of Jamaica website. "Okay, the site is quite user-friendly, so I'll leave you to figure it out. I'll be next door though, so give me a shout if you can't see what you need."

Preddy scrolled through the pages and found a collection dedicated to the parish of St James. He scrutinized the black-and-white photographs, many of which carried a pleasing sepia tint. Some were identical to the ones in Gavin Baccus's office and there were dozens of others he had never seen before. He was struck by the change in clothes worn over the decades. Women wore thick, elegant long dresses to their ankles, long-sleeve blouses with collars up to their throats. Men sported smart suits, with long-sleeved shirts and ties, topped with panama hats. Not a pair of saggy jeans or exposed underwear in sight. These were the early years, when horses and wagons were prevalent, the change in decades visible in bold fashionable cars with sleek rounded shapes of a kind now to be found only on the streets of Havana, Cuba. The roads, though narrow, appeared much wider because there were fewer vehicles.

With great effort he set aside his nostalgia and concentrated on the shops, searching for anything that looked like a hardware store or one that did any form of woodwork. The main streets burgeoned with tidy-looking shops. There were butchers, shoemakers, boutiques, watchmakers, jewellers, a photography studio and a bakery. For an hour, he remained engrossed in the photographs searching for clues. The closest he came to anything of significance was a furniture store from the 1970s named Hardy's.

A sound at his arm caused him to turn around.

Ellen was standing at his shoulder. "Found everything you need, Detective? Or can I help you?"

Preddy pointed at an image on the screen. "Only if you can resurrect de owner of Hardy's and get him to tell me if he's ever seen a tool like dis." He removed a photo of the awl from an envelope in his breast pocket and handed it to the librarian.

"Oh, I saw this awl on the news the other night. Murdered the poor young man just like that." Ellen shook her head apologetically as she handed it back. "Never seen one like it before, but the family who owned Hardy's is still around, at least the granddaughter is."

Preddy's eyes lit up. "You sure?"

"Yes, man. She's Mrs Vassell. Lives in Johns Haven and goes to my church, Johns Haven Adventist, so I see her almost every Saturday. Must be close to ninety years old, but she goes to choir practice on Tuesdays and runs an afternoon training fellowship on Thursdays. Real nice lady." She grinned at Preddy. "If anyone can tell you anything about the shops and traders back then, it would be her. That said, she likes to talk about God, so if you're not saved, you better be prepared for a lecture."

Preddy smiled as he stood up. "Or just lie."

Ellen laughed and her eyes crinkled. "I'm a Christian, Detective Preddy. My starting point is 'Thou shalt not lie', but I never try to press my beliefs on anybody."

"You have a phone number for Mrs Vassell?"

"I don't, you know, but if you call the church they'll put you in contact with her. Or you'll catch her on the premises tomorrow. She'll be happy to give you a Bible lesson."

CHAPTER 21

Wednesday, 9 January, 2.50 p.m.

Alone in the evidence room, Preddy stared at the crowded whiteboard. Jerome Baccus's and Eryka Malden's names remained prominent at the top of the board, side by side in death as in life, asking him to find out who killed them.

The top-tier suspects' names danced before his eyes. People who were all at the Grand Marquee, ostensibly for an evening out, possibly with the intention of committing murder. The lovelorn Tex Doran in the throes of a midlife crisis, unable to hold the attention of a young woman. The seemingly bankrupt Wesley Ashburn desperately needing to clinch the beach contract. The Livity Vendors Association members, a group of angry people led by Ras Bizzi, with sidekick Moses Fearon, a duplicitous man playing two sides. Preddy rubbed out the names of Nicki Younis and that of Suzanne Doran. He smiled wryly as he did so. Writing off women as possible murderers had almost been his undoing in the past, but Nicki had a solid alibi and Suzanne did not care enough to murder either party.

Spence was the first to enter the evidence room. She pushed open the door with her foot and greeted Preddy. Rabino followed shortly after carrying her notebook and a large bag of mints. As she caught Preddy's eye she paused and did a slow underarm throw in his direction.

"Catch, sir."

"Thanks." Preddy expertly snatched the mint from the air. He was relieved that Rabino was not antagonistic, but that had never been her style in all the years he had known her. "Not seen Detective Harris anywhere?"

"Him coming, sir." Spence sank into a chair and flopped back as if exhausted. "Him and Super outside de conference room chatting. Don't know what dem talking about, but dat white man so downright shady sometimes."

Preddy itched to take the bait. He wanted to unburden himself of his uncharitable thoughts about the secretive Glaswegian, but knew that would create unwelcome division in the team. Preddy had not even complained to Valerie, preferring to keep his girlfriend in the dark about the additional stresses on his mind. For now, only Spartan the parakeet would continue to be regaled with news of the goings-on at Pelican Walk. "We'll give him a few minutes," he said.

Spence and Rabino looked at each other in a conspiratorial manner.

"I want to run something by him when him come in," said Spence.

"What is it?" asked Preddy. "Or should I not ask?"

"You no hear de latest out of Glasgow, sir?" said Spence. "University of Glasgow, I should say."

"No, what?"

"They're talking reparations money," said Rabino.

"Oh yes, I did catch something on de radio." Preddy held up a hand to silence the detectives as he heard approaching footsteps.

A dishevelled Harris entered toting a cup of hot coffee. "Sorry about that, guys. Just got held up for a few minutes." Harris seemed aware of the continued silence that followed him across the room to his chair. He adjusted his seat and glanced at each of his colleagues in turn. "Wha' happen?" he said in his best Patois.

"We were just discussing de University of Glasgow." Preddy moved away from the whiteboard. He pulled out a seat directly in front of Harris and sat rapping his fingers on the tabletop. "All dat slave money, eeh?"

Harris's face began to reflect the tell-tale signs of his embarrassment. He studied each face as if trying to work out which one of the detectives had raised the matter.

Spence caught him staring at her and returned his gaze. "You always talking 'bout all de things going on back in Glasgow, but dat one missed you?"

Harris grew redder as he sipped his coffee, failing to hide his discomfort behind the emitting steam. "They plan tae give back the money tae UWI through grants and scholarships. That's a good thing!"

"I seem to remember last year you telling me dat Scottish people had nothing to do wid slavery," said Preddy. "Yet your alma mater can account for two hundred million pounds earned off de backs of slaves."

Rabino's expression was one of outrage. "Two hundred million? Jesus."

"You no shame?" Spence was warming to her subject. She turned her chair to face him and delivered a withering glare.

"Naw, I'm naw 'shame'." The blood percolated under Harris's face, darkening his pale complexion. "I'd be ashamed if they didnae offer tae give it back."

"You shoulda shame." Spence spread her fingers and clutched at her heart as if feeling pain. "If ah did me, me woulda shame so till!"

Harris glared at each officer in turn. "Is this a joke?"

"No," said Rabino coldly.

Spence narrowed her eyes and raised her voice. "Detective Harris, you think slavery is a joke? But is wha' dis me ah hear?"

"Whoa!" Harris held up an open palm as if to ward off attack. "I didnae say that. Slavery was wrong and shouldnae have happened. People were cruel, greedy and uncaring back then. I'm disgusted, but I wasnae alive in the seventeenth century."

"Everybody fold deir arms now and say, 'I wasn't dere.'" Preddy set his jaw. "How convenient, eeh?"

"All I can do is apologize for my ancestors." Harris shifted uncomfortably. "Naw sure what more ye want me tae do?"

Spence said, "You could contact de university and demand dat dey make reparations to we too . . . de police force."

"Eh?" Harris looked at her in confusion. "The university didnae ask for suggestions on where the money should go . . . It's going tae UWI so Jamaicans in education will get their share."

"And what about the interest on the money?" asked Rabino.

"Yes, dey must have plenty more millions to distribute." Spence gave him a death look. "You need to tell dem dat de Jamaica Constabulary Force needs money."

"Good idea." Preddy nodded. "We need new vehicles, better weapons and all of de wonderful modern high-tech equipment dat you like to tell us about."

"Yes, we could get a national fingerprint database and a DNA database," added Rabino. "Build more police stations than churches . . . You'd like that."

"Hold on! I dinnae think that's how reparations work." Harris removed a tissue from his pocket and wiped away beads of perspiration trickling down his neck. He reached across the table for the oscillating fan and turned it squarely onto his face. "They're naw going tae take suggestions from any Tom, Dick and Harry."

"So you don't even plan to try, eeh?" Spence kissed her teeth.

"And I thought you were different." Rabino shook her head solemnly. "When it boils down to it, you don't really want to help us."

"Och, come on!" protested Harris. He straightened his back and sat forward in his chair. "I'm just one man. I cannae—"

Preddy snorted and choked on a laugh. Spence threw back her head and joined him, slapping the desk in delight. Rabino grinned and chastised them both. "You two! You're useless! I hadn't even got started yet. Cho!"

"Hah! Hah!" Harris slumped back in his chair, relief evident in his face. "Jesus! I thought ye were about tae pull yer weapons on me. That wasnae funny."

"It did funny no rass!" Spence chuckled and dabbed at her eyes. "Is because you couldn't see your face or hear your voice."

"Never mind," said Rabino to the flustered Scotsman. "None of us are going to search any historical records looking for people named Harris who got rich off slavery."

"Speak for yourself, girl," said Spence, earning herself a playful elbow from Rabino.

"Don't worry," said Preddy. "Nobody is holding a thing against you, Detective Harris. Well done to Glasgow University for doing de right thing."

"I'm actually astounded they admitted to it," said Rabino. "Just think about it though. That's one single university. What about all the other UK universities? What about the other businesses built on slavery?"

"Dey'll never confess." Spence spoke with sureness. She reached for the table fan and turned it pointedly so that it again began showering air over everybody. "Scotland probably owes us a billion pounds, but nobody going offer a penny."

"Can we pick on England now?" asked Harris.

"Next time." Preddy clapped his hands together and picked up a black marker. "Right! Attention, people. Any luck with Wesley Ashburn, Detective?"

"I asked Ashburn tae come and see me, but he surprised me by inviting me tae his home in Fairview." Harris drained the last remnant of coffee and reached for his notepad. "He's dropped down the list of suspects if the only motive we're attaching tae him is money. I've seen his financial records. He does have money. He owns his house outright."

"So not a mortgaged-to-de-hilt mansion den?" asked Preddy.

Harris shook his head. "Nice place he's got, but quite modest . . . inherited from family. Four beds, three baths. Showed me the legal correspondence and the deeds. He was quite open, much more relaxed at home than he was at his office. He admitted he lied about some of the miniature models he showed us. Some of those deals collapsed long ago, but he keeps the designs on display tae showcase the work they can do. Apologized for misleading us."

"So he's got no mortgage to pay at home, but what about the Miranda Hill studio?" asked Rabino.

"He showed me the lease for Miranda Hill and his bank records. The mortgage is steep, but it gets paid every month, never missed a payment."

"So where is all his money coming from?" asked Preddy.

"Again, inherited property. His deceased dad owned a huge chunk of land in the Bogue Industrial Estate and built commercial property on it. Apparently, there used to be a massive sugar plantation down there in the fifties. Anyway, Ashburn collects decent rent from four sets of business tenants."

Preddy frowned. "Den why do his bank accounts show such large overdrafts? Both de personal account and de one for All Angles?"

"Ashburn hesitated over that one. Had tae press him a bit," Harris explained. "Those are local Jamaican accounts. He also has accounts in the States. It's all tae do with tax avoidance — 'tax planning', he called it. Something his accountant advised him tae do and arranged. Ashburn's clients tend tae be wealthy expats and people who still reside in the States but buy land here. Most of the money All Angles earns gets paid in US dollars tae an account in the States. The client account has close tae four million US dollars in it. Ashburn's personal account has eight hundred thousand US dollars."

"So Gavin Baccus was wrong about that," said Rabino. "Wesley Ashburn is minted. He wasn't desperate to get the Sugar Rush Beach contract at all."

"Might still have been vex 'bout how Jerome treated him on social media though," suggested Spence. "All dat taunting would make Ashburn mad as shad."

"I didnae read him as a vengeful man." Harris looked thoughtful. "His business is doing very well without the beach contract. It isnae hard tae ignore attacks on social media when ye're quietly successful. He said it himself before, he's a big man. Jerome's a boy. He had naw need for sparring back and forth on the internet."

Preddy fell into quiet contemplation for a moment. "I think you're right. I don't doubt dat de posts annoyed Ashburn because dey were nasty. But he knew something Jerome and Gavin didn't for all deir amateur sleuthing . . . He's practically a millionaire."

"And he doesnae know Eryka. On the night Eryka died, he was dining at Margaritaville with potential clients and I've got their numbers. If the sole motive we have is that Jerome said nasty things tae Ashburn, it's a very weak one. We have nothing that ties Ashburn tae either of them."

Preddy nodded. "Gavin Baccus suggested Ashburn could have sent Moses Fearon to apply for de usher job at the marquee, but now dat seems unlikely. Too much effort and planning for a beach contract dat he doesn't really need."

"So we take Wesley Ashburn out, sir?" asked Rabino.

Preddy hesitated and turned to the whiteboard. "Dere are way stronger suspects. I certainly want to know why Moses was waving militant placards on de beach one minute and carefully arranging white plastic chairs de next."

"Do we know where Moses is yet?" asked Harris. "I know he hangs around a lot with Ras Bizzi, but do we know where he lives?"

"We can't find him and we no have no address," said Spence, her voice heavy with frustration. "Ras Bizzi say Moses live in Glendevon area, but him don't know de address."

"A lady selling beach balls did say he could've gone to St Elizabeth to buy coconuts," offered Rabino.

"More likely Moses made himself scarce because he's heard on de street we want to question him," said Preddy. "See if we can get a couple of constables to help look for him. I want him in here before de weekend. He has a lot of questions to answer about his whereabouts, and I'd also like to know if he's acquainted wid Tex Doran."

"Yes, sir."

"I've had nothing useful on Eryka's car," said Preddy. "No sign of a struggle. Her DNA and Jerome's are all over it as expected. She got out of dat vehicle under her own steam, but didn't make it to her front door."

"What happening wid de car, sir?" asked Spence. "It attracting plenty attention."

"I'll say," said Harris. "I think every young constable in the building is interested in it."

"I know," said Preddy. "Her sister Alina isn't interested in it though, doesn't want anything to do with it. Mr Doran hasn't enquired about it either, so it will stay here for now. He has papers for it, so if he wants it he can take it."

Preddy picked up an evidence bag containing the awl and scrutinized it. "Earlier today I came across de name of an old hardware store called Hardy's. A high-street store popular in de seventies and eighties but long closed since. Dere's an Adventist lady associated wid it . . . a Mrs Vassell, who allegedly is de fount of information on de old town. She may have some ideas on where de awl came from."

Spence smiled at him. "So, you going church Saturday, sir?"

"No. At least dat wasn't my plan. I'm hoping to track her down tomorrow in Johns Haven. She has a class teaching Bible studies or something."

Spence placed an elbow on the table and a hand to her jaw while giving Harris her best side-eye. "Some people 'fraid church bad. If dem set eye pon Bible, dem head look more to explode."

"Aye, some people are like that, Detective Spence." Harris delivered a radiant smile with mockery in his tone.

"Good that we have different beliefs, but can exist happily together."

"Speaking of beliefs," said Preddy, "you free for church tomorrow, Detective Harris?"

Harris crushed his empty plastic cup beneath his fingers. "I was hoping ye wouldnae ask."

"Boy, Spence was right." Preddy smiled. "Some people really 'fraid ah church."

CHAPTER 22

Thursday, 10 January, 10.20 a.m.

As Preddy made his way to the Seventh Day Adventist church in Johns Haven he felt the need to get in the mood for what was to come. Finding gospel channels on the airwaves was not an easy feat and it took the detective a good while to succeed. Although there were more churches per square mile on the island than anywhere else in the world, that appearance of righteousness was not reflected on TV or radio. Only on Sundays were the airwaves filled with baritone voices giving dire warnings about the future for people who refused to turn to God.

Religion did not play a big role in his daily life. He had avoided church since his Sunday School days, attending only for weddings and funerals. He believed in the existence of a God, but often wondered exactly what He was doing. Every time there was a mass murder in the world, or a devastating earthquake or catastrophic flood, Preddy would feel less convinced of God's omnipresence. He had no idea how to explain it to his children other than spouting the mantra learned when he was a child: "*The Lord works in mysterious ways.*" Prior to his divorce he or his wife would take Roman and Annalee to Sunday School every week in Discovery Bay, St Ann, but since then the teenagers went only if they felt like it. Forcing them would only breed resentment and, in his view, religion was something they would either gravitate towards or not, without interference. Even when they stayed with him at Ironshore he did not mention church and neither did they. They were far more interested in worshipping the sun, sea and sand on the nearest beach.

Preddy smiled wryly. It would probably be a good while before he could head for Discovery Bay and entertain his offspring for the weekend. Luckily, they had grown to be quite understanding of police work. When Annalee was little she would stamp her feet and complain if he suddenly had to disappear on police business, but as she had grown older she would encourage him to go catch the suspect. Roman seemed to find the profession tiresome and had vowed to have nothing to do with work that always involved devastated, crying people. That was one way to look at it. It was a depressing part of the job and one that Preddy dreaded most, but there was also the good part, when he could bring some form of closure to distraught friends and relatives by confirming that the perpetrators had been captured.

A small Chinchillerz frozen-food outlet, whose bright orange-and-red frontage was conspicuous even from a distance, caught his attention. It had been many years since he had driven to the small village of Johns Haven, which was about five miles from the city centre, and there had been no Chinchillerz on this part of the highway back then. The frozen-food empire was expanding apace despite the fate of the two male heirs, one of whom was deceased while the other was incarcerated. He had not seen the owners, Terence and Ida Chin Ellis, since the sentencing, and he hoped for their sakes that they had come to peace with the tragic events of two years ago.

Off the main highway, the roads leading to Johns Haven became narrower and more winding, with few cars in sight. The area was almost entirely residential, with only a few untidy-looking minimarts dotted in between the small houses. Rush hour had passed, and the working people were likely to have already headed out to the commercial zones of the city, while others would be forced to travel as far as Lucea, Negril and Falmouth for employment. Preddy switched off the religious music and slowed down as he passed a primary school, from which high-pitched voices could be heard chanting the National Pledge. Vendors were camped outside the school, handcarts laden with sugary sweets and greasy snacks despite the "*No vending between these signs*" warnings installed by frustrated school administrators. The economy was such that everybody was hustling nowadays, and no amount of threats would make defiant vendors move on.

The small post office was boarded up, its dilapidated sign hanging sadly in the breeze. Rough weeds covered the gravel path that led to the damaged front door. Political slogans had been painted on the abandoned outer walls in the green and orange colours of the rival parties. There were no signs indicating the direction of the Adventist church, and Preddy wondered if he had already driven past it. He wound down the tinted windows and glanced from side to side as he drove, slowing to a crawl to peer at various properties, aware that many churches did not have the archetypal steeple, stone walls and stained-glass windows of yesteryear.

He continued up the winding road, and as he breached a corner he saw a line five cars long before he noticed the church. The vehicles were parked half on the grassy verge, half on the asphalt, there being no pavements on either side of the road. On an elevation above the vehicles was the church, set back a good distance from the roadside.

Preddy was pleased that it met his description of what a church should look like. He disliked the bland buildings indistinguishable from houses that were popping up in many towns following disputes between power-hungry church members. This church had character, being built of grey stone blocks, stained-glass windows and an attractive red steeple. An abundance of low-hanging trees provided welcome shade from the sun, and he could see some church members sitting on benches under them. The wooden gate did not allow for vehicles to pass through or get anywhere near the well-tended lawn.

The soft tone of a woman's voice emerged as a tinny sound from a microphone. The lack of excited noise was to be expected, as Seventh Day Adventists tended to operate on a much lower key than Baptists and Pentecostals. No bench-flinging, hand-flailing or talking in tongues, and certainly no running up and down the aisles or screaming, "Hallelujah!" Preddy did a U-turn, narrowly avoiding a ditch, and drove back down the road, pulling over behind the last parked car.

He retrieved his briefcase, straightened his suit and adjusted his tie as he walked through the open gate. A smartly dressed young couple on a bench were staring in deep concentration at something on a phone, their Bibles lying discarded. Preddy headed along the stone footpath and stepped off onto the grass to greet them.

"You know if Mrs Vassell in dere?" he asked.

"Yes, she inside, sir." The man gave Preddy a look that suggested he had endured enough preaching for the morning. "She's de one you can hear reading right now. Supposed to soon finish."

"Good, thank you. I don't know what she look like, but I don't want to miss her when she come out."

"Oh, she have on a long, bright green dress," said the woman. "You can't miss her. Only about twenty people in dere."

"Great, thanks."

Preddy continued up the path, stopping under a tree by an unoccupied bench. There he sat enjoying the gentle breeze while listening to Bible verses being read in a solemn tone. All around him the land was peaceful, with only chirping crickets and playful birds interrupting the flow of commentary. He rubbed his tired eyes. The strain of fast-forwarding through hours of CCTV footage at Pelican Walk was beginning to have a negative effect. He blinked rapidly a few times then closed his eyes and fell deep into thought.

As expected, every single male detective had paid a visit to Eryka's Audi, spending time admiring the wheels and chassis. Some sitting in it and pretending to drive, revelling in luxury they were never likely to experience. Every detective, except one. Only Iain Cotner had been missing from the parade of eager eyes. Cotner, who drove a modest car to and from work, had shown no interest in the high-end vehicle.

A tiny frown grew into a deep etch on Preddy's brow, and he opened his eyes in annoyance. The roaring sound of an engine increased in volume, polluting the serenity of the church grounds. He stood up. Harris was manoeuvring his motorbike through the gate. Preddy glanced at the church windows and could see a few heads leaning out. He winced and walked quickly towards the Scotsman.

"Whe' de rass?" he muttered.

Harris switched off the engine, removed his helmet and shook his ginger locks free. "Ma lip-reading skills arenae that great, Preddy, but I dinnae think that was 'good morning'."

"You annoying de church people, man."

"Och, sorry. Didnae realize it was that loud."

Preddy stared at him from head to foot. "Why you dress like dat?"

Harris set the pedal stand and climbed off the bike. He looked down at his khaki chinos and white polo-shirt. "What? They look all right tae me." He held out the hem of his shirt and used it as a fan, exposing his bare midriff. "Feels lovely and cool when ye're riding, but when ye stop, the heat sets in right away."

Preddy clenched his palms together, irritated by the man's jovial attitude. "Dis is a church, Detective Harris. I asked you to wear a jacket. You couldn't find one?"

"I'm hardly naked, am I?" Harris tucked his sunglasses into his pocket. "Och, come on, Preddy. It's naw as if we're going inside, is it?"

"You mean you wanted to avoid going inside." Preddy stared into Harris's unapologetic green eyes. "Look around you. You don't think a suit would have made a better impression?"

Harris brushed off the criticism with a grin. "Old ladies are always impressed by me for some odd reason. Mrs Vassell will be just fine."

United voices filled the air, a slow and mournful chorus that sounded as if the small congregation was flagging in both voice and spirit.

Preddy made a mental effort to stem his annoyance, which was not solely a result of Harris's informal appearance. The Scotsman had not graced Pelican Walk with his presence all morning, and Preddy wondered where he had come from — where his secret investigation had taken him. "You found de way all right?" he asked.

"Took a few wrong turns along the way, but it wasnae that bad. Signage could be better. I dinnae know how ye'd find somewhere like this in the dark."

The screech of wooden benches being dragged along stone floors grated on their ears. For Preddy it brought back memories of Sunday School, when the benches would be drawn closer together and the children were made to sit at the front to reduce the chance of misbehaviour. When the service was over, those who had behaved impeccably would be rewarded with a busta — a small, tough sweet made from dried coconut, sugar and ginger. Those children who had been unable to stifle giggles or keep still for an hour were escorted out by their upper arms with no treats.

The babble of indistinct conversations grew louder as members began to emerge from the Adventist church to the strains of the organist playing uplifting chords, as if to invigorate their legs and encourage their departure. Preddy studied them. The members were a mixture of the well-heeled and the middle class, most of whom were of retirement age, the men in tailored suits and women in formal dresses. It crossed Preddy's mind that some of these parishioners probably no longer lived in the district but had been brought up in Johns Haven and remained drawn here by pleasant memories, even though there were other Adventist churches more conveniently located in St James. It seemed natural that they would want to return to where they were most comfortable, and with the familiar face of an elderly teacher whose voice they knew and trusted. If he ever felt the need to rejoin church, he too would rather go all the way to his family village in Westmoreland.

"I think dis is her," said Preddy.

"Which one?"

"In de green dress, carrying a silver walking stick."

The elderly lady used one hand to clutch the arm of a young man and the other to manage her walking stick. Her hair was completely white and pulled up into a neat bun at the top of her head. She was plump, and her exposed, swollen ankles were evidence of circulation problems. Her long-sleeved dress was buttoned up to the neck, yet despite the soaring temperature, her appearance was unruffled. The young man gently released Mrs Vassell's grip on his arm and went back into the church.

Preddy watched impatiently, wishing she would continue towards him, but she stayed put, smiling and nodding with the parishioners. Her young escort returned and handed Mrs Vassell a Bible, which she took and squeezed his hand. She then set off down the incline moving at a decent pace with the aid of the cane.

"Let's meet her halfway." Preddy set off towards her.

"Aye, before she gets stopped again."

A female member caught up with Mrs Vassell before the detectives did. She grasped the old lady's hand and kissed her on the cheek. The detectives stopped and stood waiting as unobtrusively as possible for the cheerful conversation to end.

"She's like an ancient rock star," muttered Harris with pained smile. "Wonder if I can get her tae autograph ma notebook?"

"Good morning, Mrs Vassell," said Preddy as soon as the other lady had moved on. "I'm Detective Preddy and dis is Detective Harris. We're from Pelican Walk."

She looked up at him through rheumy brown eyes then reached for his hand. "Hello, Detective Preddy. How you do?"

Her voice was strong and her grip firmer than Preddy had imagined it would be. "Very pleased dat I got to meet you."

She loosened her grip and stared at Harris. "Detective Harris?"

"Aye, Mrs Vassell, that's me." He shook hands with her.

"You live in Mo Bay?" she asked.

"I do." Harris smiled. "Originally from Glasgow, but I'm based at Pelican Walk for a few years."

"Let's have a seat on de bench over dere for a minute." Preddy pointed at the seat he had recently vacated. "Rest your legs for a bit while we talk."

Mrs Vassell's gaze landed on the motorbike near the bench. She looked from Preddy to Harris and back. "Is one of you was making up that whole heap of noise in the place?" The elderly lady made little attempt to hide her displeasure.

Preddy smiled at her then looked at Harris, savouring the familiar creep of red flooding the white man's face.

"Sorry, I wasnae thinking, tae be honest, Mrs Vassell. Sort of got used tae riding around without having tae think about noise."

The old lady lowered herself onto the bench with Preddy's help. "You ride that big old noisy thing to your church, sir? Pastor must well vex!"

"I'm naw a church man, ma'am. Ride it tae work sometimes. I dinnae think it disturbs ma colleagues."

"I going pray for you, sir." She shook her head and looked at him with pity. "You need to get Jesus into your life."

Harris sat beside her and shuffled uncomfortably. "Thank ye, ma'am. That's, er . . . very kind of ye."

"None of you have on wedding ring. You not married."

"Divorced," said Preddy. "Might do it all again in a year or two though."

Mrs Vassell gave him an encouraging nod. "Yes, sir. Good idea. And you and your wife must stay in church." She glanced at Harris, who averted his gaze. "What about you, sir. Not married?"

"And naw looking tae go back there again, ma'am."

"Chuh, once is nothing. Some people do it two or three times. You have children?"

"Aye, naw in Jamaica, but I have three of them."

"And none of them don't know God?"

"If they do, they forgot tae mention him," said Harris. "They tend tae tell me about most of their acquaintances though."

"Young people nowadays don't have God in their lives. That's why Jamaica stay so. We need people to pray and repent. Turn to their Bibles." She squinted at Preddy. "You have God in your life, sir?"

"I was raised a Christian," said Preddy. "Not in de Adventist Church though."

"Good. I don't worry about which denomination people choose as long as they choose God." She turned to glare at the wilted Harris. "You know that God is in foreign too, not just Jamaica?"

"So I hear, ma'am," said Harris. "I'm sure God is giving all foreigners as much attention as they deserve, and who am I tae take up His time?"

"Sound like the Devil strong inna you, man!"

Preddy decided that Mrs Vassell was warming too much to her calling of preaching, and besides, Harris had suffered enough. "Don't worry 'bout him, Mrs Vassell. Detective Harris happily attends our morning devotions at Pelican Walk, so I'm sure he'll soon be drawn to a church on weekends." He ignored Harris's raised eyebrow. "As police we can't only rely on God. As you know, we need evidence and witnesses to catch de people trying to destroy innocent lives. Right now we're trying to find out who took de lives of Jerome Baccus and Eryka Malden."

"Those poor young people." She bowed her head in reverence at their memory. "I'm telling you. Some parts of this parish have changed so much over the years. Fewer people come to night service nowadays. As it get dark they don't want to come out again. I come out. No gunman will make me cannot leave my house when I want to. I tell you, the young people have a lot of anger towards one another though. Any little argument them start shoot."

"We're doing our best tae stop it," said Harris. "Jerome and Eryka were good friends, and we think they were killed by the same person."

"I did hear something about it on the radio." Mrs Vassell cradled the handle of her stick with both hands. "Sad to say sometimes the bad news doesn't stick in my head anymore. Unless I directly know the person."

"I know what you mean." Preddy took out his phone and brought up the gallery. "This shop, Hardy's, looks like a hardware shop. You know it?"

"Of course I know it. Papa's shop!" She smiled, clasped his hand in a firm grip and moved the screen further away from her eyes. "Those were the days. I was a young woman back then. So many nice shops on the high street selling quality goods. My father was one of the first Black men to own his shop." She chuckled with pride and a glint of light crossed her eyes. "People called Papa 'hard ears' because they were against the idea of him opening a shop, afraid he'd lose his money. He was stubborn, didn't listen and decided to call the new shop 'Hard Ears' to annoy them. When he ordered a sign for it, the sign maker thought he'd said 'Hardy's'. Mama saw the first proofs and decided that name sounded more appropriate and wouldn't let him change it. People used to come in and call him Mr Hardy, but our family name is Turner. Some people of my age still call me Miss Hardy."

Preddy liked the animated look on her face and the happy sound of her voice. He hated to interrupt her reminiscing, but solving the murders had to be his priority. He carefully extracted his hand from her grip and scrolled through the phone gallery. This time he held the phone a good distance from her eyes. "Have a look at this tool, Mrs Vassell. You ever see one like it? It's an awl. Very old. See it has a point with a small hole in it and de handle with a turtle pattern. We're told it's made of lignum vitae."

"We were thinking maybe yer dad would've worked with lignum vitae back in the day," Harris added.

"Hold it up little."

Preddy did as she asked.

She squinted. "Wait, that turtle . . . Father Jesus! Papa did make some like it, not to sell. Mainly to amuse people's children during school holidays. This design wasn't his standard practice at all. There was a large workshop at the back of the premises where he kept some tools. He would carve animals into the handles of tools that never left the shop. It was like his personal stamp." She twisted Preddy's wrist to view the photo from another angle. "Back then nobody really followed any health-and-safety rules, children were always in and out of the shop playing. I guess the parents were just glad to be rid of them."

Preddy leaned towards her as adrenalin rushed through his body. "Dere were more tools, like dis one?"

"I remember him carving the designs on an awl, a hammer, a plane and a saw. So he had a turtle, cow, mongoose, pig." She smiled. "Boy, you taking me back a long time now, but I remember as clear as anything. He loved his work and he loved having people around him while he worked."

"What happened tae the tools?" asked Harris.

"If I remember rightly, he gave them away." She thought for a good while, her lips pursing then evening out as she reflected. "When ill-health took him he sold the shop to another merchant. The tools went to a sandals maker who had a small shop just a few doors down from ours. That man had children always hanging around too — his kids, and others that I'm not even sure who they belonged to. Sometimes you'd see a few little girls, but it was many little boys playing around, throwing stones at one another. Two unruly boys were always moving around the tools in the sandals shop. Sometimes the poor man used to come and borrow tools from Papa, particularly the awl, to bore straps in sandals." She stared off into the distance and smiled wistfully. "When the boys wanted money they used to make up little poems and songs to perform for Papa. You want to see them beating tin can, making rhythm. Then he'd give them pennies and they'd be off to buy blue draws!"

Harris paused his pen above his notebook and raised an eyebrow at Preddy. "Should I ask?"

"It's a form of dessert made mainly of sweet potatoes, green bananas and coconut milk," explained Preddy. "Taste nice. Spence makes it sometimes." He turned back to Mrs Vassell. "Dat man who used de awl to make sandals must have passed away long time?"

"Long-long time! Papa outlived him." She waved an acknowledgement to a couple of elderly churchgoers heading towards the gate. "The boys would be in their late sixties by now. Big grey-back men!"

"Do ye remember their names?" asked Harris.

She stared up into the tree above her head while she thought. "No, sir," she said eventually. "Wish I could remember, but I can't. Little devils, the lot of them."

Preddy took some photos from his briefcase. "Okay, I know dis is a long shot, but look at dese photos. Do any of dese men remind you of de boys?"

He handed Mrs Vassell two photos and she shook her head. "Uh-uh. Poor me to go remember faces from decades ago."

"De one in your right hand is Terrell Doran . . . People call him Tex. De other one is Wesley Ashburn, who runs a company called All Angles. Names mean anything to you?"

Again she shook her head. "No." She pointed at Doran. "He needs to stop with the black dye or use a lighter colour. This makes him look foolish."

Preddy rustled around in his briefcase again and pulled out a copy of the *Western Mirror*. "Dis is a photo of de Livity Vendors Association members. Look at de four men closely. Any of dem remind you of de boys?"

She squinted and studied the individual faces. "No, sir. This one have bald head. That one is Rasta. This other one looks like he has locks too. One have on cap, I can't even see his face too good. Two of these men don't even look so old."

"True," said Preddy. "I was thinking dey could be related to de boys you knew — deir sons, perhaps?"

"Oh, I understand, Detective. My granddaughters look like me, yet my daughter doesn't look anything like me. Strange, eeh?" Mrs Vassell moved the newspaper back and forth from her eyes, trying to get a better focus. "You should see my pictures from I was a girl, they look nothing like me as a middle-aged woman and nothing like me now."

Preddy watched her, waiting hopefully as she studied each face in turn.

"Everybody hair grey now. Everybody taller, some fatter, some slimmer." She looked across at Harris. "You look now like you looked as a boy?"

"Naw," Harris conceded. "Had freckles back then and huge cheeks. I'm glad they're gone."

"Do any of de names under de photo bring back any memories?" asked Preddy.

Mrs Vassell mumbled the names to herself as she read. "I wish I could help, but I was never that good with names anyway. Not great with names or faces. I'm better with voices. You know, I have a very keen ear. As soon as I pick up the phone and someone says hello . . . as long as I've spoken to them before, I know who it is."

The young man who had retrieved Mrs Vassell's Bible for her earlier walked up to them. "Come, your taxi reach, Grandma!"

"Oh, I'm coming," she said. "Tell him to wait a little. You need anything else, gentlemen?"

"Not at de moment, Mrs Vassell." Preddy tucked the newspaper back into his briefcase and closed it. "Thank you for your help."

Harris helped Mrs Vassell to stand up. "If ye do remember any names or anything at all, do let us know."

"Yes, sir, I will." She pinched his arm with a twinkle in her eye. "You going find God, Detective Harris. I will see to it. I know you not looking for Him, but I going see to it that you find Him!"

CHAPTER 23

Thursday, 10 January, 12.10 p.m.

Moses Fearon's time had run out. Officers throughout St James had been notified that he was a person of interest, and although residents of the volatile community of Glendevon denied knowing who he was or where he lived, a sighting had been reported elsewhere. The elusive Moses had been spotted leaving a wholesale store at Westgreen Plaza touting bags of plastic straws and was now said to be in the plaza's car park, where his cart of green coconuts stood next to a burger stand.

Spence and Rabino were patrolling One Man Beach at the opposite end of the city. Upon hearing the news on the police radio, Spence did a U-turn in the unmarked police jeep and drove at high speed along the boulevard.

"At last. Dat blasted man!"

"No wonder we couldn't find him. Wouldn't have thought he'd get great sales down Westgreen where there are no beaches."

"People thirsty everywhere and de people down dere must tired ah box drink and soda," replied Spence. "Him will make money, man. We going show him dat you can run, but you can't hide."

They turned into the car park that serviced the small plaza of shops, which included a laundrette, pet shop and supermarket, as well as a few eateries. Spence rolled down the windows and both detectives scouted the area.

Rabino sniffed in the air. "My nose is telling me that's the hamburger van over there. They said his cart is behind it."

Spence parked adjacent to the bright red food van with "*burga*" and "*hot daag*" scrawled like graffiti all over the bodywork. The overwhelming smell of sizzling meat and onions hung in the air. A youth wearing a white apron and white hat was tending to a queue of customers from the nearby business places. Some patrons held umbrellas over their heads to shelter from the relentless sun.

The detectives climbed out of their vehicle and walked past the customers. To the public, the officers looked like any other casually dressed women — Spence in black trousers and red sleeveless blouse, Rabino in blue jeans and orange short-sleeved blouse. Both wore dark jackets to disguise the guns in their waistbands. Rabino's large camera hung from a strap around her neck.

"See de devil over dere." Spence whipped her handcuffs out of her pocket and held them behind her back as she walked towards him.

"We arresting him?" whispered Rabino.

"If him won't come willingly, I going arrest him arse for illegal vending. Anything to get him back to Pelican Walk. Me tired ah him already!"

An unsuspecting Moses Fearon was demonstrating his expertise with the machete for his new customer base. He cleanly chopped the top off a large green coconut and the husk flew to the ground, exposing the tasty white flesh inside. Colourless coconut water spilled from the opening and splashed his arm. He laid the machete on the cart, placed a straw in the coconut and handed it to a grateful customer.

Rabino clicked a few noiseless shots of the handcart from different angles, before lowering her camera. As the two detectives drew closer, Moses looked up and smiled.

"Coming to you, ladies, just join de line." He wiped his hands on a greasy-looking rag hanging from his cart and turned back to his waiting customers. "What price coconut you want, sah? Nuff water in de big one and dem well sweet."

Spence clapped her hands twice, demanding his attention. "We not joining no damn line. We no want no blasted coconut."

"Seh wha', lady?"

"Moses Fearon, isn't it?" said Rabino.

He frowned and looked from one to the other, as if trying to force his fuzzy brain to explain the presence of these women.

"Pelican Walk Police," said Rabino.

Moses licked his lips and gulped as he stared at her. "Laad God."

"God might well be female, but I'm not Her. It's Detective Rabino and this is Detective Spence."

The customers murmured among themselves as they watched the face-off.

"Two day now we ah drive up and down in de hot sun looking for you." Spence waved the shiny handcuffs under his nose. "You can come on you two leg, or you can come on you belly. Is up to you."

Moses twisted the damp flannel in his hands. "Me hear seh you looking for me, yes. What me do?"

"Why didn't you call or come in and ask that question?" asked Rabino. "Most people with nothing to hide call the police when they hear that they're looking for them."

Some of the customers in the adjacent line for the burger van turned to listen to the conversation. Even the young man selling the spicy fast food leaned out to see what was going on.

"Sorry, Officer," Moses mumbled. "Ask me what you come to ask me. Ah work me ah work, but me can talk."

"Look here!" Spence glared at him. "We no come here to negotiate wid you, you know? You coming wid us right now. Detective Preddy have questions for you."

Moses looked at the surrounding faces as if hoping one of his patrons would speak up for him, but no one seemed inclined to challenge the officers. "De Norwood detective?" he whispered.

"Yes, him same one," said Spence. "We ready."

A young woman seemed to be enjoying the confrontation while acknowledging her plight. "Look like we nah get no coconut today!"

The woman behind her chuckled and shook her head in agreement. "Bwoy, it no look so."

"Wha' 'bout me cart!" wailed Moses. "If me leave it here so dem will tief it."

"Nobody no business wid you rass coconut," said Spence. "Ah murder business we ah deal wid!"

The hamburger van owner called out to Moses. "Gwaan wid dem, boss. Me will watch de cart! Nobody can't take it 'way."

"Thank you, man!" Moses retrieved a piece of tarpaulin the size of a large tablecloth from the bottom of the cart and spread it over his produce, trying to conceal as many coconuts as possible.

Spence jingled the handcuffs close to his ears, which encouraged an increase in speed.

"Me coming, Officer. Me coming!"

Moses reluctantly climbed in the back seat of the jeep grumbling incoherently.

Rabino half-turned in her seat to look at him. "You have something to say, save it until you get to the interview room."

"Me no know wha' Preddy coulda want wid me." The nervousness was evident in his voice as he perched on the edge of the passenger seat.

"Detective Preddy to you," snapped Spence. She started the engine.

"Dat wicked man kill off plenty man ah Norwood and now him want me. Me see him last week, him and one white man, but me never 'fraid cause me know him cyah do nutten when white man ah watch him." Beads of perspiration appeared on the man's glistening brow. "You better make sure you in de room too, you know? Cause next ting you going hear lie dat me attack him and him haffi shoot me!"

"Nobody not going shoot you," said Spence with little attempt to calm his nerves. She eyed him while adjusting the rear-view mirror. "Sit back in de seat, sir. Me no like how you close up behind me."

"Seatbelt on," ordered Rabino.

Moses sank back in defeat, fastened his seatbelt and rubbed his moist palms on bare knees.

"Don't worry," said Rabino. "There'll be cameras on you at all times and another detective will be present. If not one of us, it will be Detective Harris. That's the Scottish man you seem to think is your protector."

"Yes, Detective Harris him name," said Moses. "Dem better keep him at Pelican Walk. If him was at Norwood, Pred . . . Detective Preddy couldn't shoot up nobody."

"Ah whe' de rass." Spence slowed down and turned sideways to shoot him a death stare. "First of all, Detective Preddy never shoot a soul. Secondly, Detective Harris was not on de island at dat time. And thirdly, if you mention one more word 'bout Norwood I going make sure you never sell another rass coconut in de whole ah Area One!"

"That's St James, Hanover, Westmoreland and Trelawny," added Rabino.

"All right, sistren. All right!"

"You chat too much 'bout white man dis and white man dat, and me no wah hear it," warned Spence. "Like say white man can make Jamaica better."

"Me hear you," muttered Moses. He avoided her steely glare by gazing at the blur of passing vehicles as the jeep gained speed.

"Don't bother make plan to lie to de white man neither," said Spence. "Just because you see him look so? Him ah no fool."

"No, me not going lie to him, Officer." The man lowered his eyes as if fearful that Spence could see into his mind.

"Me no have nutten to lie 'bout. Me is a good man. Never murder a soul inna me life. All me do is walk sell coconut and heng out wid Ras Bizzi. Him can tell you. Never do a ting dat coulda make police want me."

Rabino offered him a half-smile. "I'm glad you plan to cooperate. You can tell Detective Preddy all about what you did and didn't do."

Spence pulled up at Pelican Walk. She climbed out and yanked the back passenger door open. "Make haste!"

The fugitive obeyed and glanced nervously at the lobby entrance, where a ram goat stood staring inside as if contemplating whether to sneak past the desk officer. "Wait, you have goat pon duty at dis station?"

His attempt at humour was shot down by Spence. "You going wish goat did a run tings, just wait."

"Come on, Mr Fearon." Rabino moved aside, allowing him to precede her. "I'll put you in an interview room. You won't have to wait long." She jerked her head in Spence's direction. "She wasn't joking by the way. Don't get smart in there. Tell the truth and you just might get to spend tonight in your own bed."

* * *

Preddy pushed the door without knocking and entered the interview room with Harris close behind him.

"Well, Mr Fearon, we didn't get much of an introduction de other day, but I take it you remember us?" Preddy sat down in front of him and slammed a file on the table. "Detective Preddy and Detective Harris."

"Yes, sir," said a meek Moses. "Me remember when you was talking to Ras Bizzi."

Harris nodded politely at him as he pulled out a seat. "Hello again, Moses."

"Hello, Detective Harris." His relief at the white man's presence was evident in his voice, and his heaving chest gradually settled.

"So." Preddy switched off the table fan. "What's your version of what happened at de Grand Marquee?"

"Version? Me no have no version!"

"Seems as if you've been a busy man, Mr Fearon." Preddy removed two photographs from a manila envelope and pushed them across the table. "Is who dat wearing black trousers and white shirt?"

"Ah me, sir." Moses blinked rapidly and ran an index finger over his chin.

Preddy tapped the second photo. "And is who dat in shorts and vest waving a placard reading, '*No vendors, no peace, no apartheid beach*'?"

"Ah me dat too."

"Care tae explain?" said Harris.

"And please, no bull," added Preddy. "It's been a long day and we're not in de mood."

Moses kept his eyes on the photos as tiny beads of perspiration grew on his shiny scalp. "Me know dis look bad, Officer, but is not what you thinking. Is just some extra money me was looking. Time hard. Me hear pon street dat one employment agency looking for workers, so me quick-quick go downtown go register. Dey wanted people ready and willing to work wid Misser Baccus, so me sign up."

"Ye signed up tae work with the same man who's apparently hated by all of the Livity vendors, just tae earn a few extra dollars?"

"Ah truth me telling you, bossie! Me no love de Baccus man, but me no hate him neither. An' my pickney, dem have to go back to school. You know how much notebook cost, and den to go find bus fare and lunch money? It hard, man!" His imploring eyes looked from one detective to the other, finally fixing on Harris. "Is just two hundred dollar an hour dem was paying, but me couldn't turn up me nose at dat."

"Ye were there from at least six o'clock that evening. And then a few hours later, Jerome Baccus was dead, stabbed through the heart. Ye expect us tae believe that was just a coincidence, eh, Moses?"

"Laad God!" Moses slapped his palm on the table and tossed his head. "Me know is de Baccus man murder you wah pin pon me! Me know it!" He wailed and pressed his forehead on the table. "All when dem woman detective don't want tell me nutten, me know!"

"Calm down, Moses." Harris rapped on the table beside the suspect's ear. "Look at me. Look up. We're going tae do this our way without the dramatics."

Moses raised his head reluctantly. "As dere is a God! De only time me talk to Jerome Baccus was when him come hand me a badge wid me name on it dat afternoon. Him say all ushers must wear badge at all times. Never see him again in de evening. Me never kill dat man. Is not me!"

"Ye've been hiding from us for days. What did ye think we wanted tae see ye for?"

Moses ran both hands over his bare head as if searching for a cap he was not wearing. "Is a girl me did ah try talk to inna patty shop, pretty girl. She run me. Me and her start cuss. She tell me her man ah police and she going fix me business. Next day me hear say police looking for me."

Harris shook his head in disdain.

"Is true me telling, sir! Me never know is murder you want talk to me 'bout till todeh. Me no deal wid murder."

Preddy leaned closer towards the agitated man. "We want to believe you," he said. "Maybe it wasn't your plan? Maybe somebody put you up to it and you went along wid it. Times are hard, eh, Moses?"

"No, sir!" The suspect shook his head even more vehemently. "Nobody no put me up to nutten. Not even ten million dollar woulda get me murder nobody. Dem woulda haffi give me whole heap more money, fake passport and visa fi run go foreign!"

"Och, really? That's yer price?"

Moses quickly added, "But, ah no me!"

Preddy pushed another photograph at him. "You know dis man?"

"No, never see him before. Is who?"

226

"His name is Terrell Doran, also known as Tex."

"Don't know him at all, Misser Preddy, no, sir."

"What about dis one? You know him?"

Moses pulled the second photo closer. "Of course me know him. Me no *know him* know him. Me see him pon TV. Is Wesley Ashburn, another big man looking to capture Dowdy Beach . . . and run off Livity people from sell tings. Ashburn and Baccus wicked together. None of dem don't care 'bout poor people."

"So ye've never met him then, Mr Ashburn?" asked Harris.

"Not up close, like how you and me sit here so. But believe me, we did plan to go look fi him." Moses spoke with more than a hint of venom. "Him going put up a marquee and do a presentation too . . . sometime dis month. We will be dere to complain. Me no know how politician just make big man come walk all over likkle man, just because dem have money. Is years some of we hustling. Dem run we from beach to beach, run we from Sam Sharpe Square, run we from main road. Wha' dem want we fi do?"

"I'm sure yer concerns are being considered," said Harris. "Sometimes it takes a while tae get around tae everybody."

"No, bossie." Moses snorted. "Dat is not how tings work inna Jamaica. We haffi take de fight to dem! If we no take it to dem . . . dog nyam we supper!"

Preddy studied the irate suspect. "And if Wesley Ashburn advertises for ushers to lay out seats for his presentation, you'll turn it down, of course?"

"Turn it down?" Moses shot Preddy a defiant look. "You think me can go home go tell my woman dat me no want rich man money? Woman no want man widout money."

"Ye're afraid she'll give ye bun?" said Harris.

Moses stared at the Scotsman in surprise. "Same way, bossie! And me love my woman. Me no want she gimme bun!"

"No clash of priorities and morals for you den, sir," said Preddy in a mocking tone.

Moses showed no sign of embarrassment. He shrugged and stared at Harris as if seeking endorsement. "All me know say . . . me no want nobody come mash up me dolly house."

"Did ye know Eryka Malden, the lady that was killed at Cherry Walk?"

"No, Misser Harris." Moses placed a hand on his heart. "As God is my witness, me never know her. Me was home all night. From de state of emergency start rum bar close-up early-early. Me no even bother go road most night again and me no really have beer money fi spend like one time. Me buy few beer from supermarket, put inna fridge."

"Ye have someone who can provide an alibi?" asked Harris.

"Provide wha'?"

"Proof that ye were at home that night. Somebody who saw ye?"

"Yes, sir." Moses brightened and sat upright. "My woman and kids, and de two neighbour next door. We did outside a drink and reason till late. Den we lock up and put de kids to bed. Me go to my bed by midnight. My car inna garage since before Christmas, so if me to go reach Cherry Walk me woulda haffi flag down taxi. Only ah eediat woulda do dat!"

"What your father do for a living?" asked Preddy.

Moses frowned. "My daddy was a school caretaker from since me born. Him a old-old man, retired long time. Why?"

"Give us a minute." Preddy gathered the photos back into the envelope and rose. Harris followed him out the door and into the adjoining room. Rabino and Spence were there watching through the reflecting glass.

"What do you make of him?" asked Preddy.

"He's convincing," said Rabino.

"Aye, he is that," agreed Harris. "Doesnae want tae get bun, but is happy chatting up a policeman's girlfriend. Still, I'm naw getting 'murderer' from him."

Spence shrugged. "Time hard, but it seem funny to me dat he would take a penny from Baccus. Most people wouldn't do business wid an enemy for no amount of money in de world. Me wouldn't do it."

"Moses isn't that discerning," said Rabino. She moved closer to the glass and pressed her nose against it, staring at the interviewee. "Money is money to him. Doesn't matter whose."

"'He who pays de piper calls de tune,'" quoted Preddy. "We only have one piece of solid evidence . . . de awl. Unless we can tie it to him, we have nothing. We'll let him go, but keep a tail on him. See if he tries to get in contact wid any of de other suspects."

Rabino reached for the door handle. "We'll find a couple of constables to follow him."

"Blagrove and Mitchell are usually quite helpful." Spence followed her out. "Check de canteen."

When the female detectives were long out of sight, Harris opened the interview room door and beckoned to the suspect. "Time tae go, Moses. Ye're free."

The man was on his feet quickly and almost ran through the door.

"Hold on!" Harris backed up to avoid being knocked over by the eager man and whipped out his phone. "Give us a contact number before ye go."

Moses mumbled the number and Harris instantly called it. Moses took the ringing phone from his pocket and waved it in the air. "See, me not lying, Misser Harris."

"Good to see," said Preddy.

"Me tell you, me no have a ting to hide, Misser Preddy. Not a ting."

Moses strode away at pace and cast a nervous glance over his shoulder before he reached the exit.

CHAPTER 24

Thursday, 10 January, 2.30 p.m.

The four detectives had eaten lunch at a seafood restaurant on the beach less than a mile from Pelican Walk. Its popularity with the locals had a lot to do with its reputation for not diluting spicy flavours to cater for the unadventurous palettes of tourists, preferring instead to stick with traditional ways of cooking. Preddy was also keen on it because the operators resisted the temptation to play music of any kind, leaving patrons free to enjoy the soft sounds of the sea and the caws of the expert terns that fished in it, as well as their own conversations. Most other beach diners blared reggae or soca from noon till dusk, and for Preddy, more often than not, it was an intrusion into his thoughts.

The bar counter contained remnants of shared plates of fried snapper fish, bammies and festivals. Preddy had done his best to steer their lunchtime chatter away from work and onto the frivolous things in life, an effort which usually succeeded once they were off the grounds of Pelican Walk and away from the radar of the lurking superintendent. They had swapped the grey walls and discoloured white ceilings of the police station for green bamboo walls and a thatched roof, through which glimpses of blue skies could be seen. The breeze was pleasantly strong and pushed frothy surf up onto the warm white sand that petered out mere metres from their padded bar stools. Yachts and catamarans bearing contented tourists and well-off locals glided past in the distance.

Preddy glanced at his watch. Soon they would have to get back to work. Murder was the dark cloud that would forever shroud the island's inimitable beauty.

"When I win Super Lotto, is one like dat I going buy," declared Spence, pointing at a glass-bottom boat. "All of my time will be spent on de sea. No more fighting traffic in cars."

"Not all of us have trouble getting through traffic," said Rabino with a glance at Harris.

"Och, ye havenae noticed then? Didnae ride the bike this morning."

"Is what happen to it?" Spence shook her glass of orange juice, rattling the ice, and took a long drink.

"Er, nothing. It's working fine." Harris carried a look of slight embarrassment. "I've been assigned an unmarked car, a grey Corolla, for now, but I want a jeep — better on the roads. Have tae wait a few weeks."

Preddy sipped his carrot juice while watching Harris and decided to remain silent. He waited for the expected verbal onslaught from Spence, but it did not arrive. She was still gazing wistfully at the sea. Preddy smiled to himself. This was the ideal place for Harris to throw these sorts of grenades, as the sea and air were able to quell the explosion of indignation. Later, Spence was bound to cotton on that Harris now had two vehicles when some officers had none, and the resentment would surely flow.

Preddy wanted to recline and enjoy the peace, but instead he straightened his shoulders and inhaled. "Time to get back, people." He waved at their waitress, indicating that he needed the bill.

"That was good stuff," said Harris. He wiped his fingers on a napkin. "I need tae learn tae cook like this and do ma own fried fish. I cannae get it right."

Rabino rose and stretched her arms skywards, bending her waist from side to side. "You'll never do it."

"Yer confidence is noted, Detective Rabino."

Spence got up and brushed the festival crumbs from her blouse. "Some ah you too 'fraid ah spice. Your fish coulda never taste so."

"I'm naw 'fraid ah spice' at all!" Harris was indignant. "Far from it."

Preddy allowed himself a faint smile. "Anyway, you know de cookshops would miss you badly. What would deir weekly takings be without you?"

"True. Cannae find the time tae practise anyway."

"Me belly full!" Spence groaned and fingered her tightened waistband. "If I did wear belt wid dis trousers, I would take it off and bore ah next hole."

"I know what you mean," said Rabino. "I need to go for a long walk."

Preddy stared at Spence. His eyes went to her waist, focused on the belt and his face took on a faraway look.

Spence subconsciously drew in her stomach and grinned at him. "Give it two hours, sir, it soon go down." She slid her bag over her shoulder and dangled her keys in front of Rabino. "Come, girl, is you driving."

"Evidence room, half an hour," said Preddy.

Preddy paid the bill and drove back to Pelican Walk with Harris. He glanced at the Scotsman's grey Corolla in the car park. It appeared to be in excellent condition. He wondered who Superintendent Brownlow had deprived of the vehicle at such short notice to give it to the foreigner, but did not dwell on the matter.

Harris climbed out. "I'll just grab some water and be with ye in a bit."

Preddy was distracted and did not respond. He moved swiftly through the lobby, ignoring Officer Wilson, who raised his head from his newspaper as the detective rushed past him. Preddy leaped up the stairs two at a time and strode to the evidence room.

He donned rubber latex gloves and pulled a large transparent bag from a cabinet, checked the contents then pushed it back. That bag contained the clothes from Eryka's bed — her shorts, vest and sweater. He pulled out another bag and slid the contents onto the table. Jerome's logo shirt emerged with trousers and a leather belt, the clothes that he had left on a chair at Eryka's apartment. Preddy held the belt up to the light. He was still studying it when the other detectives entered the room.

Rabino pressed her back against the cool wall. "What's with the belt, sir?"

"Holes," said Preddy.

"Holes?" Harris tossed back his fringe and used his unopened water bottle to cool his face, rolling it over his warm cheeks.

Preddy waved the belt in Spence's direction. "It was something you said." He opened a drawer and removed the bag containing their only piece of physical evidence, which he held aloft. "Suppose de awl made holes in Jerome's belt?"

The three detectives stared at Preddy with blank looks on their faces.

"I don't get it, sir," said Spence.

"Extra holes," explained Preddy. "If you needed to add extra holes to a belt, you wouldn't take it back to a shop. You'd bore your own, wid something pointed and sharp like a nail or an ice pick or . . ." He paused deliberately, waiting for confirmation.

"An awl," said Rabino. "I've never added extra holes to my belts . . . worried I'd spoil them, but I've wanted to."

"Me too." Spence patted her distended stomach. "Like today."

Preddy nodded. "When we spoke to Eryka, she said something about Jerome putting on weight, you remember? Dese holes don't look uniform to me . . . de two end ones?"

Harris donned a pair of latex gloves and slid the box along the table towards Spence. He took the belt from Preddy and squinted at the holes. "I think ye're right."

Spence and Rabino took turns studying the pierced leather, while Harris flicked over the pages of his well-worn notebook. "Eryka did say that she bought presents for him . . . a leather wallet and belt."

Rabino glanced at Harris. "You still have that magnifying glass?"

"Aye." Harris walked over to a drawer and returned with the glass.

Rabino moved it slowly along the leather strap. "I see. These two aren't as uniform as the others, but it's a pretty good job.

"The human hand isnae as precise as a mechanical boring machine, naw matter how skilled the craftsman."

"What does it all mean, sir?" asked Rabino.

Preddy placed his palms together and stared at the ceiling. He ignored the evidence of rain encroachment, small patches of dried water turned brown against the white gypsum. "We know Eryka saw or heard something dat night, something dat triggered a memory. Something on de seven o'clock news, most likely. Suppose she remembered where she'd seen de awl before? Suppose she remembered who used de awl to bore extra holes in Jerome's belt?"

Rabino looked thoughtful. "She didn't specifically mention a belt to her sister. She said she was going home for clothes."

"Agreed," said Preddy. "I think she was going to pick up Jerome's clothes, and not because she was thinking about Tex finding dem. No, I think she was going to retrieve de belt and bring it to me."

Harris picked up the awl and measured it against the holes. "Looks like it could be the tool. We never got any prints off it, but might be able tae get some prints off the belt."

"Dat would be good." Preddy looked around at his team. "So, maybe Eryka and Jerome are out walking one day — maybe after a big lunch — saw someone wid an awl and asked him to make de holes?"

234

"Some random person?" said Spence.

"Or a person they saw in the area all the time?" said Rabino.

"I'm thinking it would have tae be someone they knew on sight," said Harris. "I know all sorts of things get carried around in Mo Bay, knives in particular. I imagine a few people are concealing all sorts of pointed tools, including screwdrivers and ice picks, but I cannae imagine someone just walking around with an awl on display for anyone tae see."

"You'd be surprised," said Preddy.

"Aye, guess I shouldnae be," conceded Harris. "After all, there's coconut sellers like Moses openly carrying machetes and naw one seems tae think that's odd or dangerous."

Spence shrugged. "Dis is Jamaica. People sell jelly coconut ah road."

"Never had any fatalities around sellers either," added Rabino.

Preddy again stared into the broken ceiling and this time focused on a piece of sagging wood borne down by the weight of water over many years. He averted his gaze from the eyesore. "Okay, focus, people. Eryka saw de awl on TV and left home around ten. Maybe de murderer was also watching de seven o'clock news and saw de murder weapon. He thinks she'll remember it and remember him. He goes to her apartment—"

"How did he know where she lived?" asked Harris.

"You never see her social-media pages?" Spence looked at him with disdain. "De Cherry Walk apartment is all over it, and de Audi. Young people nowadays don't keep a thing private. De whole of Jamaica could find her apartment, no trouble."

"I agree," said Preddy. "De murderer goes to her apartment to find her, doesn't know she's wid her sister. Maybe he tries to get in. Or maybe he looks around, doesn't see de car and decides to wait around. He gets lucky when de car appears."

Pain stabbed in Preddy's chest at the thought of Eryka dying because she went to retrieve evidence to help solve the murder of her beloved friend. For the hundredth time, he wished he had not been so keen to hang up the phone on her that night.

"Poor Eryka." Rabino let out a long sigh. "She arrived home at the worst possible time."

Harris wrapped his hands around the back of his neck, his elbows sticking out to the sides. "So how do we work out who'd be carrying an awl, who Jerome and Eryka would've felt confident enough tae approach in the first place?"

Preddy held up a palm. "Mrs Vassell said de tools were given away, most likely to some boys who hung around de sandal maker. So we could be looking at an older male, maybe sixties, or someone younger who inherited it from him. Somebody who treasured it and had it for many years, wouldn't give it away. Maybe carried it all de time."

"Somebody like . . . ?" asked Harris.

"We haven't eliminated Tex Doran from the equation," said Rabino. "Who knows what he did for a living before he became a wealthy man?"

"If Eryka saw Tex anywhere near when she was with Jerome, she'd have avoided him." Harris shook his head. "There's naw way Tex Doran would be punching holes in Jerome's belt for him."

"But would Tex punch holes in his chest?" Preddy massaged his temples. "We definitely need to speak to Mr Doran again as soon as possible. It's hard to find any background information on dat man. I want to know what he was doing from de time he was a sweaty schoolboy until he got rich, and how."

"I'd like tae have a face-tae-face with the man, since I missed the last one," said Harris.

"Okay, see if you can pull him in." Preddy put the belt and clothes back in the bag and locked it in the cabinet, then secured the awl in a drawer. "Try and sweet-talk him in. He's been cooperative so far, but he might start shouting harassment if he gets worried, and I don't want him to lawyer up. Maybe he'll respond positively to a foreign voice and face."

Harris straightened up. "I'll do ma best."

CHAPTER 25

Spence and Rabino stood in the adjoining room watching attentively through the reflective glass as Preddy and Harris entered Interview Room One and closed the door.

"You think we'll get a confession?" whispered Spence.

"That would be so good," said Rabino. "Clear up a double murder and give us chance to catch a breath."

"Until de next one, girl."

The men pulled out chairs in front of Tex Doran. Smartly attired in tailored brown trousers and grey designer sports shirt with sleeves buttoned around his wrists, he looked dressed for a sales convention. He sat, stretching his legs out beneath the table and flexed his right knee. He rested his elbows on the table and clasped his hands together. The corners of his lips were turned up slightly, yet his eyes remained flat.

"Looks like my room has been upgraded, Detective Preddy. Thank you."

Interview Room One was indeed a vast improvement on Room Four, where Preddy had first encountered the businessman. Both rooms had the same uninspired grey walls, white plastic tables and matching chairs. But not only did Room One have more space, a decent standing fan and a large window allowing for plenty of light, it was also blessed with fresh air from a vent and there was no odour of damp or decay. This room was Harris's choice.

Preddy placed his notebook firmly on the table. He drew the fan closer and turned the casing so that the pleasing draught from the blades was hitting only the detectives' side of the table. "We try our best to make all visitors as comfortable as possible."

"So I see," said Tex with a sneer in his tone.

"I'm Detective Harris. Nice tae meet ye, Mr Doran." The Scotsman reached across the table to shake the suspect's hand and was forced to switch hands mid-motion when Tex unexpectedly offered him a left.

"Hello, Detective Harris. Still on the island, eh? Never thought I'd get to meet you in the flesh, so to speak."

"Wish it was under better circumstances." Harris placed a folder of papers in front of him and stared at the inter-viewee. "What's wrong with yer eye?"

"I was in the front yard under the apple tree trimming a few branches and an apple fell." Tex dabbed at his reddened eye with his fingertips. "Careless me. It's not as bad as it looks."

Harris scrutinized him but said nothing.

Preddy sat forward and tapped his open notebook repet-itively with his pen. "You seemed so cooperative last time you were here, but subsequent information leads me to believe you weren't dat open. Now, I want answers."

"To what I can't imagine." Tex sat upright and craned his neck as if trying to read Preddy's notebook upside down. "I've told you everything I can think of. I don't know who committed the murders. Doesn't matter how many times you ask the question, I'll give you the same answers."

"You told us you injured your knee falling on the plane steps at Sangster. You want to try dat one again?"

"So, you've been looking at CCTV footage, I guess? Very thorough, detectives. Well done." He shook his head. "My, oh my, you really think I killed my own woman!"

"Eryka wasnae exactly yer own woman, was she? That's Suzanne Doran, unless I'm missing something?"

Tex Doran fell silent, bowed his head and stared at the table, his greying eyelashes perfectly still. The creep of a bald patch on his head was visible through carefully placed hair dye. The only sounds to be heard came from unseen vehicles moving around in the courtyard below.

"Answer de question, Mr Doran."

Tex muttered something under his breath.

"What was that?" Harris leaned closer to the suspect.

Tex raised his head and cleared his throat. "Any chance of getting some water in here?"

"NWC lock off de water," said Preddy. "When we finish you can try de canteen. Right now, we going talk about your lies."

"I've had a bad right knee for years." Tex examined his fingertips, his voice barely a whisper. "Usually it's fine. If you ever see me walking normally, it's one of the rare moments when it isn't acting up. Prior to the airport accident my knee would seize up, mainly when I'd been sitting for long periods. I'd been sitting for half-hour before they called us to the boarding gate. That's why you will see me on video limping and stretching my leg. And whether you believe it or not, I did aggravate it at the airport when I slipped."

"Why did ye feel the need tae lie when ye were asked about it before? If the explanation is so innocent, why lie?"

"I don't think I lied last time." Tex refused to meet the Scotsman's gaze. "I was asked a specific question by Detective Preddy and I answered it. Didn't think it was that big a deal, to be honest. Thought you lot would go after the real killer and leave me alone. If I had realized you'd be off investigating my movements I'd have saved you the time."

"We like people who save us time," growled Preddy. "We don't like people who waste it."

"Look, Detective Preddy—" Tex exhaled heavily — "I will give you the name of my physicians in Jamaica and in Fort Lauderdale. You need permission to see my medical

239

records? You've got it. I want to get my name out of this mess. I'm not an idiot. I know why I'm top of your list, but it wasn't me. You think I hurt my knee struggling with Eryka, right? I loved Eryka. You hear me? I loved her."

Preddy stared at him, thinking about Valerie and wondering if he could ever feel jealous enough to want to hurt her, to kill her. Suppose she went back to her husband? Women did, and men went back to their wives. Suppose she cheated on him? Could he ever bring himself to hit her? He could not imagine it even in a fit of rage. Even through years of a rocky marriage to his now ex-wife he had never once thought of raising hands to a woman.

"Did ye grow up in Mo Bay, Mr Doran?" asked Harris.

"Yes, born and grow. Spent most of my life here. Wasn't till in my late twenties I moved to Kingston for a few years for education. After that I moved back to Mo Bay."

"Any craftsmen or leatherworkers in yer family tree?" asked Harris.

"Not that I know of." Tex frowned. He leaned to one side, slowly removed a handkerchief from his trouser pocket and wiped his hands. "My father was a merchant seaman and his father before him. I prefer to stick with dry land. My first business was a scrap-metal dealership."

"Is that how ye made yer money?"

"It was a good business, but I got an offer I couldn't refuse and sold it. Started travelling from here to the States and investing. That's when I started making real money, about seven years ago."

"Investing in . . . ?" Preddy stared at him. "Do you invest in beach design and development companies by any chance?"

Tex's eyes flitted nervously. "No. At least I don't think so."

"You don't know?" asked Preddy.

"I'm pretty sure the answer is no," said Tex. "I have colleagues in the States and we pool our resources. We invest in start-ups and in established companies with potential. Neither Baccus Designs nor All Angles were on my radar, although I can't say they never were. We invest in maybe a hundred promising companies. I don't want to swear to anything though. My computer is in the footwell of my car outside. I can pull up my investment records. You can go through the list."

"Dis 'we' you mention — are dey guys who grew up wid you in Mo Bay?"

"No. One was born in the States and lives there. The other was born in St Catherine and I met him at an expo in Kingston many years ago. It's just the three of us who work as a partnership with business scouts to identify targets for investments."

"All right. We'd like to look at de computer," said Preddy. "Give us your car keys. I'll send someone to go get it."

"Sure, I didn't lock it. Who locks a car at a police station?" Tex tried a smile that collapsed as soon as it began in the shadow of Preddy's malevolent glare. "It's a burgundy Land Rover Evoque parked by the front bins."

Preddy turned and gestured at the partitioning glass.

Tex stared at the glass for a few moments and lowered his eyes again. "I guess it's like I'm on TV in here?"

"Something like dat," said Preddy. "It's common practice."

"For your main suspect? I knew I did something to merit an upgrade." His short laugh carried no mirth. "Whoever is out there watching and listening, it wasn't me. Not. A. Murderer."

Spence knocked on the door and handed Preddy the laptop before retreating. Tex powered it up and spun it back to face the detectives. "Scroll down. You can see all the investment names, past and present."

Preddy and Harris sat shoulder to shoulder as Preddy scrolled down through the vast list of business names and individuals, few of which were familiar.

Tex dabbed yet again at his smarting eye. "Told you. No Gavin Baccus, no Wesley Ashburn. I have nothing to do with those men, nothing to gain by whoever wins the beach contract." His hands shook as he struggled to remove two business cards from his wallet. "One is my doctor at G-West Medical Centre, down Fairview. The other is my Fort Lauderdale doctor. I'll instruct them to tell you whatever you need to know and send you whatever records you ask for." He took a deep breath. "I loved Eryka Malden and I want you to catch whoever killed her."

"Thanks." Harris took the cards, studying the suspect's shaking fingers. He kept his eyes on the man as he placed the cards in his file. "Tex, are ye feeling all right?"

"I'm fine." Tex Doran snatched back his hands and placed them under the table away from view. "Not comfortable being here, that's all."

Harris turned the fan towards the interviewee, who sat up straight and inhaled as the blast of cool air hit him. Preddy glanced at Harris with annoyance. He did not want his prime suspect, this man who could be a murderer, feeling comfortable at all, and Harris was well aware of it. For a moment he thought about spinning the fan back around, but he could not afford to let his suspect detect a split in the united front.

"We're going tae get ye some ice water." Harris sounded as if he was speaking to a small child. He gestured at the reflexive glass. "It'll just be a minute."

Preddy tried to keep a poker face while finding it hard not to gnash his teeth. He fought the urge to kick the Scotsman in the shin. There must be good reason why Harris had suddenly decided to show sympathy for this man, but Preddy could not imagine what the reason could be.

Outside the door in the adjoining room, Spence and Rabino were incredulous at this turn of events. Spence folded her arms across her chest, a look of defiance on her face. Rabino shrugged and headed for the canteen.

"Is there anything ye think we should know, Tex? About the case or anything else?"

"No."

Harris gave him a pleasant smile. "How's the knee feeling now?"

"It's okay," said Tex. "Having my legs stretched like this is fine. If I sit with them bent . . . that'll be the end of me."

"Ye know, Tex, sometimes people think they cannae talk tae others about what's really going on," said Harris. "That strangers willnae understand or believe them."

Tex Doran wriggled in his seat and concentrated on flexing his knee. "Not sure what you mean. Nothing is going on. Everything is all right."

Rabino knocked on the door and placed three bottles of cold water in front of Harris. She shot a quizzical look at Preddy, who gave an almost imperceptible shrug.

Tex grabbed his water without waiting for it to be offered. He struggled to remove the cap, twisting it the wrong way. He paused, took a deep breath and made a second feeble attempt, which also failed. Harris reached for the bottle and untwisted the cap, grimacing as if in difficulty, then pushed the open bottle back towards the interviewee. Tex gulped as if the water was a lifesaver. He drained the entire half-litre in one go and licked his lips. "Thanks, I needed that."

"Och, these arenae easy, are they?" Harris made a show of struggling to open his own bottle. "Ye have tae wonder why they do this." Following Tex Doran's lead, he drained his bottle.

"What was so urgent to do in America dat you had to go away?" Preddy ignored his water and beat a pen on the table.

"Just went to shop, as I do from time to time." Tex massaged his empty water bottle. "Bought some clothes and shoes, mainly for Suzanne. Keep her sweet, you know?"

"Might keep her sweeter still if you didn't mess around wid other women."

"I hope you find the murderer, Detective. You need to eliminate me and move on. You must have other theories or God help us."

"We do have a number of theories," said Preddy. "As you would expect, we are going to investigate each one thoroughly."

"I would expect nothing less," agreed Tex. He looked at Harris again. "We done now?"

Harris handed him a business card. "If ye change yer mind and want tae talk, please call me. Night or day."

Preddy raised an eyebrow. He had expected Harris to be more probing, but instead he seemed keen to let the suspect go. Preddy opened his water bottle with ease and took a sip. "If you're sure we're done?"

Harris stood, reached across the table with his left hand and shook Tex's hand. "Come, Tex, I'll walk ye out. Ye can take yer computer, we willnae need it. Here, I'll carry it for ye."

Preddy nodded at Tex as the two men left the room. He waited until they started descending the steps then followed a few paces behind them. Spence and Rabino were at his shoulders within seconds and all three detectives crept down the stairs into the lobby.

"What de hell just happened, sir?" asked Spence.

"I have absolutely no idea." Preddy cracked his knuckles. "When Detective Harris returns, he can tell us."

"Can't wait to hear," said Rabino.

* * *

Preddy propped his shoulder against the lobby wall as he watched the Scotsman and the suspect chatting beside the Land Rover. For once Harris was not wearing his sunglasses, instead using his hand to shield his eyes. Ten minutes ticked by, which Preddy endured by changing his gaze from Harris to the packed noticeboard beside his head. It was filled with posters of wanted people, mainly gang members, as well as photo-friendly shots of community events that the officers had participated in. A faded collage of missing people dangled by a single drawing pin at the end of the board. Preddy's eyes returned to the men. Harris was patting Tex Doran's shoulder. Preddy frowned.

Spence took the opportunity to exchange pleasantries with Officer Wilson while keeping one eye on the entrance for Harris's return. Rabino remained just behind Preddy and he glanced at her. She had shown him no resentment since his demand for the real estate brochures and seemed to have returned to her normal diplomatic self, yet Preddy knew she had not forgotten the incident. Forgiven, maybe — forgotten, no chance.

"How's everything wid you?" he asked.

"Can't complain, sir." Rabino stared straight ahead, sharing the same point of focus as Preddy. "Well, I guess I can, but I won't."

"We're good, right?"

"Right." She indicated towards Harris with her chin. "Wish I could hear you say the same about you and him."

The top-of-the-range vehicle finally purred away down the drive and Tex Doran was gone. Harris stayed put, waving at the car until it turned onto the main road.

Preddy stepped straight into Harris's path as he entered the lobby. "Well?"

Harris mopped his brow and pointed at the canteen door. "Let's go in here. It's empty."

The three detectives followed behind him and took up seats on the nearest table. Harris stood in front of them and surveyed each face. "Tex Doran isnae a murderer. He's a victim of domestic violence."

Silence from his audience. The air was heavy with the voices and sounds of kitchen staff undertaking their daily tasks — running water and the clanking of pots on the sideboard, followed by an admonishment for wetting up the floor and a frustrated demand to pass a mop.

"A whe' de rass?" Spence finally exploded, her eyes widened.

"Is this for real?" asked Rabino.

Preddy stared at the Glaswegian. Just when he thought he had heard it all, Harris threw a curveball. "Explain it to us, please, Detective," he said. "You have de floor."

"The signs are there if ye know what tae look for. A bad knee? Maybe innocent, maybe not. Shaking hands, nervous looks? Could be down tae being under scrutiny in a police station." Harris began to pace back and forth as if he was a college professor lecturing a room of attentive students. "He's right-handed. Used his right hand tae wipe his face, tae power the laptop, tae try tae open the bottle. Shook hands with his left hand. Why? My guess he's in pain, didnae want me tae squeeze his right hand. He was sweating, could easily have rolled up his sleeves, but ye notice he kept tugging them down. Hiding bruises."

"What is dis me ah hear," breathed Spence.

"A bruised eye from an apple? What bloody apple? There wasnae a single apple on any tree in that garden." Harris stopped pacing. "Fuck! That broken vase in his house was the first clue. I missed it because I was looking for signs of him being a murderer, naw being a victim."

Preddy leaned forward, his expression one of disbelief. "You're saying dat tiny Suzanne Doran who is barely bigger dan a twelve-year-old has been beating up her big, tough husband?"

"Ye said it yerself, remember, Preddy?" Harris turned abruptly to face his leader. "Right after we first met her. 'I bet she attacks him behind closed doors,' ye said. I know ye meant verbally, but I'm betting she's physical too."

Spence waved her hand at him in a silent request for permission to speak. "Okay, I know I said I'd kill my husband if he ever did what Tex did, but dat was a joke. No beating, no killing, we'd just go our separate ways. You're saying Suzanne's reaction is to beat him up when she feel like it? And she just became dis violent harpy a year ago?" Spence made it sound as ridiculous as possible. "What can go so?"

"Who says she just started doing it?" Harris stared at her. "She could've been violent for years. Suzanne's behaviour could be the reason why Tex turned tae somebody like Eryka. Somebody he could talk tae and pamper. A non-violent woman who needed him, and he was glad for the attention. He wanted tae feel loved and needed."

Rabino shook her head. "I'm having a hard time believing he wouldn't just hit her back. I mean . . . the size of him.

246

He clearly still works out. You could see his muscles through his shirt — chest and arms. I can't imagine any woman, even his wife, picking a fistfight with somebody built like him."

"That's the thing though," said Harris. "If he hit her once, hard enough, she'd probably be dead. He knows it. She knows it. She probably taunts him with it. He hits her and everyone is instantly on her side. Naw one is going tae believe him. Trust me, this happens."

Spence shook her head. "Not inna Jamaica."

"Aye, inna Jamaica," replied Harris. "Look, naw offence, but this is a pretty macho society. It's bad enough trying tae get men tae come forward in Glasgow, but at least trained officers are familiar with the behaviour there. In Jamaica, men are taught tae be tough. If they say a woman beat them up, they'd get laughed at and taunted, so they shut up and live with it." He paused as he took in their facial expressions, which varied between concerned and sceptical. "He's naw a violent man. He runs off shopping tae America buying things tae pacify Suzanne. When he can, he stays there, as far away from her as possible. They have nae kids, they're high-society people, they'll smile and hold hands at events tae keep up appearances. Both of them admitted tae basically living separate lives at home."

Preddy nodded. Slowly he was beginning to accept that what Harris said made sense. "I remember dat."

Harris placed his palms together and brought his fingers to his lips, closing his eyes briefly. "Remember ye told me he said something about washing his own clothes in the washing machine and ye scoffed at him? He probably does do his own washing. Wouldnae be surprised if Suzanne told the washerwoman tae naw wash his clothes or even hid the laundry from her."

"Wow!" Rabino flapped backwards in her seat.

"Upstairs just now, Tex mumbled something before he asked for the water. I wasnae sure I heard clearly what he said. Thought he said, 'Should've got rid of her,' which sounded like a strange admission when ye're accused of murder. But the more I think about it, that's exactly what he did say." Harris reacted to their blank stares by concluding, "He was talking about Suzanne. Saying he should have divorced her."

"This did not turn out like I expected," said Rabino. "At all."

"Dere's an understatement." Preddy bowed his head and massaged his temples, trying to force his palpating brain to accept the idea of Tex as a battered husband.

"So if Suzanne is dis violent menace, you think is she kill Eryka?" asked Spence.

Harris shot her a long, thoughtful look. "That's naw her MO. Her violence is directed towards her husband, naw at her female competitors. She didnae kill Eryka Malden. Neither did Tex."

Rabino exhaled. "If what you say is right, what do we do about it? What can we do about it, for him?"

"Tex is nae admitting tae anything being wrong right now. I'm hoping he'll want tae open up and phone me. I'll give him a week and see what happens." Harris removed two cards from his shirt pocket and waved them. "If he doesnae call, these are his medical contacts. I'll take him up on the offer of getting his medical records and take it from there."

Spence stared at him warily. "Dis is Jamaica, you know. You can't get involved inna man and woman story.'"

"Aye, I can," said Harris. "And will, when it's a man and woman horror story."

CHAPTER 26

Thursday, 10 January, 8.40 p.m.

Instrumental reggae music emitted from the speaker of Preddy's CD player as he lay slumped on the sofa at home. Roman and Annalee had mocked him for hanging on to the entertainment equipment, which they considered extinct, but Preddy had no intention of getting rid of it any more than he had any intention of getting rid of his thirty-year-old record player. The vinyl albums, mainly Studio One music, sat in their leatherette box next to it and were played mostly on weekends. Nothing sounded as good as vinyl to his ears, and no modern technology could beat the earthy sound of old tunes spinning on the turntable.

It was dark outside, yet still early, and he could happily have gone straight to bed, but sleep would have proved futile as he could not free his mind from the murders. Yet again he had failed at his annual New Year's resolution not to take work home. He was reading case files, scouring his own notes, trying to determine who was most likely to have taken the lives of the young victims.

The phone rang. He turned off the music and snatched it up as soon as Valerie's name appeared. "Hello, baby," he said.

"Hello, my love. What's up? I didn't hear from you today."

A warm feeling ran through his heart, followed by a tinge of guilt. It felt good to have another person care so deeply for him. He loved this woman with his whole being, but sometimes, when the darkness of his job overwhelmed him, he ended up neglecting to communicate with her, something she had chided him for more than once, and something he knew was his duty to correct. He had messed up badly last time and had an ex-wife to show for it.

"I was just going call you," he lied. "Got back late, grabbed a shower and not too long finished dinner."

"Oh, well, glad to know you're eating, Ray. What did you have?"

"Er, curried chicken and Irish potatoes." He guessed that Tuesday's leftovers were still edible, but had not opened the tubs in the fridge to check.

"Good. Make sure get your greens too. I going clean couple bags of callaloo for you to put in de freezer. Takes five minutes to steam."

"You too good to me, baby," he said, guilt once again digging him in the ribs.

"And I want you to be good to yourself, hun. I really hope you not working on any murder business?"

"No, man. Listening to music and tidying up de place. Not even bothering wid de TV. I'll be in bed in half-hour reading through my best Christmas present. Dis guy Beatty is honest and funny."

Valerie chuckled and the sound cheered him up immensely. "I'm glad you like *The Sellout*. You need to sur-round yourself wid more joy in your life."

"You are de joy in my life, woman. Always will be. How you doing anyway? Overrun wid work at de lab?"

"Wasn't too bad today, although we do have a huge backlog from the holiday break. Only one or two customers pressing me for sample results, but dey'll have to wait till next week. My work is spread through de team and everybody pulling together. As it should be, Ray."

"I hear you, Val." Preddy smiled and wished he could hug her for failing to hide her obvious concern. "I swear dis case has all hands on deck. I'm not doing it alone."

"So, you and Detective Harris getting along like butter on bread, eh?"

"Well, I wouldn't quite put it like dat, but he came up wid an interesting theory today dat really have me looking at him in a different light."

"A good light?"

"Let's say he's more intuitive dan I thought."

"He still not telling you which detective he investigating though?"

"No, and I've stopped asking him. Now, I just try to watch where he goes and listen in on his conversations whenever I can."

"Make sure you stay safe, Ray. Whatever is going on, you look after you first. You hear me?"

"Loud and clear, ma'am. I love you."

"Love you too, hun. Call me tomorrow, you hear?"

"I promise. Sleep well, baby."

Preddy put the phone on the sofa. He stretched his aching body skyward then reached across the coffee table for a glass of not-so-cold soursop juice. The ice had melted and condensation sent droplets of water to the tiled floor, which he ignored. As the sweet liquid soothed his throat he wished that he could indeed pick up Paul Beatty's satire and lose himself in the words, but the victims of Montego Bay's latest violent streak were calling out to him and would not be silenced.

He turned off the light so that the only illumination came from the communal lights outdoors. He lay on the sofa staring up at the whirring blades of the overhead fan. An array of faces, male and female, suspects and victims, trotted through his brain — Eryka, Jerome, Gavin, Tex, Wesley, Moses. Eventually he fell into a fitful sleep, but even that did not diminish the visions. There was Suzanne throwing pots at Tex, who raised his arms in front of his face to stave off the missiles. Suzanne, ignoring Preddy's orders to stop the assault while he pointed a gun at her.

The detective sat up with a start and glanced at the clock. It was nearly midnight. He mopped his brow. He should be glad — at least he was not dreaming of Norwood.

He made his way to the bedroom and flopped down onto the bed, where he twisted and turned, trying to think of nothing. He doubled up his pillow and pressed his head into it. Now the dreams became more lucid. A group of Livity vendors angrily waving placards in front of Pelican Walk station, threatening to storm the building. Ras Bizzi patiently trying to quieten the raised voices. Even Harris made an appearance, running away from him with that bronze laptop clutched in his fingers, his ginger hair flapping around his ears. Each time Preddy stretched out a hand to grab the laptop, Harris sprinted even further away and mocked him for being unable to keep up.

Dawn could not come quick enough.

CHAPTER 27

Friday, 11 January, 6.50 a.m.

Preddy returned from jogging, his vest drenched, his chest heaving and falling as he headed into his apartment. Little breeze was circulating, and the cloudless blue sky indicated that this would be another blistering day. He kicked off his sneakers and socks and savoured the coolness that came with bare feet encountering tiles. He pulled off his damp clothes, but did not quite make it to the bathroom before Spartan demanded entry, hitting the windowpane energetically with his beak.

Preddy tossed the clothes into the top-loading washing machine, thinking of Tex Doran and Harris's comments. Washing clothes was no big deal for Preddy since his divorce, and he was sure that plenty of single men did it without thinking twice. The machine did all the work. Tex was a married man, a rich and busy businessman, flying around the world, who did his own laundry even with a wife and domestic helper at home. Tex, a victim of domestic violence, afraid to fight back. Preddy closed the machine and stared through the glass cover. He had to accept that his prime suspect was actually a victim and not a murderer.

Preddy sighed deeply as he filled the kettle. He packed a large mug with green ganja leaves and left the hungry parakeet on the kitchen countertop gorging on ground corn while he took a shower. Afterwards, he pulled on a short-sleeve white shirt and tan trousers and headed to the fridge. Rarely did he have any appetite for cooked food in the mornings — except on Sundays, when tradition would always have him frying dumplings or boiling bananas to eat with ackee and saltfish or mackerel. If the teenagers stayed over he had no choice but to cook or let them make a mess of the entire kitchen, and cleaning up was not their thing. Their healthy appetites demanded hot food as soon as their eyes opened.

He picked up two cool tangerines, spread a cloth over his shoulder and approached the countertop. "Why you won't help me, son?"

Spartan immediately flew onto Preddy's protected shoulder. The detective ruffled his tiny crest, earning a soft headbutt to his cheek. "You eat my food, and you listen to de goriest tales, but you won't tell me what I need to know."

Spartan cheeped as if in apology, then squawked as tangerine rind sparked acidic drops in the air. "Sorry, boy." Preddy quickly moved the tangerine as far from the repulsed bird as his arms would allow. "Never mind, finish you corn."

The parakeet gave up all interest in the remaining crumbs and remained settled on Preddy's shoulder, nestling into the cloth towel. "Good boy. Despite your silence, you and I make a good team. And although Super will never admit it, you save de JCF plenty money. Psychologists are not cheap." Preddy scooped up bits of scattered corn and returned them to the saucer. "Dere's a double murderer walking de streets, Spartan, and I have to get him. Tell me what to do." He held the second tangerine under the table to peel it and popped a few pegs in his mouth. "Talk, no?"

Spartan remained silent and bobbed his head from side to side. Preddy heard a tapping sound from the front of the apartment. He got up, taking care not to dislodge the bird, and inched towards the window. Another pair of parakeets were looking in. "You've been in here too long, Spartan. See your friends have come to check where you are." As he opened the window the visiting parakeets chirped and quickly took off with Spartan close behind them.

"Birds of a feather flock together," muttered Preddy.

He watched the three of them playing in the leaves of a royal palm tree across the road, their bright green wings standing out against the dark green fronds, which barely moved when brushed by their lightweight bodies. The creatures could probably fight off a predatory bird together, united in holding their ground. A thought flitted through his mind as he watched the lively performance. The Livity Vendors Association was a united team. Maybe Ras Bizzi could tell him more about the individuals within the group. The Rastafarian had spoken with certainty about the nature of the people he mixed with regularly, but that was before Eryka's death. If not Moses, then one of the other men in that group could well be the person he was looking for.

Preddy fastened his watch to his wrist. Ras Bizzi would probably be hauling his cooler of ital drinks to one of the free beaches, if he was not already there. The Rasta man had been forthcoming and helpful before and might be willing to divert to Pelican Walk headquarters for half an hour.

* * *

Preddy crunched on a mint as he entered Pelican Walk lobby. He was surprised to see Mrs Vassell sitting on a bench by herself with a stack of church pamphlets and a Bible in hand. A large tote bag was beside her with more pamphlets sticking out. Her walking stick was propped up against the wall.

Officer Wilson gave Preddy a tortured look and mouthed, "Save me." The detective grinned at him and nodded at the Adventist lady, whose broad smile deepened when she spotted him.

"Hello, Mrs Vassell. Good to see you. Everything all right?"

255

"Yes, sir. You look strong and well, Detective Preddy!" She squeezed his arm. "I'm not here to see you though. I've come to see Detective Harris."

"Oh, he's expecting you?"

"No, when I woke up this morning the Spirit said to me, 'Go see that ungodly white man,' so here I am." She beamed, and as her hazel eyes lit up he caught a flash of her youth. "This Bible is for Detective Harris and these tracts will help him learn about God."

"He'll be absolutely delighted." Preddy felt a warm glow of satisfaction that reflected in his face. "You make yourself comfortable, Mrs Vassell. I'll ask Officer Wilson to call him for you."

"Already done, sir." Officer Wilson glanced up from whatever document had garnered his attention. "Him coming down in a minute. 'In a tick,' he said."

"Oh good," said Preddy. "You need any ice water or anything, ma'am?"

"No, sir, I'm ready for my ministry." She patted her Bible with enthusiasm. "I had my lemongrass tea and plantain porridge for breakfast. I don't need a thing else."

As Detective Harris came down the stairs, Preddy acknowledged him with a big grin and edged closer towards Officer Wilson. He leaned against the reception desk and watched Harris approach the elderly lady.

"Oh, dere's a Rasta guy waiting for you upstairs, sir," Officer Wilson said. "Say him have an appointment. Ras Bizzi. Wouldn't tell me him real name, 'bout him don't use slave-master name." The policeman kissed his teeth. "Me put him in Interview Room One."

"Hmm, yes." Preddy had fixed his attention on Harris's increasingly reddening face.

"See, he leave a cooler full of drinks dere cover up, sir." Wilson pointed at a bench on the other side of the lobby. "I told him we don't allow people to store drinks here, but him say you wouldn't mind because is you send call him and him can't leave dem outside."

Preddy glanced at the pink cooler. "Dat's okay," he said. "It can stay. I won't be wid him too long."

Mrs Vassell pressed the Bible into Harris's unwilling hands.

"Thank ye, Mrs Vassell, but I dinnae think I'll have time tae read it."

"Of course you will have time, Detective!" she insisted. "God has time for you. You can find time for Him."

"I'll try ma best." Harris tried to stand, but Mrs Vassell grabbed his hand and dragged him back onto the bench.

"You must come to church on Saturday, you hear? I want you to experience a service."

"Er, I dinnae think I'll be available, ma'am. Things are very busy here at the moment, as I'm sure ye'll understand."

Mrs Vassell nodded. She clung to his hand and pumped it up and down. "I understand, Detective Harris. If not this week, then maybe the week after, huh?"

"Um . . . maybe."

Mrs Vassell stared at him earnestly. "I'm not going to stop until you come, you know, sir? Anybody who knows me will tell you that I don't stop."

"I'm getting tae realize that." Harris mopped his brow and looked Preddy's way. His eyes implored him to act and Preddy surprised himself by feeling some sympathy for the Scotsman. Religion should not be forced down anyone's throat, and although Harris was not likely to swallow it no matter how hard it was pushed, Preddy decided to intervene.

"Hate to interrupt your ministry, Mrs Vassell," said Preddy, "but I have to borrow your new disciple now for urgent police business. Hope dat is all right?"

Preddy handed the old lady her walking stick and she smiled at him. "All right, sir. I hear you. You and Detective Harris doing good work, and I know you working hard."

"Ye can make it home okay?" Harris picked up her handbag and gently hung it over her shoulder.

"Yes, man. I'll walk out to the road and hail a taxi. That's how I got here." She stretched her limbs. "I get around by myself quite well. I might look weak, but thank God, I'm not too bad. I'll be fine." She gave the Scotsman's hand another squeeze. "See you soon, Detective Harris."

Out of the corner of his eye Preddy noticed that someone was descending the stairs.

"Oh, you reach, Detective Preddy?" said the Rasta man. "Me just come down to grab a drinks. You want one?"

"No, I'm fine, thanks, Ras."

"Lady, before you go you want drinks?" the vendor asked. "Ah good ital drinks, no preservative, good fi you body!"

Mrs Vassell waved an apologetic hand. "No, sir, I'm good."

Ras Bizzi's loose dreadlocks cascaded down his face as he bent over his cooler box and started to sing to himself. Mrs Vassell, who had been making her way out with Harris as escort, squeezed his hand so tightly his eyes flew to hers.

"Are ye okay, ma'am? Sit back down. Come on, sit." Harris led her back to the bench and she sat heavily. He used one of the pamphlets to fan her cheeks while she stared ahead wide-eyed.

Preddy followed her gaze. She was focused on Ras Bizzi's back as he knelt rattling around in the ice. The woman appeared to be in a trance. Ras Bizzi continued to sing, a lively melody about marching men, a tune Preddy did not know. The Rasta man grabbed a bottle of Irish Moss and headed back up the stairs. "You ready, sir?" he called over his shoulder.

"Right behind you, Ras," said Preddy. "Soon come."

When the creaking of his footsteps dissipated Preddy walked over to Mrs Vassell and crouched low in front of her. He took both her hands in his and felt them shaking. "You know him, don't you? Dat Rasta man?"

Harris looked confused at first and then breathed a sigh of relief. "Och, I thought she was having a stroke or something."

"Nearly did have a stroke," she whispered. She eased her right hand away from Preddy and used it to massage the delicate skin on her throat. "I haven't heard that song in many years, but I'll always remember it. That Rasta man . . . he has long grey hair now, and the voice is much deeper." She inhaled deeply. "Those cheekbones are just like his daddy's, though. No mistake. He was one of the boys who used to sing and recite for Papa back in the day."

"Ras Bizzi?" Harris frowned. "Are ye sure?"

"It's him." She nodded firmly. "Skinny same way. The shape of the face is just like when he was a boy. I would never have thought he was a Rasta man now."

"You remember I showed you a newspaper photo of de Livity Vendors Association?" asked Preddy. "You didn't pick him out. His given name is Bennett Shaw."

"That wasn't a good photo, couldn't see the cheekbones," she said. "Anyway, I told you I'm better with voices than faces. When I have the two together I wouldn't make a mistake. He was singing that marching song he made up. You know, kids always like to mimic soldiers marching and beating drums?"

"Stay here a minute, ma'am," said Preddy. "You going to talk to Detective Harris for a while, you hear? Tell him all dat you remember."

"Yes, sir. That surprise took the energy right out of my legs."

Harris continued fanning the elderly lady. "Ye'll be all right soon. We'll have a wee chat and then I'll get a cab for ye."

"I'll send Rabino down." Preddy stood upright and whipped out his phone. "Spence and I will deal wid Mr Bennett Shaw."

* * *

Preddy and Spence headed towards the interview room while Rabino grabbed a drink and headed for the lobby.

"You really think Bizzi is de man?" asked Spence. "She's an old woman and we're talking many decades since she last saw or heard him."

"She sounded certain though. His face hasn't changed."

Spence tried to keep pace with her striding leader. "You think he will admit to anyting?"

He patted a padded evidence envelope. "We'll see what he has to say about dis."

The detectives fell silent as they approached the door behind which sat their new prime suspect. Preddy pushed it open. "Sorry about de wait, Ras."

"I and I want to help Babylon, no matter how dem a fight Rasta man." Ras Bizzi directed an admiring glance at Spence and lingered on her braids. "Wha'? Hello, Empress. Looking regal. Me love de natural ting."

"Hello, Ras." Spence smiled as she took a seat. "Can't bother wid de chemical ting again or de wig. You done know how it go already."

"Dem no good fi de body," agreed Ras Bizzi. "Ah so me love see sistren represent demself well."

"Sorry to take you away from you work, sir," said Spence. "I know you want to be outta road selling."

"Not a problem, sistren."

Preddy studied the calm-looking Rastafarian, with his thin face and perfect white teeth. He had never paid attention to the man's cheekbones before, but now he could see that they were indeed high, giving him chiselled features reminiscent of rapper-turned-entrepreneur Snoop Dogg. He wondered who this cheerful man with the engaging smile and flowing locks really was. A man who could plunge a pointed instrument straight into another man's heart and leave him to die? A man who could use a stone to bash in a woman's head and drag her into a filthy gully?

Preddy's stomach churned. "We won't take up too much of your time, Ras. Just hoping you could help us wid some questions about de other men in Livity."

"Ask whe' you want ask, sir. I and I will try answer."

"How well do you know dose guys . . . deir background? I mean, I know you know Moses, but how well do you know de other two?"

"A good man dem, sir. Me tell you dat already." Ras Bizzi rubbed his beard locks. "Maybe three or four years me know dem, so me can't really say me know dem background so well, but ah no man what drink or smoke or gwaan bad."

"How long you know Moses?" asked Preddy.

"Long-long time, from we ah likkle youth. Me would swear for him, man. Him is one of de good guys. Him wouldn't hurt a soul, neither man nor woman."

"Don't swear for anybody," warned Spence. "You know how many people lose millions in bail money, 'bout dem swearing for people?"

"Ah true too, sistren." Ras Bizzi nodded soberly. "Only youself you can swear fah nowadays."

Preddy sat back in his chair and kept his eyes fixed on the Rasta man. "You see, it's our understanding dat Moses was quite a little troublemaker. Used to hang around de craft shops downtown wid other youngsters making a nuisance of himself."

"Who say dat?"

"An elderly lady was just telling us all about him. Mrs Vassell." Preddy smiled in a friendly manner as he said her name. "She remembers Moses from way back when. Her father used to have a craft shop downtown and dere were always little boys hanging around, playing wid his tools. She says dey would recite poems, sing, bang tin cans?"

"Who?" The Rasta man shuffled in his seat. "Dat lady downstairs?"

"She same one." Preddy made a steeple with his hands. "Nice lady. Some people know her as Miss Hardy."

Ras Bizzi eyes moved swiftly to Spence then back to Preddy. It was enough for Preddy to sense fear. The Rasta man opened his bottle of Irish Moss and tilted back his head, letting his locks almost touch the ground. He took his time drinking the liquid while staring at the ceiling.

"Ever seen her before?" asked Preddy. "I think she was Turner before she married?"

"Dat's right," said Spence. "Miss Turner now Mrs Vassell. She's an Adventist, from Johns Haven?"

Ras Bizzi licked his lips and slowly capped his bottle, studying the crude label a long while. "No, man. I and I see hundreds of people every day, but I never see her before."

"You know, she thought she recognized you from somewhere, but she couldn't remember where." Preddy kept as pleasant an appearance as he could bear. "I told her she probably bought drinks from you on de beach, but she says she can't recall."

"Oh . . . well, maybe so. I and I sell a whole lotta drinks to a whole lotta people."

"She had an appointment, elsewhere so she had to leave, unfortunately," said Spence, "but she'll be back tomorrow so we can have a proper conversation, see what she remembers about Moses and Hardy's. You and him used to hang out back den?"

"Not much." Ras Bizzi wiped his lips with the back of his hand. "Old people sometimes remember tings wrong. Moses is hard-working from him ah youth till now. I never hear nobody complain 'bout him behaviour at no time."

"You remember Hardy's store?" asked Preddy.

"Me remember when dem did have one Hardy's downtown. Dat time I ah likkle-likkle bwoy. Look how long dem place gone. I and I never really go round dere much, you know? Too much wood shavings getting up I nose." He gave a nervous smile.

"I know how you mean." Spence leaned forward as if she was enjoying his company. "And back den I bet no one used face mask, no true? Is not like now when people more health conscious. I'd never let my kids go playing around any place wid sawdust and sharp tools."

"Speaking of tools, remind me to bring dis for Mrs Vassell to have a look at." Preddy opened the padded envelope and drew out an evidence bag. He removed the awl, his eyes remaining fixed on the suspect. "You ever see dis before?"

Ras Bizzi went perfectly still. "No," he croaked. He cleared his throat. "No."

"Dis is de murder weapon used to kill Jerome Baccus," explained Preddy. He twirled it around in his fingers, as though to mesmerize the Rasta man. "Somebody slid this point through his skin, right under his ribcage. Somebody . . . maybe Moses, eh?"

The suspect looked up at Preddy with something resembling hope in his eyes. "If him do dat, him woulda wicked."

"Moses doesn't think he ever met Eryka Malden," said Preddy. "You think it's possible dat he knew her?"

"Oh, dat lady what get kill a Cherry Walk? Him never mention her to me." His dilated eyes seemed to be trying to read Preddy's. "You really think is Moses do it?"

"We haven't found anything to tie him directly to her yet, but we're gathering information. You never really know how two people are connected sometimes."

"True," added Spence. "Sometimes people have to rack deir memory to see what comes out. My granny — God rest her soul — used to tell some story 'bout people she remember from she was seven. She pass at ninety and her mind was still so sharp. We think Mrs Vassell will be key to our investigations."

"Old people love good-old-days story." Ras Bizzi tried to smile, but the result was a pained expression. "Even when days wasn't good, dem remember it as good. Dat old lady will all remember tings dat never happen. None of de young bwoy in de old days used to bad."

"People can change over de years." Preddy waited a beat, hoping that the man would finally give it up and explain himself. "Sometimes things happen in deir lives and dey become violent. I mean, you're saying you never saw Moses violent, but Miss Hardy remembers him throwing stones at boys, so right dere we know he has a tendency to hurt people."

"Me understand wha' you mean." The Rasta man stared at his empty juice bottle, his mind apparently elsewhere. He seemed startled when Preddy tapped the table lightly and rose to his feet.

"Well, if we can scratch Moses off our list tomorrow, dat would be good." Preddy tucked the awl into the bag and returned it to the envelope. "We'll see what de old lady has to say."

Spence followed her superior's lead. "Thanks again for coming, Ras. Follow me. I'll show you out."

Ras Bizzi pushed back his chair and rose as if his slender frame had gained weight. He held onto the back of the chair for a moment, with his head bowed. Preddy waited, willing him to confess. He desperately wanted the man to take the opportunity and unburden his soul. If he did not, Preddy predicted there would be a long and dangerous night ahead for everybody, particularly Mrs Vassell.

Ras Bizzi pried his hands from the chair. "Me coming, sistren."

"You going walk beach now and look some sale?" asked Spence.

"Dat I going do, yes." Ras Bizzi held his empty bottle by the neck and beat the body against his bare knee. "Need to empty out de cooler and go restock for lunchtime."

"Sun hot, you soon sell off." Preddy glanced at him. "Oh, and don't tell Moses about Mrs Vassell, will you? She may turn out to be a key witness."

The Rasta man stopped beating the bottle. He opened his lips, but no words came out. He turned and followed Spence from the room.

CHAPTER 28

Preddy and Spence were in the evidence room waiting for Rabino and Harris. Preddy erased the names of suspects and possible motivations. Wesley, Tex and Moses vanished in swift strokes. Now there was much more white space. In large bold letters Preddy wrote "*Bennett Shaw aka Ras Bizzi*" and made notations under the Rasta man's name. Spence sat on a chair with her feet up on a small storage cabinet and filled her boss in with her own observations.

"You no think maybe Moses did help him, sir?"

Preddy shook his head. "If Moses had helped him he'd have thrown him under de proverbial bus and sought leniency for himself. Bizzi was scared stiff."

After what seemed like an age, but was no more than half an hour, the door opened. Preddy looked up in eager anticipation.

Superintendent Brownlow put his head in and glanced around the room. "How you doing, Detective Spence? Long time, no see."

"Fine, sir." Spence smiled politely as she carefully lowered her feet and sat upright.

"Haven't heard much from you, Preddy, so I've come to see what's up. How is everything going?"

Preddy wanted to throw the marker pen at the man's broad head. "We're making good progress, sir."

"You're supposed to be reporting, and I haven't heard much recently." Brownlow kept a stubby hand on the door handle as if contemplating whether to enter and shut the door. "The commissioner has been on my case, and I want to be able to tell him that we have some promising leads."

"You can definitely tell him dat, sir," said Preddy. "We've narrowed down de list considerably."

The superintendent glanced past Preddy's shoulder and squinted at the whiteboard. "So, you've taken off Wesley Ashburn? Good. I can imagine all manner of mess if he was involved. I knew he was bigger than that though."

"Yes, sir. You were quite right." Preddy maintained a rictus smile and tapped his pen against his thigh. He wanted the man to leave before Rabino and Harris got back. Having the brass sit in on team discussions and strategies was something to be avoided at all costs. There was nothing he wanted to tell the superintendent until he was sure what the plan for nabbing Ras Bizzi was, and maybe not even after that. Brownlow would want to play by the rules, and the rules sometimes had to be broken to get desired results.

"And Mr Doran has gone too? I don't know him that well, but by all accounts he is a good businessman, clean as a whistle."

"So we believe, sir." Preddy cleared his throat. "I can fill you in dis evening, sir."

The superintendent remained firm. Instead he put a foot further into the room and continued reading the board. "'Bennett Shaw also known as Ras Bizzi'?"

"We're working on a strong theory dat he was involved in both murders, sir," said Preddy. "Just trying to get some corroborating evidence."

Footsteps could be heard coming down the corridor. Brownlow turned around and moved away from the door. "Oh sorry, I'm blocking you. Come in, detectives."

Rabino and Harris acknowledged him as they squeezed past his ample frame. Brownlow noticed the Bible in the Scotsman's hand and gave him a wide smile.

"I'm delighted to see you're coming around, Detective Harris."

"Aye, sir." Harris smiled back. "Resistance is futile."

Rabino sank into a chair beside Spence and fanned herself with a notebook. Spence gave her a knowing look and said nothing. The room was silent. Preddy squeezed his toes together in his shoes and fought to prevent himself from tapping them.

Superintendent Brownlow's lips curled slightly at the edges. "I'll make myself scarce, shall I? Wouldn't want to interfere with progress." He backed out of the room. "We'll speak later, Detective Preddy. A full report by close of business."

"Yes, sir." *Business never closes*, thought Preddy, *except for people in the top echelon with desk jobs and no real threats to their careers.* For them, business was nine-to-five. For Preddy, even twenty-four hours was rarely enough.

Preddy listened to Superintendent Brownlow's plodding footsteps growing fainter before speaking. "Ras Bizzi has not confessed to murder or anything else. Not to knowing Mrs Vassell. Not to ever seeing de awl before. So, tell me de old lady hasn't changed her mind?"

Rabino glanced at Harris, who inclined his head in a gentlemanly fashion indicating that she should speak first.

"We hid her in a side room so Ras Bizzi couldn't see her as he left. She could only see his back then, but she swears she saw enough of his face earlier to remember him."

"She's prepared tae sign a statement," said Harris.

"We need more," said Preddy.

"I thought Mrs Vassell recognized him on sight?" said Rabino. "She can pick him out of a line-up, surely?"

Harris shook his head. "He'll lawyer up and his lawyer wouldnae stand for that. He'll say she picked him out because she saw him right here in the lobby. Probably say we put her up tae it."

"So we can't use de fact dat she knows he handled de awl as a youth?" asked Spence.

"It's good, but I don't think she'll be taken seriously," said Preddy.

"Agreed," said Harris. "She's eighty-odd. The defence will say she's mistaken, and Bizzi will never admit tae the awl being his. We've got naw fingerprints from the awl or Jerome's belt. She cannae put the awl in Bizzi's hands from decades ago. It's all circumstantial."

"We'll get him." Preddy had been staring at the ceiling, thinking about the Rasta man while they spoke. The rage of the disenfranchised extended way beyond the young men of the island. It affected the old too — those who should be looking forward to retiring and who probably never would, such was the need to keep earning just to stay alive. This ageing Rasta man who claimed never to touch animal meat or skin had once bored holes in a leather belt. He had killed twice and would kill a third time.

Preddy lowered his eyes to meet those of the Scotsman. "He'll go to Johns Haven to find Mrs Vassell tonight."

Harris stared back at him. "How'd ye work that out? Or should I naw ask?"

"I let him know she could identify him and sort of hinted she's likely to be dere."

"Ye sort of hinted?" A flush spread over Harris's face as his tone hardened. "Ye're going tae use the old lady as bait? Are ye out of yer mind, Preddy?"

Preddy gave him a death stare. "What was dat, Detective Harris?"

Harris sank his fingernails into his palms and took a deep breath. "What I meant was, do ye think it's wise tae take that risk?"

"We'll protect her," said Spence. "We'll put eyes on de house, starting from now."

"Och, really? Remember what happened when we put eyes on Antwon 'Tuffy' Fraser?"

"Dat was a different matter," snapped Preddy. "Tuffy put a target on his own head de minute he joined de Benbow gang and picked up a gun. Bizzi won't go near her till night-fall and he don't have no gun."

"And ye know that how, exactly?" sneered Harris, his green eyes glowering.

"Nobody wid access to a gun would use a stone to beat somebody to death. He killed Eryka wid a stone. He killed Jerome with a blade. Up close and personal is Bizzi's way."

"That's some theory ye're going tae be testing, Preddy."

"We going do a stakeout tonight." Preddy put down the marker pen and cracked his knuckles. "On my head be it."

"Do ye naw think ye should run this by Brownlow first?"

"No, I don't."

A distinct chill fell on the room and a few seconds of pain-ful silence passed by. The fans whirred against the heat, which was winning the fight. Footsteps sounded in the corridor out-side the room. Spence discreetly nudged Rabino with her foot beneath the table. Rabino pretended to be reading something intriguing in her notebook, but her eyes were unmoving.

"I may have tae be . . . elsewhere tonight," said Harris. "Something important came up earlier."

"Dis is de most important case for all of us right now. Where could you possibly need to be, Detective Harris?"

Even as he asked the question Preddy guessed the answer. For the man to suggest a possibility of being absent from a stakeout, it could mean only one thing. The J Lane investigation had neared conclusion and the MOCA men were ready to act. They would just have to do without their foreign stool pigeon tonight.

Preddy waited, his eyes challenging Harris to explain himself.

Harris cleared his throat. "I'll see if I cannae . . . change things around a bit."

"You do dat, Detective Harris."

"This could all go so badly wrong," the Scotsman warned.

"It could." Preddy turned to Spence and Rabino. "Listen up, people. Dis is what we're going to do . . ."

CHAPTER 29

The moon was barely visible, a small sliver of light in a pitch-black sky over Johns Haven. The few shimmering stars did little to illuminate the sparsely populated area, which was dense with trees and bushes. Invisible crickets made their presence known, chirping incessantly as if they had waited all day for an audience to do so.

Preddy had been in position for almost an hour now, parked beneath overhanging bushes a fair distance from Mrs Vassell's house, waiting and watching with both front windows lowered. He wished he had a pair of the night-vision goggles that Harris liked to rave about, that the JCF could ill-afford.

So far the night had been uneventful, the narrow asphalt road mainly traffic-free. Either Johns Haven did not have many Friday-night revellers or they had not yet set out in search of entertainment. The air smelled fresh, too far from the sea to carry any salty odour and far enough from the city centre's pollution from jerked grills and car exhausts.

The police radio crackled and he held it closer to his ear. Spence and Rabino were in position inside the old lady's house and reported no unusual movements. He had heard nothing from Harris since his promise to arrive by eight o'clock, which time had long passed. An officer had conducted surveillance duty outside of Mrs Vassell's house all day and kept Preddy up to date every hour. The elderly lady had been reading on her verandah most of the day. She had received only two visitors during the afternoon — a fruit-basket delivery from a supermarket and an electricity-meter reader. Although Preddy could not see her from his vantage point, he knew Spence and Rabino would not allow anyone to breach the windows or doors. On the other side of the house was a road where two other Pelican Walk officers, Mitchell and Blagrove, sat in an unmarked vehicle.

Officer Timmins had been given the task of tailing Ras Bizzi all day. He reported that the Rastafarian had gone through his usual business of walking the beaches selling cold juices. By early afternoon, Bizzi had closed his cooler and tried to wave down passing taxis, which had ignored him. Eventually a pickup truck had stopped, and the suspect had hauled his cooler into the back and leaped in after it.

Preddy had ordered Timmins to follow and not let the vehicle out of his sight. No one had any idea where Bizzi lived and it unnerved Preddy to think that a brazen attempt could be made on Mrs Vassell's life in broad daylight. It had been an anxious twenty-minute wait before Timmins had finally called Preddy to report that Bizzi was not heading for Johns Haven. He had trailed the man to the unstable Rosemount community and seen him entering a small wooden house. Later Bizzi had emerged to tinker with the engine in a green Honda Accord, which Timmins had described as "tired-looking" with grey patches of unpainted bodywork.

Preddy could feel the adrenalin coursing through his veins. A vision of Superintendent Brownlow flashed through his mind. If this stakeout did not to go plan, the superintendent would hand Preddy over to Commissioner Davis, who would not hesitate to throw him under the bus. Preddy swallowed the bile rising in his throat. He would never allow Spence or Rabino to go down with him, whether they were acting on his orders or not. Harris would no doubt be immune — although in his defence, the Scotsman could rightly claim his objection to the entire plan had been overruled.

Preddy checked the time again. For Harris not to make contact at all was unusual, and particularly for a stakeout like this, which was effectively a life-or-death matter. At the very least he would have expected a voice or text message. A prickle of tension ran through Preddy's temple and a chill spread over his body. Had something happened to Harris?

He bashed the steering wheel with his fist. "Rassclaat!"

He jabbed at his police radio and contacted Officer Mitchell. "You and Blagrove need to keep circling de house. I have to move from here, but I'll be back."

Mitchell's voice came back with a tinny crackle. "Will do, sir."

Preddy phoned Spence and spoke urgently. "I have to leave de scene for a while. You've still got Mitchell and Blagrove for backup."

"What happen, sir?" Spence's voice was immediately suspicious. "And don't tell me 'nothing'!"

"Harris no reach here yet."

Preddy could hear her relaying the information to Rabino, but he could not hear the latter's response.

"Well, him did say him have somewhere to be, sir."

"I have to go. You know what to do." Preddy made a sharp U-turn and gunned the jeep's engine.

* * *

The Unity Hall district was one of the more prosperous regions on the borders of Montego Bay. The roads were evenly tarred and the large homes well maintained with exquisite gardens. Most of the properties included two or three acres of land, room for pools and plenty of fruit trees. Preddy had long returned all the real-estate brochures to

Rabino, and as he drove towards the Unity Court complex he followed directions from memory.

Preddy cruised past the enormous main structure with its towering walls designed to keep out intruders and sight-seers. The smart lighting from well-placed streetlights illuminated the area, something which would have pleased the detective in normal circumstances, but he needed darkness.

Two security guards were staffing the huge iron gates at the front of the complex. Both were dressed from head to toe in black, with yellow writing on their baseball caps declaring their official status. Through the railings Preddy could see an array of high-end vehicles in the car park. A sprawling stand-alone building was marked "*Leisure Zone*", and the frontage held a digital billboard flashing images of sporting facilities. He caught a glimpse of tennis rackets, bowling balls and snooker cues.

Preddy cursed under his breath as he went by. The premises appeared more secure than the General Penitentiary in Kingston, and he wondered whether it housed as many criminals. There would be no sneaking onto the grounds of Unity Court tonight. He drove to the end of the road, his eyes darting from side to side as perspiration prickled his brow. If tonight was the night the MOCA men planned to take down a rogue detective, where were they?

The detective pulled over on a half-built plot of land and sat thinking, his brow knotted as he stared at his silent phone, willing it to ring. Harris must be in trouble or he would have made contact by police radio or private phone by now.

Preddy checked that both his service weapon and concealed backup weapon were ready to use. He took a deep breath and turned the vehicle around, driving straight up to the closed gates of Unity Court. One of the security guards tipped back his cap and lowered his head to peer into the vehicle.

"Detective Preddy, Pelican Walk Police." Preddy waved his badge at the man. "Open de gate, please."

The security guard straightened and shook his head. "You cannot come onto de premises widout permission, sir. You visiting somebody?"

Preddy sank his nails into the steering wheel. The guards had been trained to look out for scammers and interlopers and would not roll over so easily. Ordinary people opened up gates without question when they identified police officers, but this complex was clearly not for the ordinary.

The other guard watched Preddy, a suspicious expression appearing on his round face. "Sir, if you tell me who you visiting, I'll call dem, and if dey say it's okay, you can come in."

The lights of the billboard bounced on his windscreen, and the image of the bowling balls flashed into Preddy's vision. A hundred thoughts invaded his brain, and there was no time to arrange them in any logical order. "Call Iain Cotner."

"Who?"

"Detective Iain Cotner. He's Pelican Walk too. Him not expecting me though."

The guard took out his phone, turned his back and moved away from the gate. Preddy leaned his head out of the window, straining to hear the conversation. The voice was too low. He wiped away perspiration with his shirt sleeve as he waited. If his deductions were wrong and Cotner was not a Unity Court resident, he did not know who to ask for.

The guard pushed his phone into his trouser pocket and approached Preddy's window, his face set. Preddy's heart sank in anticipation of a curt refusal of admission.

"Turn left and take de space in yellow block." The man pointed in the direction. "De blocks have colours, just look for de signs. Mr Cotner soon come down." He pushed a button and the gates purred smoothly along the ground track as they drew apart.

Preddy exhaled a long, silent breath. He crawled through the gates and drove past a sign declaring that visitors were restricted to yellow block only. He cruised through the delineated regions eyeing the parked vehicles: red block for management and staff, green for penthouse owners, blue for all other residents. No sign of Harris's car or motorbike. Having completed an almost complete circle he was soon back in front of the guard, who stared at him with unbridled annoyance.

"See de sign mark '*Yellow block*' right dere, sir!"

"Oh, sorry, man." Preddy feigned ignorance and waved a hand in apology. "I see where it is now."

Preddy parked in the designated area and climbed out of the vehicle. Spotlights blazed down on empty tennis courts towards the rear of the property. A glass structure beside the courts revealed cross-trainers, treadmills and rowing machines, some of which were in use. Two white women in sports leggings and vests were running on adjacent treadmills, their ponytails swinging from side to side.

He looked towards the entrance of the single-tower residential quarters. Tall pine trees stood like sentinels on either side of the automatic double doors. A familiar figure emerged from between them — the dark-skinned, athletic form of his colleague Iain Cotner, who was casually dressed in blue jeans and red polo shirt. Two muscular men were by his side, dressed in dark suits and ties, both wearing serious expressions.

Preddy stared at each face. The eyes of one bodyguard were hidden beneath expensive dark sunglasses. The lights in the car park were strong, but there was no need for dark glasses at all. Thugs and posers trying to look cool were the only people Preddy knew of that wore shades at night. He assumed both minders were concealing weapons, licensed or otherwise.

Detective Cotner smiled and stuck out his hand as he neared. "Wha' happen, Raythan, man? How you reach up here?"

Preddy did not smile back. "Iain." He shook the man's hand. "We need to talk."

"You sound serious, eeh?" Cotner smiled again.

"In private," added Preddy.

"Sure, follow me." Cotner waved away the men at his side. They moved aside a few steps yet stayed in close proximity. "Let's go up to de penthouse. Good views up dere."

Preddy glanced up at the ninth storey. "Let's make it ground floor." He fixed the man a solid gaze. "Accidents can happen up on high, you know?"

"All right. Let me think now." Cotner rubbed the stubble on his chin. "Okay, come."

Preddy followed him into the stone-flagged entrance hall with its white-tiled walls. A stainless-steel lift stood beside the wide staircase, otherwise the spacious lobby was bare. There did not appear to be any apartments at ground level. Cotner entered a code into a numbered panel, which opened a side door off the hallway, then held the door open for Preddy to go ahead of him.

The two bodyguards followed them down a corridor of walled glass. Soon Preddy realized they were in a walkway connecting them to a lavish leisure complex. They passed a games room where two Asian males were playing snooker, watched attentively by their friends. A ping-pong table took up a great deal of space in the next room. Preddy slowed down as they walked past the bowling lanes, all of which were occupied by couples and groups. Recessed lights over the pins highlighted the tracks.

Cotner slowed down and looked behind him. "You a sporting man, Ray?"

"Not much."

The sounds of splashing water and shrieks of laughter floated in the air. Preddy smelled chlorine long before he saw people bouncing on a diving board and plunging into the waters of the large swimming pool. Other residents drifted by on inflated rubber tubes. People of all complexions were present, but most were white or varying shades of light brown. The majority darker population of Jamaica were rarely adequately represented in ownership of luxury properties like these.

Cotner opened a door. "Dis is one of our nicer lounges, and it's empty so we'll have privacy for now. Everybody's in full Friday-night mode so no one will come in here."

Preddy stepped into the room, an overwhelmingly white space — the walls, floor, leather sofas, glossy tables, all white marble. A blue Smeg fridge freezer stood beside shelves of expensive-looking liquor bottles. A line of tasteful sculptures ran across the back wall, adding a splash of variety. The overall effect was still too stark, and Preddy could not imagine anyone spending hours in the lounge relaxing. There was not a book or a magazine in sight. It felt more like a sterile clinic.

Preddy indicated the bodyguards. "Dese guys have to go."

"Of course, no problem. Have a seat."

Preddy walked towards the floor-to-ceiling window and looked at the residents milling around in the garden outside. No one cast a glance in his direction, even though he could have been no more than five feet away from some of them. He frowned as he realized this glass was similar to that of the interview rooms at Pelican Walk. He could see out, but no one could see in. Unease flowed through Preddy and he swung around to see Cotner with his head partially out of the door whispering to his men before closing the door behind him. Now they were alone.

"So, what brings you here, Raythan?" Iain Cotner moved towards the fridge. "You want a drink, man?

"Where is Detective Harris?" said Preddy.

There was no discernible change in Cotner's countenance despite Preddy's strong tone. He continued to smile as he reached onto a shelf and removed two glasses and two small bottles of rum. "Why would I know where Detective Harris is?" He opened an ice bucket. Using a gleaming pair of steel tongs, he placed small chunks of ice into the glasses and poured the liquid slowly. "You lost him?"

"Cut de rass foolishness!" snapped Preddy, his eyes blazing. "If anything happen to him, you done!"

The man approached Preddy slowly, a glass in each hand. He sipped from one and extended his hand to offer the other. Preddy ignored it and stared into his eyes.

"Where is Sean Harris?"

"How would I know? Him not here. Last time I saw him was sometime dis morning." Cotner raised the drink towards Preddy's face. "Here, drink dis and calm down, Ray. You try calling him?"

Preddy swiped at the tumbler, which flew from Cotner's fingers. It smashed against the floor, scattering glass shards and liquid everywhere.

"You've got a bumboclaat nerve!" said Cotner. The smile disappeared from his face. His eyes narrowed and nostrils flared. "Go find your fucking white man and don't come asking me nothing 'bout him! You no hear me say, me no see him?"

"No?" In two swift movements, Preddy whipped a gun from his waistband and another from behind his back. He aimed one squarely at Cotner's temple, the other at the closed door.

He walked closer to the man, breathing heavily. "Harris has a pair of custom-made shades. Right now, dey're on de face of dat ugly fucker outside dis door."

The two men stared at each other. Eventually, Cotner averted his gaze and walked over to the bar. "Dat fucking eediat," he muttered.

"Listen to me, Iain. I don't know what you doing, and I don't want to know. Not my business. I'm leaving here wid Detective Harris one way or de other."

Cotner poured more white rum onto the ice in his glass, swivelled it and swallowed in one gulp. A *pah* sprang from his lips as the sharpness hit his throat. He sank onto the sofa and put his hands on his knees, staring at the floor deep in concentration.

"You have time to get away." Preddy's eyes never left the man and he did not lower either of his weapons. "Hand him over and go 'bout you business. If not, I going light you up long before your backup get in here and I going fix dem too. What will it be?"

"So dis is going to be another Norwood?" sneered Cotner. "You going blitz de place wid bullet?"

"Call it whatever you want call it."

"Okay, you say you don't want to know what I'm doing?" Cotner patted his knees and waited. "You do though, really — no true, Ray?" He lifted himself off the sofa, shuffled towards the window and looked out at the oblivious residents strolling in the grounds. "De JCF can't get me dis standard of living, can't get us dis standard of living. I deserve to live dis way. You deserve it too. I can help you get it. All of dis and more, Ray. Think about it."

"Not interested." Preddy shook his head. "Tell me where Harris is."

"Come on now, Ray. Don't pretend like you've never imagined yourself driving around in a brand-new Porsche, flying to small islands on de weekends, staying in any five-star hotel you feel like, not having to budget for anything."

"Get Detective Harris." Preddy cocked his weapon. "God help you if him not alive."

Cotner turned and stared into the gun barrel then into Preddy's hard face. "Relax, man. I'll get him for you."

"I'm coming wid you."

"No need." Cotner reached into his back pocket.

"Don't do it, Iain. Don't." Preddy waved his weapon at the detective's forehead.

"Wouldn't dream of it, Ray." Cotner carefully removed his phone, holding it at arm's length for Preddy's benefit before speaking into the device. "Bring Harris down to de exec lounge."

Preddy kept the gun trained on him as he waited. The other weapon stayed on the door.

"Don't worry, nothing's wrong wid him. Murder isn't something I've ever been involved wid. Can't say I've never thought about it though. White man must learn to stay outta Black man business. Sean Harris too fast."

"Him doing police business," said Preddy. "Just like me. Just like you use to. Is what happen to you?"

"What happen to me?" Cotner's eyes mocked him. "What happen to de JCF? Ten years' service I've given to dis country and what do I get? Even teenage bwoy fresh outta high school have Mercs to play wid and money to burn."

"And most of dem will be dead before dey hit twenty-five."

"Well, I reach forty, so I beat de odds already." Cotner smiled wryly. "You sure you don't want think about it, Ray? Dere's still time. We can get rid of Harris. My men caught him snooping around earlier. He managed to get over a back wall and disable one of de rear security cameras, completely ruined it." He watched Preddy as if hoping for signs of agreement or at least understanding. "Could've shot him for breaking and entering. Believe me, dat idea crossed my mind. Nobody saw him come in except us. Nobody could blame me. I disarmed him. Could've claimed self-defence. What you think?"

"Where's his weapon?"

"Under lock and key upstairs in de penthouse." Cotner's voice was filled with hope. "It will disappear, like him. No one will know he was ever here."

A clock that Preddy had not noticed before ticked loudly in the silence. Inside the ice bucket, melting ice cubes were slowly being displaced. They rattled as they parted and sank in the cold water.

"Tell your thug to bring de weapon too."

Cotner pressed redial and did as ordered.

"We've been trying to get out of Harris what him doing here. Says it was his own initiative and no one else knows." He studied Preddy with suspicion. "And now, see you here . . . his partner, which tells me something is going down."

"You wrong." Preddy lowered both weapons and pointed them at the floor. "I don't know what him doing here. Not a soul know him come here. I tracked his car to de adjacent street because him supposed to be on a stakeout wid us in Johns Haven right now."

"I did catch on de radio dat you guys were hunting down a murdering Rasta." Cotner folded his arms across his chest, his expression challenging. "Thing is, how you know to ask for me by name, Ray? How you know I stay here? My name not on any deeds. Nobody at Pelican Walk know I'm here. De only property on my file is my little house in Red Hills, and dat's where my service vehicle and private vehicle are registered."

"I didn't ask for you by name," lied Preddy. "Told de guard I was a detective from Pelican Walk and asked to be let in. He's a nice guy, friendly. He said dere was a Detective Iain Cotner from Pelican Walk on de premises too, and if I wanted to come in he would call you and get you to authorize entry."

Cotner winced and shook his head. "Management employ some right fucking fools to work on security."

A knock came at the door. Both men immediately focused on it. Preddy fingered the triggers on his guns.

Harris entered the room first with the two bodyguards behind him. His apparel took Preddy by surprise. He had never seen the Scotsman dressed from head to toe in dark clothes before. Clad in black jeans and a matching long-sleeved shirt, Harris looked more like a cat burglar than a cop. His face was paler than usual, almost a light shade of grey, and his eyes were reddened, but to Preddy's relief, he looked otherwise unblemished.

Preddy eyed the pieces of shiny metal the bodyguards were holding at waist-height behind Harris. "Put away de gun!"

He raised his own weapons, one pointing straight at Cotner, the other at the guard sporting the stolen sunglasses.

"Nobody panic and everything will be fine." Cotner showed his palms. "Put away de tools, guys."

The men tucked the weapons in their sides beneath their jackets.

Preddy walked towards Harris. "You okay?"

"Aye, I've been better." The shaking voice did not sound much like its owner's usual easy tones.

Preddy waved his gun at one of the men. "Give Detective Harris his gun and get over by de window, both of you."

The thug looked at Cotner, who inclined his head. "Give it to him."

The man reached into the other side of his waistband and pulled out the firearm, which he handed to Harris by the handle. Harris snatched it and glared at his captor as the man sidled crab-like past him. A bodyguard now stood on either side of Cotner by the window.

"You're free to go, my friends," said Cotner in a tone that suggested the night's events had all been a misunderstanding and easily explained. "Just remember — no warrant, breaking and entering private premises. Harris is unhurt, and it's our word against his. All my guys are licensed firearm holders. You say no more about it, Ray, and neither will I. We'll put it down to crossed wires."

"We'll do dat." Preddy backed up to the door.

Harris pointed his gun in the direction of the three men, anger etched on his face. He strode towards them purposefully, catching Preddy by surprise.

"Wait! No, Sean!" Preddy shouted.

"Whoa!" yelled Cotner.

"I willnae shoot the fuckers."

Harris snatched his sunglasses from the man's face and tucked them in his shirt pocket. "Dinnae fuck with ma Ray-Bans, ye scrote! Ma radio and phone, now!"

The other hoodlum removed the police radio and phone from his pocket and handed them to Harris, who backed away. As soon as Harris was in the hallway, Preddy tucked his weapons away and turned back to Cotner. "It's all over, Iain," he said. "We'll forget about it, as you say."

"See you around, Ray."

* * *

Preddy grabbed Harris's arm and almost ran along the corridor. They emerged outdoors into the humid air, where plenty of witnesses were strolling by, and a feeling of relief washed over him.

"My jeep is over dere." Preddy looked sideways at Harris. "You sure you're okay?"

"They didnae hurt me." Harris's voice was cold and bitter. "Said they would though. Said—" His voice broke off in a choke. Preddy glanced at him and could see the tortured eyes of a man who had thought he was close to death.

Preddy opened the passenger door. "Get in, quick."

"How'd ye find me?"

"I might tell you some day. Let's get out of here." He ran around to the driver's side and jumped in.

As they approached the gates, Preddy gave a sharp toot. The security guards looked around at him and one of them pressed the button.

"Don't go outside the gates!" shouted Harris.

"Why?" Preddy slowed to a crawl. "You outta you mind? We getting out of here now!"

"Just wait, Preddy! Make sure he cannae close it."

Preddy stalled the vehicle with the two front wheels over the gate track. "Wha' de rass is dis?" he hissed.

The guard tapped on the window. "Move along, sir. Is what happen?"

"Sorry about dis." Preddy pressed an empty space on the footwell. "De accelerator jam or something."

The other guard walked over to them, grumbling with each footstep. "Push it over de line. It can't stay here. De gate must close now." He and his colleague walked behind the vehicle and began to push.

"You better tell me what we waiting on," said Preddy. He pressed down the brakes while the vehicle began a rocking motion.

"Them. Listen."

Preddy heard it. The sound of police sirens, plenty of them. Within seconds, their headlights were dazzling Preddy's eyes.

"Now ye can move!"

Preddy pulled out of the way and turned his body around 180 degrees to watch the unmarked police vehicles piling into the Unity Court complex. The stunned guards barely had time to move out of the way.

"My God," breathed Preddy.

"Nope, MOCA actually," said Harris, sounding more like his old self.

"Where de hell have dey been?"

"Well, I was a wee bit early." Harris keyed his phone and placed it under his ear as he spoke urgently. "Aye, penthouse. I couldnae see what code they input." A pause. "Ye'll never kick off that door. Bring the battering ram."

Preddy tried to follow the one-sided conversation but the noise around him was deafening. Vehicle engines, wailing sirens, loud voices, boots on the ground.

"Sure, naw problem." Harris cut off the phone.

"You going back in wid dem?"

"They dinnae need me, Preddy." Harris shook his head. He stretched his arms out straight ahead, then brought his hands up to his head and pushed his fringe away from his brow in a slow movement. "Naw for now anyway, it's their case."

Preddy stared at him. It was as if the ginger fringe had been infused with hundreds of white hairs within a matter of hours. "What MOCA have on Cotner?"

"Gun running. They've connected him tae more than one shipment. If the intelligence is right, there's a huge stash hidden in a compartment behind the skittles in the bowling alley — J Lane. His cronies come bowling every time new stock arrives and collect their share. Their cars are here. Apparently, our Detective Cotner is well on his way tae becoming a US dollar millionaire."

"Figures." Preddy nodded. He looked Harris up and down. "You were 'a wee bit early'?" he said with scepticism. "I imagine you and dese MOCA guys had a plan wid dates, times, locations, a warrant. What made you early?"

"I was trying tae dismantle the electricals so I could get inside and look around. Thought their system was identical tae the one at Pelican Walk. Turns out theirs is a bit more complicated."

"You come up here before, yes?"

"Aye, twice, with an estate agent. He's going tae be mad when he realizes there's naw sale and naw commission." Harris exhaled a long, drawn-out breath and flexed his right hand. "One set of cameras went out all right, but I thought it was all one unit. Turns out there are two, and I guess I got spotted on the cameras that were still working. Hurt ma hand trying tae get away, but they were on me before I could escape."

"I'll take you to Cornwall." Preddy floored the gas. "Can get a doctor to look at it. You look shaken. Maybe you should stay in overnight, make sure you're okay?"

"Naw," said Harris. "Naw hospital, naw doctor. I'm fine. Take me tae ma car, I'll drive maself home."

"Sure. Where you park? I have business in Johns Haven, so I can't follow you home."

"Och, fuck!" Harris looked crestfallen. "Mrs Vassell!"

"Yes, Mrs Vassell. My phone hasn't gone off so I know Bizzi is not dere yet. Spence and Rabino are inside her house. Mitchell and Blagrove are outside. She not dying tonight, Detective. At least, not by de hand of any fake Rasta."

"Let's get tae her, Preddy!"

"If you not up to it, I can explain all dis away," said Preddy. "Say you sick?"

"Just step on it, Preddy, or shove over and give me the damn wheel!"

"What about your car?"

"Fuck ma car. Let's get tae the old girl, before Bizzi does!"

CHAPTER 30

Friday, 11 January, 11.32 p.m.

The sleepy district of Johns Haven had transformed into a hive of activity. Every light in Mrs Vassell's house was on, and urgent, indistinct voices cut through the once-silent street. Disturbed dogs from opposite households barked in anger at the intrusive movements around their territories.

Preddy screeched to a halt as an alarming vision caught his eye, the sight of a slender, dreadlocked man running from the building and leaping the fence.

"Me rass!"

"Och, shit!"

Spence and Rabino dashed out behind the fugitive as he fled down the dark road.

"Suspect on the run!" screamed Rabino.

"Make we get de car!" shouted Spence.

The two female detectives changed direction and headed towards their concealed vehicle parked off the main road.

"Bennett Shaw!" Preddy hung his head out the window and pointed his weapon at the fleeing Rastafarian. "Stop! Police!"

In the distance old Mrs Vassell could be heard shouting, "Mercy! Mercy, Lord Jesus!"

Preddy was relieved she was alive and in good voice. "Don't make me shoot you, Rasta! Stop now!"

Ras Bizzi paused only to grab a large stone and take aim. Preddy withdrew his arm and, using both hands, swerved in anticipation of the incoming missile. The accuracy of the stone's flight was such that it shattered much of the windscreen, turning it into a mosaic.

Preddy's gun fell into the footwell as he made an abrupt stop and held up his hands to protect his face from possible splinters. Harris was propelled forward into the dashboard, slamming into it with his shoulder. The Scotsman struggled out of the vehicle, drew his weapon and made a valiant attempt to chase after the suspect, but Bizzi picked up speed and sprinted away, increasing the distance between them.

"Man on de run!" Preddy shouted into his radio and pressed on the accelerator. Using the handle of his weapon, he beat on the fractured windshield trying to improve his damaged sightline. The glass wobbled, yet much of it held firm.

Harris continued the chase on foot, but eventually lowered his weapon and stopped. He panted heavily and rubbed his aching wrist just as Preddy's jeep arrived at his shoulder.

Preddy pushed open the passenger door. "Get in, quick."

Up ahead, a car door slammed. The fugitive gunned the uncooperative engine, which gave a grudging whirr but did not fire up. Just as the two detectives were almost upon it, the engine revived and Ras Bizzi peeled away.

Preddy put his foot down and drove with his head partially hanging out the window, his view severely impaired. A quick glance in the wing mirror revealed Spence's vehicle coming up behind them. Another jeep approached from the front and Preddy gesticulated wildly at Officers Mitchell and Blagrove.

"Dat's him! Turn round!"

The officers obeyed, doing a sharp and noisy U-turn. The convoy trailed the fugitive, sirens blazing, lights flashing, as they sped through winding roads, leading further away from the metropolis. As the roads narrowed, the potholes became more prevalent and unavoidable due to broken or non-existent streetlights.

Harris squinted into the darkness. "Where the hell is this?"

"Seems to be Cambridge." Preddy skidded around a corner. "Or heading out of it."

Preddy tooted his horn as he closed in on Ras Bizzi. He thought about running the Honda Accord off the road, but endangering his fellow officers was not part of the plan, however desperate his need to apprehend the murderer. The two police vehicles following his were too close and all were going at speed. Taking out Bizzi might cause a major accident, and any pile-up on this narrow road would be an unmitigated disaster.

The area was pitch black except for the broken tail lights of the fugitive's vehicle, which, judging by its struggling engine, was finding the going hard. Ras Bizzi suddenly swung onto a tiny asphalt lane that appeared fit for the use of handcarts only. His engine gave a loud bang and the vehicle spun out, sending up a thick cloud of dust.

Preddy pulled up behind him and grabbed a flashlight from the glove compartment. Harris coughed and climbed out, gun in hand. The back of Ras Bizzi's straw outfit was barely visible as the man disappeared into the dense undergrowth.

Harris brushed at the dust obscuring his view. "He's got good camouflage."

Spence and Rabino came to a halt behind them followed by Mitchell and Blagrove.

"Sorry we didn't get him, sir," said a breathless Rabino. "He came through the roof quiet as a cat and surprised us."

"Damn man can run too!" said Spence.

"Him gone up dere." Preddy indicated the narrow track with his flashlight. He looked at Mitchell and Blagrove. "You two stay here. If he doubles back, you better hold him. Shoot him if you have to, but take him alive."

"Yes, sir."

With Preddy leading the way, the four detectives struggled through the rugged terrain, following what they hoped was Ras Bizzi's route. A strong, undeniable smell infiltrated the air as they advanced further into the dense brush.

"Do ye smell that?" asked Harris.

"Couldn't miss it," said Preddy. For anyone attuned to the odour, the pungent smell of burning dried marijuana was unmistakable.

"Somebody lives up here?" Harris sounded incredulous. "Wouldnae have thought round here was inhabited."

"I'm not even sure where we are," said Rabino.

"Me neither," said Spence. "Some bush, but look dere . . . People live up here, man."

The light up ahead came from large balls of flames, which rose from tightly wound wads of paper stuffed into kerosene cans dangling from trees. The smell of burning dried marijuana became stronger and was now mixed with the lighter odour from an abundance of thriving green herbs. In the distance, watchful dogs let out bloodcurdling howls of warning to visitors and residents alike.

An unpleasant feeling crept through Preddy's veins as he calculated their location. They had turned off at least a mile north of Cambridge and travelled a good way by foot, ending up in a village. Bizzi had taken a tortuous route, but Preddy had no doubt where they were. He had heard stories of this place. A peaceful commune away from the hustle and bustle of the city, where residents kept themselves to themselves, living without electricity or piped water, where militant residents harboured a long-running grudge against police officers and did not accept their authority.

"Detectives—" Preddy came to a halt and waved his flashlight ahead — "We're in Sereno, de Rastafarian indigenous village."

"Oh no," murmured Rabino.

"Is this bad?" asked Harris.

"Could be," said Spence. "Very."

Preddy turned to face them with a sombre expression. A shoot-out in Sereno would be a career-ending event for every single person on his team, regardless of whether they apprehended Ras Bizzi or not. "People, put away de guns. I don't want to see even a glint of metal. We're going in, in peace."

* * *

In the heart of the village were small wooden huts painted red, green and yellow, some on stilts, with thatched roofs made from wattle and daub. No unsightly electricity wires ran through any of the buildings. The makeshift lamps swinging from the trees provided better lighting than most streetlights. There were no signs of even a standpipe. Instead, giant kegs of water stood beside each hut. A few long-abandoned car chassis were piled up beside sturdier-looking handcarts and a few wheelbarrows.

The detectives were met with the unpleasant stares of at least twenty Rastafarian men and women. Some of the men held machetes at their sides, menace and distrust in their eyes. Mongrel dogs ran around their heels barking loudly, until one of the men shushed them. A wood fire burned close by, and the savoury smell of roasting yams flooded the air, mixed with the heady scent of weed.

"Ah who you? Wha' you want?" said a Rasta man with undisguised venom. A full crown of grey locks was piled at the top of his head. A long black robe with red-and-green stripes hung from his frame, and he carried a wooden staff.

"Detective Raythan Preddy, Pelican Walk Police." Preddy tucked his flashlight in his pocket and held up open palms. "We don't want no trouble wid you, Ras."

"We no want no Babylon inna we place!" said another man. The group slowly moved closer to the four detectives.

"You betta leave Rastafari alone." The speaker took a huge draw of his cucumber-sized spliff and blew a cloud of smoke into the air. "Babylon no have no business here."

"We're here for a man who goes by de name of Ras Bizzi. Real name, Bennett Shaw." Preddy scanned the group, but there was no sign of the fugitive. "We know he came through here. We just want to take him and go."

The cloaked Rasta man waved his staff at the detective. "Dat nah happen."

Preddy spoke as politely as possible. "What's your name, sir?"

"Ras Sonny is I name."

"Ras Sonny, dese are Detectives Spence, Rabino and Harris." Preddy flourished a hand as he introduced each of them.

Ras Sonny's eyes scorched the Scotsman. "De white man whe' dress like tief a Babylon too?"

"Aye, I am." Harris stepped forward and stretched out a hand toward the leader. Ras Sonny kept both hands on his staff.

A middle-aged woman walked up to Ras Sonny's side and folded her arms across her ample chest. Her locks were hidden under a colourful head-wrap, which matched her ankle-length dress. "Dem come here dis time ah night? Baby ah sleep and now dog bark, wake dem up. Babylon no have no decency!"

A younger woman, who appeared to be a teenager, stepped forward. A gold-coloured head-wrap shrouded her locks and a sullen expression covered her face. In one hand was a thick piece of wood that looked like an old table leg. She clutched at the neck of one of the agitated dogs and stroked its head when it sat at her feet. "And dey bring two Babylon woman too." She glared at Rabino and Spence. "You think you can take any ah we?"

Spence narrowed her eyes. "Look here, missis—"

Rabino patted her colleague's arm. "The only plan we have is to take Bennett Shaw into custody."

"He killed two people, a man and a woman," said Preddy. "Dat's de only reason why we're here."

"Who him kill?" asked Ras Sonny.

"Jerome Baccus and Eryka Malden," replied Preddy. "Stabbed Jerome at de Grand Marquee late night on de first of January. Eryka was killed less dan a week later . . . bashed her around de head wid a stone."

"You see him do it?" Ras Sonny's tone was accusatory. "Babylon always ah come beat and kill people, and tell lie seh Rasta man do dis and Rasta man do dat. All when dem don't see is who do it."

"We have good evidence dat he was involved and we need to bring him in," said Preddy. "De court will deal wid him. If him not guilty, him will go free."

Ras Sonny raised his voice. "Ras Bizzi, come here!" There was silence for a while. "Bizzi? Come here, me say!"

The fugitive emerged from behind a hut. He walked slowly towards the group and stood behind the imposing figure of Ras Sonny.

"Babylon say you kill somebody . . . two people. Wha' dem talking 'bout?"

"I and I don't know nutten 'bout murder," said Bizzi. "Jah know! A lie dem a tell! Run dem out!"

"Run dem out!" The community members chanted the refrain and waved their arms, a few with machetes aloft. "Run dem out!"

Ras Sonny raised his staff and silenced them. "Detective Preddy, take you sistren and you white man and gwaan back to you lawless city. We no have no murderer in dis village."

Preddy took a deep breath. His wiped his moistening palms on his side. Behind Sereno village were untamed hills and mountains, vast spaces for Bizzi to hide out in, for years if he chose to. "Can't do dat, Ras. Him have to come wid we, right now."

"What you going do?" asked Ras Sonny. "Shoot we? We just hear a gunshot lick and know dat is must Babylon coming, because nobody else woulda come up here ah shoot."

"We didnae shoot," said Harris. "Bizzi's car backfired."

"Bet you did want to though, eeh, Babylon Harris?" Ras Sonny sneered at him. "Shoot we inna we chest, shoot we inna we back. History tell we exactly wha' white man good fah. You cyah tell me nutten!"

Ras Bizzi nudged Ras Sonny in his side and pointed at Preddy. "Dat one kill off de young bwoy dem in Norwood a few year back. You must did hear 'bout him?"

"Yes, me hear 'bout him." Ras Sonny nodded and narrowed his eyes. "Look like nutten don't change from Coral Gardens, 1963, till now . . . except is Bald Head dem slaughter inna Norwood, not Rasta."

Preddy bit his lip and fought to maintain his composure. He wanted to shout, to defend the position he had taken on Norwood, to shut down any further criticism of that deadly night. He forced his brain to go elsewhere, to focus on what really mattered — arresting a cold-blooded murderer.

"Well now, let's talk 1963," he said. "Ras Bizzi, tell us all 'bout Coral Gardens."

Ras Bizzi's face was blank. "Wha'?"

"Come now," said Preddy. "De Coral Gardens Massacre is known to every Rastafarian in Montego Bay whether he is eighteen or eighty, probably to most Rastas in Jamaica. You must know de story?"

Ras Bizzi's voice took on a high pitch. "You ah try trick me to seh someting. Me ah no eediat."

Ras Sonny turned and stared at him. "You really don't know 'bout Coral Gardens? You moving around wid us for years now and you don't know our history wid Babylon?"

The under-fire Rasta man shrugged. "Me no really study history like some ah you."

"Bennett Shaw is not a real Rastafarian," said Preddy. "Trust me."

"Him is one ah we!" shouted a male voice. "Rastafari fi life!"

"For convenience, you mean," said Rabino. "This man who says he doesn't touch dead animal skins was happy to punch holes in leather belts. Turns out he's done it for a lot of people. Wouldn't surprise me if he eats meat too."

"He's had a varied working life over de past forty years," said Preddy. "Used to sell beach balls and seashells, made bead necklaces, tried his hand at carving gourds for a while, before migrating to juice vendor and now murderer."

"Dis fake Rastafari business is just to sell drinks to tourists who love de locks and de clothes," added Spence. "Nothing to do wid your beliefs or religion. Him is not one ah you, him a murderer."

The group of Rastafarians began to murmur among themselves in indistinct voices, while Ras Bizzi vehemently pleaded his innocence.

"He tried tae kill a third person tonight," said Harris. "That's why we chased him up here."

"It's true," said Preddy. "He tried to murder an old Adventist lady, a Mrs Vassell, though some know her as Miss Hardy or Miss Turner."

The woman who appeared to be Ras Sonny's partner frowned. "Miss Hardy, dat nice church lady?" She pinched her man's arm. "Is she always handing out tracts and trying to get we to go church. Say we must bring de grandkids on Saturday."

"Me know is who." Ras Sonny nodded. "She come buy callaloo and carrot up here before. Why Bizzi would try kill her?"

"Ask him, Ras." Preddy pointed a finger at the fugitive. "We don't chase people for fun."

"Neither by day nor at midnight," said Spence. "Dis is no joke."

Ras Sonny regarded the suspect. "We see you run go hide before dem come. What you do, man?"

"Nutten." Ras Bizzi stared sullenly at his feet. "Not a thing, as Jah is I witness!"

"I remember de first of January." Ras Sonny grabbed Bizzi's shoulder and shook him. "You came here late at night. De dog didn't make a sound, but me see you, carrying a plastic bag. Thought you would come over and say goodnight to us, or join we play likkle Ludo, but no. You went behind de storeroom."

"No, is not me!"

"Ah you! After me no blind?" Ras Sonny stared at Preddy. "Him wasn't behind dere for long, but him leave in different clothes."

Preddy's heart beat as though it would jump through his chest. "Where is de storeroom?"

"Come, I will show you."

As Ras Sonny began to lead the way, Ras Bizzi set off at pace in the opposite direction.

The teenage Rasta girl drew back her arm and threw the table leg as if it was a boomerang. The tool slammed into the back of Bizzi's knees. He screamed, fell flat on his face and lay sprawled in the dry dirt.

Spence ran over, sat on the man's back and pulled his hands behind him, while Rabino fixed handcuffs to his wrists. The crowd of Rastafarians murmured, but none moved forward to assist the detainee.

"Nice work." Spence smiled at the girl. "You can come join JCF anytime."

The girl grinned and retrieved her weapon. "Me no love gun, ma'am!"

Preddy and Harris followed Ras Sonny to a windowless hut containing ground provisions. Preddy shone his torch at the undergrowth behind the storeroom. Harris took a few tentative steps into the unknown and jumped, startled by a rat that ran over his foot and scuttled deeper into the bushes.

"What's dat?" Preddy waved the light at a dark object.

Harris felt around and emerged with a large black plastic bag tied securely at the neck. Preddy reached for it. Inside were a soiled T-shirt and chequered shorts.

"Looks like dried blood tae me," said Harris.

A look of dismay crossed Ras Sonny's face. "Dose are Bizzi's clothes. Dat's what he had on, de first of January."

The three men returned to where Rabino and Spence had detained the fugitive.

"Well, well — look what we found." Preddy tossed the bag on the ground near to Bizzi's face. Bizzi raised his head and glanced at the bag before silently placing his cheek on the soil.

"I'm betting Jerome's blood is all over dis?" said Preddy. "You murdered him because you were tired of being pushed off beaches. Every venture you ever tried failed, and when you finally got de juice business off de ground nobody would fit you into de new beach development. What happen dat night? You told Jerome to ask Gavin to reconsider and him laugh at you? Him tell you to go away and leave him alone?"

"I and I no have nutten fi seh to no dutty Babylon," murmured the captive.

Machetes glinted in the lamp light as the group of Rastafarians began to mumble and curse the murderer in their midst.

Harris hauled Ras Bizzi to his feet. "Guess we better get ye out of here, before ye come tae some harm."

"Yes, take him wid you, sir." Ras Sonny's voice was full of disdain. "We no want nothing to do wid no murderer." He stretched out a gnarled hand towards Preddy, who clasped and shook it.

"I never shoot a soul in Norwood, Ras. Don't believe what you hear," said Preddy. "And when Coral Gardens happened, I wasn't even born yet — none of my team were. It shouldn't have happened and it will never happen again."

"I believe you. Thank you, sir." Ras Sonny turned around and reached out his hand to Harris. "Thank you too, Misser Detective."

Harris smiled and shook it in a firm grasp. "I'll dress more appropriately next time, sir, I promise."

The four detectives set off down the dark track towards their vehicles with the reluctant fugitive shuffling in front of them.

Preddy glanced at Harris. "Now, feel free to tell Super what's been going on."

"Ye do realize that with our improved clear-up rate, Super might insist that I stay permanently at Pelican Walk?"

"Oh, is dat so?"

"Ye could have faked enthusiasm, Preddy," Harris chided him with a grin.

"Where de hell have you been anyway?" asked Spence. "We said eight o'clock in Johns Haven and nobody no see you."

Harris cleared his throat. "Had a little business tae take care of, that's all."

"So, is it taken care of?" Rabino posed the question to Harris, but her eyes focused on Preddy.

"Aye, it is."

"Looks like it." Preddy held Rabino's gaze. "Pelican Walk is going to be one detective short from now on."

"Wait." Spence stumbled and almost tripped over the uneven ground in her eagerness to quiz the Scotsman. "No tell me say you finally going home to Glasgow for real?"

"Ye sound almost sorry." Harris chuckled. "I'm flattered."

"We're losing somebody else." Preddy pushed the malingering Rasta man ahead. "Iain Cotner. Detective Harris can tell us all about it when we've got dis one locked up."

"Dis me well want hear," said Spence.

As they approached their vehicles, they spotted Mitchell and Blagrove anxiously watching out for them. Preddy looked at Harris. "You know is Saturday morning now?"

Harris frowned. "And?"

"And in a few hours, it will be time for church. Mrs Vassell is expecting you. Say, nine o'clock?"

The four detectives laughed heartily.

THE END

ALSO BY PAULA LENNON

PREDDY & HARRIS SERIES
Book 1: MURDER IN MONTEGO BAY
Book 2: MURDER UNDER THE PALMS
Book 3: MURDER AT SUGAR RUSH BEACH

Thank you for reading this book.

If you enjoyed it please leave feedback on Amazon or Goodreads, and if there is anything we missed or you have a question about, then please get in touch. We appreciate you choosing our book.

Founded in 2014 in Shoreditch, London, we at Joffe Books pride ourselves on our history of innovative publishing. We were thrilled to be shortlisted for Independent Publisher of the Year at the British Book Awards.

www.joffebooks.com

We're very grateful to eagle-eyed readers who take the time to contact us. Please send any errors you find to corrections@joffebooks.com. We'll get them fixed ASAP.

www.ingramcontent.com/pod-product-compliance
Lightning Source LLC
Chambersburg PA
CBHW032153190626
46814CB00005BA/1977